I0692735

VER'NOVA

Evergreen Sunlight — Part One

Forrest C. Richard

VER' NOVA
Evergreen Sunlight — Part One
Copyright © Forrest Richard, 2025

All rights reserved. No part of this publication may be
reproduced, stored in a retrieval system, or transmitted in any
form or by any means, electronic, mechanical, photocopying,
recording, or otherwise, without written permission of the
author and publisher.

Published by Forrest Richard, Edmonton, Canada

ISBN:
    Paperback   978-1-77354-713-8
      eBook   978-1-77354-728-2

Publication assistance by

PUBLISHING
PageMaster.ca

TO ASHLYN

CONTENTS

PROLOGUE

The dominant tree species grows at an alarming rate,
using small structures for its foundation. They have
been recorded to reach lengths that should, in theory,
topple over its mass.

Janak paused at the end of his note, observing the incredible sponge-like vegetation molding right in front of him as he stood over a growing stump. Over the hour that just passed, the stump grew past his pronged feet and above his hips. It was wide enough that if he were to wrap his arms around it, he would just be able to touch the ends of his fingers. The air smelt of fresh rain, and the moss under his soles was damp. This was the usual weather for RES 9.

These unusual trees, found in many biomes all over the planet, have been fascinating to watch every single visit. Their surface occupation crawls across the planet like slow clouds and harms nothing they wash over. They simply grasp onto any ragged rock and grow a massive mossy tree with angular branches. Growing past two hundred feet seems to be its breaking point, but it should be less due to the density of its structure. An individual tree's life cycle is short—Even shorter when the herd is hungry.

Janak glanced up at the alien forest, watching the peaceful leviathans graze over this endless supply of food. These giants were the first living beings he encountered when he landed on planet RES 9. Their sheer size fascinated him so much he almost forgot to appreciate the planet's beauty on his first landing. The creatures floated softly over the treetops, grasping large mouthfuls and moving onto the next trunk. As they swam closer and closer to the thicker lower trunks, their finned tails bobbed high above their rounded bodies and gaping mouths. The sound of their low-pitched wails, paired with the occasional gust of their large fins, made for a peaceful morning. They didn't seem to mind Janak and his Talener. The long and sleek recording scope was no harm to them. Initial contact communication was quickly discovered to be a dead end. The creatures were less sentient than Janak hoped for. The giants just wanted to follow the crop, feast, and find a mate; not share universal information like he had hoped.

> *Recorded to reach lengths that should, in theory,*
> *topple over its mass.*

An amateur biased conclusion; Janak didn't like the way it sounded. A lifetime of archiving the universe should have taught him to know better. There were things in the vast void that couldn't be explained... or could be explained. The nature of research meant that sometimes it could take a hundred years to solve its riddles. Crawling sponge trees that were a vital food source for floating leviathans were something he could figure out with enough time. Hopefully not one hundred years. The trees have a purpose, just like every other living and breathing organisms in an ecosystem. Balance is achieved when every form of life does what they are intended to do. Evolution brought these two living entities together over hundreds of years to coexist and create balance. What was it like for the trees or the whales before? Did the vegetation begin as a rampant dominant mold before it evolved into a creature's diet? That time had passed and Janak was studying what was in front of him.

His presence here could be seen as a virus, so he kept his interference low enough that nothing would be imprinted when he moved onto the next planet. An intruder could be eradicated as easily as it could destroy the entire system. Regardless, the sponge trees and the leviathans live in unison, as the trees need to be grazed, or their structure will topple in on itself and kill the parent crop. The giants make sure the trunks are always clipped.

> *Using small structures for its foundation... and*
> *appears to be a vital dietary source for the leviathan*
> *class mammals... no... delete paragraph.*

Janak deleted the paragraph; editing his notes was something he despised. Jumping from statement to statement always made his editing process tedious. However, recording was his purpose in this grand galactic ecosystem. It could always be worse. Janak walked over to his Talener and set it to auto record the crawling mass of life. He made sure the machine had enough power to last the week before proceeding to trace his path back to his vessel. Janak took his time on his return. He spent the hike pondering the leviathan's ability to float. In a moment of curiosity, he removed the vial of brown sponge from his jacket and held it beneath his mouth. He rubbed his mandibles together, tasting the air the moss emitted. Confirming his guess, the trees had a complex chemical structure of light gases. The leviathans must have evolved from a land dwelling creature to a beast that carved through the sky like it was water. The tree's high gas composition must be to thank for that.

As fast as his own sensory organs were, the information that Janak pulled from the moss was instantly coded into his recorder and sent to his vessel. The Seekers perfected Janak into the explorer they needed; they gave him extraordinary tools to do all the heavy lifting. But he didn't mind ingesting the smells and tastes with his own senses. An explorer is what they made him, and an explorer is what he would be. Nothing could take away the feeling of awe that came with every new discovery. Maybe that's why the Seekers chose living explorers instead of machines.

Janak rubbed off the remaining odour from his mandibles and returned the vial to his coat pocket. He bounded over jagged rocks covered with a thinner reddish moss and walked down the hill towards his vessel. He could see the sharp chrome body shining in the distance; a ship of impossible invention lay in front of him in this new frontier. There would be a lot of work to follow in the coming months. Archiving everything recorded up to now would be boring work; looking for sentient life would be the interesting part. The Talener was set to follow the herd, and now he would spend the remainder of the day looking for tomorrow's research.

Janak scuttled to his base camp as it came nearer. His vessel shimmered upon his return. Janak clicked in harmony with his Voidante to mirror the greeting. This machine, the Seekers, this universe, all gave him the purpose he wanted: to explore the stars and find life. The void was endless and growing. Its size was incredible, like the leviathans. But its sheer and incomprehensible expanse was a death sentence for the undiscovered life that existed in his time. How long could a civilization hold out until they made contact? The weight of his mission was heavy, and comparing it to the Seekers' responsibility seemed near impossible. They wanted him for their mission and he always felt scared he would fail. His flaws, however, didn't matter to them; they saw the bigger picture. They saw him as an explorer for a terrifying universe. It was a frontier he was willing to face for the promise of expanding a better life.

Janak returned to his Voidante to submit the morning's research before flying off to find what else the planet offered.

CHAPTER 1

It was the first day of rain in two weeks and the wildfire smoke was no longer burning Joel's eyes. The mixture of rain, fresh cut cedar, and smoke created a sweet and nostalgic smell, making his morning a bit more enjoyable. It was a staple memory of when he first started working in the Cadiaheim mountains.

Surrounded by snowy peaks, towering cedar trees, and a dense under-foliage of ferns and moss, Joel and five other coworkers hiked through a familiar landscape they had been assigned. Rain ran off their wide brim hard hats and soaked the sleeves of their reflective jackets. The wildfire smoke from Sandy Bank would have obscured the whole mountainside, but the rain forced it to a milky haze that held no higher than the trees they were paid to cut down. The cold rain was enough motivation for the crew's desire to return to a warm bed in a cramped city.

"Tag these last three here and then we can pack it up for the day," Michael, their foreman, said. It was their last shift before their days off, and the shared agreement to get out of the cold was unspoken. No one minded the silence between them, which Joel appreciated. It let him listen to the sounds of the coniferous canopy, forest floor and everything in between. Even the loudest, over-sharing coworkers of his could periodically take time out of their boastful stories to admire the quietness around them. It was difficult to find nature's true silence when opportunity is whittled down to competitive wage labour or the nepotistic life of riches.

As he was grabbing the fluorescent ribbon, Joel caught a small blur in the corner of his eye and traced it to a standing dead tree next to him. It was entombed in a swath of bright green vines with heart-shaped leaves. Bell shaped purple flowers bloomed in the dozens, adding a uniqueness of colour to the surroundings. A small hummingbird jumped from flower to flower. Its green coat had a reflective hue to the light, and a red underbelly as dark as blood. Joel watched it hover seamlessly as it fed into the nectar rich stigmas. The roof of the old forest gave the bird some safety from the frigid rain.

He watched the bird in stillness. There was no need to get closer, as this was the closest he has ever been to a hummingbird his whole life. There was an odd calmness to watching something so tiny trying to survive.

He was soon interrupted by the mumbled noise of his coworkers conversing about rumours within management, which distracted him long enough to miss the bird's exit from the flowered vines. Joel marked a handful of desirable trees with cuts of ribbon and regrouped for the hike back to the shuttle bus.

The shuttle was parked in the familiar gravel lot which was now drowned in mud. It took the crew another two hours to just push the bus out onto solid road. The company would most likely not cover that as overtime. Joel boarded the bus last and sat behind his foreman, Michael, who was driving. He started the steep drive down the mountain road faster than Joel was comfortable with.

"Mr. Robson! Did ye call your lady; let 'er know you're late?" the old man yelled.

Joel grunted. "No, not yet. We have an understanding when I am this far from the city." A sharp jab of guilt shamed him for not calling Beth. Either way, she was working a late shift and wouldn't be free to talk. "She's also sort of mad at me."

"Should have picked 'er some of those pretty purple flowers ye were admiring. Can never go wrong with flowers."

Joel nodded in agreement while staring down at his mud-caked boots. Flowers could make the rift between them better for a short while, but Joel wondered if that rift was even worth mending. The past month has been a series of battles between them. Five years of history together that was toppled in a small fraction of time. The nasty things he has said to Beth could not be forgiven, and he didn't deserve to be forgiven. Joel knew he was being neglectful and toxic, but he still couldn't figure out how it got to this point. He felt like a burden to her. "Yeah. Should have picked those flowers."

Michael sighed heavily in agreement. Joel knew he was about to get some old Fyken'Isle wise tale about courting a woman you loved. It wouldn't be the first time, but Joel respected Michael as a boss and friend, so he'd listen to his tales without objection.

"Had this lady once back on the island. Caught me lookin' at those navy girls, the ones that passed through the channels that spring. Anyways, I was in all heaps of trouble. Picked 'er a flower each day, but still she was madder than a bull. So after I picked apart me mum's whole garden I went all the way to the mainland to find the most beautiful flower. It was gorgeous, lad. Purple with these white stripes. I put it in resin so it would last for a long time. And when I got back, I gave it to one of those navy girls." Michael let out his toothless smile and turned to catch Joel's reaction.

Joel let out a small chuckle and shook his head. "I don't see how any of that helps, Mike."

"Eh, I was just trying to make ye laugh. I was never good with the ladies anyways, so don't take any advice from me." He paused to drink out of his thermos while still keeping focus on the road ahead of him. "I'm sure she will forgive ye for whatever ye done. Keep showing 'er you're sorry, Mr. Robson."

The shuttle managed to make the hour-long descent off the mountain without getting stuck. Michael's driving became more forgiving once they merged on the narrow highway back to Blackpine. He yelled at his crew to prepare their work visas for the upcoming checkpoints ahead. Security checks far from any city were relatively easy to get through, but the officers would make your night hell if anyone was unprepared. Michael had gotten pretty good at keeping his crew in shape after a couple bad experiences.

It was already dark when they arrived back at the compound. No one wasted time in getting into their personal vehicles. There was an impatience from the crew to give the company less time than they deserved.

Joel's first and only notification when he turned on his phone was from his older brother, Harvey, asking him for a call. Joel couldn't figure out if his tone was urgent or not. Harvey was easy to talk to, but the sense of dread flooded through his gut. He sat down on a stripped log that has been rotting outside the office trailer since they set up the compound and rang his brother. "Hey Harv," Joel said quietly, "how have you been?"

"Joey, sorry to call you so late." Harvey sounded exhausted. "I just wanted to call you and let you know Mom is in the hospital, probably for good this time. She's been in hospice care for the last few months, but she was rushed to emergency last night."

Joel felt nothing. He knew mom was sick but didn't feel the need to visit her. It would just make their last moments together more unbearable than the last time he saw her.

"Oh…I'm sorry, Harv. Is Dad okay?"

"He's been quiet… maybe you should come and see him? I wouldn't mind seeing you either."

Joel dreaded the offer. He could list thousands of reasons to excuse himself. But as he lingered, he could feel Harvey's disappointment grow. If Harv was right, this would be the last time he would be asked to return home for the sake of their mother. "Yeah. I'll come down these days off. I'm not supposed to be back at work till the seventeenth, so yeah, I'll come down."

Harvey thanked Joel and followed with a long silence before their familiar awkward goodbye. Usually he would ask how Beth was doing or bicker about the ongoing Revenland blockades, but Harvey always knew when talking was appropriate or not. Joel sat on the damp log for another minute in silence before getting in his car to drive home.

No remorse was held for his mom. His entire childhood was worthless because of the abuse he and his brothers had to endure. If anything, he should feel angry that he might not get the chance to say one last "fuck you", or relieved that she will finally be gone. His thoughts were overcome by a mad coughing fit. Probably something caught from the rain. He peeled out of the compound in a race to get back to Blackpine. The long drive home was spent trying to repress memories as they piled on top of one another, threatening to crush him under their weight. He wanted to give her nothing, even on her deathbed. All he could give was an absent relationship because of a robbed childhood. No parent should raise their child to become this bitter. Maybe that's why he found it difficult to love Beth.

The drive through rural Cadiaheim was littered with dozens of small towns on the cusp of being completely abandoned, if not for the stubborn farmers or the newest meth lab. The life that still hunkered in these towns probably had no descendants to inherit the soon-to-be derelict homes. Each only had a handful of street-lights to signal that life still existed there.

Joel was born in a similar small town back in Yarford. His parents had the unfortunate experience of the 2033 housing collapse that forced them all to move to Golden. He was too young to remember anything from before Golden; most of his childhood was spent in that landlocked city. He used to bike through the river valley daily with his brothers to try and find the coolest tree or walking stick that looked like a wizard's staff. At this point, the idea of life outside a city was uncomfortable to Joel, and none of these towns advertised a better quality of life from what sad excuse he already had.

He once had a dream of buying a farm and raising some animals along with sectors of cropland as a main source of income, but he wouldn't know how the hell to do it in the first place. Besides, Ignot Blight was a guaranteed career suicide for farmers and that seemed to be found everywhere.

The greater metropolitan area of Blackpine was surrounded by three other municipalities that made Blackpine look much bigger than it actually was on the map. There were Perrin, Sudrow, and Terrace Heights. Most of the wealthy executives and higher class families preferred them, as their tax dollars went to kicking out overdosed junkies or to freshly paving roads.

Joel's townhouse was near the harbour, a little north of downtown Blackpine. From there, he could watch the bay traffic of large container boats and walk to a variety of local bars. There was a park hosting a disgustingly large tent city a couple blocks south, but the homeless didn't wander far from the shelters offering three meals a day. The one million residents who weren't unhoused were all crammed into highrise apartments or townhomes that hugged the coast like a concrete spine. The practically non-existent transit system usually made traffic a headache, but it was quarter-after-one, which made for a smooth welcoming without any bumper to bumper lineups.

As Joel parked his car and pulled his duffle bag from the backseat, he noticed his living room lights were on. Beth was home and could be seen sleeping on the couch through the main window. He could feel his gut already dropping. He must have forgotten her schedule; he thought she was on night shifts. Joel wondered if he could enter quietly enough not to wake her to avoid reopening the debacle they had before he left for work two weeks ago.

His mom already gave him enough on his mind and he was too exhausted to quickly form some apology he had days to prepare. This would have been so much easier if Beth wasn't in his life; if he was alone in solitude and never had to find the effort to care for someone else. Anxious thoughts raked down the back of his head. They taunted him to get back into the car to find a motel, but he was too tired.

Careful not to make any noise, Joel crept through the front door and left his bag at the basement door. He tiptoed upstairs and soon found himself taking a hot shower, wondering if Beth would be outside the bathroom door to greet him. Thankfully, that wouldn't be the case as he walked himself to bed alone. The moment his head laid on his pillow he could feel his body melt. The exhaustion from two weeks of cutting and loading timber deep within the mountains washed over him and gave the addictive comfort of a much appreciated thoughtless sleep. No dreams would remind him of Beth or his mother. True peace occurred in these moments.

Joel woke up early out of habit and couldn't bring himself to sleep in. Instead, he laid in an empty bed while stewing in a hole of self-pity. Eventually, he forced himself to go downstairs and found Beth sitting cross-legged on their couch with a cup of coffee. She was watching a documentary series about smugglers during the fourth Aross war. Joel had already watched it during a slow shift in the mountains.

"It's not bad, eh?" Joel said as he grabbed his cup and filter to make his own coffee. Beth turned towards him with a disappointed stare. A stare he could immediately recognize. He gestured if she wanted more coffee and she remained still. Joel silently accepted the refusal and slowly continued to brew coffee for one. Once it was ready, he made his way over to the couch to join her; she paused the episode the moment he sat down. He felt like a deer that just waltzed into a trap. A stupid fucking deer.

"You couldn't say hello? I wouldn't have minded you waking me up…but seriously?" Her frown grew angrier with each word.

"I'm sorry, I didn't want to wake you. I thought you were still mad."

Beth let out a deep sigh. He could tell she was frustrated.

"No, Joel. I forgave you a few days after you left. That's all I can do in this relationship and that makes me a fool. I always keep forgiving you, every single time we have a fight."

Joel's heart sank. She wasn't wrong. Joel couldn't count the number of times he had apologized to Beth for walking out during a fight. With every apology was a promise to stay, hash it out and forgive. He could never follow through on that promise. Tears began to burn behind his eyes. "I didn't mean to, I'm sorr—"

"Stop apologizing. You left me for two weeks to think about the things you said. You always do this and it breaks me a little more each time. Nothing about this is fair to me. All I ask is for you to finish a conversation like an adult. And I fell for your shit again, thinking you'd come home a little happier. But no, you just passed by me on the couch without saying hello." Tears started to well in her eyes, but she managed to hold them back in front of him.

"I don't know what to say; can we please just pause this?" He couldn't lock eyes with her out of shame. She couldn't see his tears.

"You had two weeks, Joel. Two weeks to figure out what you wanted to say." Beth lightly put her mug on the coffee table and walked upstairs without another word. Joel could hear her start the shower.

He took the chance to carry his coffee to the porch and peo-ple-watch in the cold of the morning. He stayed there until the sun rose high enough to warm him up and coerce the wind to draw in the distant wildfire smoke that he desperately wanted to avoid. It would still be there during his time off to remind him every day what he would be returning to. There was no will in him to return to work, but he also reserved none to be at home. This city had its cuffs on him for the next week, and he would just have to suck it up.

When Joel returned inside to brew another cup of coffee, he found Beth in her scrubs packing her work bag with lunch snacks. Her eyes were slightly puffy; he hated when she had to go to work upset. Joel attempted to break the tension but immediately regretted the words as they came out.

"I hope you have a good shift. Hopefully, it's not too rowdy."

Beth looked at him with a silent stare again, but this time wore a face of defeat. As much as he loved her, nothing could mistake that look of complete loss of faith in him. She was too tired to explain how she felt.

"We don't have to unpause. Just please don't leave like that again." Even Joel could see that she didn't believe that. Beth has always been vocal with Joel about seeing a problem through to the very end. He had failed her multiple times now; the trust she had in him was gone. She closed the door behind her just before he could utter, 'I love you'. He stood there with an empty cup of coffee, feeling like a horrible cancer that would not go away. He set his mug down and remorsefully carried himself back up to bed.

He found his antidepressants set neatly on a freshly made bed. Joel hated this brand, as they made his joints feel weak and sore. He placed them back where he last left them in the nightstand cupboard and curled up to rest. Sleep was the only remedy for his guilt-ridden mind. The place where he could forget all his problems and find a fresh approach for when Beth got home. Instead, a sudden coughing fit overcame him, forcing him to sit up and clear his throat. The wildfire smoke had been dense, making his lungs work in overdrive. The coughing would not settle as he tried to peacefully drift into the dreamless void.

CHAPTER 2

Joel was woken up by the obnoxious horn of a passing train. His phone showed it was noon, and the regret of wasting his day to sleep was seeping in. The nap helped calm the emotion of returning home, but his head was pounding and his throat tasted of copper. He forced himself out of bed and put on jeans instead of sweatpants so he wouldn't look like a rock bottom bum. He decided to capitalize on the small trickle of motivation and leave the house for errands.

The nearest grocery store used to be owned by a friendly Yandian ma and pa, but they had to shut down and sell due to the disproportionate property tax and lack of groceries on the shelves. He could still walk to the next grocery store, however, it would take him the better part of his afternoon and he risked getting mugged at every second street corner.

Nothing but TV was keeping Joel home, so he risked the walk instead of driving. More regret piled onto him when he noticed how long people were lining up for their groceries. Food shortages and an overpopulated city has put some constant stress on necessities, and Joel was kicking himself in the ass for not arriving right before the store opened. Once he finally was in, the pickings were slim and every aisle had a store employee enforcing how much you could take for the sake of 'hoarding prevention'. Every TV and overhead radio was playing the most recent terrorist attack on Royale Point, which showed him nothing had changed in the owner's taste of media since the last time he was here. Vallan had publicly condemned the terrorist group named Saddars two years ago, and it was still the media's favourite cow to milk.

After collecting what he was allowed and paying half a day's worth of pay, Joel braved his walk back home, hoping not to get jumped for the groceries he needed for his apology dinner. He passed his regular liquor-store, questioning if Beth would disagree with him mixing alcohol with his antidepressants. It had also occurred to him that he would have to lie about taking the medications in the first place. He bought a case anyway and agreed he would deal with that issue when he was faced with it. Luckily for him, there was no shortage of booze and it was forgiving on his wallet.

A dark rum would help with the new body shakes and headache he woke up with. His mom had an old cold remedy of eating a radish and chasing it down with the strongest vodka you could find. But colds weren't stopping mom from finding time to drink and she was paying for that by being on death's bed. How would he break the news to Beth?

His walk home would have been uneventful if it wasn't for passing by four police officers trying to revive an overdosed junkie. The guy was pale blue and looked beyond saving. The police officers still tried to wake him with multiple drug-reversal kits and cursed silently as they could not succeed. Someone's kid just added a little more trauma onto four people trying to save him, all because he wanted the newest batch of meth released right after their bi-weekly welfare checks showed in their accounts.

Joel tried not to think too hard about it. It wouldn't be the first time he witnessed a failed revival. He had issues of his own, and he needed to think about what to say when Beth got home. How could he begin repairing five years of damaged trust? Walking out on every fight, refusing to amend, and calling her awful names may have killed what he worked so hard for. Beth used to be his purpose and now he felt like she was a fleeting chapter in his life.

It wouldn't be long before she returned home. Joel began to prep his ingredients while nursing one of his beers and casually listening to the TV he put on as background noise. It started off with a regular season hockey game but somehow switched to a reality show about an unhinged rich family suburb in the Julliettes. He would have switched it, but he found one of the daughters comically gullible and that was better than having to listen to more current news.

When he heard Beth come through the door, an uneasy wave of nerves washed over his stomach and tensed his spine. She came into the kitchen carrying her work bag and a saggy pack of dirty scrubs. She looked to have more energy than she had when she left the house this morning.

"Is that butter chicken? Smells delicious." She eyed the beer can while passing by, but had no comment.

"Feels good to cook something. The camp food has been laughable recently, so whatever we have on the shelves here will always be better." He awkwardly followed her to the laundry room, looking for a window to get her attention. She had her arms deep in the washer when he broke the news.

"I didn't have anything to say this morning because my moms in the hospital. She probably doesn't have long." Joel waited as he watched Beth stop her chore and quickly stand up. She covered her mouth in shock, with her other hand on her hip to brace herself.

"Joel I'm so sorry; are you okay? Is she going to be okay?"

"Harv sounded pretty serious on the phone, so no, I don't think she will be okay. I'm going to go visit them this week and if you want to come, you can. I'm more so going to see Dad and the boys, but I think I might have to say goodbye to her." Nothing in Joel's body wanted to say anything to that woman.

"Of course I'll come. I can call in sick." She slowly took him in an embrace. "I know what she meant to you, but I think your dad will really... Your skin is burning hot. Do you have a fever?" She placed the back of her palm on his forehead, looking at him like she looks at her patients.

"No, I'm fine. It's probably just a bad mix of the smoke and rain. Listen, you're under no obligation to come. I know I hurt you again. I fucked up and I'm trying to figure my life out. There's no excuse for what I put you through, and I'm sorry." He tried to reciprocate the embrace, but she stepped away.

"Joel, we don't have to hash this out now. I know what I preach, but you are allowed to process this thing with your mom first." She followed him into the kitchen as he backed away to the steaming pan. Keeping his hands busy while he thought seemed more important than facing her.

"I know. I just want to be better. If I can't figure out how to talk to you, how am I supposed to face my mom? Do you really want to be there to see that?" He stirred the orange bubbling sauce a little too hard, spilling a spoonful over the side of the pan. "I don't want to go home. I don't want to be at work. And I don't want to be *here*. I've been so confused lately that my thoughts are a fucked mess, and I've been taking it out on you. It's like...I always expected myself to get to this point, thinking I'd find a way to avoid it. Avoid being like my mom. But now here I am, and I'm lost."

"We can get you back into school if you need a career change; it doesn't have to be logging camps forever. There's also couples' counselling, which might take a few months to get a slot, but if we apply now..."

Joel slammed the spatula on the counter, splashing sauce over the backsplash, "And then what happens if nothing changes? Those aren't realistic goals if I'm still going to hate myself at the end." The silence between them held for what felt like an eternity.

"Well, then at least you tried."

"This would be easier if you'd just leave me." The rock in his gut expanded till he couldn't breathe, waiting for her to bite back.

"That is not a solution. For the hundredth time, that is not how we fix ourselves. Please, stop saying that." He could hear her voice quiver. It took him a second to notice his own tears and the vice on his throat.

"I need to leave." The tension grew with every step towards the front door. Joel grabbed his jacket and didn't bother looking behind him. He half expected for her to call after him, but was given nothing. Maybe she had finally lost her will to chase his ignorance.

The walk to Wayther's Pub was relatively short compared to the others, and it gave him an excuse to walk on the harbour front. Joel felt a blanket of exhaustion on him and hated that he couldn't peacefully rest. He continued down his path, crossing by the bright neon screen ads from the car insurance complex and the family-owned kebab shop. Soon he would round the corner of the halfway home and hoped to see the older Yandian woman sitting on her balcony, humming old melodies in her native tongue. The sudden weather change to a crisp light rain made that unlikely.

The city, this street, his townhouse should have felt more like a home to Joel. It's where he lived for the past five years and yet it left the feeling of just another stop before the end. As much as he wanted his chapter with Beth to close, he dreaded the thought of her leaving. Joel needed her, and the history they've made together would end up as waste if he continued to refuse changing. He truly did love her. She has always been good to him. But love wasn't what he deserved; hatred and suffering was his birthright and it would only be erased upon death.

Joel rubbed the bridge of his nose, feeling the weight of his heavy eyelids. He had texted an old friend, Hayden, the moment he left the steps of his house. He regretted that decision, but he was tired of drowning in self-pity. Hayden would fill the silence Joel would bring. This whole night already was awful, and he wasn't even in his bed to begin the next day. Sharing drinks with Hayden would only delay that.

The familiar green and yellow glow of Waythers shined off the wet sidewalk, already greeting Joel with the stale smell of cheap beer. Joel saw Hayden standing outside the pub sharing a cigarette with an older bearded man with an obnoxious laugh. Another candidate that wanted the nightly title of drunkenly sharing too much of their past, hoping to get some form of sympathy from Joel. One friend was never enough for Hayden to enjoy a night out drinking.

"Fuck this," Joel said out loud. He turned around and debated his next stop. Maybe being alone was better than a crowded sports bar. About an hour later, Joel had embraced the blind journey of his search for a warm place to sit and eat. It was much easier to distract himself with whatever was in front of him. He slowed his pace and looked out towards a park path with dancing lights.

Blackpine had its sights but would always be a city plastering itself with the shiny bells and whistles of a phoney influential fantasy. It had a few notable sights that gave it some uniqueness; a bunch of architecturally impressive towers that were three-quarters empty, but always interesting to look at from the boardwalk. He missed the river valley back home in Golden. It was the perfect place to escape as a teenager. He would always wander through the closest park, which sheltered hundreds of tamarack trees he loved to look at and climb. They would only serve as nostalgia now. Those walks were only inspired after a drunken comment from his mom during family dinner and hearing her scream after him as he ran out the door. Blackpine was supposed to be a fresh start, but now he was just reliving the past with a failing relationship instead of an alcoholic parent.

This city was temporary. It always has been. He imagined he'd live here until he was offered a position that required him to relocate. At the pace he was moving with his employer, another ten years was his estimate. To wake up, work, and go home, on an endless cycle, fourteen days on and seven off. The thought made him hopeless. His endgame shouldn't be looking forward to moving to a new city with enough savings to keep him alive. Life was easier when he was living in his youth, back when Golden was his whole world. Every day was filled with the pleasures of adventure and no responsibility. Now his only pleasure of the day was a mediocre coffee. No one told him adulthood was a routine of devoting his life to a company and trying to decide if your personal time should be spent on more work or impending responsibilities.

Joel noticed he had stopped walking while he was lost in his thoughts. The decorative lights outlived his interest, and he continued along the sidewalk that hugged the park. Maybe it was time to turn around or loop around a different block to get home. He had soaked in his sadness for long enough and was ready for a deep sleep. The phantom weight on his back begged him to find a place to lay down, and his joints felt like they belonged to a ninety-year-old tumbling down a hill. The walk home made him regret how far he went. The night air dropped low enough that it froze his wet shoes, and his cough came back for another relentless round. All he could focus on was his warm bed. He hoped that Beth was asleep so he could avoid another argument, just for tonight.

'Mercer.' He thought. Maybe a new city wasn't such a bad idea. An idea that would start him fresh and put distance between him and Beth. Leaving her would add on to his already big enough shit list, but that would end the constant damage he left on their relationship. Beth needed someone who wasn't so goddamn miserable all the time, and it was clear he wasn't good enough to make her happy. A sliver of him hoped she would beg him to stay when he announced he would leave. He pictured the conversation in his head and then ran another hundred conversations on how the breakup would go. Joel remembered that same feeling of hope when he told his mother he was leaving Golden. She was quick to disappoint him.

When Joel finally reached the steps of his apartment, he could feel the bearing weight on his legs and back. His feet, nose, and hands were wet and frozen. It didn't help that the ongoing cough was making his throat scream. It was time to go inside or he would pass out, right in front of his own stairs. When Joel stepped inside, he was greeted by the warmth of his place and the looming tension of confrontation. He silently walked to the bedroom and found Beth already asleep. The conversation would have to wait. The couch seemed a more appropriate a place to lay down and rest his head. He didn't realize how guilty he felt until he actually sat down.

Beth was never tough on him and didn't deserve to go to bed angry. He should have stayed, and either buried the argument or come to some solution. Trying to suppress his cough was proving difficult and only agitated his throat more. It occurred to Joel as he sat down that he was running out of sick days. He began to mentally plan how many days he needed to recover before his last day off. A cough was manageable, and he wasn't bedridden yet. Joel threw back cheap pharmacy cough syrup from the bathroom cabinet and returned to the couch to call it a night.

When the seven o'clock alarm sounded from his cellphone, Joel felt an instant piercing throb shoot through his ears that rocked his brain. His mouth was completely dry, and when he tried swallowing, it felt like gargling sand. He turned off the alarm and rolled onto his side so he could stand up. Pain shot through every joint and muscle, but he could only let out a weak groan. It was difficult to focus on standing up, and he only realized he had lost track of time when Beth was shaking his shoulder, ordering him to wake up.

"I can't move," Joel groaned. Even opening his eyes was impossible, as a thick crust had locked them shut. Beth must have walked away at some point. After hearing movement from the kitchen, he felt a warm cloth clean off the gunk on his eyes.

"Gods you look awful," she softly spoke. "You must have caught a cold from your walk last night."

"I need to leave for Golden today." He tried to blink through as she continued to clean around his lashes. Once he could open his eyes, he saw the clock was already thirty minutes past. Beth looked tired and upset. Joel couldn't imagine that she wasn't angry with him. It made him feel guilty. He was an asshole who couldn't even decide what he wanted from their relationship. There was so much that bothered him, but blaming Beth to be the root cause was just cruel. He thought back to last night's fantasy of leaving her. Guilt rose and crashed like a violent wave. "I'm sorry," he said.

"Sorry for being sick or sorry for being an ass?" she asked sarcastically, looking at him from the corner of her eye.

"Both."

Beth placed his phone on his chest and silently looked down into her steaming coffee. "I would like to finish our conversation, but it would probably feel like kicking an injured dog. I left some medicine on the coffee table; please try to get some rest before you leave... I think it's best if I stay home."

No surprise there. Why would he bother begging her to join him?

Beth gently rubbed his shoulder, picked up her purse and made for the door to start her day. Joel wished her a good shift and faded back into a slow fall of discomfort and fatigue as she closed the door. He felt his mind melt deep beneath him and then violently tense into a spasming migraine. The pain continued for what felt like hours. Looping back and forth between numbness and burning until the void was nothing but a raging storm.

CHAPTER 3

The station started to hum with the sounds of the furnace, waking up to work against the cold Mercer fall. Sadie felt the electricity surge from the power box, through the building's frame, and then divided into dozens of different requests. The draw needed from the furnace to the computer she was using was small, but enough to slightly irritate her. Sadie ignored the glitch and silently listened to the static noise of the station. Anyone could listen to the sounds of electricity with the right attention, but it made a unique tune only for her. Each and every form changed slightly by its origin, always staying true to its base familiar tune and revealing its hidden lyrics to Sadie.

This building's voltage reverberated like waves, probably caused by the rows of computers running expensive software. The waves outlined each wire that carried glowing currents, tracing its foundation while singing its song. She had never visited Mercer before, but this was still the same soft hum that she has been listening to since she discovered her abilities.

FORREST C. RICHARD

She took a moment from the computer's file archive and watched Lyas's imprint move his way through the halls by unlocking the card access locks. He made his way into the large room where officers would write their reports; he was carrying two cups of stale hot coffee.

"Only one of these cops has actually seen our friend, and they chalked it up to just seeing shadows," Lyas said as he sat beside Sadie and placed a cup beside her. Sadie picked it up and felt the warmth melt into her hands.

"I found seven statements mentioning our friend; I even mapped them out for ya," Sadie kindly smiled as she turned to Lyas. She commanded the computer to print her map of the sightings around Mercer. She nodded her head for Lyas to grab it from the printer. Lyas grabbed the map and paced around the officer's desks.

"There's no pattern here," he frowned at the page. "That kind of makes my next plan garbage."

"Lyas, each report is more concerning than the last. He's testing his limits, and we might be out of time. Maybe you should call the others to meet us here." Sadie watched as Lyas turned his back to her. It was in times like these where she wished she could be the one to read minds. She never knew what plans he was coming up with next.

"Not yet. The guy could just be confused and scared. Think about when you first discovered your abilities. There was no one there to guide you. We were skeptical of Natasha, and look where she's now. All we need to do is catch him at the right time, in the right place."

Saide glared at him in confusion. "That was a really stupid comparison. Natasha never meant to hurt innocents. These reports reek of intended violence. Is it so hard to admit that this man might be different from the rest of us?"

"Different?" Lyas faced her. The morning sun was casting orange across his face.

"This man might be too far gone. He might like this new life, and we are not equipped to apprehend someone who won't come willingly. I know that you've thought about this scenario. Time is something we cannot afford if there continue to be victims around this city."

Lyas stared approvingly at her while nodding his head. She could easily forgive him for initially disagreeing with her. The handful of friends they have recruited over the years have come under their own freewill. Sadie had always prepared for potential conflict on each introduction, but each of their friends were found within a couple of days. This disappearing man was making their mission increasingly difficult. She trusted Lyas to make the right decision.

"I'll call in Rowan; she can track on the north side of the river while we cover the south," Lyas said.

Mercer was a large city to cover, and Rowan's help would aid them greatly. The city was known for being a gateway between Golden and the rich oil fields in the most northern parts of Cadiaheim. For decades, an oil rush dominated its economy and convinced droves of money starved adults from neighbouring provinces to move there. The real estate and downtown core exploded in growth, enveloping the small towns around it and forcing the citizens to build a giant ring road that made the city look like a melting clock. Sadie found Mercer quite boring, but had found an ongoing streak of delicious restaurants over the week they've been there. Her favourite so far was a green onion cake food truck.

Lyas picked up his satchel and downed his remaining coffee. "Let's head out. I felt a memory of a delicious pho place not too far from here."

The two left the empty room and made for the exit. As they passed the lunchroom, Sadie could feel the cellphones of each officer ringing together in an uncoordinated symphony. Lyas had them lined up, staring blankly at a rerun hockey game on the television. Sadie had turned all of their radios off earlier, as the constant static screams of their transmissions pinched her nerves.

As they had left the building and entered the rental car, Sadie switched the building's security cameras back to life. She watched as Lyas closed his eyes and took a long, deep breath. It only took him a second to recollect his own thoughts and release the dozens inside the station. The hum of the car's life sparked as Lyas started the engine. Sadie watched the glow pulse through the wiring and into every device that kept the machine functional. In the next couple of years, the rental company would have to replace the car's fading battery.

With no other leads, the two made their way further into the downtown core for an early lunch.

* * *

It was a few days later when the next sighting came in. Sadie watched over the city's river as she waited for Lyas to finish his phone call with Rowan. They stood atop a steep bank that displayed Mercer's picturesque skyline; the river was glittered with broken ice that had not yet fully froze. Their mission had drastically changed with the brutal murder of a young man late last night. Grief weighed on Sadie that morning, knowing full well that she had the capabilities to prevent an unnecessary death, but Mercer's phantom proved impossible to find. She waited anxiously for Lyas to give her some good news.

"...okay sounds good. Stay safe, I love you." Lyas hung up his phone and walked up next to Sadie to join her on the scenic overlook. "Rowan came to a dead end at the Old Court. She has a couple of ideas for baiting this guy, but I'm worried we would lose more time."

He let out a long sigh, followed by complete silence. Sadie could see the frustration lingering on his face. When Lyas first met her, he presented this hopeful idea of a clean slate if she joined him. Accepting his offer was overwhelming and terrifying at first; she had never left her home country of Arsacadia back then. But he promised guidance through the screaming storm that was her newfound powers. Sadie knew this wraith that had just tasted blood would not get the same offer.

"How do you see them? See gifted, like us?" she asked.

"Large, populated areas look like beehives. Every individual mind glows bright and zips around as they go about their day. If I don't tune the voices properly, it all sounds like bees; that's why I thought I was schizophrenic back when I was alone. But when a person, like us, finds their abilities, they sound... look... feel completely unnatural. As if the beehive was infiltrated by a wasp that wasn't invited. That's how I found all of you, except that this ghost keeps disappearing before I can pinpoint him and take control of his mind."

"Is that where you're at? To force him to stop?" She looked at him gently. She was worried her question was unintentionally too judgmental.

"I promised to never enter the minds of my friends without their permission, but this ghost has killed an innocent, and that makes him my enemy," Lyas said.

Sadie nodded in agreement. Every one of their friends had committed unique levels of damage to themselves or others when they first discovered their abilities. Lyas held them accountable by giving them the option to learn control and work together to prevent chaos that trailed fear. Who knows what she would have done if she had to learn all alone? The longer left to their own devices, the more dangerous they would become, and Mercer's ghost had found unstable independence with violence. She knew deep down he couldn't be saved.

"Let's jump to where the body was found," Lyas said.

Sadie cusped the back of his elbow and let her stomach drop. The two of them collapsed into Sadie's world, where she was shown millions of channels that were wires, batteries, and nodes that all acted as her personalized transit. She had always preferred travelling within cities as energy flowed within a localized space, giving her a tall dome that could carry her wherever she wanted. They had taken the form of a ball of kinetic energy that would have rushed away in every direction if it wasn't for her conscious grasp. She focused Lyase's essence close to her, jumped them into the tail end of a news helicopter and pivoted at forty-five degrees to land themselves beside a detective's cell phone. Sadie pulled the two of them back into their physical dimension, startling the group of detectives and forensic analysts standing around the dark alley. Lyas silently sent them away once he regained his balance. The unnecessary eyes walked out of the crime scene in unison with blank stares and forgetful memories.

"Oh, no… Is this all part of the body?" Sadie gasped. The extent of the gore settled in as her sight adjusted to the dark lighting. The man's body had been torn across the road and dragged ten feet up the building's side, leaving a trail of blood and dismembered bits that were spattered with a heinous rot.

"Is that…mold?" Lyas asked.

"They haven't even recovered his torso yet," Sadie pointed to the hanging corpse glued to the brick wall. It was maimed from the ribcage down, blanketed by a thick layer of the rot.

"I say this in the most respectful way possible, but we are lucky they haven't moved the body yet. Take me up."

Sadie stepped beside Lyas and took his elbow again. Instead of collapsing into particles, she excited the air around her and collected charges. As she placed them around Lyas and herself, they lifted off the ground, trailed by fingers of lightning reaching out to whatever metal they could touch. It was a slow and unstable form of travel, but was useful in unique instances.

Sadie lifted Lyas until he was face to face with the murdered man. His skin was littered with spores and a bouquet of mushrooms was sprouting out of his eyes and mouth. The stench made Sadie nauseous.

Lyas reached forward and placed his palm on the man's head; it would take him a few minutes to read the last moments of the man's life. Sadie studied the man's face, believing that his death could have been prevented. He could have made a meaningful life, but was ultimately given a death written in nightmares. Her guilt clutched and shouted within her chest, forcing her to remember every detail.

"There's not much left; the majority of his brain is decayed. There's only an image of a deer's head in his final moments," Lyas sighed. She knew what discomfort came with reading a dead brain, as he had told Sadie about the experience after his first time doing so. "He felt scared, and incredibly helpless. Whoever did this to this kid made him suffer slowly."

"This mold, this blight, is the obvious anomaly. I don't remember seeing anything like this at the other scenes."

"Maybe he was trying to hide it. Now he's resorted to display." Lyas scratched his dark beard. "He must be using the fungus or spores to disappear so quickly."

Sadie lowered them back to the concrete. The lightning dissipated once she released the charges. "If that's true, then our friend has endless escape routes."

"The details of this murder are going to draw too much attention. Our window has closed." Lyas scrunched his nose and peered back up towards the body. "How in the hells does a deer fit into all of this?"

Sadie had a difficult time trying to guess this murder's motive. The kid's body was burned into her mind, haunting her with the prospect of fungus leaching out of every orifice. This death was not honourable, only smeared with horror and humiliation. A regular person could not match the strength and power of someone like her, or her friends, as if displaying what horrors were committed was proof of weakness without. Whoever was behind these attacks, this murder, would feel the full extent of the horrors she could create.

She thought there was hope in bringing in the rest of the team to help. "Do we call in the others?"

"No. Rowan told me they're occupied in Lavendy. I won't pull them out."

"We need to find this guy before he kills again. The next victim won't be granted any more mercy than this kid was given. Call the others," Saide urged.

"Sadie!" Lyas snapped. "This is our new reality; to be stretched thin and thinner as more of us are discovered. I can't call in the others because maybe they're going through the same shit we are."

"We are no longer in the quiet here." Sadie sternly looked at her friend. "All of Mercer will know something sinister is among them within the next few hours."

"I tried! I tried to reach out, to make contact, but I failed. I thought I could meet him before the world would beat me to it. Sadie ... I need an ally right now, not a critic," He sighed.

Sadie exhaled deeply. The world was dangerously close to discovering the miniscule fraction of gifted among them. Mercer's Blight was about to be the spark that would rupture the safety blanket of their hidden lives. An introduction wasn't supposed to happen like this.

"Let me comb a part of the city. I can jump through each alley, each street. Anything to change our current plan, we have been too slow at this. Please, once I see something abnormal, I'll call you," she spoke with assurance. She knew Lyas was dismayed, but would be open to solutions.

"You have two hours, then you meet me on eighty-sixth and one-o-fifth. We'll regroup there," Lyas ordered.

Sadie blinked back into her kinetic form, zipping through the building's galvanized wire and up towards the tip of the network tower. She looked towards the south-west area of the city and ran the currents of every telephone wire and flood light that overlooked the most hidden of places. She listened to the hum of the city, hoping to catch an excited spike of chatter. Searching every corner she could think of would be time consuming, but more ground was covered.

She thought about what Lyas said about how the phantom could travel. Any spore or fungus patch could be this guy's gateway. In contrast, it wouldn't be so different to how Sadie used her own abilities. She zipped through traffic lights, noting dark corners and empty spaces. Wherever this phantom would be found, it would be on his domain. To Sadie, that meant she had to get the jump on him first.

Chapter 4

The blood was no longer fresh and had almost dried to the old hangar floor. It stuck to the bottom of Morwin's boots like wet glue and cried with a crackled squelch with each step. Humid air that tasted of aged copper and musty rain filled his lungs as he walked towards his sample. Morning sun shone softly through the skylights and canvassed the trail of red that leaked like a river from the samples' wounds. It was the warm welcome that Morwin needed after a long night.

He knelt beside the sample's body and examined the growth made overnight. Spores and mold had completely eaten the man's feet and had crawled up to his chest; he was glued to the floor by a blanket of withering green and blue filaments. Morwin held the sample's hand that was chained to the metal post. it was raw and bleeding from his wrist.

Weak and soft. Couldn't even escape.

"Wake up," Morwin uttered. He shook the man's face to help rouse him. The sample's eyes fluttered weakly and tears began to fall. Morwin could feel the sample's brain jolt in fear.

"Please…help me," he cried. Morwin prodded his mind for a memory of a name.

"Your name is Negan, ya? How fast did it take you to give up?"

Instantly. Gift him death.

"What? I'm sorry, I'm so sorry…" Negan sobbed. "I don't know what I did. Please let me go home."

Morwin sighed and looked at the sample with curiosity. Negan was an impressive specimen, but failed spectacularly. Now he was just additional proof that the human body was too fragile.

Move on and find a new sample.

Feed us.

"In due time," Morwin waved his hand. "When I left this hangar, I gave you the option to escape before the mold reached you. You're still here, half rotten with no feet. I want to know what happened."

"I couldn't…" fungal tendrils hung from his nose, carrying snot from his blubbering. "It was too painful! How did you expect to break me out of this chain? I want to go home!"

"I had faith you'd figure it out," Morwin said sorrowfully. "Being strong and smart doesn't mean anything when you can't escape from a simple trap. A real survivor would have pulled their chained hand right off the bone. It's extreme, but I would have regrown you a new one."

"What the fuck are you talking about?" Negan's voice was raised in anger.

Don't let him speak to you like that.

He's beneath you.

Morwin stood up from the blood stained concrete and mulled over Negan's body. He could feel every single spore running through the arteries and veins, digging into deep layers of membrane. Each spore was now becoming a permanent part of Negan, and furthermore, a part of Morwin. The body reeked of fear and adrenaline, like stale piss on a carpet. This sample's time had expired; a new one would need to be discovered.

"I want to admit something Negan, you're the only one I know who will listen," Morwin said. "I killed a criminal last night. Dragged him across an alley and up a wall. What bothered me the most was how easy it was for me. Not in the way his arms bent like plastic straws, or how he ruptured with just the push of a finger. But how it was so easy for me to take a life; he was my first."

He looked at Negan's face to see if he had his attention. His tears had turned red.

"Since I've changed, I had to come to terms with being above what I once was. I've evolved out of your species, and I know more like me will surface. There's going to be trial and error in my methods, there will be more death. I hope there is some solace in knowing you're not alone. Thank you for being my second."

Morwin allowed the mold to finish the remaining tissue. It quickly crawled over Negan's head as Morwin stepped away. The sounds of hunger being satisfied annoyed him; there was too much to plan with little time.

He stepped outside the hangar and watched the morning sun burn away the dense frost. A cigarette would have been wonderful to calm his nerves. Morwin watched the Mercer skyline wake up and dreaded the work set ahead of him. Control would not be presented on a platter, it required commitment. He fantasied how wonderful it would be to just skip to the end.

FORREST C. RICHARD

We need more.

He's learning.

Morwin smiled. "Finally nice to have some recognition. I think it's time we look for our own kind."

More feeding, we need the data.

"That would be a waste of time," Morwin said. "I know how to cripple them. I showed you that with ease last night. What I need are friends who understand. I can't save this world alone."

But what about control?

"Control is what we want. I thought that's been established."

Of the mind.

To influence.

Morwin pondered the words. Control could be accomplished easily amongst the humans, but what about the new race? He assumed whoever else was enhanced would adopt the same responsibilities burdened to him. The world, his home, was becoming a toxic cesspool caused by weaker versions of his past-self. It needed saving, only by those who could actually bring change. To be gifted such incredible skills and ignore the duty attached was a crime itself. Maybe negligence amongst the new race was a real and frightening possibility that fell within his duty to face. The traitors would need to be persuaded, with force.

"I need to learn control of the mind," he said. The words fell out in a panic. "Where do I begin? What do I need to do?"

More samples.

Strong minds will suffice.

"We will learn to influence their wills, then we find some friends." Morwin donned his deer-head hide over his face and dissipated into a nearby fungal growth. The mycelium carried him through the blighted dirt, searching for the next sample he needed for his newfound purpose.

* * *

It wasn't long before Morwin located a handful of samples with healthy brains. He had difficulty in choosing the three top candidates, so he took them all.

Morwin studied the bodies plastered with rot against the hanger walls. He had grown enough blight to restrain them from the neck down. They wouldn't be up there for long, anyway. On the left was a young man with a similar physique to Negan. In the middle was a thirty-year-old woman, and on his right was a marathon runner in his sixties. All three relentlessly screamed and cried for help. Morwin covered their mouths with a thick film to stifle the noise and focus on the task at hand.

He chose the mind of the young man first to compare to his most recent sample. Looking back, he wished he spent more time with Negan's brain. Morwin searched for the deepest spores that had latched themselves within the brain's core. He prodded the tissue, searching for the function of each button he pressed. Once he was finished, he moved onto different areas, discovering the lobes responsible for memories, motor actions and speech. Each region presenting a unique purpose for Morwin to experiment with. He even found an interesting button that caused extreme rage when enticed.

Hours later, Morwin finished studying the boy's mind. He could have finished much earlier, but perfecting skill was more important than a quick tour. By the end, the man was reduced to a drooling meat bag. An expected consequence by the wringing and exhaustion of every cell. The body was disposed to feed the hunger.

Morwin chose the woman next, but wanted a different approach. He closely inspected her structure to compare to the boys, finding similar and unique connections that they shared. Pressing buttons was easy, but now Morwin wanted instant obedience held on autopilot. The process angered him, as the woman was constantly trying to resist. On top of this, the experience was like holding a handful of wet eels together without dropping them. Exposing the subject to pain for compliance took too long as he needed the process to be effortless and quick. He spent hours rearranging the woman's brain, looking for the perfect formula to create his desired ability.

The countless attempts ultimately fried the woman's life, forcing Morwin to move onto his next subject and try again.

CHAPTER 5

The drive to Golden would have been near impossible if it wasn't for the cocktail of pain relief drugs. There were plenty of small towns in between his drive to make pit stops, but Joel brought ten-hours worth of extras, just in case.

Joel debated staying home; his headache made his knees weak and vision blurry. His brothers would have been disappointed if he cancelled, not to mention his father. He had hoped the long drive would be enough time to recover from whatever head cold he was battling. The pain had already died a little since this morning.

The journey from Blackpine to Golden was a long trek, but unfairly beautiful. The surroundings, for the entire ten hours, were picturesque mountains with snow-white caps, crystal blue rivers, and ancient spruce trees. A lack of potholes was the bonus. The province was obsessed with maintaining these roads to keep them smooth; they were greatly favoured over any other highways that the tourists weren't using. The towns between this stretch were known for their ski hills and rentable cabins that would rob a couple months' pay from you.

Joel had three checkpoints to get through; at least three that he remembered since the last time he visited Golden. The province loved to squeeze whatever change they could grab off of visitors. If only they knew there wasn't any important enough infrastructure between these cities that were of any interest to extremists.

By the time he was half an hour away from Golden, Joel felt that his car had had enough and was making concerning noises that shouldn't be ignored for long. His attention was diverted when he found himself at the back of a traffic jam that stretched a few kilometres before the entrance of the city limits. Another checkpoint. Joel's eyes were already heavy enough to put him to sleep, and the night was getting late. All he wanted was a bed and a hot shower to loosen the aches and tension building up within his body. His head had refused the pain meds, making the migraines spike with each flash of another car's headlights. Joel was thankful he hadn't rolled his car in a ditch yet.

As he finally pulled up to the gate, Joel grabbed his papers when an officer approached his window. He could only see the bright light from the officer's flashlight.

"Papers and open your trunk please," the officer asked.

"My trunk? Why do you need to check that?" Joel said. He was confused, as he has never been asked that at a checkpoint before.

"There have been missing persons that the Mercer Police Service are treating as connected. We have escalated our authorities to help the search but there's been no risk here in Golden. If you refuse, you will be asked to turn around and not to enter the city."

"Umm, I guess; go ahead." Joel opened the trunk for the officer and waited. Mercer was a few hours away from Golden, but still close enough for their issues to leak into his old home. The officer quickly returned to his window, handing Joel his papers.

"Thank you, sir. Local boy eh? What brings you home?" The officer said.

"Family shit, I don't think I will be long here," Joel softly smiled. He wanted nothing more than to be in his own bed.

"Well, I hope it goes well. Good luck with ya and stay safe." The officer stepped back and waved Joel on.

Joel continued into the city, trying to ignore the stabbing aches from his spine. Luckily, his childhood home was only a few more minutes away. He soon pulled into the driveway of where he grew up, hoping that his father was asleep. Joel wanted to stay in his car for a few more minutes, trying to avoid the inevitable small talk, but all he wanted in that moment was to lay his head.

As he made his way up the steps, Joel's father, Wesley, opened the front door to greet him. "Hey kid, can I take your bag?" His dad smiled. He was in his pyjamas and looked exhausted.

"Dad, it's two a.m. You should be asleep," Joel said stiffly.

"I wanted to get you settled in. Drive was longer than usual, eh? Gods you're almost green, are you feeling alright?"

Joel walked into the familiar living room where he and his brothers used to watch their favourite TV shows. He threw his bag on the floor and sat heavily on the old couch that reeked of mothballs. "Just a little carsick. How are you?"

"I'm doing okay..." the two of them sat in silence for what felt like minutes to Joel. The last time Joel left this house ended in vulgar accusations and salt rubbed in old wounds.

"Are you going to ask how she's doing?" There was carefulness to his words.

Joel waved his hands in a sarcastic surrender. "How's mom?"

His father stared at Joel without a word. Joel knew his dad wanted a better reunion, but he was tired and ill. He didn't mean to disappoint him this soon; they could catch up after an awfully needed rest.

"The guest bedroom is set up for you. I'm going back to the hospital in the morning; you should come along." Wesley left Joel alone in the living room to return to his own bed.

Joel laid down on the couch, debating whether he should rest there now that he had silence. His eyes faded into the black as he let the pain wash over the remaining life left in him.

* * *

Dad's classic rock playlist filled the silence on the drive to the hospital. The two of them shared small updates over breakfast, and now they had run out of things to say. He could tell Wesley was treading deep within his stress. Joel wondered how grief and loss would change his father. Wesley acted as if mom was fine, as if she would be discharged from the hospital any day. From what Harvey told Joel, that wouldn't be the case. Denial was an interesting emotion to watch unfold when Joel was absolutely certain he wasn't its victim. He believed he would try to be there for his dad when the time came.

The mixture of coffee and pain meds was making Joel feel jittery. His hands were uncontrollably vibrating and his head was being squeezed by an invisible vise. He told himself it was his cold, but he knew it was the anxiety of seeing his mom. Joel ran through every scenario on how their reunion could play out. He wanted to stand up for himself and refuse her the last word, but he didn't want to upset dad. It would end up being a shitty meeting, like it always did. He just had to push through this last stretch, and then he would never grant her another thought for the rest of his life.

The walk to the hospital, from where they parked, was long. Wesley didn't want to pay the outrageous parking fees and Joel couldn't find a flaw in that argument. Wesley brought him to the family care unit waiting area where he was reunited with his older brother Harvey and younger brother Martin. They had brought their better halves. All the familiar faces made Joel miss Beth's presence.

"Joel, nice to see you, man." Harvey took Joel into a friendly embrace. "Didn't want to fly the distance, eh?"

"The delays probably would have made me late by one more day. Nice to see you Harv," he hugged his brother back and then moved onto the others. Joel couldn't describe the love he had for his siblings. They all had to endure the same abuse; what made them better than Joel was that they stayed. Despite the shared mental and physical torment, they still held their bond.

The group of them shared notable changes over the past few months, obviously avoiding the large elephant in the room. Joel dodged questions about Beth by saying she couldn't get the time off work. He wasn't even sure if she would still be at home in Blackpine when he returned. His family didn't need to know about their issues. Joel's father soon placed a hand on Joel's back and nodded to him. The two of them stepped to the side where they could talk privately; Joel was curious why his dad couldn't have said what was on his mind while they were in the car.

"Look, Joel, your mom might get better for now, but I don't know how long you'll be home. This might be your last time and she's been sober for a while…can you go talk to her, please? But be civil?"

Joel felt a pinch of annoyance over his father's trust. "You don't nee– Just give me some time alone," he stuttered. "I don't have much to say to her, anyway."

Joel stormed off to his mother's patient room to get the last words over with. He refused to give her any satisfaction or forgiveness. If his dad wanted civility, then he should have intervened twenty-seven years ago. He walked into a room full of medical equipment and the sounds of vital sign reports. The room heavily stank of rubbing alcohol, covering the scent of roses that his father had brought her. Joel approached the bed and found his mom almost unrecognizable. She was frail and gaunt. The white of her eyes had turned yellow and her skin had become a leathery grey. He had to remind himself this woman in pain was the same woman who beat him throughout his youth.

"Simone," he said with sternness. Joel was trying incredibly hard not to let the shaking surface.

His mother slowly turned and met his eyes. She gave him a smile, showing him rows of yellowed teeth. "Hey sweety."

Joel watched her with unease. Despite her current state, this woman terrified him. He hated her. "I came to say goodbye, because Dad asked me to. Whatever you have to say to me, say it now."

"Can you sit? Stay with me for just a little?"

"No."

"I know I was cruel to you boys. I got sober, then I got sick. I never got my chance to make it up to you. I'm sorry," she cried through the words.

"I'd never forgive you, even if you had all the time in the world to try. I guess the narcissist in you thought this would go differently. No, you'll get nothing from me, mom."

"Please, just hear what I have to say. Your brothers, they listened–"

"That was their choice! You'll get nothing from me. I thought I could bear through this, but I can't. You need to just go. Fuck you, mom."

Joel stormed out of the room, holding back iron hot tears. The grief and pain overwhelmed him like a rocky avalanche. Nothing about his last words was satisfying. It just felt empty. He pushed past his dad who was trying to console him. Joel needed to be alone and unscramble his thoughts. Years of hatred had just been whittled down to a minute-long goodbye. Old memories jumped out of the shadows to make him relive his most terrible moments, watching that woman demean him to nothing. Joel wanted to scream.

The stabbing aches in his head clashed with his hatred for his mother and for himself. Boiling hot rage tried to pry its way out, to show the world what she had created. Joel found an empty stairwell and pushed the anger down. He sat for what felt like hours, breathing through the pain, forcing himself to stop. He would not give her anything.

* * *

It was a couple days later when she finally passed. His father was there by her side for her final moments, but Joel had refused to visit her again. Once he heard the news, he drove to the hospital to pick up his dad and bring him home. He was quiet the entire drive. Joel knew he was angry with him. Wesley had begged Joel to try talking to his mother again, but couldn't convince him to. The last two days carried tension of unspoken grief and disappointment.

Joel filled his time with making meals and cleaning the house. His cold was recovering, and the pain had reduced to a manageable headache. He would soon have to drive home, but he hadn't spoken to Beth since he left Blackpine. He didn't know what to expect when he returned and assumed the worst. There was no place he could seek peace amidst the death of Simone.

Wesley had asked his children to meet for dinner to discuss funeral planning and their mother's assets. Joel expected to get nothing, and would refuse whatever was offered. He told Wesley he would stay a few more days to help, but needed to return to Blackpine. His dad had no objection. Joel pushed off a pinch of betrayal as he told himself his dad would never know what he endured under Simone, but he felt he wasn't wanted in either of his homes. An urge to leave pulled at him.

The dinner with his father and brothers was quiet, occasionally broken by knives scraping on ceramic plates and jabs at the Golden Wolverines attempt at the playoffs. Joel looked around the table, seeing his family in front of him. He loved them, but at that moment he felt like a stranger, waiting to move along. The feeling should have been irrational, but the familiar faces around him had unfamiliar recognition. He wondered how long it would take for his father to forgive him. The silence was broken with Wesley setting down his utensils and clearing his throat.

"I wanted to go over mom's will tonight," Wesley said. "What assets she had left were passed to me, but she had prepared a letter for each of you."

Wesley set down the will in the middle of the table for them to read and followed with handing individual letters to Joel and his brothers. His brothers were handed small sealed letters. Joel was handed a large orange envelope. He looked over his mother's handwriting of his first name and contemplated opening it in front of his family. Joel decided to wait, and his brothers followed suit.

They finished their dinner and said their goodbyes late in the evening. Once Joel heard his father enter his bedroom, he took his envelope into the living room to discover what his mother had left him. The room was dark, with only a single lamp casting warm light to reveal the contents. Joel opened the sealed envelope and pulled out a thin booklet. It was a children's book; the cover had a simple drawing of a toddler sitting in a bathroom, making a mess with the toiletries around him. The story was about the toddler making messes all over the house, but still being loved by his mother.

The one and only time Joel was read this story was when he was seven. He had broken a soup bowl and quickly left the house before his mom found out. He took his bike and rode the trails of the river valley, trying not to think of the broken bowl. When he returned in the early evening, his mom was already drunk and beat him with a wet towel. Even though they were innocent, his brothers were given a lashing before him and forced to watch Joel receive his.

Simone threw Joel into his room, refused him dinner, and made him sit in silence to think about his mistake. Joel crawled into bed a few hours later, but woke when his mother came into his room and began to apologize. She had the children's book in hand and offered to read it to him. Joel didn't have the courage to say no. He sat and listened as she read the story, and all he could think about was what life would look like without him. How his mom would be happier and he would no longer have to endure the pain he caused. Despite the numerous times she broke her apology and the beatings continued day after day, she never read him that story again. The one and only time he was read this book was engraved in his mind.

Joel flipped the cover of the book and found a short written paragraph in his mom's handwriting. It read:

Joel. I wish we had more time for forgiveness. I hope you can look back on this book and remember the times of love we had for each other. I have so much to make up for, but my final wish is that you can look past my flaws and hold the good memories dear. I love you, son.

Rage flooded Joel.

The book dropped to the old carpet as he stood up from the couch. His hands and face boiled hot with the clenching of every muscle. It took all of his will not to scream or laugh; he wasn't sure which would happen if he let go. Tears began to blur his vision. Every part of him strained with misery, wanting to cry out. But he would not give Simone that, not even in death.

That woman had no clue of the pain she caused, he thought. The book was nothing but a thorn of a memory to him, and she believed it was an olive branch. All of his suffering could be traced to her, and she wanted forgiveness. His rage was fuelled with the realization he couldn't throw the book back at her. His mom had robbed him of everything.

Joel's mind was racing, and he tossed his clothes back into his backpack. He must have made too much noise, as his dad had come into the living room.

"Joel? What's going on? Are you leaving?"

Joel bitterly looked at his dad, locking eyes. "Why did you never stop her from beating us? You just stood by and let it happen."

"Son…" Wesley let out a long sigh. "It's more complicated than that. Your mom, she was suffering. She never meant to hurt you."

"Bullshit. You could have stopped her. You knew how evil she was, how every night she would get so drunk and beat us for any little mistake she could find. She ruined my life, Dad!" Anger flamed hotter as he screamed at Wesley. Joel needed to run.

He grabbed his bag and stormed out of the house. His dad followed him, quietly begging him to stay. The pounding pulse of rage drowned out Wesley's pleas. His car struggled to turn over but started after a couple tries. Joel peeled out of the neighbour-hood, with his dad standing on the sidewalk watching him drive away.

Dozens of memories raced through his head, forcing Joel to remember each insult and hard slap. He knew she was to blame for her abuse, but the small voice in the back of his mind still reminded him it was all his fault. Death was the only cure to bring Joel peace.

It was only until he was ten minutes out of the city that he realized he wasn't heading back towards Blackpine. He was heading north on the highway to Mercer. He felt a pull to go there instead of home; nothing in Blackpine was waiting for him. Mercer called his name, offering a restart. He noticed his cellphone had been vibrating consistently. He had multiple missed calls from his dad and brothers. Joel tossed the phone out of the car window and watched it bounce on the asphalt. He didn't want them trying to track him.

The night was getting late, and Mercer was four hours away. At some point, he decided he would pull over and sleep in his car, but he still had the will to drive on. Tomorrow he would be in Mercer and put his mother's abuse behind him. His rage quietly endured as he followed the pull northbound.

CHAPTER 6

Janak gloried at the night sky above. The atmosphere on RES 9 held a deep sulphur dioxide layer that painted a pink-orange sky during the day and varnished the stars above a warm amber during the night. Every planet he visited had unique gaseous combinations, creating horizons across the colour spectrum. Each one was more beautiful than the last.

No clouds blotted the stars above, revealing the body of the galaxy ROCI 210 to the fullest this planet could offer. Only the massive bodies of two Leviathans, floating in stasis, blocked the view behind them. Janak didn't mind, he was here for them. The stars were just the bonus. Janak named them Derithian-Yen in the Celeste Tongue. Janak had exhausted the Idelvin glossary long ago, but he still gave the giants nicknames from his home. Many other incredible discoveries were named by his true tongue, and he was proud to carry the Celeste legacy.

He had nicknamed the two Yen above Vrit and Wex, a male and female immersed in the five day long mating ritual. His

Voidante was parked underneath their mammoth tails, collecting data and organizing the catalogue of the Derithian-Yen's habits. Three of the planet's four moons reflected an amber red hue against the ship's sharp chrome hull. He was surprised the giants paid no concern to the alien machine.

Janak watched and recorded with his Talener as the two Leviathans floated in unison. They held each other still by overlapping their fins, making a small space in between their bellies to hold the dozens of embryonic bubbles. Janak was close enough to the lowest of the bubbles to see every detail. The Derithian-Yen fetus was as large as Janak stood; it floated in clear fluid, surrounded by a thin translucent shell that seemed incredibly fragile. Still, the parents never once crushed an egg by accident. This would be the third day of the Yen's birthing ritual. On the last the mother would part with every fertilized egg stuck to her belly. Thus would begin the five hundred year journey from birth to death.

Janak still hadn't observed enough to determine if the Leviathans mated for life or how many times they would mate in the solar rotation. They were an incredibly fascinating species, but their size made them slow. He would soon need to move on.

Janak set his Talener to auto-record and picked up his pack off the damp moss. He walked until he found a hill overlooking the valley. From there he could see the two Leviathans and his ship settled underneath, miniature in comparison. Janak pulled his heater from his pack and turned the lid. The coils instantly heated, casting a warm radiance over his body and illuminating the ground around him in a fiery glow. Janak set it on a flat rock and held his bluish grey fingers above it. The dampness in the night air was tolerable, but still felt frigid. His Idelvin roots were always there to remind him of his habituated dryness.

The wind brought a warm breeze that Janak sensed early with his antennae. He watched as the giants let the draft carry them eastbound, slowly. They were no longer directly above his Voidante, but that was of no concern. Janak pulled a rectangular meat ration from his jacket pocket and set it on top of his heater. The meat instantly started to sizzle inside the foil, causing Janak's mandibles to quiver in excitement. The food he was allowed to bring on expeditions was decent, but didn't come close compared to the home-cooked meals. His eyes spotted the quick movements between the rock crevasses. Tiny insects emerged from the ground, following the scent of a delicious new prospect. Their search for his meal would be quashed the moment they got too close to the radiator. Then it was a race back underground to makeup for the moisture they just lost.

Janak set his hand in the path of a tiny wanderer and lifted it to his view. The creature scurried across his hand, disoriented from its intended route. Dozens of stringy legs blurred around its pointed oval-shaped body. A bushel of twirling hair hanging from its thorax pointed towards Janak's face, revealing the cluster of eyes at the end of the hairs. Janak returned the insect to the gravel; it would return for another attempt at his meal once it replenished its body with the desperately needed moisture.

Finding a planet with life was a proud achievement; finding a planet with life uniquely evolved, was a true honour. Bacteria would always be interesting to find, especially when the planet's nature theoretically should kill any living existence. But being the first to see centuries of a complex structure of evolution was an unexplainable fascination. RES 9, and every other planet with life, owned its differences in the great expanse of the universe, and he was there to witness what was on offer. Observing creatures that blotted the sky, onto something as small as a grain of sand, reminded Janak not only of the gift of being a Voidante, but the gift of discovery. He would forever be indebted to the Seekers for the purpose they gave him. He dreamed of the day an expedition would lead him to sentient life.

Janak scarfed down the meaty ration and sat on the damp ground for a few more hours before he would return to his ship for rest. The stars above called for a witness, unblemished and shining, without a cloud in the sky. The stars called when no one else on this rock could answer, except him.

* * *

The silver and chrome belly of the Voidante reflected small, dark ponds as the ship sailed through the prairies. Janak was leaning out of the cargo door, holding onto a handhold and watching the ground blur past as his ship steadily glided. The ground below was littered with hundreds of circular pools, punched through the short brown grass in an almost perfect grid. The gaseous moss refused to grow this far north. Rocky and desolate tundra would soon dominate this part of the hemisphere. With no food, it made no sense to Janak why the Yen would make this journey to these lands. His intuition wanted more.

After documenting the birth of newborn Yen, Janak spent the next three of the planet's days looking for more of the giants to study new behaviour. He found a group of five males, one of ancient size and age and the others ranging from young adult to mature. He found this odd, as he initially recorded males to be introverted and territorial. He followed them for many days as they flew northbound at a comfortable pace to match the speed of the elder. When they arrived at the grasslands, the Yen drifted above the dense white clouds and did not descend for days. They just floated in stasis, puzzling Janak with this new behaviour. Nothing in the area could sustain their diet and the water below was poisoned with deadly minerals and possibly lethal if consumed. Janak was keen to find the Yen's intention, bringing him to finding the horizon spanning a grid of circular pools of water.

Janak flew his Voidante across the prairie, cataloguing the ground and sending down instruments to gather intel. He soon discovered that the pools were created by shy creatures and below the grass sat a vast ocean of alloy rich water. The ship would be supported enough if he had to land, but Janak chose to study high in the air. After many hours of zipping above the pools, Janak had his ship come to a halt and hover. He sat on the edge of the cargo door and let his legs dangle in the cool breeze. Janak pulled out his tablet and took pictures of the landscape below. These would be just for his personal collection, as the ship was constantly gathering images and models. Personal pictures allowed the kind of creativity he would be proud to show off.

Droning cries above caught Janak's attention. He watched as five enormous bodies descended, splitting the clouds like hands parting sand. As they slowly floated down, Janak noticed that the four younger males were clustered below the elder, using their bodies to gently cushion his fall. The elder laid in stillness and its monstrous eyes had glassed over. Janak was witnessing a funeral.

The leviathans lowered their ancient one until their bellies almost scraped the ground below them. The young males rolled away, letting their elder softly glide to the grassland as its final resting place. With its size, the elder's body covered kilometres of land and hundreds of pools underneath. The ground buckled and bowed, causing water to flood out of the holes and surround the elder's body in a shallow bath. Janak was surprised the ground didn't rip apart entirely from the weight of the creature. The four young males returned to the sky, but circled the body of the elder. They pointed their noses to the blanket of clouds above and hovered as still as the dead ancient one. Janak sat there in awe at the ritual. These leviathans continued to gift him with incredible glimpses into their life. These sole giant rulers gave this planet its beauty, from the day they are conceived to the day they take their last breath. The gift of discovery, the pure awe of life, would always remind Janak of the gift of purpose.

As the ancient leviathans body settled the waters until the waves ceased, every circular pool began to tremor lightly. Droves of the shy creatures emerged from the pools. The Yen's body dwarfed them in size, but they looked to be as big as Janak in comparison. Janak used his tablet's zoom lens to get a clearer image and looked upon the newly discovered species. They had a hard and black exterior that covered a thin body and four long, double-jointed legs. The head protruded out of its torso like a slug, but Janak couldn't see eyes. They were particularly ugly creatures, and shared no beauty like the Yen. Thousands crawled out of every pool that bordered the elder and soon covered it until the body was a withering, black mass. Scavengers. Evolved to deconstruct the Yen and return it to the planet.

Over an impressive thirty hours, the carrion hungry creatures tore and shredded every surface of the Yen's body. They spared no waste as each part of the elder was broken and dragged to the ocean below. Janak watched the entire feast, amazed how fast the creatures worked. The ground below the body straightened from the bow as the mass was removed, and all that was left was a bloody stain in the wet grass from where the leviathan was rested. The creatures, given a scientific name of Derit-Caro, gradually returned to their pools once there was nothing left to take.

The funeral ritual was complete, and the four males turned their mountain sized bodies southward for the journey home. Janak watched them slowly distance themselves from each other as they disappeared into the horizon, returning to their lonesome company. Their duty to carry their respected senior was over, and would return with the next Yen to be rested. Janak was amazed, but puzzled. The Yen gained no benefit from carrying the elder all this way and then staying for the rapid feast of the carrions. Not only was it undeniable proof that the Yen had enough intellect to mourn their dead, but whoever took part shared a deep respect for the old. And whoever was lain was given as a gift to a different species with no reciprocated value.

The entire series of events made Janak believe the nature of the Yen delved deeper than what he initially believed about their race. Life, on any planet claimed its own uniqueness, but truly shared connections on many levels.

Janak remembered burying his brother two cycles ago. He had watched Kolen grow of age, far past the age of when Janak's parents passed. He would visit Kolen after every expedition and stay with his family before being called upon for the next cycle. Prolonged life was sometimes a curse and a blessing. Janak would see planets beyond comprehension, but in return, he had to watch his brother die. It wouldn't stop with Kolen. The curse would continue with Kolen's kids, and their kids, and so on. The brutality of it made Janak second guess his decision to become Voidante.

But the brutality wouldn't dominate the blessing. Janak was given the gift of being with Kolen in his last days. In that time, they reminisced about days of old and grew the love they had stronger. Memories of youth and their parents were shared. They looked back at times of laughter and times of anger. The grief was painful, but those final moments were an undeniable beauty of sentiment. That gift allowed Janak to dissolve the doubt and believe in the purpose given to him. He would continue to explore the void and stars in between carrying his brother's memory. And with that memory, he had watched the funeral of a giant.

CHAPTER 7

Trailer trucks and vehicles going well above the speed limit roared past Joel as he walked the thin shoulder of the highway towards Mercer. Attempts at hitchhiking stopped about an hour ago when he realized that no one was willing to slow down in the unexpected blizzard that had soaked his clothes and shoes. Joel was sure that someone would eventually lose control and ram him into a ditch. This highway was not made for pedestrians.

Joel's car had finally croaked some seventy kilometres back, turning what would be an hour long drive to a full day of hiking. He had left the vehicle on the side of the road, knowing it would be eventually towed and ticketed. He didn't care. That was a problem for the future. All he grabbed was his passport, a bag of clothes, and resumed the journey to Mercer. Farmland and large billboards were veiled from the thick screen of blurring white; he couldn't even see the asphalt twenty feet ahead. Drivers paid no mind to him, mostly because they didn't see him until the last second.

The storm continued late into the evening, and Joel was only halfway to Mercer. The snow had slowed him to a snail's pace. He was forced to huddle inside an abandoned gas station on the side of the highway and make a fire out of rotten baseboards. He quashed a creeping feeling of being rock-bottom. The past day felt like a fever dream to Joel. Hundreds of screaming thoughts would have crippled him if they weren't droned out by his determination to reach Mercer. With no phone, no car and no family, he didn't even know what he awaited there. Mercer was his destination on a blind path.

The pathetic fire he made on the cement floor was warming his hands. Joel wanted to sleep, but spent the entire cold night keeping his fire alive without an ounce of exhaustion. He tried not to think too hard about it. He could already feel the panic edging over the border of his sanity. His decision to drop everything felt like a weightless rock, just waiting for an opportune time to remind him of his situation and break his will. A part of him cried for warmth, for family, and for guidance. The rock would soon drop and he would face the reality of when one gives up. It was difficult to ignore the impending panic when he wasn't trying to put one foot in front of the other. All he had as a distraction was attempts to dry his socks.

When Joel realized the sun was rising, he stomped out the remaining embers and continued walking northbound on the side of the road. The blizzard had ceased, but as the sun warmed the morning air the snow turned to slush beneath him. Every car that passed, caked him with slurry, muddy snow. His clothes quickly returned to being drenched.

When Joel finally reached the outer limits of Mercer, the sun was returning to the horizon. A checkpoint similar to Golden's had lined up drivers bumper to bumper for the last kilometre. Joel could feel their eyes follow him as he walked past each car, feeling their judgement for cutting the line. The border guards loosened their questioning pressure once he had explained his car's demise; all they cared for was his passport and sent him through once they were satisfied. Joel continued to make his way into Mercer until he came across a bus shelter. Night was creeping in and his clothes had not dried. Joel's feet ached as the soles of his shoes began to peel away from the rest. He thought sitting was a nice break, but some sort of shelter would be necessary soon. Joel couldn't help but see the past few days as only a blur.

His world had flipped to an uncomfortable mess, all because of his stupidity. Nothing about leaving everything behind was freeing to him, and he only began to realize that when he finally sat on the bus bench to rest. His best-case scenario for tonight would be just to freeze to death.

A bus pulled up next to the bench with a flashy LED destination of downtown. The driver opened the door for Joel, holding a look of impatience as Joel considered the ride. He was quickly convinced once he felt the heated air rush over him. The driver didn't bother asking for fare once he noticed Joel's shoes. He just gave Joel a look of gracious tolerance, most likely forced by a policy allowing free rides to homeless in freezing weather. The unspoken payment was just to sit in silence and not cause problems. Joel knew the only bed available to him in this city was at a homeless shelter, if he didn't want to shell out the money for a motel. He wished he had a friend that would offer their couch.

The bus had dropped Joel off deep in downtown. Mercer's core was packed with highrises, restaurants and traffic. A surprising amount of people were out despite the weather. Groups of smiling couples and laughing friends hopped from one bar to the next, each striking a quick glance at Joel's questionable attire. It took Joel a few spooked looks to remember a murderer was on the loose within Mercer. That fine line between wanting normalcy and paranoia was as plain as daylight. His shambled outfit definitely didn't help his case.

Rows of neon signs advertised numerous bars and pubs. For half a year the city halted to a frozen hibernation, limiting hobbies to drinking and more drinking. Distilleries all around the city took these opportunities to experiment with a range of fruity or sour alcohols, displayed on posters outside their bar doors. A similar culture existed in Golden and Blackpine. Joel wondered how many were actually worth tasting and how many tasted like garbage. It's not like he had the interest to sit and buy a pint, anyway. The smell of deep fried appetizers had no effect, either.

Past the core revealed the district of homeless shelters and streets that locals probably warned others not to venture alone. Crowds and tents packed the sidewalks outside the shelter doors, directly rejecting that option without hesitation.

Joel continued walking until he came across what looked to be a cheap motel. He tried not to think too hard about what clients had come through these rooms; all he needed was a bed to last him till morning. Joel entered the stale smelling lobby and found the front desk run by a fat, older gent with a brown stained moustache and yellow fingers from smoking too many cigarettes.

"One room, please," Joel said somberly. The man leaned forward with a bothered groan, scanning Joel from his head down.

"Can you pay?"

"Of course. On credit please," Joel tried to ignore the criticism. The man's doubt slowly became more glaring with each failure and 'denied' text on the pay machine. Joel's bank must have immediately flagged the purchase as suspicious and were probably trying to call his phone that was lying in a ditch. He went to pull his debit from his wallet, and found it missing. He must have accidentally tossed the card when he rushed to leave his father's place.

"I ain't a charity man. Doors' right there."

Joel looked at the man with defeat. With no money, he knew he'd be sleeping rough tonight. No banks were open at this hour. Joel left the motel, embarrassed at the cluster of failures following him since his attempt at starting anew. He rounded the corner into the back alley and found a thick blanket hanging from the dumpster. Joel couldn't smell it without smelling himself.

He pulled the blanket around his shoulders and slowly lowered himself to the icy concrete. Joel didn't feel tired, but felt the weight of defeat hooked and sunk his will far below his pride. He knew the cold would eventually dull his body until he froze to death; he didn't want to fight it either.

Joel had made it to Mercer, and was worse off than he had half expected. Regret laughed in his face, pointing out his stupidity until he traced his decision back to his mom's parting gift. Simone got the last twist of the knife, and he would die the failure she always predicted him to be. He imagined his father and Beth standing over him, confirming their doubt solely created by Joel's negligence to change. He let his eyes close and waited for death to take the reins.

"What have you led me to? Is this the prospect?" A voice creeped from the darkness. Joel quickly sat up and faced a man standing over him with a rotting deer carcass fitted over his head. Joel didn't even remember hearing the stranger's footsteps. "It's true… I can feel his fire."

"What the fuck? Stay away from me, man," Joel snapped angrily. He shuffled across the concrete to make space between them.

"I thought my search was pointless. I thought I was alone." The man crouched and locked eyes with Joel. The stranger's eyes held firm but glazed over, hiding behind sockets ripped in the deer's hide. The stranger refused to look away. "I can see your confusion. I am not here to harm you."

"Leave me alone, freak. I am not in the mood to be fucked around with." The stranger's presence brought a lingering tension. Joel wanted to rush away but was cornered by the garbage bin and motel wall. The stranger tilted his head, holding his lifeless gaze.

"But you're a freak, like me. You haven't felt it yet, have you? The sleepless nights, disappearing hunger, sickness and pain coursing through your body. These are all signs you've lived, no?"

Joel's confusion couldn't silence the immediate awareness of the stranger's words. The last few days held a heavy toll, and distress triggered all sorts of labour on a body. Joel knew he couldn't sleep or wasn't hungry. These were just the motions of losing his mother and leaving his life behind. "So I look like shit, lucky guess. Can you leave now?"

"My guess doesn't come from your appearance. I can feel your life. It's different from the rats around us. You've evolved into a greater being, like me, and I can help you. Look deeper, beneath the pain. Look for the power that flows through your blood."

"Shut up," Joel felt his anger growing, but doubt pricked his mind. Beneath the fury surged an unfamiliar intensity. Waves of nausea creeped from his stomach as the stranger continued to predict what Joel was battling. "I am not like you."

"In many ways, you are."

"Fuck you." Joel stood up to walk away. The stranger rapidly threw what looked like a wet rope and tightly wrapped it around Joel's ankle. Before he could yell, Joel was pulled underneath the stranger and his neck was gripped by cold hands.

"Resistance isn't tolerated with me," the stranger grimly said. "Willingly or not, you will help me."

Joel struggled to pry himself out of the stranger's grasp, but the man was incredibly strong. He could feel his neck being crushed by his hands. As Joel kicked and turned, a strange sensation began to vine within his head. Fear screamed within as he could feel his memories and thoughts become violated. An uninvited guest was inside his mind. His will was waning. Joel forced the rage beneath to defend himself.

A hot flash of green violently pulsed between Joel and the stranger. Joel closed his eyes as rage rushed through his body, overpowering every feeling and thought under its own control. He flipped to his side in a panic and felt an explosion of debris strike his body. Joel was completely disoriented.

As the rage settled, he realized the stranger was no longer gripping his neck and was absent from his mind. Joel opened his eyes, looking at the destroyed wall of the burning motel and the stranger was nowhere in sight. He began to pat down his body for wounds and found solid steel when he reached his head. A helmet enveloped his entire skull, leaving two slots for his eyes. The steel pressed firmly against his skin. Claustrophobia squeezed his lungs until he couldn't breathe. Joel tried to pry the helmet off his jaw and failed. It held securely.

Was this given by the stranger? He thought. Joel began to panic and smashed his head into the concrete in an attempt to free himself. Hot flames, eating the motel walls, cast orange light over him as he repeatedly slammed his head down. He couldn't even put in a dent.

Shouts echoed from the parking lot, and the motel owner ran into the alley to see the source of the explosion. He was on the phone with 911 and was screaming orders for every fire truck in the city. Joel stood on his feet and ran. Throbbing thoughts of fear drowned out the shouting behind him.

Joel ran until he noticed a derelict house; its smashed windows and doors were boarded with fresh plywood. Distant sirens of first responders echoed. He could see their lights cast over the rooftops surrounding the motel. Joel jumped the fence and pried off loose plywood from a basement window. Once he was able to slip in, he pulled the wood covering back and scanned the room. The house was silent. It was mostly empty, except for a burning barrel and a couch that may have been brought in by squatters. Joel let himself fall to the ground, holding his head in his hands. The cold steel was smooth beneath his palms. He could feel small grooves across the mouth and scalp.

He thought back to the stranger and the explosion. He didn't think anyone was hurt, but the chaos made him unsure. Images of the stranger and his deer head flashed in his memory. Joel began furiously recalling the details of the recent encounter and how the stranger breached his mind. He didn't realize his breathing had heightened and his hands were uncontrollably shaking. Panic was taking the wheel. Heat deep within surfaced again. Joel let himself breathe slowly, shifting his focus of the helmet and stranger to nothing.

An hour passed before the shaking settled. Sirens still wailed on in the background, but no one had followed him. He felt calmer, but painfully aware of the lingering events that occurred. Without warning, a portion of the helmet opened over his eyes. In the following second, it opened over his mouth and jaw. Joel patted his face, feeling his skin, nose, and eyes. He reached for the back of his head but couldn't find the helmet. It had completely disappeared. Was this a trick of the stranger?

Joel moved himself to the dirty, dusty couch and laid down. His clothes were still wet from the snow and slightly burnt from the fire. Joel considered using the fire barrel for warmth, but knew it would attract attention. He lay in silence, convincing himself that he could sleep. Another restless night ultimately went by.

CHAPTER 8

A couple days had passed in the stale basement of the abandoned home. Joel hadn't slept or eaten. Each minute that passed without the feeling of exhaustion and hunger grew a terrifying belief that the stranger knew more about Joel than he realized. He wanted to leave the basement, get some money, and leave the city. But then he risked being found by either the authorities or the deer carcass freak. Joel wondered if the faint pull that had grown stronger since he reached Mercer, was the stranger calling him.

The first morning after the motel incident, Joel had noticed small aches on the palms of his hands and soles of his feet. He initially thought he just had slivers from plywood, but looking closer, he found metallic circles seamlessly embedded within his skin. They surfaced enough to just level with the palm and soles, and felt like the same cold steel that had once enveloped his head. In a panic, he attempted to pry one out with a rusty screwdriver found on the floor. He quickly quit when it became apparent he couldn't cut his own skin. He since recklessly ignored their presence, but failed to stop unconsciously feeling their outline.

The helmet, the rings, the stranger's words, all became too much to comprehend. It was a nightmare he couldn't wake up from.

The days that had passed continued to be beaten by a blizzard bringing in thick damp snow. Joel's clothes had finally dried and revealed the horrible stench of lacking hygiene underneath. He wanted a hot shower badly. Joel continued to pace around the empty basement rooms, trying to distract himself with the details of items left behind by the previous owners. Reading the scribbles of graffiti was enough to keep him busy for a while, until sudden sounds of footsteps upstairs drove him out the small window. His hiding spot had outlived its welcome.

The snow had piled high, reaching above his ankles and spilling into his shoes with each step. Rooftops and tree branches were plastered with white, and grey clouds cast dull light over. Joel walked in the opposite direction of the motel, knowingly avoiding the downtown core. Daylight had revealed the state of this neighbourhood and how many homes stood derelict. One day it would all be torn down and replaced with highrises. Joel continued walking until he reached a Lavendy bakery. A waft of coffee and fresh pastries was inviting, but not to fulfil an absent hunger. Joel entered and was greeted by a younger cashier, most likely the daughter of the owner. The store was packed with exported goods from the Lavendy state.

"I'm sorry, but can I use your phone?" Joel asked with embarrassment. The cashier smiled and pointed to a landline. A relic from his past. He remembered stealthily jumping in on his brothers' calls to prank them and their friends. "Thank you."

Joel picked up the phone and let the dial tone sing. He wished he could remember his dad's or brother's numbers. Newer phones made him lazy when it came to his contacts. The only number he knew by heart was Beth's. He forced himself to memorize it when he started at the logging camps. Reception was poor in the mountains and the camp only had a satellite radio for emergencies.

Would Beth want to speak with him? He thought. Joel was certain Beth had started to cut all ties with him. Even if he called her for Wesley's number, he would open an undeserving wound. She didn't deserve that pain, regardless of the situation he was in. Joel held the phone to his forehead, debating the worth of her aid. As far as he knew, Beth thought he dropped off the face of the planet. Maybe that was a better ending than finding out he was trapped in Mercer, hunted by a psychopath, and becoming his crutch again. Joel was painfully aware of his situation, but couldn't bring himself to dial her number. Beth would be better off with him gone forever. Joel could feel tears welling in the corner of his eyes. He set the phone down and wiped his face with his torn jacket. He quickly left the store, refusing the free pastry the cashier tried to offer him on his exit.

Joel continued his blind journey through the city, passing by busy streets and donair shops. He soon found himself in an old warehouse district packed with brick buildings and abandoned refineries. His walk ended abruptly when he was grabbed from the back and thrown through a concrete wall.

Joel rolled over broken rubble and scattered rail ties. A sensation of knives grazed his mind and was cut off with an unexpected forging of the helmet. Joel was certain his body was broken from the sheer force, but he couldn't feel any injury. He quickly planted himself to stop the roll and jumped to his feet. Joel furiously scanned the room, expecting the stranger to attack again. He was nowhere to be seen.

"Show yourself! What do you want with me?!" Joel shouted through the helmet. Seconds passed before a voice creeped from the rafters.

"I cannot see into your mind. Why is that? Is it your helmet that refuses me passage?"

"What have you done to me?" Joel demanded. He clenched his fists, darting his eyes to every corner. The stranger was hiding from him.

"I've underestimated you, Joel. It's time for a proper introduction." The stranger rapidly materialized from the ground up, forming from vines and lichen.

As he stepped into the light, Joel noticed his right arm was amputated from the bicep. Tendrils were intertwined and hanging from the stump. "You injured me badly. My own arm has proven more difficult to grow back than I expected."

"I did nothing to you. That explosion was your doing."

"No. That was you. You're discovering the chaos of your abilities," the stranger walked closer to Joel. His eyes would not divert. The lifelessness of his gaze held without a blink. "My name is Morwin. I have been blessed with gifts, and so have you."

He stopped when he reached a respectable gap between them. Morwin held out his arms to his sides in a surrendering gesture. "I'll be the first to admit that my methods yesterday were a bit too forceful. I didn't expect that raw power from you. I was just going to dominate your mind, and you've clearly shown me you appreciate your own free will."

"Of course I do. I could feel you dig through my memories. You changed me somehow. I can't eat, sleep or hurt myself. Undo whatever you did, now," Joel gnashed his teeth. Rage bubbled through the surface.

The deer carcass began to unravel, revealing Morwin's face. His hair and beard were dark and thin. Pale skin stretched over his cheeks, showing dark veins spreading underneath. Despite his sickly look, he held a grin of confidence. "The only deed I've committed is to peer through your mind. You shut me out before I could really grasp control. Everything else is your own doing. Your own evolution. Don't you realize that these changes come from deep within, long before our first meeting?"

Joel shook his head, but belief that Morwin was right crept through. "Why am I like this?" Joel's breath rattled.

"I do not have that answer. I was lost like you too, but quickly accepted my new purpose. Don't you see that we have been gifted the opportunity as heralds of the new race?" Morwin stepped back and sat down on a large chunk of broken concrete.

"I feel unnatural. My body aches with uneasiness, like I'm about to blow up at any minute. This is no gift."

"I'm amazed that you're so cynical about this. I've seen your mind. I know you yearn for change. The world is in decay according to your perspective, and you choose to ignore the very power that can bring that change," Morwin said. "You've cut ties from your old life. Your past is behind you, from your own choice. Fate and fortune have paved the way for you to wield this new purpose."

"I want to be left alone. I want nothing to do with you or these 'abilities'. You speak like a madman, and frankly, the way you dress doesn't help your case," Joel said.

Morwin laughed. He nodded in deep thought. "I disagree. This world, our bodies, life itself crawls with bacteria. From birth to death, we and our tiny travellers are returned to the dirt. I can manipulate… the rot. It's what feeds the nervous system of our planet. Our Aross. You'd understand its beauty if you could see its wide connection." Morwin's smile disappeared, replaced with solemnity. "I wear the hide of our planet's creation out of respect. In death, the deer still feeds this life."

"Are you behind the murders? Are you Mercer's killer?" Joel said. He pondered Morwin's motive. The man was clearly unwell.

"I prefer to refer to them as my sacrifices. I needed them to learn."

"What do you want with me? Did these lives that you took also have abilities?"

"No," Morwin said disappointingly. "The first few were like tests. I was blessed as a herald and I am only bringing the strong with me. Humans fail spectacularly. They break under the slightest touch. That's why I need the strong, like you, alongside me."

"You're a fucking monster," Joel snapped. Anger boiled under his skin. The silver circles vibrated with anxiety. "You're killing innocents. Do you not understand that?"

"They have no innocence. Like you, I've watched the human race destroy this planet and themselves. They bitch and squander about every issue without enacting any actual change. Aren't you tired of the games they play? The rich continue to fatten and the poor choose ignorant bliss. No one stands up? That reality is beyond innocence. They've had their chance, Joel." Morwin stared further into Joel's eyes. His words carried commitment to his belief.

"And how will you be different?" Joel said grimly.

"Because we have the opportunity to avoid the same mistakes and have a clean slate for our new race by eliminating the pathetic failures before us. Do you really believe that we could change Aross with the current systems they've created? Very few have tried and tried again to enact real change. They're silenced each time, by every class. No one cares. It costs too much money to care. I can't stand by anymore. I know for a fact they won't accept us, or what we have to offer." Morwin's words carried defeat in his rant. His eyes drifted to the cracked cement below his feet.

"I don't disagree that this world needs change," Joel spoke with carefulness in his words. "I'm tired too. I have so many issues of my own, I've stopped caring about the bigger picture."

Morwin locked eyes with Joel. Silence held between them.

"But I won't kill an innocent," Joel firmly stated.

"Then you'll join them in the dirt where you belong," Morwin's rotten head draped over. In quick succession, the ground below Joel burst with shattered concrete and tendrils. He was thrown backwards into a stack of creosote soaked planks. They splintered under the force of his impact.

Joel rushed to find his bearings. He reoriented himself from the ground and attempted to run. He quickly found his leg stuck in place. It was glued to the concrete by a wet mold, moving up his leg. Another blow he didn't see landed on his chest, pushing him through the rail ties and into a metal support beam. The beam split like a twig as his body flew through.

As he landed, Joel grabbed a rail tie to stop his momentum. He felt disoriented. He should be dead from the impact. Joel rushed to his feet and sprinted to an open back exit. He was five feet from the exit when something gripped around his neck and pulled him backwards. A tendril had grabbed him, choking his last breath out of his lungs. Joel was pulled across the empty warehouse until he was at Morwin's feet. More tendrils restrained his body till he was kneeling. Joel's hand pried at the vine around his neck, but it held tight.

Morwin stood over Joel and gripped his head with his intact hand. Joel could feel Morwin trying to force open the helmet. His fingers pried from Joel's neck as he furiously struggled. The tendril around Joel's neck squeezed tighter as Morwin yanked at the steel. His vision blurred more with every tightening shift. Fear and rage screamed from within. Morwin wouldn't grant him death. He knew his body would be used as a puppet. Panic filled his mind.

"This helmet will come off! Even if I have to decapitate you!" Morwin screamed. "You're just like them. Selfish pricks who have chosen not to care!"

Joel let out a voiceless scream from his empty lungs. He could feel the chaos within, forcing its way through his fleeting control. He threw an empty hand upwards and grabbed onto Morwin's collar. Rippling energy flowed through his palm, exploding in a bright neon light. Joel could feel Morwin release him, but his own arm shot outwards, letting a hot beam of green cut through the walls of the warehouse with ease and up towards the roof. The green ray roared out of control, cutting everything in his path like scissors on paper.

The roof began to collapse. Joel closed his hand to stop and threw himself forward, releasing the tendrils from his neck. He rolled to his side and shifted his vision towards the exit. Picking himself up, Joel ran for the direction that could save him. He waited for Morwin's attack on his retreat, but made it outside without another assault. Joel sprinted between the warehouses until he was out of breath, leaving Morwin behind in the crumbling building.

CHAPTER 9

The motel had been cleaved against the floor and up through the building's furnace. The explosion most likely occurred from flames sparking the gas line. Sadie and Lyas were standing in the back alley assessing the damage; they were waiting for Rowan to regroup with them.

"Is this pull nearby?" Lyas asked.

"It feels close, but fleeting and far." Sadie stood next to the charred wall and examined the slash closely. The cut was clean. Whatever destruction occurred disintegrated anything it touched. "Our murderer seems to have developed his abilities further."

"This pull... Can I examine it?" Lyas carefully asked. She knew the courage it took to ask for that permission.

"Of course," she said. She let Lyas stand directly in front of her, and she felt her mind feathered with a soft touch. Lyas soon stepped away and shook his head.

"I don't see anything. Well... maybe. It's very faint." He scrunched his nose as he thought.

"I'm sure it's there. That spike of energy pointed directly here, same as what drew me."

Sadie looked up towards the clouds and let the soft snowflakes fall onto her cream coloured skin, melting onto her brown freckles. This blizzard reminded her of an Arsacadia early spring. Her sisters and brothers would take Sadie to the lake and ice skate late into the night. The winters were too cold to be outside, but springtime made the night air enjoyable. Her hometown of Skjerrel took pride in the last snow melt; the festival of Mainnus spiralled the town into a week-long binge of drinking and partying. But she was far from home, and far from spring. Mercer was about to dive into a cold winter, and soon everything would be frozen under a minus forty wind.

"This murderer is evolving faster than I anticipated. Whatever hit this motel practically split it apart like nothing," Lyas said as he examined the back wall.

"No blood was found. You think whoever he tried to attack ran away?"

"It's too early to say. You'd think a civilian, just attacked by a fungus wielding sociopath, would be crying loud enough for me to hear." Lyas rubbed his nose with his fingers. "The longer this chase goes on the more confused I get. His actions seemed coordinated, then suddenly he lashes out at random? The guy must be losing his grip on reality."

"Maybe Rowan can share what she found," Sadie nodded towards Rowan, walking towards the two. She looked completely normal in her attire; she would blend in well with the public. Only the closest friends to Rowan knew of the arsenal of deadly weapons hidden within her clothes.

"This city is offensively ill-designed," Rowan said as she joined them. "You know how many times a car almost hit me? It's like they strategically planned on phasing out sidewalks for more car lanes."

"What'd you find?" Lyas sounded impatient. Rowan just rolled her eyes back at him.

"Practically nothing. There's a few more corners I want to check. Utility tunnels, old airport, abandoned museum," Rowan said. "What'd you find here?"

"Our killer destroyed half a motel last night," Sadie glazed over the demolished wall. "You see anything we might have missed?"

Rowan looked over at the wall and scanned the alley side to side. Lyas and Sadie watched as Rowan crouched near a dumpster bin and brushed aside some snow.

"He attacked someone last night. Dragged him right here, you see? There's mycelium residue," Rowan traced remnants in the snow. She looked up at Lyas. "Are you sure you didn't hear an attack?"

"Just a surge of power."

"Have you even slept yet? You look exhausted," Rowan said.

"I don't need sleep yet. I'll sleep when we catch this guy," Lyas grumbled.

Sadie felt an awkward tension between the two. She quickly spoke to change the subject. "Lets go talk to the building owner."

"No," Lyas said. "Let's move on from this place."

Rowan nodded and said her goodbyes to her friends. Lyas watched Rowan walk away before speaking up. "Take me to that old estate. I want to check there next."

Sadie frowned at Lyas; he had dismissed Rowan so quickly. She grabbed onto Lyas's arms and collapsed them into the kinetic stream.

* * *

"Look harder, Lyas. I'm absolutely sure I can feel him," Sadie said. She was crouching over the rotten body of a young female. When they had finally discovered the killer's lair, they found bodies scattered over the walls and floor. Mold and wet growth plastered whatever remaining skin they had. Half of their bodies were already consumed. No one was left alive. After searching the entire building, they had counted ten dead, and three possible remnants of a completely decomposed grave. Sadie wanted to move the bodies to a resting place more respectable than the nightmare they were left in. Lyas refused.

"I'm trying. I think he disappeared again," Lyas sighed. He was sitting crossed legged on the ground, leaning into a meditative trance. He shot Sadie an annoyed look as his focus broke. Sadie ignored his rudeness and looked back at the girl's body. The only parts remaining were her head and rib cage. Everything else was eaten. Her face was petrified with a scream; Sadie guessed she had died in horrible agony.

"I can still feel his pull. He didn't disappear," she said sternly.

"Sadie, no offence, but why can't you just tell me the general direction instead of doubting my search?" Lyas stood up and approached her. She could hear the shortness in his words.

"I would tell you if I could, but it's like following a needle on a faulty compass," Sadie had felt a pulling feeling in her mind about two days ago. Sometimes the feeling would spike with energy.

Her main theory was the killer becoming stronger with each kill. However, the feeling was hard to track and harder to describe. Lyas looked for her with his mind almost every minute of the day, but couldn't pinpoint the source. "I can try jumping through the city, following its tow?"

"You've tried that already."

"Yea, but not with this new feeling!" She was growing angry with Lyas's stubbornness.

"No, Sadie. This time, we're doing this my way," Lyas said as he crossed his arms.

Rowan swung down from the rafters and softly landed on her feet, making no noise. She holstered her bow around her back as she joined them. "We can ambush him here. He will probably return at any minute."

Lyas stepped closer to Sadie. "This lair, right here, is our best shot. If I split us up then our chances of capturing this killer drastically drops."

"Capture? What happened to killing this freak?" Sadie said sharply. "Look at their bodies, Lyas. These people suffered. Slowly and painfully. Why does this killer deserve our goodwill?"

Lyas scoffed. "He'll get no goodwill from me. But I also won't let my emotions break my judgement."

Sadie glared at her friend. With every passing day, tension grew between them. Rowan was a kind buffer, but Sadie was furious with their failure to stop the killings sooner.

Rowan cupped Sadie's back and lightly encouraged her to walk away. She walked to a stack of plastic pallets across the warehouse floor and sat down. She released the band from her ponytail and let her bright blonde hair fall down over her shoulders. Keeping her mind busy, she ran her fingers through her scalp, collecting loose strands and braiding it back together. Rowan silently approached the pallets and sat right beside her.

"Tactically, you know this ambush is the best chance we got," Rowan said.

Sadie nodded. "I know. But I'm being drawn into a foggy direction. You can't feel it? Is it just me?"

"Yes, just you. Lyas nor I, feel a pull. Maybe it's just your ability to sense raw energy?"

"This feels different," Sadie muttered.

Rowan sighed. "I hear you, Sadie. But we can't prioritize a feeling we are just learning about. Waiting for this monster, right here, is our smartest option. Lyas will make sure he won't get away."

"I'll make sure he won't," Sadie solemnly said. "You can see the fear in their eyes. How their killer tortured them and fed them to that blight. No one deserves to die so dishonourably. These killings are pure evil, and I don't care how we stop him at this point."

"I know you do care, Sadie. Killing this monster will only serve as a reminder of your past."

Sadie finished twisting her elastic band and turned towards Rowan. "Let's say we capture him. What if he escapes and continues killing? What happens if we can't subdue him and he kills more? Each death, including the ones already dead, falls on our responsibility. We have incredible abilities that allow us to stop threats like this blight, and Lyas has stalled us for time, all for foolish reasons."

"Rushing into a threat can have its consequences too," Rowan softly spoke. "We always do our best. No matter how difficult the problem is. The fact that you care so much for these dead is the very proof I need to understand you're made for this life. Mercy is what makes us different from the cruel."

Sadie let out a small smile. She knew Rowan was torn between supporting either argument. Rowan loved Lyas deeply, but also loved her friends enough to see when they were struggling. The effort she put into their friendship was enough to listen to her reason.

"I'll follow Lyas's lead, but if I so much as see him slip, I will burn this killer to ashes."

"And I'll join you," Rowan smiled back.

As they walked back to Lyas, Rowan pointed out each potential advantage point from the rafters and second story decks. She explained she wanted Sadie next to Lyas when the killer appeared. Rowan showed her where she would perch herself for a kill shot. They agreed Sadie would incapacitate the killer with a strong, unexpected current, followed by Lyas dominating the killer's mind. Rowan was hidden out of sight, on standby as collateral, in case the killer didn't react to Sadie or Lyas.

They all hunkered down in their chosen spots. Lyas was silent and barely spoke a word to Sadie. He looked exhausted and irate. Two weeks of tracking had them all on edge. They all had a high stake in this capture, and a failure would greatly cripple them.

Hours passed as the three waited in tense anticipation. The afternoon sun weakly broke through the grey clouds and shone through the broken frames of the skylights, cast on a group of plastered, eaten bodies. Their faces haunted Sadie from afar, screaming to be released. The silence of their horrid trance was broken by Lyas.

"Something's happening. There's frenzied chatter near downtown," he said.

Sadie continued staring at the twisted faces, waiting for the impending moment the killer would arrive. She felt a rising tide from within. In a second, the tide became a rushing surge. The pull that had been following her imploded into a grip, tracing to a fountain of raw energy that cried out. The power overwhelmed Sadie. What had been a trickle had turned into a terrible torrent. She could feel the rage. She felt a similar impression the night of the motel attack, but nothing of this scope.

Sadie turned to Lyas and noticed he was already staring at her. She knew he could feel a part of the torrent. She wondered if he would reach into her mind and absorb the sensation in full. Lyas slowly shook his head, locking his eyes with hers.

"Don't," he said.

"I'm sorry."

Sadie collapsed into pure energy and flew towards the source of the rapids.

Chapter 10

Joel's foot slipped from under him as he rounded the corner of the community arena. He had been running for what felt like hours along the icy roads. It felt as if he could keep running; he didn't feel winded at all, but the helmet still mounted his head. Passing people weren't shy to stare. He needed it off.

"Go away, go away," Joel whispered quickly. He tried to pry the faceplate off again, and failed.

Morwin's words echoed in Joel's head. How much of his mind did he really see? He thought. Joel braced himself on the wall and peaked around the corner. Nothing strange stood out. Another pedestrian strolled by and stared at Joel, unknowingly letting her mouth droop open. Joel spun around and ran to the edge of the parking lot. Ahead of him stood a stand of pine trees, followed by a steep cliff into the river valley.

Before he could reach the drop, Morwin rose from the ground. The antlered deer carcass hung over Morwin's scalp, but Joel noticed a part of his jaw and cheek was completely burned off. Morwin's eyes flamed with rage as he lunged towards Joel, screaming madly. Before Joel could react, Morwin grabbed his arm and tossed him through the arena wall. Joel rolled through a locker room, into a rink board and stopped somewhere along the empty, smooth concrete.

Wildly looking for an exit, Joel could only see the hole he had just been tossed through. Around his feet grew a circle of bulbous, leathery spheres. They expanded until they reached the size of a balloon and exploded with a cloud of amber dust. Joel waved his hand in front of his mouth, expecting to immediately breathe the spores in. The air continued to smell untainted.

"Your mask helps you in many ways," Morwin deeply spoke as he rushed towards Joel. "You can't hide behind it forever!"

Joel braced his feet before Morwin grabbed him. He expected to be tossed like a rag doll. Joel grabbed Morwin's jacket and absorbed the blow. Morwin let out a grunt and came to a sudden halt. The two pulled and pushed into each other's weight, trying to gain control. Joel was taken by surprise when Morwin landed a solid fist that rattled his brain.

Joel stumbled backwards, disturbing the spore cloud around him. He felt a tight grip wrap around his ankles. His body flew from under his feet and his head smashed into the concrete floor. Joel's vision became painfully blurry. It took him a second to realize he was hanging upside down. Joel tried to move his arms, but found them pinned against his ribs. Morwin stood facing Joel, watching him swing side-to-side.

Morwin breathed heavily. He watched as Joel struggled with the tendrils restraining him. His body twisted in the vise, squeezing the air out of his lungs. Morwin stared silently, watching the life slowly leave Joel.

Sirens began to cry distantly, and sung louder as they drew nearer. Joel felt a pinch of hope, but suddenly realized they would be running into a meat grinder. Morwin turned his head, listening to the approaching cries.

"Take your helmet off," Morwin said grimly.

Joel continued to swing as he fought against the tightening grip. The sirens shouted over the screeching of wheels. Joel could hear shouts from outside.

"Whoever comes into this building will die. I'll tear them from limb to limb. All for you to witness. Unless you take off your helmet."

Joel tried to shout, but his lungs strained empty. Images of flesh being dismembered flashed in his mind as he continued to struggle in the restraint. Innocent lives taken, blamed on his weakness. He needed to get out.

"Their lives are on you, Joel," Morwin said. He turned his back to him and began to walk towards the sirens. "Embrace the curse of responsibility."

Blood boiled through Joel's body. He was helpless. People, unknown to him, were about to die. The approaching reality of their deaths was judged on him without his choice. Anger within him surfaced in a frenzy, eager to lash out in every direction. Joel lost control of the remaining will he had left, and in a second, a roaring barrage of wind and thunder enveloped him.

The shearing of metal and splintering of wood cried out under the bellows of the thunder. Daylight instantly replaced the darkness of the arena. The tendril wrapped around Joel's body split apart as he fell to the ground and curled into a huddle, trying to protect himself from whatever hell was unleashed. The thunder quickly died, but followed were the wounded screams of people.

Joel raised his head and found the arena completely flattened. Only rubble replaced its existence. Morwin was nowhere to be seen, but fire trucks and police cruisers circled around him, chewed apart and destroyed. Joel could see people crawling through the rubble, covered in dust, and dragging blood behind them. The damage stretched past the parking lot and into the street. The trees that hugged the arena were snapped at the stump. Blame set on Morwin flared within Joel as he took in the extent of the damage. However, he soon realized the surge of violence came from within him. He knew he had set free his overwhelming anger in an attempt to stop Morwin. He looked at the dead and injured bodies of the people buried by rubble. The fault was his.

Joel's stomach dropped, expelling hot vomit out of his mouth. He could feel it splash the inside of the helmet and trickle down his jaw. He tried to wipe it away with his sleeve, but only felt the solid metal against his arm. A pile of bricks and steel joists shifted slowly in front of him. Morwin stood up, holding his ribs with his intact hand. Large slivers of wood had pierced his body, oozing dark blood from their cuts. Morwin grunted as he pulled an arm sized splinter from his side.

"You're just full of surprises, aren't you?" Morwin rasped.

"What did I do? These people, they need help," Joel pleaded.

"They were too weak to begin with. Dead or dying, they've already lost their right to live."

Joel stared at the wounded. He could see fear paralyzed on their faces. One cop, covered in blood, was hunched over a pile of bricks, trying to pull out someone from the rubble. He abruptly fell backwards, holding a dismembered leg in his hands. Joel stumbled towards him, desperate to help. Morwin rushed towards Joel, shouting.

"No!" He pushed Joel, forcing him to fall to the ground. "What, do you not understand?"

Joel could feel intense pressure pinned to his ankle. Morwin stood over him, anger flaring in his eyes and blood dripping from his clothes.

"You have been blessed with incredible gifts," Morwin hissed. "You have evolved above the species driving themselves directly towards their extinction. And you want to save them? It's fucking irresponsible. With your gifts, you could single-handedly wipe them off the map and open passage for your brothers and sisters to come."

Joel glared at Morwin. "It's just us. There are only two of us."

"No," Morwin shook his head. "I can feel more around us, like tiny spores ready to burst through the rot. They will arrive like a horrible storm if I'm not there to herald the way. I wanted nothing but to show you the truth, but you have held onto a weakness from your predecessor's selfishness."

Morwin crouched down, grabbed him by the jacket collar, and lifted him up. "I will show our siblings the truth. By my word or by force. Either way I vow to make Aross a better planet than it was in the hands of these humans. Your helmet protects you from my truth. I guess I'll just have to kill you."

Joel's vision turned black as he felt the ground underneath him give away. His world turned into the haze of a dream, tumbling through nothing. He could see veins of white stretch across the horizon, zipping past him at an incredible speed. He felt a forceful lurch that pulled him up through the sky as he watched the veins disappear below. Joel's balance broke as the world around him regained shape. Morwin remained in front of him, holding onto him, but they were now in the middle of a street of downtown Mercer.

"Let the world see you for what you really are. Watch them witness your death," Morwin said.

Joel was picked up off the ground before he could regain his stability. His body cut through the belly of a garbage truck and continued through the glass and drywall of a highrise. He landed on the street of the block next over. Gasps and shouts of people surrounding him echoed between the buildings. Their screams became louder when dozens of wet black tendrils burst from the ground, holding boulders of shattered concrete.

They all fell down onto him in succession. Joel's body ached in pain as he was clobbered. He threw his arm over his head to brace for another impact; he forced himself to hold his stance. A block of concrete broke around his arm, giving him an opportunity to roll forward. As he landed on his feet, Joel began to run. Lost by the unfamiliar layout of the city's core, Joel sprinted towards a street unjammed with cars. He was quickly denied exit by a car flying towards him.

The unexpected impact pinned Joel to the corner of a tower. The carriage wrapped around him, but the pain was tolerable. Anger only began to boil when Joel looked down and saw the mangled body of the car's driver in the demolished cabin. Joel pushed the car off of him and viciously looked for Morwin.

Groups of panicked civilians were running away or gathered at a distance, watching Joel through the filming cameras of their phones. Heavy snow drifted down, melting on the grey asphalt of the street that was littered with rubble. Sirens wailed from a short distance.

Morwin materialized out of a blender of fungus in front of him. Joel jumped forward, seizing Morwin by the throat as he appeared. He could see the surprise in Morwin's eyes. Joel squeezed his grip as hard as he could, wanting to see Morwin's head pop off. The sociopath just smiled.

Tendrils burst from the ground around the groups of people who stayed to watch and snagged them by the legs or arms. Their grim screams rang out until they were slammed down or torn apart. The people not yet grabbed by a tendril stumbled over each other in a panic. Joel watched in horror as the street became washed in the blood of innocent lives. Anger pulsed through his body and into his mind. Joel looked down at Morwin, seeing the face of pleasure in death. Blood raged through Joel. He held onto Morwin's throat and plummeted his face with a closed fist. Joel rained down punch after punch, but the tendrils continued their slaughter.

Morwin's face quickly became a bloody pulp, maintaining the psychotic grin. Joel bound his rage into every punch, unleashing a desperate flurry to stop the killing. The concrete below Morwin's head began to crack and shake with force after each hit. Joel's fist flung thick blood outward with each raise. Morwin's laugh gurgled through the pooling blood in his throat.

Joel screamed as a jolt of fury flooded his body. His arms and shoulders shook uncontrollably; he could feel the silver rings vibrating. Joel tried to suppress the chaos surfacing and failed. He failed to stop Morwin, he failed to stop the slaughter. Rage took command, as it had in the arena, and used Joel's body as its host. Joel pointed his hands outward, towards the tendrils, and a horrible shock wave pulsed down the street, chewing up the building's glass and the street's asphalt. The wave dismembered the black tendrils at their root, but bodies of civilians were seized by its power and mangled through the flying rubble. The highrises surrounding him lost corners of their foundation. Torn metal shot through the air like arrows. Cars were picked up, crumbling into disfigured trash. The wave carried down, destroying everything in its path, until Joel closed his fists.

As the rage was repressed, guilt swiftly took its place. The damage seemed to stretch on for blocks. Screams and sirens could be heard in every direction. Bodies were scattered and pierced into the rubble of the shattered walls. Joel's breathing rose in a panic. His mind raced, trying to figure out what to do or how to reverse the destruction.

Joel slowly stood, forgetting Morwin's bleeding body under him. He looked at his palms embedded with the silver rings and watched gobs of blood fall from his knuckles. He was disguised as a terrible weapon, responsible for the deaths of many.

Ahead of him, between the destruction, jetted a bolt of blue lightning. In a flash, a woman appeared, standing safely away. She had blonde hair, tied in a ponytail, and dark brown eyes that shaded her pale skin. The woman slowly held out her arms to her side in a pacifist gesture. Her body held tense in anticipation as she watched Joel in silence. As he looked into her eyes, the pull that had been shadowing him grew tenfold. What had been a foggy feeling had turned into an anchored connection. A string locked between them, almost as clear as day. Joel didn't recognize her, but she felt as familiar as his warmest memories. He could feel her curiosity peak as she discovered the change of the pull. Everything before the woman's arrival disappeared in the background as she fell under his spotlight. Peace began to wash over as they stood.

The woman looked down at Morwin, impelling Joel to do the same. Morwin had stopped laughing, but gurgled through the blood to signal life. Before Joel could grab him, Morwin dissipated into mold, and was gone in an instant. Joel looked up at the woman. She hadn't moved an inch. Rubble and blood stretched past her, reminding Joel of the destruction brought by his violent eruption. Injured screams broke through his attention to the woman. Police, fire trucks and ambulances were rushing into the unaffected streets around him.

Joel looked at the woman. She pleaded with her eyes for him to stay. Joel turned and ran.

CHAPTER 11

The confused, scared eyes of the people noticing Joel weighed painfully on him. He had now sprinted ten blocks away from downtown, with the helmet still attached over his face. The explosion he caused must have been heard for miles, as crowds of civilians moved towards the smoke and sirens. Many had their phones out, taking pictures or calling others with more knowledge. Joel stood out like a sore thumb. His clothes were tattered, and the helmet didn't match the attire. Some filmed or pictured Joel as he ran by, recording the obvious anomaly in the horrible destruction of their city.

A sudden siren and screeching of tires shrieked from behind him. A police car, flashing its red and blues, zipped past him and quickly banked to cut him off. Two officers jumped out, drawing their guns, shouting urgent demands for Joel to drop to the ground. Joel pivoted towards a sidewalk between condo buildings. The officer's shouts became louder. Joel could see more police vehicles speeding down the street towards him.

The sidewalk in front of Joel led to a small green space that overlooked the river. He thought the river valley could hide him for a short window before the cops brought their helicopter. Joel quickened his sprint, leaving the pursuing cop cars far behind him. He crossed the green space and slid down a wet and muddy bank. He tumbled down until he reached a paved path that looked empty. Joel pivoted down the path at a rapid pace and stopped when he came across a bike trail that looked untouched since the snowfall. Joel followed the trail, listening to sirens echo over the valley.

Joel noticed a homeless camp ahead of him, signalled by a bright orange tarp sitting in a pile of scattered garbage. Joel ran up to the tent, desperately looking for new clothes to take. He noticed a homeless man lying across the garbage, eyes glazed over and drooling from the mouth. Joel could see the man was breathing, but completely impaired in a state of comatose. He waved a hand in front of the man's eyes and got no reaction.

Joel found a pair of jeans and a hoodie that looked minimally preserved from stains and dirt. Most of the clothes at this camp were wet or covered in waste. He quickly stripped down and threw on his new disguise. Right after, he crouched behind the tent, hiding from the euphoric eyes of the camper. Joel let himself breath deeply, slowing his panicked state. He tried not to think about downtown. His mind was as clear as it was going to get.

The helmet unfolded in its two part routine. Cold air settled over his skin as misty air formed from his hot breath. He wiped away the putrid remains of vomit from his mouth and beads of sweat that frosted over his forehead.

Joel, please lis...

The helmet shot back over his head. Joel looked behind him and into the surrounding trees. The homeless man was still as high as he was found. The only sounds his tense ears captured were the wailing sirens and clumps of snow falling off branches.

Joel sprinted away from the camp, using thin trails that led further into the valley park. He found a large uprooted tree on its side, providing a tall wall of roots to hide behind. Joel sat on the cold ground and let himself breathe, trying to ignore the voice that had just visited his mind. The helmet unfolded with his regained composure.

I mean no ha...

Joel commanded his helmet again. He nervously laughed as he tried to make sense of his newfound delusion. He wondered if Morwin had finally taken permanent residence within him.

Joel dug into the soft ground under the fallen tree. He could hear a helicopter approaching. As he shuffled himself under the trunk, he pulled snow and dirt back towards him, creating a soft cover. Joel laid there in silence, as he spent the next eight or so hours listening to sirens and a helicopter hover about. He desperately willed the helmet to stay on.

Night descended with a heavy snowfall, covering the tracks he made when he found the fallen tree. The helicopter made a couple passes near him, flashing its spotlight as close as twenty feet. The sirens died late into the night. Once the helicopter disappeared, the city became silent, with only the sound of falling snow to listen to.

Joel pulled himself out from his den and brushed the dirt and snow off his clothes. He sat himself on the ageing trunk, struggling to find the motivation to face the unwelcome voice. He could only leave the city with the helmet off. Joel knew he had to face the voice at some point. Joel willed the helmet off. He found only silence for a minute until he was visited again.

Please, listen.

Joel waited. Anticipating a horrible attack or visit from Morwin. His body tensed with each passing second.

I am of no harm to you. My name is Lyas, I am not the Blight you just faced.

The voice sounded unfamiliar. It was deeper than Morwins.

"How are you talking with me?" Joel said out loud.

I am telepathic. But you can seem to cut me off when you want, so I appreciate the chance to speak.

"I'm going insane." Joel held his head in his hands. He had heard about schizophrenia in the past. Morwin must have altered his mind, he thought.

No, you're not schizophrenic. I am very real.

"What do you want, then?"

I'll keep this short and simple. I'm offering you the opportunity to meet me at the cafe on one-o-one street and one-o-three Ave. In the A.M. I can help explain some of the changes you are experiencing. I can offer you safety.

"This sounds like a trap. I don't trust you," Joel spat.

I don't blame you. What you're going through is an intense experience. Especially after being hunted by the Blight. However, should you refuse, I want you to understand you will be followed for the rest of your life. You have dangerous capabilities and I can't let you leave without some surveillance to watch your every move.

Joel laughed. "So I have some pretty shitty options."

I prefer 'limited'. You have to understand that your abilities make you a planet wide threat. You can live independently, that's

fine. But you may just find yourself levelling another city, a conse-
quence of not learning control. Or you can listen to what I have to
offer.

Joel rubbed his eyes out of frustration. He thought back to when he left Golden, and how things could have been different if he just stayed with dad. This whole situation felt like a horrible nightmare that wouldn't quit.

"I'll think about it. Now leave my mind," Joel said bluntly. His mind ran silent. He waited for a response, but the visitor said nothing. Joel thought about the offer and his threat. This Lyas could still be watching from the hidden corners of his head. Joel kicked aside snow at his feet, revealing more dirt and rotting leaves. He laid down, knowing full well he couldn't sleep. All he wanted was to be at home. His life had spiralled out of control and all he could do in the moment was close his eyes and disassociate hoping the visitor wouldn't speak again. Joel donned his helmet. What was once a terrifying appendage had now become his only defence against uninvited voices or visits from deranged murders. Joel let the silence fill the air as the snow slowly covered his cloths and felt the strange pull of the blonde woman call for him.

*   *   *

Morning sun broke through seams of the clouds, reflecting light between the glass walls of downtown. Hundreds of people packed the downtown roads, shoulder to shoulder, all hoping to get a closer look at the destruction from the police barricade. Soft cries and sobs sung through whispered chatter of shared thoughts between strangers and friends. It seemed like the whole city had come to witness the tragedy.

Joel slowly made his way towards the front, squeezing between bodies as respectfully as he could. Most people moved away out of sheer discomfort once they saw his clothes and dirt smeared face. He imagined the stench he carried wasn't pleasant either. The crowd became tighter to squeeze through the closer he got to the barricade. He considered trying a different street, but each block must have been packed with an audience.

The true extent of the damage became evident once he reached the bright orange roadblock. Five blocks that ran north to south had been eaten away. Highrises surrounding the street had broken glass and ripped foundations, reaching from the ground up to twenty feet. Asphalt and water lines had been torn up; craters were pooling from uncontrolled leaks. Cars were piled over others; chassis chewed and spit out of a horrible monster's mouth. Joel even noticed a couple vehicles hanging from floors high up the tower walls.

At the end of the vicious wind tunnel sat a giant pile of rubble, clumped together by the unnatural torrent made by Joel. Cars and metal beams poked out of dark concrete, slowly being pulled apart by a large gathering of excavators and first responders. The mound crawled with searchers shouting out to awake any survivors. Joel could see a few bodies being carried off onto stretchers, but that was just a drop in the bucket. People either filmed the destruction or asked the barricading police officers if they could volunteer their help. No one was allowed through. The cops claimed the ground had become too unstable.

A loud voice obnoxiously rang out beside Joel. He looked over and saw two men conversing in a volume that was awkwardly louder than the whispering crowd of onlookers.

"It was those fucking Saddars. I tell ya, those Vallanites are going to pay for this goddamn attack," one man barked.

"Didn't you watch the news last night? Revenland claimed responsibility," another man spoke with confidence.

A woman, a stranger to the men, chimed in. "Revenland will claim anything. My cousin was a few blocks away before the attack and saw someone waving a Men-of-Bronze flag."

The three continued to bicker over each other, trying to lower their voices amongst the silence and failing. They had no idea. There was no political or radical group's hand in this. These people would never know the true reason lives were lost, but they would still spread their theories within their social circles.

The vicious cycle of blame became incredibly clear when Joel knew the blame was his. People would go on to rant and shout their theories online and to the media, spreading rumours and enforcing other incorrect conspiracies. Some would hold their fabricated beliefs close to their chest and refuse differing opinions that did not align with their truth. Uncertainty is an uncomfortable weakness. The uncertain was the most terrifying aspect when tragedy befell and it was fitting for the people of Mercer to fill the uncertain so quickly with false conspiracy. If only they knew the real terrifying truth as to why the city was attacked.

Joel turned away from the barricade, making room for more eager onlookers. He walked against the packed crowd, remembering the screams and scared faces of the victims from Morwin's attack. Joel could have stopped him, but ended up killing so many more because of his lack of control. Morwin had escaped and would hungrily hunt Joel down. His mind racked itself with the multiple predicaments he faced. Joel had no idea what to do, and soon Morwin would catch him again. He wasn't sure how many more would die next time, by his hand. He needed help.

Joel looked up at the closest intersection sign and realized that the cafe, where this 'Lyas' asked to meet, was only a few blocks away. The sun was rising above to a late morning, keeping him in the A.M. window. Even if it was a trap, Joel wondered if that would be the best solution for him. He had lost count on how many times he lost control; each incident had resulted in the destruction of everything around him. This Lyas would either make him incapable of hurting anything again, or actually follow through on his offer. Either way, Joel felt the burden to stop himself for the sake of the innocents he murdered, and for anyone unfortunate enough to fall within his path when he lost control again.

CHAPTER 12

The delta river flowed beneath the body of the Voidante as it glided down from the lower level atmosphere. Janak had originally spotted it on his first approach survey of RES 9 and noted it for a later visit. Signs of life showed on the heat map, but the delta's formation alone made it a unique natural territory.

The Voidante sprayed mist and gravel into a flurry as it touched down. Readings showed the ground soft but stable, unlike the prairies he had just finished surveying. Even watching an enormous mass lay on the grasslands wasn't enough to convince him he could land his ship on that land. Deep water made him slightly uneasy.

The ship's hanger seamlessly opened, revealing the bright sunlight shining through the pink cloudless sky. Janak grabbed his pack and activated his Talener to auto-follow. The moment he stepped on the black gravel, he felt his foot sink a couple inches, enveloped by the clear mountain water. Hundreds of rivers of all sizes surrounded him. Janak crouched and let his hand dip into a thin creek, feeling the cold glacier water wash over his hard shell.

The delta was an anomaly in relation to natural geographic formation. The rivers draining from the melting mountain glaciers was normal, however; it was the coastline that caught his eye. At the end of the river, mouths formed two perfectly shaped lines in the form of a triangle. The river water didn't drain into a large body of water, but a gigantic landmass of dense moss instead. The moss prairie stretched past the horizon, only broken by a few dips and hills. This species of moss absorbed the watershed and stored it beneath kilometres of stacked organic layers so deep that you'd never have guessed an ocean sat under it. Janak was amazed as the volume of water should have flooded these moss prairies. This planet continued to surprise him.

Janak peered through the scope of his Talener as he shifted his focus back to the life heat signature. He was shown activity within the rapids, but he couldn't see anything yet with his naked eyes. Janak walked back to the cargo ramp and sat down, keeping his feet out of the water. The ship's body provided shade from the glaring sun; being so close to the equator made a drastic temperature shift from what he was used to. He pulled out a sealed pack of quay nuts and snacked away as he watched the Talener crawl across the river flats. He wondered if the noise of his ship's landing spooked the creatures into hiding. A little waiting would change that, he thought.

It was only about ten of the planet's minutes that passed before the river creatures scurried from the waters. Unlike the ocean scavengers, these creatures were bright and hard shelled. A bulbous, bone white husk, sat on top of a shallow stomach with four tentacled arms. They slithered across the gravel at a weirdly fast pace, irrespective of their boulder sized bodies. Janak had the Talener zoom in on the creatures, watching from his tablet. He couldn't see any eyes on the body until he captured an image of dozens of holes on each tentacle. On all four arms were littered sockets and dark eyes. Sometimes a creature would stretch an arm high above its shell, acting on alert for any dangers around.

The creatures shuffled across the delta in straight formations, staying close to their peers but also avoiding contact. They used their arms to drag in piles of gravel towards their shell, using their hidden mouths to swallow the rocks up. With the Talener's x-ray scope, Janak watched the creatures swish buckets of gravel within their fine haired stomachs, scraping off any algae for sustenance. With the amount of filtering the water goes through, it made him think about how clean it truly was once it reached the subterranean ocean.

He could tell that the creatures understood his presence as irregular because they avoided coming anywhere near the chromed ship. A few even became frustrated with the alien obstacle, letting out barked grunts when they found their paths were interrupted. Feeding was the most important job they had; an interstellar ship paid no importance to their day, except when it blocked their meal. For hours Janak watched the creatures surf across the delta, clearing any bits of algae out of the water before it reached the giant moss sponge. He even managed to record a quick tussle between two males who accidentally crossed paths fighting over territory. They were a truly interesting species to record, but a part of Janak missed the Yen-leviathans' presence.

Something about their sheer size and behaviour gave this planet its unique quality. Regardless, he still had a job to do, and he would have the chance to say goodbye to the Yen.

Janak typed out his daily report, deciding to name the river dwellers: Derian-Perulucan. They were the ninety-eighth warm blooded, and the one thousand five hundred and sixty-two totalled species now discovered on RES 9.

※ ※ ※

The sun had just passed the horizon when Janak decided he archived enough notes for the day. The fading light cast orange and dark purple tinge over the wispy clouds. Night would slowly overtake the beauty in a few minutes. The Perulucan barked in a chorus to signal the return to the deep river waters. Janak watched the creatures scuttle across the gravel to find a watery bed; they would return to fresh crops of algae in the morning.

Janak closed the ship's cargo and threw off his jacket. He could feel his sweat-glands under his shell quiver for moisture. An afternoon of sitting under the sun and immersed in his notes made him forget to hydrate. Janak pulled out a water tube from his ration locker and sucked it back as he unclipped his duty belt. There was a certain satisfaction to taking off his equipment when exhaustion called for rest. Janak leaned over the pilot chair and turned on his favourite playlist. This was his time to relax.

An artist from the Southern hemisphere on his home planet played over the speakers. It was a mellow, waxy tune, made by a younger generation of Idelvin. Janak loved the style but enjoyed all kinds of genres from his home. He just preferred something more relaxed after a long and dull day of archiving. Janak grabbed a cup from the kitchen and walked to the laboratory wing. The room was filled with Seeker equipment that practically carried the heavy weight of complex research into any sample or data. But at that moment, he was more interested in the fermenter he brought from home.

The Seekers had strict rules about foreign items being carried to other planets and ecosystems. Most of the equipment on the ship was Seeker technology to begin with. Janak presented his case to being allowed his fermenter on his Voidante after his first cycle. The Seekers offered a design of their own, but it didn't give the same results Janak was looking for. They finally caved after they witnessed his passion for brewing firsthand. It was an acceptable compromise that came with a lengthy set of rules on contamination. Janak was just happy he could brew his favourite liquors on long cycles.

He crouched down to look at the purity percentage. It was as finished as it was going to get. For this batch, he used a synthetic copy of Bon Root. The plant had become extinct some years before the Seekers found the Illithen System, and many before Janak was born. When the Idelvin finally accepted the Seekers, Bon Root was one of the first plants synthetically returned to their planet. Brewer enthusiasts used the root to bring back the beloved drink called Bonmoc. It was one of the first drinks Janak's father gave him. After that, Janak fell in love with the craft of distillery.

Janak began to fill his cup and listened to the pipes groan. The yellow liquor made the air taste of wood and citrus. He let a small amount pour into his mouth for a test and was immediately satisfied with the batch. The sweet, tangy taste reminded him of his home and family. It was perfect for long expeditions into the deep reaches of the universe. Janak walked out of the lab and to his cot with the cup of Bonmoc. He sat cross-legged and leaned back into the ship's hull. He listened to the silent hum of the ship beneath the lazy waves of the artist's song. Moments like these filled the ache of when he missed home.

Janak closed his eyes and breathed in. Aromas from the Bonmoc filled his senses, making his mandibles and antenna quiver. He brought the cup to his mouth and took a deep sip, appreciating the chemical makeup of the root's juices. It made him crave something meaty, but he wanted to finish his drink first before making dinner. He was broken out of his meditative trance when the ship chimed softly.

Janak grabbed the adjustable screen over his cot and moved it down towards his face. The ship sensed an incoming storm within the next twenty-two hours. The notification read in a non-urgent banner. The storm posed no threat, but it would delay research into the delta. He would just have to leave a probe behind in his stead. Janak used his hand to bring up a planetary model on the screen. He zoomed in and out of areas he had yet to explore, finding the next landing. He was approximately sixty-four percent done on this planet. Archiving had gone quicker than he thought, probably due to the smaller planetary diameter.

He dropped a pin far in the Northern hemisphere a few kilometres away from the polar ice cap. The initial readings found nothing but barren tundra, but the specific area was below sea level, and he needed deep geographic samples. Extinction events were one of his preferred areas of study, and he felt he needed a break from organism discovery. Tomorrow, he would fly to his selected pin and begin another drill.

Janak threw back the rest of the Bonmoc and jumped off the cot. He tossed a meat ration into his heating oven and hurried to the lab to pour himself another cup. Tonight he would spend the rest of his free time listening to tunes from his people and drinking the batch of Bonmoc he had been distilling for weeks. The joy of being alone was filled with the appreciation for priceless craft, and Janak was more than happy with that.

CHAPTER 13

The cafe sat facing a busy street swamped with construction. It was an older building, run by a local chain. Joel was surprised it was still open, being so close to downtown. The entire city felt tense and quiet. No one knew whether to go to work or not when their worst tragedy in history befell them.

Joel shifted between his feet, trying to keep his toes warm. The idea of a trap raced in his thoughts as he debated with himself on entering. Facing this man named Lyas was his penance, and if it was Morwin in disguise, then he knew he could never outrun Morwin's terror. The only comfort in the decision to enter was the pull he had been feeling since he got to Mercer, and it led straight towards the cafe.

Joel hesitantly stepped forward and opened the frosted door. The warmth of the building immediately hit him, followed by the smell of burnt coffee and old carpet. Utensils and plates clashing rang from the kitchen. The cafe was close to empty, except for a few older couples sitting in silence over a hot breakfast.

Hidden in the far corner sat a man and a woman that looked to be around his age. The man had long black hair curled just above his shoulders. His beard was neatly trimmed and full below his sunken eyes and brown skin.

The woman he instantly recognized through the strange pull they shared. He knew it was her before she turned around in her seat to face him. He could feel her curiosity peak, along with a vigilant tension. The blonde woman stared at Joel with a stern expression, no doubt feeling what was stewing under his surface. She wore the same outfit she was wearing when they met on the bloody streets of downtown: a thin navy blue jacket with a light scarf around her neck.

Joel, rubbing his hands together to warm them, slowly walked to their table and stopped beside an empty chair between the mysterious man and the inexplicable woman. The man motioned to the chair and gave Joel a friendly smile.

"The waitress should be back soon with a fresh pot," he said. Joel stood for a moment, trying to fathom the situation. He stared coldly into the man's dark brown eyes, looking for any hint of a threat.

"You Lyas?" Joel said. His hands twitched in anticipation of an attack. "What do you want with me? How did you speak in my mind? Are you with Morwin?"

Lyas raised his hands in surrender and smiled. "I see you have lots of questions. I think I can help answer some, but yes, I am Lyas. Please sit."

Joel's eyes darted between the empty chair and the two strangers. The unexpected friendliness from the two threw him off guard. He was still expecting Morwin to jump out from under the table. He sat down slowly, keeping his hands on his lap to quickly defend himself if he had to. The man named Lyas shifted his chair to face him.

"I can tell you a hundred times we are not here to hurt you, and I think that won't make a difference. What that Blight, this Morwin, did to you has put you on edge. I promise you your mind will not be touched by me. You can leave anytime, but I want to extend an offer." Lyas sipped his coffee after he spoke. He smiled when the waitress arrived at their table and refilled his cup. She set down a cup in front of Joel and filled it without asking. A thick steam raised from the surface, smelling freshly brewed.

Joel waited for the waitress to leave their table before speaking. "Are you with Morwin?"

"No," Lyas said. "In fact, we came to Mercer to find him. You just happened to show up unexpectedly."

Joel looked over at the woman. She was studying him with her brown eyes. "So who are you then?"

"My name is Lyas Kattian, and this is Sadie Theon. We are gifted like you, just in different ways."

"I'm not gifted," Joel snapped. He shot his eyes back at Lyas. "Something happened to me; I can't control it. It can be reversed, right?"

"Unfortunately, no," Lyas softly said. "Your life has been altered and I can't explain why. You just happened to fall in a microscopic group on this planet that can wield immeasurable power. I am here to offer you control, and a family that shared the same fear you carry when they first discovered their abilities."

Joel looked at Lyas confused. "I levelled downtown and killed innocent people. You're not here to arrest me?"

"What happened downtown…" Lyas looked down at his cooling coffee. "Was awful. But our family is not innocent of hurting people either. The abilities we wield are incredibly intense, and were out of control when we first discovered them. I hold myself accountable by seeking out others, like us, and guide them. It's our duty to learn control for the burden of souls lost by our hand."

"I didn't mean to kill those people. The power overwhelmed me. I killed them trying to stop Morwin," Joel said somberly.

"I understand," Lyas nodded. "He is a monster. He provoked you. Come with me and I promise you we will take him down."

Joel scowled with disgust. "Are you kidding? Do you know how insane all of this sounds? A family of 'gifted people'," Joel scoffed. "I don't believe for a second you can offer me anything. You didn't feel the rage I felt. You didn't see the destruction happen right in front of you. I need to leave… to somewhere secluded and off grid. Somewhere I'll never hurt anyone."

"You can't outrun the burden of the accident you caused. It will haunt you forever," Lyas spoke.

"If I go with you, my only burden will be whatever payment I owe for your 'offer'. You just want to use me, like Morwin."

"I don't want to use you, Joel. I only want to teach you."

"I don't want to learn anything about 'this'. This power should not be in anyone's hands. I'll make sure it never sees the light of day again," Joel said sharply.

"So what happens when you lose control again? Or if Morwin, or another with nefarious purposes, finds you?" Lyas's tone sounded annoyed.

Joel scoffed. "Someone like you? I know you can't read my mind with my helmet on. I know it blocks you out. Your 'promise of following me' is a bluff, because I know I can hide. And if I can hide from you, I can hide from others."

Lyas leaned forward on the table, over his crossed arms. "At some point, the helmet will have to come off."

Joel clenched his fists. He wanted to laugh at this man's vain confidence.

Before he could stand up, the woman named Sadie spoke.

"Joel, wait," her voice was stern and calm. "Living a life alone is no life at all. I was angry like you, back when I first discovered my abilities."

She paused, as if she was offering Joel the opportunity to listen or interject. Joel shifted to face her, staying silent. Through the bond, he could feel her anticipation in the words she carefully chose.

"I killed an entire hospital when I first lost control," Sadie solemnly said. "It was a couple years back, the Skjerrel Incident in Arsacadia, do you remember? I was scared and my entire body felt like it was being shocked with hundreds of volts. My parents brought me to the emergency clinic. The doctors thought I was faking. I tried to suppress my fear, but it got so bad I just… let go. The entire hospital, with everyone in it, burnt to ashes. My parents were the first to go. They were standing right next to me. I thought I was dead, or if it was all a bad dream. None of it made sense."

She paused again to bring her cup of coffee closer to her. Her voice became heavy. Joel could feel the pain of her grief through the pull.

"Lyas found me some days after the incident. I was a mess. He helped things make sense in a way. He offered me safety in a time where I needed it the most. Lyas and our family taught me how to wield this power and use it in incredible ways. I can't bring back what I lost, but what was given in return saved me. I owe it to those people, to my parents, to make sure no innocent dies by my hand again. And I'll fight to the last breath to make sure of that promise. That's how I hold myself accountable."

"Lives were lost because I tried to save them," Joel said. "That makes me dangerous. And if we are anything alike, we have no right to be saving anyone."

"I disagree. What of the lives lost because you didn't bother to intervene? With abilities like yours, you are given the opportunity to prevent worse things that could happen," Sadie said.

"People with power say that to justify their destruction," Joel grumbled.

"People with a tainted heart, yes. But yours is good. I can feel it." Sadie leaned forward. "Let us help you."

Joel paused in thought and realized he was tapping his foot excessively. She felt truthful, but Lyas could be manipulating his mind. Joel wondered if anything was real, if he was really in a cafe. Had Lyas already dominated his reality?

He wanted to believe Sadie.

"Explain why I'm like this. How did we get these powers?" Joel asked.

"That's one answer I can't give you," Lyas spoke up. "We have no idea why we are like this. There is no proof we were given these powers or born this way. It's like one day the planet started to pop out humans with powers."

"But there's a small amount of us?" Joel asked.

"Very small. And surfacing at an increased rate. You will meet all of them if you come with us. Morwin is the first to..." Lyas paused in thought. "He won't be given the opportunity to repent. He found a liking for killing, and if we don't find him soon, he will kill more."

"Why can't you find him?"

"His mind and body, wanders. It's difficult to track. Gifted people can be found when I concentrate, an exception being you; but Morwin is a fog amongst a hive. We spent days trying to find him in Mercer. Then suddenly, you appear. In and out, like a lightbulb. I've never seen anything like it. You're the closest we've been to capturing that monster." Lyas took another sip from his cup.

"He needs to be stopped. The man is mad. He believes he's some sort of saviour," Joel said.

"I completely agree. He is proof that hearts and minds of evil intent are not immune from our gifts. I wanted to help him, but he has given us no choice but to apprehend him. You can help us."

Joel lowered his head into his hands. He never expected any of this. A few days ago, he was with his family, living somewhat of a normal life. A life he hated. A life he didn't deserve. But now he was living a nightmare.

"How do I know you're not manipulating my mind? Morwin got to me. So can you," Joel said grimly.

"I have made a promise to each and every single member of our family. I promised to never enter their mind without their permission. I will never alter their will unless they ask. I only entered your mind to speak with you, to offer you this meeting. It was necessary, but the promise is extended to you from this point forward."

Lyas placed a soft hand on Joel's shoulders. "I can imagine it's hard to trust us. Let me prove the worth of my words."

Joel rubbed his eyes until they showed stars. He could feel his wariness disarming.

"My life, I've already abandoned. I have nothing to lose if I go with you. I don't want any part of these powers, but I will let you teach me control. After that… I have no idea what happens," Joel said.

"That's a good start," Sadie said.

Joel lifted his head and decided to take a sip of the coffee in front of him. The hot brew calmed him for a second. He realized it was the first thing he ingested since he left Golden. He could actually feel a slight tinge of hunger.

"What happens from here?" Joel said.

"Myself and my partner Rowan are going to stay in Mercer, for maybe a day or two. I want to see if Morwin will try anything. He might be easier to find now that I know what I'm looking for. Sadie is going to take you to the farm, to meet the others and get settled in," Lyas voice rang with a suppressed relief.

"Where will I be going?"

"We live on a secluded farm in the middle of The Rown Isles. It's peaceful, I bought it years ago from my uncle. Sadie can take you there instantly."

"We can go whenever you want, Joel. If there's anything you want to bring, it needs to be small and on your person," Sadie said.

"I don't have anything on me. I got these clothes from a homeless guy; they're not even mine," Joel mumbled.

"We can get you new ones," Sadie smiled.

Lyas stood up and took out a few bills for the coffee and a generous tip. He zipped up his jacket and walked to the edge of the diner table. "Your world has changed, Joel. It's strange and terrifying. I promise you I will make things right."

Lyas walked himself out the entrance and Joel watched him through the window as he walked down the street. Nothing seemed to change; the diner continued to act normal with no changes to his reality. He realized he was actually itching to leave Mercer right away, now that he had the opportunity. Even if he changed his mind, Sadie would supposedly take him far away from Morwin's reach. He looked over at her; she was staring into his eyes silently. He wondered what the pull between them meant, or how it began, in the first place.

"You feel it too, don't you?" He said.

"I do. I have no idea what it is, but I'm hoping Lyas and my friends can help figure it out," she said softly. She stood up from the table and nodded towards the entrance. Joel stood up and followed behind her. They stopped on the sidewalk and faced towards downtown. He looked over at the plumes of black smoke and lines of emergency vehicles filling up the downtown core. Thick clouds had formed since the morning, and a heavy snow was beginning to fall.

"Their lives will be with you forever," Sadie spoke. "You're not going to fail them."

"I already have," he whispered.

Sadie sighed in sympathy. "Take my hand," she said. "Don't let this experience alarm you. It only takes a second."

Joel looked down at her extended hand. He had no idea what was to come. He grasped it and felt the warmth of her palm. She softly smiled at him, and the world collapsed around him in a blue flash.

Chapter 14

Morwin shot out of the mycelium realm and landed violently on his chest. Thick blood spat from his mangled mouth as he gasped and coughed. The pain was unbearable as it vibrated throughout his entire body. He rolled over until he was lying on his side. He had instinctively brought himself back to his warehouse. He only recognized the familiar layout through his partially swollen eyes.

Morwin ran his hand over his face and felt the severity of his wounds. His mouth held only a few teeth, and his lips had split in many directions. Half of his jaw was missing from Joel's devastating cut. He wondered if he would ever be able to grow it back properly. As he felt further up his face, he found multiple bleeding gashes and his eyes were swollen like purple tumours. Pain rang with every touch on the exposed nerves. He let out a loud and angry groan to dull it.

Someone was here.

Clotted blood flung off Morwin's face as he spun around to face the intruder. He tried to force his eyes open, but his vision remained blurry. Morwin reached out with his mind, prodding every corner for signs of life. All he could find were the dead brains of his experiments.

"Show yourself!" He screamed. The shout echoed through the abandoned building. Nothing but silence followed.

They have left. This place is no longer safe.

Run now.

Morwin steadied his breath and smelled the air. Through the layers of the rotting corpses were traces of the stranger's bacteria. They had walked all over his home, leaving trails of dead cells for him to find. He traced each step along the floor and concluded that three strangers had breached his home.

He was surprised when he discovered they carried a smell different from humans. More evolved specimen? He thought. All this time he spent searching, and he missed them by mere moments. Despite his injuries, Morwin felt eager to meet them. They could help him bring down the traitor, Joel.

You fool. It's a trap.

They will want to kill us.

"We don't know that yet. I can convince them to help me. I can show them the truth. Welcome them into the design."

Heal our body. We are too injured.

"I must meet them," he gasped. "Joel will get to them first and slander my name. They came here to meet ME."

Morwin dived into the veins of the dirt and traced the trails of the visitors' scents. Now that he signalled out their individual cells, he knew what to look for. As he raced across the city, he realized the visitors had travelled in almost every street and avenue. They had traces multiple days old; he was hidden from them without him knowing. How could he be so blind? All of his focus was spent hunting down Joel, and instead he could have been recruiting more gifted.

Seconds later, he found them. Their minds glowed with supreme pathogens, like his and Joel's. It was crucial to convince them of the design. The plan to rise above the vermin. Only they could herald the world into an age of peace. Aross needed to be purged of its parasites. Joel included.

What if they hate you?

Like Joel did.

Then I'll dominate them. Morwin ruthlessly thought.

Like you tried with Joel?

Joel was an exception, right? Not every evolved specimen could resist his mind. He had trained for this; they would join him willingly or by force. He needed allies. Doubt raced through Morwin's mind, forcing him to ease his approach before the visitors. He peered through a small patch of mold attached to a dumpster, while absorbing the light and sound around to see the visitors as they huddled in a group.

"We should be downtown, clearing the rubble," A Yandian woman said. "Forget those two. People are hurt."

"No, we need to find the masked one. I can't see his mind. Sadie, you should have followed him!" A Tunland man said.

A blonde woman quickly responded. "Lyas, you need sleep. Look at you, you're exhausted!"

The man named Lyas breathed deeply in thought. The two women looked at him, waiting for a response. Morwin's hope was quickly diminishing.

"Okay," Lyas regained his composure. "Rowan, track the masked man. I am confident he had nothing to do with the warehouse murders. Sadie, return to the warehouse and if the Blight returns, quickly grab Rowan and I for backup. I'm going to find a spot to meditate. See if I can reset my focus."

The Rowan woman ran off without questions. The one named Sadie blinked out of thin air in a flash. Lyas stood alone, bracing himself on the wall as he closed his eyes. Morwin felt the incoming touch of a wandering mind. He quickly fled until he was far from the mind reader, but he could not return to the warehouse. Disappointed, Morwin had just confirmed they were hunting him. He was alone. Each and every gifted person was against him. He decided to strike the mind reader while he had the chance.

NO. You are injured and weak.

He will dominate you. Hide now.

They were right. He felt faint and wounded. Once he returned to his physical form, the pain would double. Anger rushed through him as his opportunity to gain allies was once again ruined by Joel. He needed to heal his body, and then he would strike.

* * *

The ancient barn was far enough from the city that Morwin was confident he wouldn't be found. It was small and half-collapsed. It was close enough to Mercer that he could zip back and keep an eye on the visitors who were hunting him. But he didn't linger, for the sake of his injuries.

His time in isolation was spent healing his wounds; even his hand started to grow back properly. Grey pale skin replaced what was lost, reminding him of the wounds sustained. The process took effort. He had to focus cells to reprint the structure dismembered; it was slow and made him vulnerable. His hunger cried out.

We need food, now.

Feed us.

No. Morwin thought. He needed to be careful. Watchful eyes were on him. Any disappearances might lead the mind reader back to him. He made sure whenever he returned to the city, to spy on Lyas, he kept his distance and left at the first hint of detection. The more he listened to their conversations, the more he discovered how many false beliefs were shared about him.

The day following Joel's attack, the blonde woman disappeared and Joel was nowhere to be found, like they vanished out of thin air. Morwin shifted his focus to Lyas, and the woman named Rowan. Through short pieces and clues, he concluded that the three visitors came to Mercer to 'save him'. Once they realized he was behind the murders, they branded him an enemy. Morwin desperately wished he could explain his actions. If he had the chance to reveal the design, they would join his side. The murders were only to advance the new race. He had no evil intent.

From the murky depths, Morwin watched Rowan and Lyas search for him and set traps. Their search was exhaustive to no avail, completely unaware that he was watching them closely. Lyas came close a couple times. When he reached out with his mind, Morwin would quickly flee back to the barn. It took all of his will not to introduce himself and plead his innocence. But he maintained restraint, as he would be forced to dominate them should they refuse.

A couple days later, Morwin took a break from healing and found Lyas from the mycelium realm. He watched Lyas and Rowan through the walls of a decent motel room. Lyas was sitting on the bed, hunched over, half-asleep. It would have been the perfect opportunity to dissect his mind, but he was outnumbered and not fully healed.

"Lyas, please. Let's go back to the farm," Rowan pleaded. "You've strained your mind. Morwin is long gone from Mercer."

The young Tunlanden coughed. "He could be hiding. I can't return home yet, I failed to find him."

Rowan placed a hand over Lyas's cheek. "You didn't fail. You found Joel, he's safe now because of you."

"Joel's arrival was unexpected. We came here for Morwin," Lyas said. He gracefully took Rowan's hand off his face and placed it on his knee.

"Morwin is proof that we can't win every time. Failure was bound to catch up to us one day. When you look at our family, you realize how good of a run we had. I know you knew that eventually someone would refuse our call. We would be stupid not to consider enemies could exist."

"I just didn't think it would happen this fast," Lyas said. "For a minute, I truly believed only good people inherited these gifts. Like we were specifically picked. The reason for our new responsibilities becomes more and more of an anomaly to me with each new gifted. Random or not, we now know that horrible people can also have this power. Morwin will go on to work against us, and he won't be the last. I have no clue how to handle... villains."

A villain? No. Traitor.

Morwin's mind buzzed with raging voices.

"Villains only exist in our childhood comics," Rowan smiled. "You exist to show people their greatest selves. We grow from failure, you told me that. Let's go back to the farm, start teaching Joel."

Lyas nodded. His head looked heavy. "Okay. We will go back. Did you hear from Callum or Veronica yet?"

"They're still in Seraleveli," Rowan said. "The gifted there is hesitant. Still doesn't know if he wants to join."

"Alright, but the first hint of Morwin becomes a priority, okay? I'll call Sadie."

Rowan nodded.

Morwin watched as Lyas closed his eyes and sat in silence. Morwin felt a wave of consciousness fly past his mind, and in seconds, they vanished one by one in a flash of blue lightning. Morwin faced an empty motel room, reeking of the traitor's scent. He reached out far with his mind, but couldn't see them. They were taken somewhere far; a place where Joel was settled. He returned to the physical realm at the barn and braced for the rush of pain from his healing wounds. He let out a long groan as the pain rooted itself.

Our plan has failed. We are an enemy now.

Feed US.

Poison has been spit in their ears.

Morwin punched the rotting floorboards in a fit of rage. He had failed. Those who should be on his side see him as a monster. He knew they just didn't understand, but the chance to convince them had passed. Joel had laid his roots and got to them first. He laid his head on the ground and began to sob.

"What do I do?" he cried.

Find us a snack.

Their minds can still be enslaved.

"I tried that!" Morwin screamed. "I tried, and I was almost killed!"

He stood from the floor and paced around the dark, musty room. He doubted that he could ever dominate the minds of gifted like him. Could he have tried Lyas? No, he thought. Lyas has a strong mind. Morwin's mind raced as his thoughts rambled over each other, trying to formulate the next step in the design. His hunger... his responsibilities needed to be satisfied.

"Wait," he stopped in his tracks. "What did the Rowan woman say again?"

VILLAIN.

Seraleveli.

He had heard of that state before. It was off the central coast of Lavendy.

"There's a gifted there," Morwin said excitedly. "Unsure and doubtful. He will be weak. He can join me."

The voices quivered with delight. He could travel there easily through the roots of the rot below. Joel was able to resist his mind, but not everyone would have the same ability. He could sweep in under Lyas's family and convince this newcomer of his plan for the new race. The fresh grey skin on his jaw folded with the curl of his smile.

The moment of bliss was interrupted by the rumbling of his stomach.

We need food.

Yes, he thought. But far from the city, he would look for sustenance. Mercer was under watchful eyes. His home had outlived its purpose, and it was time to bury it in the past.

CHAPTER 15

Joel's eyes adjusted to the bright sun as he emerged from the blue flash. Only a second ago he was standing on the snowy streets of Mercer, and now he stood on a gravel road in a lush green country. Sadie let go of his hand as he nervously looked in every direction.

"You're on the Isle of Lowhen, of The Rown Isles," Sadie said. She pointed to a lone tree sitting on a green hill with a dirt road leading up to it. "That's Lyas's farm, the border. It's about another ten minutes of walking from here."

The sun was shining beautifully over the long green grass that seemed to stretch over every hill. Ancient cobblestone fences bordered the fields in straight lines; some still seemed to act as pastures for livestock. Joel had never left The Northern Union, nor Cadiaheim. This was the furthest he's been from home. He always imagined travelling east to the Isles or to Yanda. He and

Beth played with the idea of a trip early in their relationship. Despite the current circumstances, the landscape amazed him. He looked over at Sadie and found her watching him.

"How'd you do that? You brought us here instantly," Joel exclaimed.

"Manipulating electricity is an ability of mine," Sadie said. "Took me a while to figure it out, but I learnt to piggyback on light travel. I can go anywhere, with only a few odd limits."

Joel looked down both ends of the road and then back at Sadie. "So why did you pop us so far from the farm?"

"I thought we should probably get you some new clothes and a meal before the pubs fill up with locals. I'm starving," she laughed.

Sadie walked down the gravel road leading away from the farm, subtly inviting Joel to follow. "There's a town not too far from here."

Joel caught up to her until he was alongside her pace. She wasn't wrong; his clothes reeked of body odour and whatever else hitched along for the ride. They walked in silence for a bit; Joel looked at each small farmhouse as if he was a tourist. He wanted to enjoy the peace of the country, but it was hard for him to ignore the anxious warnings of a possible trap. Only moments ago, he was ready to attack her and Lyas at the cafe.

She looked over at him and gave him an awkward smile. He smiled back, unintentionally just as awkward. What do you even ask a woman who can feel his every emotion? He thought.

"I don't think Morwin can track you here," Sadie said. "This place is safe."

Joel scrunched his brow. "What makes you say that?"

"I can sense... that you're uneasy," she whispered.

He looked at her sternly, trying to solve the hidden truths she could be hiding. "Why can I feel your presence? It's only you, no one else. Is that part of my 'abilities'?" He asked carefully.

"I don't know what it is, or where it came from. But I know I can feel your soul, or the direction you're heading. Sometimes it's so faint it's like it's not even there. Sometimes it's so strong it's impossible to ignore. That's how I found you downtown."

Guilt jabbed at Joel's chest at the thought of the blood and gore. She was there to witness his destruction, yet she treated him with friendliness. He quickly diverted the conversation.

"Probably has to do with these abilities. Ah, I have no clue. In a way, it's kind of creepy, violating my privacy and all," He chuckled nervously.

"Feeling is mutual, pal."

They continued down the road that curved over a hill, bringing them to a top view of the town ahead. The buildings were small, squared, and tightly packed against each other. Clay and wood shingles meshed together, only split by the thin streets below that fit their compact cars. It was a quaint town, somewhere that would have been a highlight for backpackers and travellers. Past the village was the ocean, as blue as the clear skies above. Sail boats no larger than a cabin cruiser floated in the still bay. The ocean stretched on forever, somehow capturing a beauty that Blackpine lacked.

"Welcome to Conqet," Sadie said. "Would you prefer a pub, or a pub to eat at?"

Joel looked down at his legs and feet. "Maybe some clothes first."

Sadie gladly nodded and brought him to a small thrift store that faced the main street. The entire town was close to quitting for the day, but Sadie managed to convince the shop owner to let them browse. The owner was an older woman with a thick accent. Despite her impatient comments about missing the pub, she let Joel pick out some fresh clothes and even let him take a shower in her flat above the store. Her kindness threw Joel off his vigilant state; he didn't know how to thank her. Sadie paid her a heavy tip as they exited the shop. He didn't realize how relieved he felt now that he was clean and in fresh clothes. It felt like an unappreciated luxury he missed so dearly.

Sadie brought him to a pub that she described as the oldest pub in the town. Tables and the bar were already filling with the locals. He could tell the town didn't get many visitors just by the quick glances. They sat by a small iron-worked table by the front window; Sadie was greeted by a middle-aged waitress who recognized her. She ordered two pints of beer and two plates of fish and chips. Joel was about to politely refuse the food, but found that he actually was hungry. The last time he wanted to eat was in Blackpine.

Sadie and Joel sat in silence, listening to folk music play over the chipper chatter of the town residents. Joel could feel his vigilance disarming around the comfiness of the culture. The pints and dishes were brought out in unison, smelling of oily batter and cooked fish.

"Better enjoy. This will be your only meal for the next couple of weeks," Sadie said as she bit down on a chip.

"What?" Joel stuttered.

Sadie looked down at him, as if she expected him to understand. "We process food differently. You only need to eat and drink every few weeks; something to do with our metabolism. By now you probably also have realized you don't need sleep as consistently either."

Joel nodded nervously. He thought he was just in shock or under a mental episode over the past few days. His situation was becoming increasingly unnatural with every discovery.

"Shouldn't we, you know..." Joel leaned in closer to Sadie. "Not talk about this in public?"

Sadie looked at her plate, embarrassed. "I forget at times that my world has changed. What was once terrifying has turned into my new normal. Whenever I'm not training or searching for gifted, I'm here living an ordinary life as if I'm not involved in some crazy reality. I'm playing pretend with folk who live a simple life." She watched over the mingling crowd, sharing drinks with one another and laughing over stories. "Their whole worlds are inside this town. Many of them will die without ever leaving. It reminds me of home."

Joel watched her, lost in thought. Her blonde ponytail spilled over her shoulder and floated around the lip of her pint. He could feel the sadness surface within her.

"But they will have no clue what the hell we are talking about," Sadie chuckled. "As long as we are not too loud, we will just fade into the background."

Joel awkwardly took a sip from his pint and cleared his throat. "I'm sorry about your parents. You didn't have to tell me about them, but you did. I can imagine that wasn't easy."

"Yea," Sadie slowly sighed. "I miss them. They were good to me."

The two of them faded into silence as they picked away at the battered fish and beer. The beer wasn't anything special, but it was the best fish and chips Joel had in his whole life. He tried not to scarf the meal down in front of Sadie.

After they finished, they walked back towards the farm. The sun was setting above the water, casting a golden glow amongst the pastures. Joel wasn't sure what to talk about, and he was sure Sadie didn't either. But he could appreciate the gentle feeling of new clothes and shoes. He would later remember to thank her.

The farm was hidden by the hill with the lone tree, and could be seen in whole at the top of the mound. It looked more like a miniature village than a farm to Joel. The property did have a barn, but a group of small cottages held his interest. Past the group of cottages was a larger house, not much different in size. Sadie pointed it out as Lyas's and Rowan's house, which also acted as the 'meeting house'. Each cottage, except two, were spoken for by members of their family. Sadie explained that most of them were gone, but would be back in a couple of days. Once they were back, introductions would be made.

She brought him over to a cottage that consisted of just a kitchen, bathroom and bedroom. Ivy vines crawled around every corner and window frame of the exterior, giving the house a comically vintage look. The place must have been built seventy years ago. Inside was mostly empty, except for a few boxes of kitchen items and blankets. Warm lighting painted the hardwood floors and tacky wallpaper that was peeling in many places. The bedroom was thin enough to fit a queen-size metal bed frame that only had a bare mattress, and the bathroom had open plumbing that looked as if it was ready to burst. Joel wondered what kind of family was living here before Lyas bought the place.

"You really get what you see here, sorry," Sadie said. "The boxes in the kitchen have most of the necessities you need to start off. But for anything else, you can visit our storage or walk to town."

Joel carefully stepped around the creaking floors, studying every detail of his new abode. Despite its age, he was glad they offered it to him; it was definitely better than sleeping on the streets. He sat down on one of the wooden chairs at the kitchen table and rested his arms down, feeling the silver rings on each palm. A long sigh escaped his chest.

"Today… has been weird. It feels like a dream." Joel looked up at Sadie. She was standing at the open door of the cottage. "What happens now? Am I forced to stay here?"

Sadie shook her head. "No, Joel. You are free to leave whenever. But truthfully, this place is your safest option right now. You're surrounded by people who know what you're going through."

"Yea," Joel said somberly.

"This doesn't have to be your home forever, but I hope you can try and see its potential. I know that's asking a lot, from strangers. Your reality has just flipped and revealed itself of its crazy existence. I don't expect you to accept it today, nor tomorrow," Her voice carried gently. They both knew of the hard truth. He just happened to finally accept it. Silence held between them before Joel mustered the confidence to speak.

"I wanted to kill him. Morwin. I should have killed him, but I stopped. He got away because of me."

Sadie walked to the table and sat beside Joel so their eyes were level. "I wanted to kill him too. For what he did to the ones he murdered."

"No," Joel forced the words out of his throat. "I didn't care for those people until I was the one who was the murderer. I only wanted to kill Morwin because he tried to kill me. I'm selfish. Now that lost lives are on my conscience, they have weighed me with guilt. What does that make me? I have no idea if I would save them, if I could go back. Morwin provoked me to attack him, and those people died as collateral. I never asked for that. I never wanted any part of that. Now they weigh on me."

Sadie watched him with kind eyes. She held no judgement, but he wanted to be judged. "I'm sorry, Joel. I'm so sorry. None of that was your fault. Grief does not need to be understood right after the tragedy happens. Give it some time and I promise you will understand who was at fault."

Joel nodded, trying to suppress the tight squeeze in his throat. He didn't believe her, but he knew she was genuine. He could feel it within her.

"I'd like to be alone now," He said.

She placed a hand on his arm and squeezed it. "I'll be by the firepit for most of the night. I won't be sleeping for a few more days still."

She then got up and left with a warm goodbye. Joel waited for the door to close before he got up to sift through the boxes. Despite not being tired, he pulled out blankets and a pillow. After he made the bed, he laid down and stared at the ceiling. He considered joining Sadie at the fire for a little bit, but he firmly wanted to be alone. The cottage was quiet, with only the calls of a couple cows echoing across the fields.

Once he was bored with the wallpaper above his bed, he returned to the boxes and found a handful of books. Most of them being nonfiction stories about harrowing wilderness survival, but it was the post-apocalyptic story about a father and his boy, journeying a dangerous road, that piqued his interest. He spent the rest of the night trying to enjoy the novel, but was continuously interrupted by sudden creaks in the walls. He expected Morwin to jump out to surprise him with each creeping noise. He became annoyed that sleep was a distant option. At least when he could sleep, he could ignore the world around him. Days and nights no longer had consistent meaning.

After pacing around each room, emptying the boxes and placing them in their preferred cabinet, the sun began to rise. In a lower cabinet, he found an old percolator with a tin of coffee grinds. His dad taught him how to use a percolator back when he was younger on a camping trip. He remembered feeling wired and made his dad regret that decision. Joel made himself a pot on the gas stove and poured some into an old teacup. Without cream and sugar, he had to drink it black, but he didn't mind. Joel pulled a chair outside and sat with his coffee, watching the sunrise over the grassy hills. He had no idea what to expect in the coming days, but he was finally starting to feel a sense of safety.

CHAPTER 16

The kettle incessantly screamed in the kitchen as Sadie finished pulling a sweater over her head. She sped to the stove and set aside the boiling water to cool down for her morning coffee. Sunlight shining through her living room windows signalled clear skies; it would be a beautiful day to catch up with her family.

A few days had passed since Joel arrived at their farm. He had spent most of that time isolated in his own house, occasionally leaving for a short stroll to take in the sights of the coast. Sadie attempted a few times to invite him to help with chores, or sit by the fire. He agreed a couple times, but reserved himself to silence. She tried to give him all the privacy he wished for, but the bond made each others presence difficult to ignore. Regardless, she felt determined to make him feel comfortable. Today she would introduce him to the rest of the family.

Late in the night, she was called back to Mercer for a quick pickup of Lyas and Rowan. Once they returned to the farm, Lyas excused himself to his bed, and Rowan followed. And just a couple hours ago, the rest returned from Seraleveli. They too carried an aura of exhaustion, but seemed happy to be home. She had the impression they didn't bring good news.

Sadie finished making her coffee and poured it into a tall mug. She carried it out of the house, feeling its warmth in her palms and strolled towards Joel's cabin. She found him sitting outside his front entrance, organizing a deck of cards and basking in the sun.

"Good morning!" She said excitedly.

Joel smiled and chuckled pitifully. "If this is what you consider morning, I guess. I still haven't slept."

Sadie sat down in the wicker chair beside him, making herself comfortable. "Eventually, you will. It's a difficult change to adjust to."

"Yea," Joel murmured. "How are you... this morning?" He said awkwardly.

"My family is home safe, so pretty relieved," Sadie said. "Are you ready to meet them?"

Joel stared ahead in silence, lost in thought. She could feel his soul nervously spin. "What should I expect from them? I can't help but think how weird this is, meeting others gifted like me. I need you to know that I'm not agreeing to join this family just because I'm meeting them. I'm doing this because you asked."

"I know," she nodded. "A few of them actually annoyed me when I first met them. But in time, I grew into their quirks. I'm not expecting you to do the same."

"Okay, let's get this over with, then."

They stood up and began to walk towards Lyas's house, the main hall. Sadie remembered how intimidating her first meeting was; there were fewer members back then, but it was still frightening. After that, she made it her duty to give newer members a warmer welcome.

Lyas's house was not much different from the rest of the cottages, other than its second level and wider floor. They used the living room as a meeting place for any critical news or just to be within each other's company. Sometimes, when their hunger cycles would line up, they would gather to share a family meal. She loved each and every one of them, but was painfully aware of how awkward and tense everyone acted when a new member was brought to the farm.

The front screen door creaked loudly as they entered and were greeted by the sounds of chatter and the rich smell of lavender and eucalyptus. Rowan loved her candles, maybe a little too much. Sadie walked towards the living room, looking behind her to make sure Joel was following. His shoulders were tense; she could feel a sharp caution within.

The moment she entered the room, her family fell silent. The four of them were sitting on rocking chairs and loveseats. All eyes moved to Joel. Sadie rolled her eyes. "Everyone, this is Joel. He's from Cadiaheim, of The Northern Union."

Everyone was silent. Only Aiden made a weak effort of a greeting by waving his hand. He was probably just trying to be funny in their embarrassing situation. Natasha gave a stern nod and Veronica continued to stare through Joel's soul. Callum stood up from his chair, dwarfing everyone from his towering height. Sadie noticed he had a new healing scar running down his nose and cheek.

Callum heavily marched over to Joel and held out a hand. Joel looked at it first before shaking. "I'm Callum," He said. Sadie couldn't help but stare at the fresh pink scar across his dark brown skin. It didn't do any favours for his looks.

Callum pointed to everyone clockwise, announcing their names to Joel. "That's Natasha, that's Aiden, and that's Veronica. I was told you've already met Rowan and Lyas?"

"Just Lyas," Sadie jumped in and looked over at Joel. "Other than Rowan, that is everyone. We are a small family, but slowly growing."

Joel nodded, slowly looking over each introduced member. "Nice to meet you,"

Veronica stood from her couch and walked over to Joel, maintaining a firm, cold stare. She took Joel's hands, ignoring his instinctive flinch. She ran a thumb over the silver rings embedded in his palms. "Do you yearn for the stars? There's a horrible gap in your soul that must be healed," Veronica eerily said.

"What?" Joel said as he pulled back his hands. He looked at Sadie with disgust and turned away to leave the cabin. She listened to the door creak shut behind him.

"Veronica, really?" Sadie sternly asked. "Was that necessary? I'm trying not to scare him."

Veronica held up her arms in innocence, rattling the collection of bracelets and rings that decorated her. "I was only trying to help him."

"No, babe, that was a bit weird," Callum's Vallan accent drawled. He sighed and returned to his rocking chair. Aiden attempted to stifle a laugh.

Sadie rubbed the bridge of her nose and sat down. She didn't expect much from them, but she also was surprised they disappointed her so quickly. "Thanks guys. I'm sure he loved that first impression," she said sarcastically.

Callum scowled but stayed silent. He returned to the couch with Veronica and they all shamefully sat in silence. Sadie was mad, but also missed them and wanted to hear any news they had to share. "At least try to be nicer next time?" Sadie said. "Let's hope he allows a 'next time'... Well? What happened in Seraleveli?"

"We failed," Natasha said begrudgingly. The heavy Revenland accent made her difficult to understand sometimes. "We spent days trying to convince the stupid man to come here. He could not make up his mind."

"And then he just disappeared," Aiden said. "Veronica couldn't trace him anymore. I felt like we were close to finally changing his mind."

"No. He was never going to come here. I don't think Lyas is happy with us," Callum said.

"Well, we didn't have much success either," Sadie mumbled. "Joel was unexpected. Turns out the original guy we were looking for, Morwin, is a psychotic murderer and was impossible to find."

"Why didn't you call us?" Callum asked.

Sadie felt a tinge of annoyance, but not towards Callum. "I asked Lyas, many times, but he wouldn't pull you from Seraleveli. We were way in over our heads in Mercer... So many people died."

"We heard," Aiden nodded his head. "I'm sorry, Sadie."

"So when do we go find this Morwin? He's still out there, right?" Veronica said.

"I'm not sure what Lyas wants to do," Sadie sighed. "Morwin is dangerous and will kill again. But Joel is here and the gifted from Seraleveli is missing. I don't remember the last time this much was on Lyas's plate, or even if there was a time similar."

The group nodded in a silent agreement. Behind the excitement of being home and back with their family, the atmosphere was muddled with defeat. Sadie couldn't stop thinking about the 'what ifs' when she was in Mercer and what she could have done to stop Morwin sooner. She didn't doubt that the rest of her family felt the same way about their mission.

"So what can he do?" Natasha asked. Sadie assumed she was talking about Joel, but even she wasn't sure what that answer was.

"Something fierce. I haven't seen it with my own eyes, but it was like an invisible wave destroyed everything in its path. Morwin started the destruction downtown, Joel accidentally made it worse," Sadie said grimly. "He can also, somehow, hide his mind. It was why Lyas couldn't see him. I think it's the helmet he can summon."

"Well, hopefully we didn't scare him off. I would like to see more of his abilities," Aiden said cheerfully.

"Let's not push him," Sadie said. "The guy is in pain. I think we can all relate to what it was like to arrive here. Try to make him feel welcome?"

"There is a storm within him," Veronica ominously said. "I could feel his violent desires. It may not be the smartest choice to let him stay here."

Saide shook her head. "If he leaves, he may do more damage than if he stays. Lyas is going to teach him control, just like he did with all of us. And please, Veronica. Don't spook him with any more witchy readings."

Sadie stood from her chair and walked towards the entrance. "I'll catch up with you guys later. I'm going to find Joel."

Before she could reach the creaky door, she felt a hand on her shoulder and turned to see Callum. She immediately recognized his stern look when he wanted to have a serious discussion.

"Suds, you need to talk to Lyas when he wakes up. We need to go back to Seraleveli, the gifted there is dangerous. No one just slips from Veronica's sightseeing," Callum said hastily.

Sadie rubbed the corners of her eyes. She could feel her exhaustion of responsibility begin to weigh her. "Morwin and Joel slipped from Lyas. Maybe this is just a new obstacle we all have to face. Besides, it's not me you have to convince."

"But you can convince Rowan. Lyas will listen to her," Callum's voice carried urgency. "The guy, Garem, will lash out sooner than later. He's scared; gave me this scar on accident. We need to go back and find him."

Sadie sighed. She didn't like going above her friends, but she trusted Callum closely. "Okay, I'll talk to Rowan." She walked away, saying goodbye to Callum and exited the cabin. The mounting pressure of everyone's situation was soon to crash over Lyas when he would awake. She hoped he would make the right decision. In the meantime, she would give Joel space before speaking with him again.

* * *

It was easy for Sadie to find where Joel disappeared to. She just followed the pull that led to the nearest beach and found him walking through shallow tides with his pants rolled up and his shoes in hand. He stopped and kindly waved at her as she stood atop the sand bank. She had no doubt he felt her coming to join him.

Sadie neatly piled her socks and shoes on the beach and rolled up her trousers. She joined him in the water, uninvited. He didn't seem to mind.

"Hey you," she said.

Joel meekly smiled back at her. "Hey."

"I'm really sorry," she said as the ocean splashed around her ankles. "Veronica can be annoyingly spiritual sometimes. Social cues are not her forte."

Joel let out a pitiful chuckle. "I didn't have to storm out. She just… threw me off. I honestly thought there would be a trap ready for me."

"This place is safe," Sadie grinned. "I never lied to you about that."

Joel slowly nodded as he scanned the ocean's horizon. Far in the distance were the tall fins of whales breaching and smacking down on the water. Sadie had seen them so many times in the past that she forgot how captivating it was for someone new to the experience. She could feel pulses of wonder soar through Joel with each whale spotted. She was happy he was here to see them wave hello.

"I've never seen whales before," Joel said. "I lived in Blackpine, it was right on the coast, but the bay was too polluted. Nothing larger than seals would swim close to the shore. I should have been able to see whales."

"Do you miss Blackpine?" Sadie asked.

Joel grunted. "No. It wasn't my home. There's nothing there for me anymore."

Sadie nodded in silence. They continued to watch the whales as they listened to the distant claps and water splash in rolling waves.

"What can they do?" Joel asked. "Your family?"

"Incredible things; each one is unique," Sadie explained slowly. "Lyas can alter minds, Rowan is deadly with weapons, Callum can manipulate metal, Natasha can summon fire that's fierce, Veronica can cast spells, and Aiden is really fast. And those are very simplified descriptions."

Joel laughed and shook his head. "This feels like a child's joke."

"It's who we are now, you included," Sadie said. "I can understand you not wanting any part of this. Not one of us asked for these powers. What you choose to do with them is what defines who you are. And I won't ever judge you for refusing to accept them."

Joel looked over at her. His dark brown eyes glimmered with the water's reflection. "But if I refuse, that will make me complicit in anything horrible that happens after. I have a burden now for the people I've killed and the people who might get hurt. I don't want to be in this position. What does that make me?"

"Anyone forced into helping people was actually never helping them in the first place," Sadie said gently. "Your burden is choosing what kind of life you want to live. Don't force yourself into a life that you never wanted, despite what everyone around you tells you to do."

Joel lightly nodded. "But I should give this a chance, right?" He said. "To know what I want?"

Sadie smiled at him. "I wouldn't mind that. I'd like to get to know you better."

Joel smiled back at her. She could feel his tension slowly disarm again. Whatever he wanted to figure out, she wanted to help him get there.

"These powers... terrify me," He explained. "But I'm open to learning to control them. Lyas can teach me."

"He's a real stickler, so beware," she grinned. Uncertainty felt wonderful when it was peeled away.

Joel took a parting look at the whales before asking her if she wanted to walk down the shore. Together they followed where the ocean retreated from the sand, comfortable enough to enjoy the silence and occasionally break it with the odd question about their lives. The whales continued to breach their fins, waving their hellos and slapping the water on their return. Soon, they would walk back to the farm and attempt another greeting with the family. Sadie hoped, this time, they would put in the effort to ease Joel with kindness.

CHAPTER 17

"You sure no one is going to hear us?" Joel asked as he and Lyas hiked up the worn path. On one side of them was a steep and rocky cliff that overlooked the blue sea and on the other green hills that rolled over one another. Wind from the ocean roared past their ears, but Joel was still unsure it would mask whatever he was about to create.

Lyas shook his head and chuckled. "The property continues another kilometre down the coast. It's quite a large farm! Besides, Veronica has a hex around the entire property. No one will be able to see or hear us."

Whatever hex or spell was cast, Joel couldn't see it. He questioned if Lyas truly knew the intensity of damage that he caused in Mercer. Joel felt like he needed more space to test himself. He examined all of his surroundings again to find any unwanted eyes. The only signs of life were seagulls and puffins glittering the skyline white as they glided through the air.

"How'd you even get land like this?" Joel said. "With this view, this must have been a fortune."

"It was my uncles. He inherited it when my mom moved to Tunland with my father. That's where I was born and raised," Lyas hollered over a gust of wind. "My parents would take me here on vacation. My uncle and I would walk this entire coast every time I would visit; he loved to teach me about world history and warfare. The man had no children. So when he passed, I was given the farm."

"I'm sorry," Joel said. "You sounded close."

"No," Lyas sighed. "He was a difficult man. I was always at fault for mom leaving to Tunland. He would constantly remind me of that. The guy couldn't go a day without a drink, ultimately dying from it."

Joel stared at Lyas, confused with this relationship. "But he still gave you the farm?"

"Clarity tends to arrive at the worst time. Like when you're on your deathbed. C'mon, we don't have much farther to go."

Lyas and Joel hiked over a large grassy hill crowned with dense oak trees, most likely planted by generations far before them. The trees made for a nice break from the travelling wind when they finally walked through. Lyas brought Joel to a clearing on the other side of the treeline and revealed the practice grounds.

The pasture sat in a shallow bowl surrounded by tall hills. Scorch marks smeared the vibrant grass in every direction, occasionally broken by open craters revealing the rock and dirt below. Enormous stones stuck out from the ground as if they were tossed by a giant. The entire pasture was a devastated crime scene. Any plane flying above would be able to spot it without effort. Lyas looked embarrassed when Joel turned to him.

"We use the field quite a lot," Lyas chuckled. He began to walk down the hillside towards flat ground and Joel followed. He stopped at a grey boulder as large as a small car.

"I can see why you wanted that hex. This place could attract a lot of attention," Joel said.

"It's best that we have someplace to test our limits in peace," Lyas explained. "A vital part of this family is remaining secret to the rest of the world. Who knows what humanity will want of us when we announce ourselves, and I am confident we are nowhere close to a reveal."

Joel slowly nodded. "I'm amazed I wasn't discovered in Mercer. I destroyed downtown in broad daylight and people immediately blamed it on anything else."

"Believing in something rational makes the soul feel a lot better than believing something completely bizarre. This family is nothing short of weird."

Joel let out a long sigh as he prepared what he wanted to say. "I want you to understand that I want to go back to being normal. This family... accepting this life is not what I want. I'm still here because I never want to lose control of these abilities again. Once I learn how, then I'm gone."

Lyas grunted as he frowned his brow. "Learning control won't happen today. This process takes time, Joel."

"I know that," Joel said sharply. "But I have no idea what to expect from all of this. Like, what do... I do?"

"Well, for starters," Lyas pointed to the car-sized boulder. "Throw that rock."

Joel looked at Lyas and then back to the boulder, confused. He held out a hand towards the rock and began to think about throwing it before Lyas interrupted him.

"No, no, no, physically throw the rock. With your hands," Lyas said.

Joel lowered his raised arm and shook his head. "I can't lift a giant rock. Those aren't my abilities."

"There's more to your abilities than you know. Throw the rock as far as you can," Lyas encouraged.

Joel shook his head in frustration and walked up to the boulder. He grabbed a crevasse at the bottom and found a notch with his other hand. Expecting to meet an immovable wall, he jumped back in surprise when the rock tilted. He didn't believe he moved it; it felt too easy.

Joel looked back at Lyas who was gesturing at him to try again. Joel grabbed the same notches, intending not to let go this time. In one swift motion, he lifted the rock over his head. He was in disbelief at the weight; it was as if he was only holding an empty box.

Joel stared up at the boulder's jagged surface above his head. He waited for the sudden stop of whatever was making him lift the impossible mass, but he continued to hold it effortlessly. Joel braced his legs and aimed the rock towards the coast as he threw his arms forward. The rock sailed high up in the clouds and disappeared far behind the hills. They both listened for the booming crash of the stone hitting the water.

Lyas smiled as the crashing clap echoed past them. "Even though your abilities are unique to yourself, some things you share. We all have incredible strength, agility, and endurance. Threats that would have hurt you in the past can no longer cut your skin. Our bodies have evolved every function we use to survive, and this is just the base of what you can do."

Joel thought back to his fight with Morwin and how he was thrown through walls and steel with no blood drawn. All of those attacks should have killed him; he knew something had changed with his body during those moments.

"Is that why I'm not sleeping and eating?" Joel asked sarcastically.

"Your body will still need sleep, and food. It's just on a different timeline that matches your metabolism and needs," Lyas explained. "Now, show me what makes you different from the rest of us."

Joel rubbed the silver rings on his palms, dreading this moment. He had no desire to unleash the destructive power ever again. Whatever Lyas had to teach him was the gateway from where he was, to where he needed to go.

"There were two. Two different powers that came up when I fought Morwin," Joel said quietly.

Lyas curiously raised an eyebrow. "Interesting. Can you describe them?"

Joel continued to firmly feel the rings. "One was like a hot green flash. I didn't get a good look. After that, at the arena and downtown, the other power was like a torrent... or shock wave. On top of all of this is the helmet that I can summon out of nothing."

"That helmet saved your life, saved you from Morwin. It protects your mind; I couldn't see you because of it," Lyas said. "May I see it? Can you put it on?"

Joel breathed in deeply. He hadn't summoned the helmet since Mercer. He let his mind clear until only the sound of the wind was around him. The moment he called on the helmet it formed around his head in its two consecutive motions. Joel watched as Lyas stared at him in awe and slowly walked towards him.

"May I?" Lyas asked with his palm extended out. Joel cautiously nodded and let Lyas place an open hand over the cold steel that covered his forehead. Lyas closed his eyes, but Joel felt nothing. "Incredible. I'm completely blocked out!"

Joel bobbed his head. "When Morwin almost breached my mind, that's when the helmet first came. Does it look like anything familiar to you?"

"No. The closest comparison I can make is a knight's helmet from the old ages," Lyas joked. "There's thin ridges running along the top. I've never seen a dark green metal like this before. Maybe Callum can examine it for you?"

"Yea, maybe," Joel said. He didn't really want to be examined like a lab rat.

"So you summoned it in a fear response, what of the other abilities?"

"I remember being strangled when it first happened. I was scared... but more angry, if anything. Each time after was a violent strike of rage," Joel said slowly.

"Anger can be shaped into determination. I can understand the fear of using rage, but we can make it into something more," Lyas said. "Isolate what makes you mad and mould it into a reaction. In time, we will turn that anger into focus."

Joel bleakly nodded as he stared at his feet. Trusting that Lyas would get him to a point of control felt impossible, but he was his only option. No cell of him wanted to lash out his rage; rage came with unpleasant memories and isolating them meant remembering the worst of them. This was the path he needed to avoid losing control again; he owed it to the people he killed back in Mercer.

Joel stepped five feet away from Lyas and turned towards the cratered field. He held out his right arm and opened his palm so the silver ring faced away from him. Joel breathed deeply through his nose and closed his eyes. With a blank mind, he thought of everything or anything that had pissed him off in his lifetime. Corruption in his home, the struggle to own anything, greed so deep it would never be rooted out. He thought back to the time and energy he spent trying to make the world a better place, and it was so insignificant compared to how the world actually operated. The hope he held onto when he was young was destroyed by suits with more money. Joel never wanted to rule the world, he just wanted to live a life that would leave Aross in a better place when he left it. That dream was denied. The promises of the generations before him had no value. All he had now was anger. All he was given was the death of his mother.

Rage rushed forward and Joel forced it outwards. What was a feeling of discomfort flashed into a beam of bright green light that cut across the field and blasted into the hillside. Once Joel closed his hand, he looked at the fresh crater. Whatever dirt was touched was completely disintegrated, and all that was left was a burnt tunnel sculpted into the hill.

"What was that?!" Lyas shouted excitedly.

"I don't know! I thought you'd know," Joel snapped back.

"Whatever it was, it ate anything in its path," Lyas exhaled. "Amazing. Now show me the second power."

Joel planted his feet firm and begrudgingly held out his arm again. No inch of him wanted to invite the aches and pains of his deepest troubles. These exercises felt as if they were for only Lyas's gain. Nothing good ever came from embracing the rage created by hate, but he had a burden to follow. Joel let his mind settle again before opening the gates of the memories he hated. This time he tried focusing on using the second power. When he was ready to release, a thunderous boom emitted from his hand and tore up the pasture ahead of him. Dirt and rocks scrambled in the tormenting cone he created, smashing into the hillside or flung far into the air. Repeating what he did with the green beam, Joel closed his fist to stop it. Dirt and rocks bounced and settled on the ground as thunder echoed across the land.

"That was insane. That blast should have sent you flying backwards," Lyas shouted. "How are you able to resist the opposing force? You're defying the very laws of physics here."

"Again, I don't know," Joel said. "It feels like my body wants to move, but I'm trying very hard to stay still."

"Interesting." Lyas scratched his beard. "Maybe later we can try submitting to the force reaction. See what happens after, right?"

"Maybe, but I don't see the point," Joel protested. The thought of being rag dolled by his own power was less than ideal.

Lyas nodded in silence as he gazed over the destroyed pasture. Joel could feel an awkward silence grow as he waited for the next exercise.

"I have no idea what to make of this," Lyas said.

Joel turned to him, confused. "What do you mean?"

Lyas approached the freshly torn up dirt and grazed it with his hand. "Sorry, I forgot to explain my theory. Each one of us represents an element or domain, right? Sadie controls lightning,

I control minds, Callum controls metal, etc. We can manipulate a very specific worldly function. I just don't know what yours is, yet."

Joel scanned over the destroyed pasture and raised his arms in question. "Lasers?"

Lyas laughed. "No, that'd be too simple. And wouldn't explain the propulsion wave or helmet. But I'm sure we will figure it out. C'mon, let's go back."

"Right now?" Joel stuttered. "We just got here!"

Lyas nodded his head as he began to hike up the hill. "Let's not push it. Besides, I want to catch up with my family."

"Lyas!" Joel shouted. "You told me you'd teach me control, and I learnt nothing today. At this pace, I'll never leave this fucking island!"

Lyas turned to face Joel, holding stern eyes. "But you did learn something. You really want to spend the rest of your day remembering shitty memories of your past that make your blood boil? This will take time, Joel."

"These fucking rings, man," Joel scoffed and mumbled to himself. He didn't like it, but Lyas made a good point.

"By the way," Lyas asked. "You just have those two rings, right? Nothing else on your body was altered?"

"No, there's two more on the bottom of my feet," Joel replied.

"Huh, I think I have an idea," Lyas laughed as he continued walking up the hill.

Joel waved his arms at his side in frustration and begrudgingly followed Lyas back up the path. He wondered what was going through that man's mind.

CHAPTER 18

D ark clouds began to brew a quiet storm above the farm. Rain spit down slowly as Sadie watched the clouds tumble into each other. She could feel charges gather above and dissipate as the storm moved with the travelling wind. She held her hand out, so it was no longer protected by her cabin's awning, letting the light shower dampen her skin. The familiar comfort of rain held a deep love within her.

She had just come back from an errand trip with Natasha. Aiden made them a list of specific items that required a trip to the closest city, Arthur's Gate. He was making Joel something to help him with his abilities, and Natasha and her were happy to leave the farm for an outing. She even found a cute, practical jacket in her favourite shade of blue.

Across the driveway, Callum exited his cabin and jogged towards Sadie. He was wearing a thick rain jacket and a hood covering his head. His shoulders were hunched, probably from the discomfort of the cold rain. Callum never liked the humidity of the Isles; he would never grow out of the dry Vallan deserts.

"Hey Suds, you busy?" Callum called out.

Sadie shook her head and opened her door for Callum. She would have preferred to stay outside, but knew he wouldn't tolerate the cold for long. He jogged inside, shaking off a handful of rain droplets from his jacket. The scar over his face had completely healed over.

"I found that gin you like in the city," Sadie said. "It's on the table."

Callum grinned ear to ear. "Sublime. Thank you, Suds!"

Sadie grabbed two mugs from her pantry and popped the cork on the bottle. She poured just enough for them to sip on and warm their bellies. "Friend tax," she winked.

Callum's laugh was short. She could tell he was distracted. Sadie had a hunch he came over to ask something of her. Callum nodded in thanks as he grabbed the mug of gin from Sadie.

"Lyas might send us to Jaussa," Callum said grimly. "He sensed a new gifted there. Had Veronica confirm it too."

"Okay," Sadie sighed. "Did Lyas say when we are going?"

Callum tilted his head and stared at her. He always looked like that when he was bothered. "Well, have you talked to Rowan or Lyas yet? Like I asked?"

Sadie shook her head no. "I haven't exactly had a moment to. For goodness sake Callum, we all just got home. I've been busy getting Joel settled in."

Callum scoffed and harshly rubbed his face and beard.

"What the hell is stopping you from speaking to him?" Sadie snapped.

"I tried. Lyas blew me off. Said he was figuring it out."

"So let him figure it out! Have some faith in the guy." She was slowly becoming annoyed. The whole family had only been home for a few days and everyone was exhausted. The weight of failure had been hitting them all differently.

"I want to, Sadie. But two dangerous people are running loose somewhere on the planet and now we are being sent to recruit another?" Callum barked. "Meanwhile, Lyas is spending all his time with a guy who just mopes around like a sad puppy. I'm beginning to question where Lyas's priorities stand."

Sadie set down her mug and crossed her arms. "Joel's been through a lot; give him a chance. Everyone, including you, was lost like him at some point."

Callum sarcastically laughed. "I wasn't like him. I realized quickly what these abilities meant to me. They gave me strength for the responsibilities that only we were bestowed upon. Responsibility, like capturing dangerous people?" Callum held out two upright fingers. "Morwin. And Garem."

"If you want to go back to Seraleveli or Mercer, be my guest," Sadie said coldly. "I'm not going above Lyas."

"We don't have to," Callum persisted. "Let him stay here. We can open the offer to the others and see who wants to help. Lyas doesn't control us. We don't have to follow him blindly."

Sadie let out a short scoff and shook her head. Not too long ago, she remembered feeling the same way Callum did. Lyas frustrated her in Mercer; she was ready to rush into whatever direction she thought was best. She had already broken his trust when she left him in the hangar to find Joel. Now that she was home, all she felt was relief that her family was back in one place, safe and together. She tried to empathize with how Callum felt, but only found herself becoming irritated by him. She looked up and saw him staring into her, waiting for her to change her mind.

"More people are going to die, Suds," Callum whispered. "We are wasting our time here."

Sadie deeply sighed. "No. I'll take you wherever you want to go, but I am staying put until Lyas tells me otherwise. I owe that to him. Not because I'm a blind follower, but he needs to be able to trust me. We have enemies now. It's time to start changing our approach, so we all come home, and Lyas is working on that."

Callum shook his head in disappointment as he stood up. He grabbed the bottle she got him from the table and stormed towards the door. "Thanks for the gin," he growled.

Sadie stood there in silence as Callum left. She listened to the rain patter on the roof and the crackle of the logs in her fireplace as she tried to make sense of her thoughts. She felt like a hypocrite. She was quick to jump to Lyas's defence when challenged by others, but she defied his command when it fell below her interest. The pull she felt in Mercer, towards Joel, overwhelmed her with emotion so unexplainable that she abandoned her friends in a murderer's lair. She tried to compare what she went through in Mercer to how Callum held himself responsible for Seraleveli. As difficult as Callum could be, sometimes he only wanted to save lives, just like her.

Sadie rubbed her eyes in frustration and tried to think of anything else. At some point, she would find Lyas and speak with him. That was the least she could do for Callum.

Sadie decided to go for a walk to clear her mind and threw her hood over her head. She trudged down the muddy road and then onto a path that led to a small cove that she loved to visit.

She preferred when the sun was out so she could lie on the beach and bask in the warmth. But seeing the storm over the ocean was a beautiful compromise.

As she rounded the sand hill that hid the cove, she found Veronica in the middle of the beach. She wasn't wearing a rain jacket and was drenched from the rain. Her dark black hair was slicked back and sticking to her shoulders. She was looking over the sea, holding her hands up and moving them slightly as if she was trying to grab hold of something. As much as Sadie wanted to be alone, Veronica's company always manifested stillness and peace. She walked down to join her friend.

"What do you feel, sis?" Sadie said as she placed herself next to her friend.

"Layers upon layers," Veronica said, without breaking sight of the horizon. "I can feel the edges of paper, but I can't flip them. I wonder what's on the other side."

Sadie nodded in silence. The world could be felt in unique ways, depending on who described it. To Sadie, she could feel the infinite flow of charges that sparked the planet with energy. She was always genuinely curious about how Veronica saw it with her own eyes.

"You felt another soul in Jaussa? Is that right?" Sadie asked.

"Yes, he glowed as bright as the sun. Do you think we will go to find him soon? I wouldn't mind speaking with my people again."

Sadie watched low clouds roll over each other as the ocean air parted and moved their masses. She could feel charges building on top and beneath, and in a split second she traced a lightning bolt as it was forced down towards the boiling water. The bolt was far from them, but she could feel every electron discharge itself at light-speed. To her, it was like watching whales breach the surface of the sea.

Sadie realized she was lost in thought, but when she turned to Veronica, she found her still immersed in whatever witchcraft she was composing. "I don't know… Callum wants to hunt down Garem and Morwin."

"Lyas has a lot to consider," Veronica whispered. "Now that Joel is at the farm and a new gifted has emerged."

"What do we do?" Sadie said desperately. "It feels like we're drowning. We can't keep up with the number of powerful people ascending. I don't even know if Joel will stay …"

"Oh Sadie," Veronica said as she turned to meet the eyes of her friend. "In time, the number of gifted arising will diminish. Destiny has written more than just finding others in our book."

Sadie noticed Veronica had fallen into another trance. Her eyes looked through Sadie's body and her words carried like a prophecy. In these moments, Sadie learnt to let Veronica say her peace and return to reality on her own.

Veronica's eyes returned to meeting Sadie's. She looked off into the distance to continue whatever she was conjuring before Sadie joined her. The trance was quickly broken. Sadie decided not to linger on what she just said. Most of the time, Veronica had no clue what she spoke of when she detached from her mind.

"Can you tell me about Garem?" Sadie asked. "Why didn't he come here?"

Veronica breathed deeply as her hands shaped into odd patterns. "He was scared. He had never left his hometown in his whole life, so he became hesitant when we extended our offer. For days we watched him, walked with him, spoke with him. We tried our best to convince him to leave. And then one day... he just vanished."

Sadie nodded. "What was he capable of? Callum speaks of him like he can kill thousands."

Veronica held her breath as her eyes widened. Fear within her was crawling out. "I watched him take the form of a brutal monster, with the strength of a god that exceeds ours all combined. Callum isn't wrong when he speaks of his concern for Garem. I've tried many times to find him again, but his soul is gone from my sight."

"Let's hope he has no reason to hurt us," Sadie said.

"If we continue to seek after him, then he just might."

Sadie rubbed the bridge of her nose. The rain had thickened and started to consistently drip down the brim of her hood. Her face felt wet from the spray. She thought about asking each member what they thought would be best, or which direction they wanted to take. Lyas was a leader to them, but he never acted on obligated command. If everyone felt the same or different about his choice, then surely he would listen.

"What would you do?" Sadie asked.

Veronica sighed deeply. "Whatever choice this team makes, I know to my core that destiny has already bonded the path we are on. There's no stopping what is ahead... but for right now, I'd like to ask my friend if she would paint lighting for me?"

Sadie smiled through the discomfort of uncertainty that pricked her. It was obvious to her that Veronica shared the same confusion about their future. Callum's pressure probably made it worse for her. Sadie set her doubt aside for another time to mull over and entertained her friends' ask. She raised her hands towards the clouds and reached out until she felt clusters of negative charges at the base of the storm. With ease, she pulled the currents downwards towards the boiling ocean waves.

In moments like these, Sadie felt like a kid again. She would pull the lighting down in funny lines or impress herself with sharp patterns. It was a fast game that Veronica loved. Sadie wondered if it was the fleeting images that lightning teased to eyes that weren't her own. Only she could appreciate the true vision that lightning burned within her, but she was happy to share moments with the people she loved.

Sadie and Veronica laughed at her creative bolts striking down until the rain became unbearably dense. They ran up the beach towards the path home and rushed back to get under a dry roof. Sadie would have felt bad for Veronica getting drenched, but knew she deeply loved the rain.

As they ran, Sadie considered what path would be safest for the family, and what Lyas may choose. Her friends trusted her, but she wasn't sure if that trust would be enough to convince Lyas of anything. She wanted to believe he would protect them.

If she learnt anything in Mercer, it was that Lyas could make mistakes. Mistakes were innocently human, but she thought about what the cost would be if one day the family was led down the wrong path.

CHAPTER 19

"Just try five feet at least," Natasha said. She had her arms crossed and carried a scowl that would have intimidated Joel if he wasn't trying to keep upright. He could imagine he looked quite embarrassing; his arms were stiff and his legs trembled underneath him as if he was standing on a tightrope. On top of keeping balance, Joel was struggling to focus on dialing down the intensity of the blasts from his hands and feet. Natasha seemed to become more and more annoyed at every cloud of dust he kicked up. Joel's feet landed roughly as he cut off his power. They had been trying to practise flying for five hours now and he had only just made it past two feet above the ground.

"I don't think it's supposed to work this way," Joel argued. "It doesn't feel right. I feel like I'm going to fall backwards all the time."

Natasha shook her head aggressively. "You need to find balance. Keep the intensity down and brace your knees!"

"I've been doing that!" Joel yelled.

"Do it again!" Natasha yelled back. Her Revenland accent became heavier with each irritated demand.

Joel laughed at the absurdity of the exercise and readied himself again for another attempt. For the past couple of days, Joel was becoming more familiar with the use of the propulsions and beams that disintegrated everything. He had found that Lyas wasn't lying when he promised to teach him. Joel found himself using his powers, more with intent, and less with memories. Lyas encouraged him to slowly move away from using past trauma as a crutch, and he felt he was keeping control with confidence. That was until Aiden gave him boots with holes at the bottom and Lyas told him to fly.

Out of frustration, Joel accidentally released a torrent out of one foot too early and his legs swept out as if a rug was pulled from where he stood. Dust from the pasture billowed around his back as he hit the ground. He could feel Natasha fiercely glaring through him.

Natasha audibly sighed loud enough for Joel to hear. He watched her jump into the air and bolts of white-hot flame burst from her feet. Joel could feel the heat immediately engulf his entire body. Natasha floated circles around Joel effortlessly, drawing a path of flames and ash underneath. She then streamed flames from her hands and jetted herself at sharp angles and pivots. The entire time she kept her eyes on Joel; he was confident she was showing off.

"Look. Watch my eyes and my body," Natasha yelled over the roaring flames. "I do not look down at my feet. I will lose balance. Try focusing on a specific thing, like a rock or tree, and don't break contact."

The flames extinguished, and Natasha landed gracefully. She crossed her arms again and waited silently for Joel to try another attempt. Joel heaved himself back upright and dusted his clothes off. He held out his arms to his sides and positioned his feet. Part of the challenge was letting the force of the propulsion carry him, instead of keeping his body stationary. He found it needed to be a conscious choice.

Letting in a small trickle of power, Joel was lifted with a sudden gust. He held the trickle in place and looked across the field at a large boulder, deeming it at his pinpoint and trying hard not to look down. Propulsions from his hands wanted to shift aggressively out of place, but he held them firm.

"Okay… good so far," Natasha called out.

Joel grunted in agreement. The urge to look away from the boulder was magnetic, and he could feel the trickle trying to become a raging river out of the mental valve he created. Every time he floated awkwardly to the side, he would anxiously correct it until he was back hovering still.

"Try going higher. Increase the intensity slowly," Natasha said.

Joel hesitantly let the propulsions become stronger. His body violently raised ten feet above the ground, but he maintained his balance. His eyes were begging to strain from looking at the boulder; the urge to look down was enticing. He knew, just from where Natasha was standing, that he was uncomfortably high up.

"How do I get down?!" Joel hollered down.

"No! Don't do that yet," Natasha ordered. "You need to become familiar with your stability!"

Joel felt his body drift forward. Before he could fix his footing, his eyes accidentally darted towards his feet. The momentum of falling forward dominated his control, and he spiralled downwards, headfirst. The ground cratered underneath his body as he hit the ground. Joel slowly sat up, picking clumps of grass off his sweater. He noticed Natasha was looking towards the treeline, watching Lyas and Rowan hike down the hill to meet them.

"Looks like you've made some progress," Lyas said as they joined them. "How are the boots working?"

Joel picked a piece of dirt from his neck and scoffed. "They have huge holes at the bottom, Lyas. I can't walk anywhere without feeling grass on my soles."

Lyas laughed, seemingly missing Joel's frustration. "Well, it's that or blowing your shoes off every time you try to use your bottom propulsions."

Joel rubbed the dirt from his hair and tried to bite his tongue. "I don't understand why I need to learn how to fly. I don't want to fly. I made that very clear."

Lyas gently smiled. He looked over at Rowan, who subtly nodded her head in the farm's direction. Joel took it as a sign that they were giving Natasha a break.

"C'mon, let's all head back," Lyas said.

* * *

Joel pulled off his dirty sweater and scrubbed his face with the hot water pouring from his tap. Mud dripped off of his beard into the sink; he could feel the coolness of the metal rings against his face as he washed away the grime. Looking into the mirror, he noticed his hair was longer than he usually let it grow. Long wet strands clung to his cheeks, and the backside was curling behind his ears. Soon he'd have to find someone to cut it.

He dried himself off with a small towel and went into his room to grab a fresh shirt. Joel threw the mud caked sweater into his laundry basket and felt a craving for a stiff drink. When he entered his kitchen, he found Lyas sitting in his living room.

"Sorry, I thought I'd let myself in," Lyas said.

"It's your place," Joel shrugged.

"But it can be yours," Lyas spoke gently. "I wanted to apologize. I felt hopeful about your potential when I realized to what extent your abilities could take you. I thought maybe if I show you that potential, like flying, you might be willing to stay. That's not what you've asked of me, but I am curious if you have reconsidered?"

"That's not what we agreed on," Joel said sharply. "I've been here for over a week now; I'm close to having control. Once I do, then I'm leaving."

"I understand that." Lyas leaned forward in the chair. Joel could sense a sales pitch for his loyalty coming. "This family faces pressures we haven't faced before your arrival. We have an enemy now, a shared enemy. On top of that, I'm trying to track down others like us out in the world. The group is tired of waiting around and I need to make a decision soon. If you stay, you can help us track Morwin."

That was the catch. Joel knew there would be payment for his safe harbour at the farm. He was surprised Lyas was asking this soon. "I will not be your bait," Joel gritted his teeth.

"No." Lyas shook his head. "You're not bait. You're a fighter."

"These powers should never be used again. All they're good for is hurting people."

"That's where you're wrong," Lyas argued. "I've seen your potential and I know deep down you can use them to save people. Terrible things will continue to happen around Aross and it's your choice, whether or not you want to help. I want you to stay, Joel. Morwin won't be the last enemy we face, and we need fighters like you to stop them."

Joel scoffed. "Have you not seen what people are capable of? No matter how many you save, people themselves will double that number, in deaths for the hundreds of causes they believe in. There is no point. I came here to learn how to avoid hurting them, not saving."

Lyas cupped his hands together and looked down in disappointment. "I'm sorry, but I don't agree with that. You could do so much more... I just hope you can reconsider."

The rocking chair creaked loudly as Lyas stood up. Before he walked out the door, Joel remembered needing to ask him a favour. His timing was painfully awful. "Lyas, wait... I want to call my dad and I can't remember his number. Can you help?"

Lyas slowly nodded yes and closed his eyes for a solid minute. Joel felt a faint invisible hand graze the back of his head, and once Lyas opened his eyes, he walked over to the kitchen counter and grabbed a pen and paper. Without a word, Lyas wrote down the number and left Joel shamefully standing in the kitchen.

Joel grabbed the note and read the familiar set of numbers pulled from his memory. He took it to his living room chair and sat for hours staring at it, wondering what to say. Lyas's ask had thrown him through a whirlwind of doubt. Joel wondered if what he wanted would end up doing more damage in the end.

Lya's spoke of potential that seemed so distant. He didn›t want this burden given to him; if there was any potential, it died long ago. Whatever choice he would make, either outcome would bring him to a lifetime of struggling.

Joel's mind was spinning. The thought of speaking with his dad was comforting, but he knew it would probably be the last time. Joel stood up and grabbed the landline phone. He set it to the private callback and quickly dialled his dad's number to avoid stalling himself. The phone tensely rang for multiple tones. Joel thought it would go to voicemail until his dad picked up at the last second.

"Hello, Wesley speaking," his father said. His rugged but kind voice flooded Joel with comfort and regret. He missed Wesley dearly. Joel held onto that moment of warmth before he realized the silence was lingering and Wesley spoke louder into the phone. "Hello?"

Joel swallowed down the lump in his throat. "Hey Dad."

"Joel? What the hell... Is that you, Joel?" His father's voice began to stutter and crack. Each word pierced his heart. Joel could feel his eyes welling. He refused to cry in front of his dad.

"Yea, it's me," Joel bit down on the inside of his cheek. "I'm sorry Dad. I'm so sorry."

"Where are you? Are you safe? Are you hurt?" His Dad asked in a flurry. "I thought you went back to Blackpine but Beth hasn't heard from you either! Please tell me where you are. I'll come and pick you up."

Joel's head fell heavily into his palm as he squeezed the edges of his face. He wished he had rehearsed something to say; all he wanted to do was apologize. "I'm okay, I'm safe. I just... I don't know what to do."

"You can come home, kid," His Dad was sobbing through the phone. "I'm not mad at you. Please, just come home."

"I can't." His breath was thick and heavy. "As much as I want to come home, it's just not possible anymore. I wanted to talk to you, hear your voice, one last time."

"Joel, I'm begging you, don't do anything stupid."

"I won't. I'm safe right now," Joel said. "It's good to hear your voice. I needed that. Can you tell the boys I'm alright?"

His dad choked on the other end of the line. "Where are you going, boy?"

"I'm not sure," Joel stuttered. "But I can't come home. No amount of apologies will make up for what I've done to you and the things I've said. I love ya always, Dad."

Joel hung up the phone before his dad could say anything back. He forced back tears that strained behind his eyes. Every bone in his body ached with regret and shame. He wished he could tell his father everything; maybe Wesley could have given wise insight into his dilemma. That moment was gone now.

Joel delicately set the phone down and sat with his head in his hands. He didn't realize how much time had passed until he looked up and noticed the sun had settled and dusk enveloped the sky. Joel grabbed his jacket and left the cottage to clear his mind. Outside, he found most of the members sitting around the campfire sharing drinks. Sadie was among them. She looked at Joel and waved him over. He could feel a brush of kindness through their bond. She knew he was in pain.

Joel turned away from the campfire, deciding to walk to town and have a beer to himself while he listened to the locals of Conqet play their folk tunes. Joel didn't deserve the company of kindness for all the pain and suffering he caused. Now that he said goodbye to Dad, all he could wait for was the embrace to smother his life and end the pain he so dearly wanted gone. Joel knew that day would come soon.

CHAPTER 20

Even though the hay bales were weightless to him, Joel's nose was continuously assaulted by loose tuffs that forced him to irritably scratch away. He had hit his limit of patience and decided it was time for another chore.

He didn't mind working around the farm. It killed time between sleep and training. No one assigned him mandatory duties during his stay, but the offer was opened and he volunteered just for the distraction alone. Some jobs sucked, some were more enjoyable. Joel decided not to pick and choose, and just do whatever needed to be done. Whatever the chore was, was miles beyond his enjoyment of training his abilities. Yet it was the training that was the only thing that would get him off this farm.

On the other side of the fence, the lazy group of cows stared at Joel without concern. All they wanted was the food he brought with him, and nothing else. As he scattered the hay around their feet and watched them tip their heads for a leisurely feed, Joel felt someone approaching. He didn't need to turn and look to find who it was.

Sadie felt cheerful as she got closer. She was wearing a dirt stained t-shirt, jeans and muddy rubber boots. Her blonde hair was tied in a looser ponytail than usual. She must have been doing chores herself, now coming to help Joel with whatever he needed. Joel, however, wasn't feeling like having company today. Trying to hide his desire for isolation would be near impossible.

"Hey you," she smiled. Joel felt an obvious dodge away from the thorn that pricked both their skin. Living with this bond would be difficult, at least until he left the farm.

"Hey," Joel awkwardly smiled back. "I'm just finishing feeding the cows, and then I'm going to patch the shingles on the shed."

"I know," she said. "I'm feeling kind of peckish. Want to take a break and join me for lunch?"

Joel shook his head. The offer was appreciated, but his mind was elsewhere. "I think I'm good, thank you. I'm not feeling hungry, anyway."

Sadie's hands rested on her hips; her look became more stern but somehow kept her familiar kindness. "Joel. Since you've been here, you have spent all of your free time alone. Please, a little bit of company is good for the mind."

Sighing heavily, Joel looked at the cows and tucked his gloves into his back pocket. At least it was Sadie forcing him to socialize, and not one of the others. He could at least feel what she wanted in the moment. Right now she felt genuine in her ask.

"Alright, fine. Meet you in town?" He said.

Sadie shook her head with a mischievous smile. "Nope. Change out of those clothes and meet outside my cabin."

As Sadie walked away, Joel resisted the urge to groan in displeasure. He debated just not showing up at all, but that would be rude to her. He waited to leave until she was halfway down the fence line and then slowly started the walk back to his cabin.

Joel changed into a clean t-shirt and his only pair of pants without holes in them. When he exited his cabin, he found Sadie waiting outside of her place. She was alone and waved him over. He had hoped others would be invited as some sort of buffer.

"Where are we going?" Joel asked. "Dundly? Conqet?"

"Neither," Sadie laughed. "I want to show you this place in Hieto!"

Before Joel could object, or even ask where that was, Sadie grabbed his hand and the world darkened around him. In a second, light returned to his eyes, leaving the blue glare that came with her electric teleporting. They stood atop a set of stone stairs with small, flat roofed shacks around them. The air was humid and smelled of rain and pine. The ocean sat below the hill they were standing on, but the coast was rockier and steeper than Lohwems'.

"I forgot to ask; do you like sushi?" She walked down the steep stairs towards the street below. "If you don't, this place has these delicious spicy rice cakes."

Joel scoffed and followed her. "Where are we? Are we even allowed to leave the farm?"

"For someone so eager to leave, you sure get paranoid when you actually step off of that farm," she laughed. "We are in Yanda. This is Rowan's hometown, Hieto."

Joel tapped her back as he caught up to her. "But seriously, are we allowed to leave?"

Sadie rolled her eyes sarcastically and smiled at him. "Of course. As long as we aren't showing off our powers and risking our identities to the world, there's no harm in exploring places we can easily get to."

Joel sighed and waved his arms in surrender. "Alright. Where are you taking me, anyway?"

"It's this little corner stand that doesn't have a name. Trust me, it's delicious."

Joel and Sadie walked down the town's main street until they came across a booth that was stuck between two convenient stores and covered with a plastic tarp. An older Yandian couple ran the grill. They seemed to recognize Sadie immediately and yelled something in Yandian Joel couldn't understand. Neither did Sadie, as she just laughed, smiled and handed over a few bills of their currency.

The couple quickly cooked up the order Sadie pointed to and worked at an impressive speed for their age. Joel thought he wasn't hungry until he smelled the searing of meats on their grill. He leaned in close to Sadie so the couple couldn't hear him; as if they could even understand.

"I, uh, I don't like sushi," He whispered to her.

Sadie turned to face him and smiled. Her eyes were beautiful at this distance. "It's okay, I kinda figured. I ordered you those rice cakes. Take em or leave em!"

Joel chuckled. A small snack wouldn't kill him. He tried to break the silence as they waited. "They remember you, eh? You like coming here?"

"There's a few places around the world I like to visit when I get hankering," Sadie said.

"And you just jump around when you want? Lyas doesn't tell you to stop?" Joel asked.

"No, Joel," she said. "As strict as Lyas can be, remember, you're not a prisoner. If you want to fly across the world to buy a postcard, then nothing is stopping you."

"I don't believe it," Joel said. "If I leave before I finish my training, I'll forever be on Lyas's shit list."

"Well, you've come this far," she winked at him. "No sense now in refusing to fly to where your stomach desires."

Joel could tell she was deflecting. Whatever moment they shared, that was all she wanted. That made Joel feel a little better about joining her for lunch. She must have noticed he was thinking too loud, as she looked up at him and pointed a finger at his chest.

"No shop talk. Just us, okay?" She said.

Joel laughed and nodded. He was okay with that.

Once the food was ready, the two of them waved goodbye to the older couple and continued their walk down the street. Before Joel opened his container, he noticed Sadie keeping hers closed. "Are you not eating?"

"I was thinking we could find a spot to sit," Sadie said.

Joel didn't even have time to ask where. A flash of blue enveloped him in darkness and a whole new landscape materialized when the light returned.

The air was sour, but the skies above were clear and bright. Sharp, shale mountains surrounded them, but a wide and open field had flattened the ground ahead. Small pools of crystal blue water spotted the entire valley. Geysers shot from the basins at random; the boiling water that was rocketed into the sky flew with the wind that grabbed it. Sadie sat down on a flat rock and opened her sushi box. She picked away at her food and looked up at Joel, wondering why he wasn't sitting down with her.

Joel placed himself on the same rock and took small bites from the rice cakes. He still wasn't that hungry, but the rice cakes had the perfect amount of spice and tang. Joel looked at Sadie and asked. "Where are we now?"

"Some conservation park in North Revenland," she said after she swallowed her food. "Natasha told me about it. I thought she was over-exaggerating, but there are literally dozens of geysers here."

"It's beautiful," Joel nodded. He spotted a herd of elk cross from a tree stand and followed the base of the mountains. "Kind of reminds me of home."

"In what way?" Sadie asked.

"The mountains, the pines, the elk," Joel explained. "You can find so many places around Aross with them, but they all carry their own signature."

"Once you see what else this world has, you begin to fully appreciate the world as a whole," Sadie smiled. "It reminds me of home, too."

"Do you ever visit home?" Joel asked.

"Not really. It's… not as easy as you'd think," Sadie said. "I want to, but maybe when the time is right."

Joel felt her heart pull away from a familiar grief. He didn't think he could ever set foot at home, either. She looked up at him, feeling the need to snap back what she just said. He gave her a friendly smile to show there was no bad blood. "There's nothing to go home to, anyway."

Sadie scrunched her nose as she frowned at him. "Not necessarily. There's a lot back home that waits for us."

Joels shook his head in disagreement. "Like what? We both lost too much there."

"What we lost doesn't change what grief has blinded us to." Sadie softly spoke, "I miss the people, the land, the culture. The life I considered home was brutally wounded when my parents died, but there's still something left there waiting."

"Sadie," Joel scoffed. "The people there are only after their own interests. Same as every corner that exists on this goddamn planet. People don't care about you, so why should you care about them?"

A prick of annoyance flared in the bond. "There are still good people out there. You really believe they don't exist?"

"Absolutely," Joel nodded. "I've seen what evil does to people. Wherever you go, you will find nothing but selfishness and hate. Rich steal from the poor, criminals walk free, parents abuse the ones they're supposed to protect. The evil that exists thrives in hunger and if any good is born, it is immediately consumed."

Sadie looked at him with disbelief. "Really? So everyone walking around these days is a murderer or rapist? I get you've been hurt Joel, but you can't name one person you believe is good? You can't even try?"

"Nope," Joel paused. "Well... maybe. I don't know. My brother Harv. I guess I always thought he was an honourable man. He took care of me in moments when others were needed. Maybe he's good, but in my experience, I'd be careless to believe the latter didn't exist."

"I don't think you believe that. I can feel the doubt within you. You love your brother, and you know he's a good person," Sadie said.

Joel rubbed his face between his dry hands. "Maybe. But that's one person out of billions. This fight is outnumbered. What's the point of trying to fix the world if it's just going to outright refuse?"

"Because then at least you tried," Sadie said sternly.

When Joel looked towards her, he could see the seriousness in her deep brown eyes. Across the strange bond, she truly held a belief that he could change.

"You think I'm a calloused man?" Joel asked.

"Frustratingly calloused," Sadie smiled and laughed.

Her joy forced a brief chuckle out of him. Maybe he was being a bit too stubborn, but his beliefs were born from lived experience. It was nice, however, to actually feel the hope within someone else. Nothing good could come from accepting that hope. Believing Sadie would only fortify his mistakes in failing the people from his past like his dad, brothers, and Beth.

Joel looked back towards the ground and studied the rings welded into his palms. "I appreciate you bringing me here, Sadie. You've been trying to make me comfortable... I just don't believe I'll ever see humanity in the same lens as you do. You don't need to convince me."

Sadie stood up from the rock and dusted off her pants. She held down an open palm towards him, offering to help him stand. "I don't need to convince you, but nothing says I can't challenge you."

Joel chuckled and shook his head. He grabbed her hand, and he was lifted from the shale boulder. "Where are we going now?"

FORREST C. RICHARD

Sadie scrunched her nose in thought. "I'm feeling a coffee… Maybe Bell'Ilcio?"

Joel grinned at her and affirmatively nodded. Their hands stayed locked and their bodies disappeared behind the spark of collapsed energy. The showering roar of geysers remained in their stead.

CHAPTER 21

The moment the ship's drill broke through the surface, putrid air wafted up and soured Janak's senses. The smell reminded him of low tides at home, when the sun would bake seaweed and dead ocean critters. He was surprised how soft the ground was this far north, and he wondered when he would hit solid levels of sediment.

The drill kicked up damp mud that was pigmented with the same dark green that could be found planet-wide. With a quick scan on his tablet, he confirmed the ground was saturated with algae. More data, for his theory in progress. Clumps of green mud shot up from the drill's spin and caked the belly of his Voidante. Whatever didn't hit the ship landed on the ground around him and slowly frosted over from the hemisphere's cold wind. The drill was now five feet down; Janak increased the reach to ten.

At eight feet, the drill detected mixes of more algae mud, gravel and volcanic ash. It wasn't long after that the drill struck solid layers of clay and slate. Janak let the drill continue down, collecting small samples for each foot of ground breached. Any large boulder in the drill path was immediately punctured through; it would take a lot of abrupt pressure to destroy the crown.

Janak's tablet chimed when it reached prime samples, and the drill slowed to a stop. As the pipe raised from the ground and folded itself, mud and algae dripped off and piled around the entrance of the breach. He noticed thin purple worms wriggle about as they were forcefully yanked deep from the ground and lifted to a bright world alien to them. Janak had seen them before on previous drill expeditions around the planet. In any world with life, worm species would always make him uneasy.

The drill collection compartment raised from the ground and met Janak at eye level. The data from the samples finished transferring, notifying him with another chime. Physical and chemical specifics filled his screen with readings, as it listed each unique composition. He flipped to the radioisotopic tab and confirmed matching ages to previous samples. Eight hundred million years old, approximately, dated back to the first stages of microevolution. That wasn't anything new.

He quickly brought up the fossil tab and his mandibles twitched with excitement as he read. Matching records for sediment and fossil layers were completed. Across the screen compared generated images of each drill exhibition completed around the planet; they showed Janak exactly what he had been theorizing. RES 9 was in the final rehabilitation stage of a second extinction event.

Janak ejected the drill sample and let the ship store its components back in the belly. He walked over to the ramp and sat down, reading over the collected data. Approximately nine hundred thousand years ago, the planet experienced excess volcanic activity that dumped devastating amounts of nitrogen, carbon dioxide, and phosphorus into the air and oceans. Most forms of life were choked out; this kind of extinction event could be found on the majority of evolving planets. However, durable strains of algae, moss and lichen benefited as the planet had just become a fertilizer breeding ground.

The planet was swiftly enveloped by algae in peak conditions and the gases they produced. Ninety-seven percent of life was killed off; the remaining three percent were organisms that thrived in its new environment. Extinction spiked incredibly early in the event, but held in a slow and stabilizing rehabilitation era right after. That gave algae the opportunity to evolve in many unique environments around the planet, and reprieve for the remaining three percent to adapt.

What Janak was most amazed by was the genome age of the Yen. The flying leviathans predated the second extinction event long before it happened. When comparing fossil records, it was clear to Janak that the Yen were ocean dwelling creatures abruptly evolved into terrestrials, and then into massive rulers of the sky. In an incredible window of time, the giants adapted to the new environment that devastated everything else. The steps of evolution should have slowed the Yen, but he was proven wrong. They were truly a remarkable species. For their size and needs, they should have been wiped from existence.

Janak sat on the ramp, compiling the data together until the sky faded into a deep dark blue. He watched dozens of clips he filmed of the Yen and their habits. He truly respected their species for their survival and adaptations. Janak wondered how they lived before the second extinction, and who they shared the waters with. He didn't realize how much time had passed until the air was colder with a lack of sunlight.

Janak jumped to his feet and walked into his ship, where it was warmer. He brought up his progress on a larger screen and updated it with his new samples. He was almost finished the preliminary stage of exploration. In only another couple of weeks, he would fabricate drones to complete the remainder of the catalogue, and then move onto the other planets in the RES system. The rest were barren; it wouldn't take him long to complete them. Once the RES 9 catalogue was completed, he would leave the system, but he still needed to attend fifty-nine other systems before he could return home for a break.

Janak's chest weighed heavily when he thought about returning home. He missed his family, but with each expedition, more and more parts of his old life disappeared. He loved exploring; he was made for the title of a Voidante. As each mission neared its ending, he would begin to feel moments of longing. Whether it was his ageing family, or the wonders he discovered across space; he still couldn't figure out what exactly made him feel this way. He would go on to see different species, different worlds. The Yen would be a memory of the past, like his family.

Sitting down in his pilot seat, Janak pulled the analog close to him and set a flight path to another ideal drilling spot. He would only need a few more samples to complete the data and the ship instantly found a list of nearby zones for him. He closed the ramp and felt the hum of the ship's engines come to life. The hull vibrated lightly as it lifted off of the tundra; within seconds it jolted forwards towards the next site. Wisps of clouds streamed past the chrome nose of the Voidante before it breached the top and revealed the clear, beautiful pink skies of RES 9.

* * *

Large, brown rain droplets pelted Janak's jacket and shell. He wandered too far from his ship and found himself caught in a sudden storm. The downpour immediately drenched him with muddy water. He would have been disgusted if he hadn't already known the water was only pigmented and not filled with filth.

He wiped rain droplets off the screen of his tablet with his sleeve and found the image he took was blurry. He would have to adjust the focus, so he peered inside the scope of his Talener again. The chrome joints of the instrument were protected from the moisture, but the brown rain smeared its shine. He covered the scope lens with his hand and zoomed in on the skittish arthropod. The one he had been tracking was looking right at him through the scope, attempting to intimidate him with a defensive stance. Janak was only amused by the small creature's bravery.

It must have been a male, as it placed itself between him and a herd of larger, slower female companions. The arthropod chittered sharply and turned to run away from the 'scary threat' that was Janak. He just chuckled and snapped a clear picture of the male specimen. Janak looked at his tablet and was presented with a list of names that fell under the creature's relative category. Their genome shared the same class of a Derit. Like the funeral carrions, Derit-Caro and hundreds of other Derit species on the planet. Janak chose Derit-Penilcim for the feisty arthropods.

Janak blinked away brown rain as he watched the male scurry to one of the females and climb up her back. The female didn't seem bothered; she just continued to pick away at the moss beneath her. The male hugged its many legs around his mate's shell and flattened its body out till he was completely camouflaged on her blue husk. Unless you were looking at the finer details, the male was completely hidden. It would only rush towards Janak when he got too close, or if another male entered its territory. The male Derit-Penilcim would switch between each one of its herd mates, using their bodies to surprise any unwanted competitors.

As amusing as the male's show of strength was, Janak had agitated them for too long and needed to remove himself soon. The Talener took a series of consecutive pictures and videos of the herd and chimed Janak's tablet to let him know the records were completed. Most of the pictures would suffice, but the dark rain was disorienting the lens settings. He decided to hike back and return when the storm would pass.

Janak bounded down the mossy hill towards his ship with the Talener crawling behind. Tiny insects, brought to the surface from the rain, fled from his feet with each step. He had already familiarized most of them, but he kept an eye out for any he may have missed. Janak jumped over a creek that was steadily flowing from the rain runoff. He noticed groups of fish with red sail fins skimming the surface as they jumped for frenzied bugs flying nearby. Those were fun to study when he first found them.

The Voidante was parked atop a hill when Janak first landed. The view overlooked fields of moss covered hills and flooded valleys. Creeks and rivers ran between each hill, running from tall, white peaked mountains behind them. Janak expected the view to be obstructed from the rain, but when he reached his ship, he found a completely changed landscape.

The mountain range was hidden from storm clouds avalanching down from their peaks and towards the fields. As they reached the foothills, they draped curtains of brown that blanketed the rolling land; every river was raised, and some even became rapids. Their crystal blue waters had turned to mud as the rain drenched the fields, tearing up moss and grass to clot the network of paths that have been carved for centuries. The storm hastily travelled east, leaving the slopes that gave them the speed it needed to journey across the land. Pink sunlight pierced the gaps in the blanket of clouds, revealing glittering hills with its rays, and the outlines of Yen floating through.

Janak was stunned. He would have missed them through the cover of the rain; he couldn't even hear their low calls. He counted four adults and three of a smaller size. Mothers with their calves. They followed the pace of the storm, staying under the ceiling and bathing in the downpour of brown rain. Janak guessed they were searching for tree crops to feast on. The shadows of their bodies dipped in and out of the storm's cover, making them nearly impossible to see. Janak wondered if they used the storm for the benefit of camouflage or a bath. Each herd of mothers and calves, in regions scattered around the planet, had its own unique habits. These were details so specific that would fall upon the drone's second wave of recording. Janak would be long gone before each herd's habits were identified. He would have been honoured to accept that role, but his time was almost up.

Janak looked down at his tablet and swiped his progress tab to the screen. In large numbers, it read ninety-five percent completed, on the first wave. His goodbyes creeped closer. The longing that weighed his chest became heavier as he watched the Yen carve through the storm. His time on RES 9 was a gift, and that made it even more difficult to leave. He hoped, for the next planet with life discovered, that it would share the same awe that was found here.

Memories of past planets were his saving grace. He remembered feeling the same weight when he finished his exhibitions on RMR 30, RAR 8991, and BMF 22. Each planet of complete marvel had the promise of a future successor. It was difficult to hold that close to his heart when it was time to say goodbye, but eventually he would find another discovery that inspired his drive. RES 9, and the Yen, would soon become a memory of pure value to only himself. The beauty of his responsibility came with that promise of more to be found.

Janak watched as the Yen disappeared with the fleeting storm. Sunlight returned over the mossy hills and dark dwelling insects returned to the dirt below. Rivers and creeks slowly drained the brown flood water towards the sea and crystal blue took its place. In a short amount of time, another storm would burst from the mountain range and flood the fields again. The cycle of the region would continue. The planet would turn and thrive. And soon, its alien adventurer would be gone in another system, looking for life unimaginable.

On his to-do-list, it read that he was to observe fifty-five species along a tree-dense peninsula, outline tectonic plate movement, and place weather sensors around the stratosphere. Janak boarded his Voidante and took off his drenched jacket. He poured a small amount of Bonmoc into a mug and sat down in the pilot seat. A map of the planet presented itself on the command screen, showing him endless opportunity in a universe of endless expansion. Janak plugged in his coordinates and sat back as he felt the hum of his home take him into the skies above. His next destination awaited.

CHAPTER 22

It had been three weeks since Joel had arrived on the farm, and the time Lyas was spending with him had noticeably dwindled. Joel felt as if he was being avoided, and with each attempt to confront him, Lyas would just brush him off. Despite his growing frustrations, Joel still needed to kill time in the long hours of the sleepless nights and days.

Sometimes he would take himself to the pasture and practice controlled intensity of his abilities without a mentor. Other times, he would join Sadie or Natasha to help with chores around the farm, trying to make himself useful. The days when small groups of the family left for an outing, they would always invite him. But he would always stay behind. He felt close to being finished with the lessons and found it was pointless to grow relationships with other members of the family. Still, he found himself bored and alone.

On a bright, warm day, Sadie found Joel at his cottage and offered to train with him. He had previously vented to her about his resentment towards Lyas withdrawing, and found that Sadie was offering more and more of her time since then. Joel had nothing better planned when Sadie approached him, but quickly regretted her offer when he discovered she wanted to train in flying. Despite his protest, she still urged him to try.

Sadie faced Joel as they rose higher in the misty clouds. She danced side to side, floating on a concentrated ball of lightning that supported her. Joel could feel his legs shake beneath him as he slowly elevated; he knew he probably looked like a child learning how to ride a bike. She made flying look so effortless. They must have been a few kilometres off of the ground now, and Joel fought with everything in his power not to look down. He kept Sadie as his focus point so he wouldn't fall down.

"Dude, relax a little! You look so tense," Sadie teased. She quickly mocked his posture and laughed at her own joke. Joel didn't mind; her humour was growing on him. He was mostly embarrassed that he actually looked like a frozen tight roper. "Look around you. The view is incredible."

Joel moved his eyes towards the sea and took in the sights. The ocean was a mirror of blue; there was no wind to disrupt its surface. Beneath them sat the rolling green hills and sharp cliffs that the Rown Isles were so famous for. The island continued to impress him, and seeing it from an aerial view was surprisingly appreciated.

"It's beautiful, but can we slow down now?" Joel nervously asked. They were passing more clouds than he was comfortable with.

"A few more hundred feet, and then we are going to move towards that pear-shaped island until we are above it. Let's try flying in a direction that's not up or down?" She winked at him. Joel just chuckled and shook his head.

Flying horizontally posed more of a challenge to him than he realized. When he needed to fly vertically, all he needed to do was stand as still as possible and control the output of the propulsion. Flying side-to-side required specific angles and corrections with his arms and legs; any small error could send him spiralling downwards. Sadie was patient with him when it was time to move; she was surprisingly helpful with her advice and even held him up from his armpits to get him started. Once he felt he was in a comfortable position, they flew forward at a decent pace. He tried to pay little attention to the distant ground moving beneath him.

"So, have you decided where you're going to go?" Sadie asked. She stayed close beside him, but far enough that she wouldn't get clipped by the propulsions. He would have preferred silence for the benefit of keeping focus on his posture.

"I thought about it a few nights ago," Joel said. "There's a lot of empty land up in the far most northern parts of the Union. Fyken'Isle or Barrowden doesn't seem so bad, except they get tons of snow in the winter. Someplace warm year round would also be nice, like Lavendy, but I don't have a passport."

"Good thing you know how to fly now," Sadie teased. "Have you considered staying? Here at the farm?"

Joel glanced over at her with stern eyes. "I don't feel welcome here, Sadie. I've thought about it, but it's best if I leave."

Sadie furrowed her eyebrows and flew closer to him. "Maybe it's because you spend all your time alone, or with me. Friendships take effort on both sides, ya know."

"No, it's not like that." Joel shook his head. "It's hard to explain, but… I don't feel like I belong. Maybe it's because Lyas has no more use for me or I always knew from the start I wouldn't stay at the farm."

He felt a tinge of disappointment within Sadie. He looked over at her, guilted by her emotions.

"You understand me," Joel quickly explained. "This bond between us allowed me to trust you. I can't bring myself to do the same with the others."

"Would you trust them even if I asked you to?" Sadie softly asked. "How can I? Lyas abandoned me right after he realized I was serious about leaving."

"Lyas is a complicated man," Sadie said. "You've met him at a bad time. He's overwhelmed with the responsibilities he's imposed on himself, and it's showing. I wouldn't take his absence personally. He's probably just trying to figure out every other problem in his head."

Joel harshly sighed from his nose. "He promised me he would teach me. Now that I'm useless to him, then he just backs off from that promise?"

"No, Joel. You've shown incredible progress in your control, so he's shifting his attention onto issues left untended for too long. Don't you feel the pressure of Morwin still being out there? You can't empathize with him on that?"

Joel reluctantly nodded. "Why can't he explain that to me himself? Why does he have to withdraw and leave me wondering what I did wrong?"

"That's always been a weakness of his," Sadie said. "Lyas is a good person, with good intentions. But he can't manage his stress well. Actions that hurt the people around him are often overlooked by the billions of voices that run through his mind."

"Then why is he leading?" Joel asked.

"Because he has a vision that will help people like us. He shouldn't be judged for his flaws."

Joel could feel a rock building within his gut, no doubt knowing that Sadie could feel it, too. He wanted to hold Lyas accountable for his promise, but the family was struggling with issues of its own. Lyas needed to be there for everyone, not just Joel. He just wished Lyas handled his rejection differently.

The two of them stopped mid-air when they were directly above the sharp, rocky island. Seagulls and puffins flew below them, completely unaware of the two humans floating above. Joel could see tiny specks that were boats across the ocean, most likely fishing for lobster or cod. The two of them watched in silence, occasionally calling out the odd whale breaching the waters. Sadie spun circles around him, trailing bolts of lightning behind her. He noticed his body was less tense and relaxed with the propulsion. Being able to feel proud of his progress felt like a nice change.

"I've been wanting to thank you, Sadie," Joel said gently... He watched her face him; her bright golden hair ribboned over her nose and mouth. "You've been patient with me. I... I needed that."

Her blush red lips subtly parted as she watched him. Wind continued to billow her blonde curls gracefully. Joel could feel a warm embrace grow across the bond between. She had an unmatched beauty, and in an embarrassed panic, he changed his thoughts back to what he wanted to say.

"Uh, I don't have anything to give you. I wish I did, but I just wanted you to know. Thank you," Joel said.

Sadie smiled tenderly. Nothing but gratitude and appreciation reverberated within the bond. "I'm here for you, Joel. You never had to go through this alone, so I'm with you."

Joel smiled and nodded. He looked towards the rocky cliffs and pastures that led back to the farm. "I think I'd like to try flying faster now."

* * *

The docks of Conqet were filled with locals and neighbours of bordering towns. Market stands, filled with goods ranging from freshly caught fish to homemade crafts, lined the entire boardwalk. The clear blue skies and warm weather lured in a bustling crowd that made the town louder than it naturally was. A month ago, a crowd like this would have sent Joel in a paranoid panic. But he didn't mind it now.

Sadie, Natasha, Aiden and Joel left the farm to pay the market a visit as an outing. Sadie explained to him that every six months the people of Lohwem would hold an outdoor market that included local markets from all over the island. Conqet was the usual host due to its large boardwalk and docks. The family used it as an opportunity to find unique trinkets and decorations for their cottages. Depending on their hunger cycle, they would buy baskets of fresh lobster and prawns to hold a special family meal. Sadie could feel stomach pains creeping in, so she carried a large tote filled with bagged seafood.

Joel watched over the carefree crowd as he walked alongside Sadie. Aiden and Natasha walked ahead, trying to subtly flirt and poke at one another without seeming too obvious. Joel and Sadie would just share humorous glances to cope with the awkwardness.

Sadie stopped at an older carpenter's booth, who she had bought small frames off of before. While Joel waited for her, he noticed a jeweller across from him. She was a middle-aged woman that carried slightly hunched shoulders. She kindly smiled at Joel, silently inviting him to browse the merchandise. Joel couldn't remember a time he felt the need to wear a ring or necklace, but looked at the wares out of kindness. She let him look without small talk, which he appreciated. Most of the jewellery was standard gold and silver. Nothing stood out for him until he came across a tray of dark metal rings.

"That's meteorite, if ye were curious," the woman said in a thick Rown accent. The colour of the metal was unique, but the price tag was revolting. Joel picked up one band to look at it closer. The metal was frigid and made his fingers feel charged with static.

"Feels cool to touch, eh?" Joel remarked. The woman tilted her head and frowned in confusion. As Joel set the band down, he noticed Callum and Lyas walking down the docks towards them.

He thanked the jeweller and rejoined Sadie. His gut told him Lyas had something important to say based on his serious scowl. Joel thought he was there for Sadie, or the others, until Lyas walked right up to him.

"I need to talk to you," Lyas said quietly. He looked over at Sadie and beckoned towards the other two. "Sadie, go get Aiden and Natasha. Meet us at The Willow Pub."

Lyas and Callum walked away without another word. It was clear Lyas wasn't asking. Joel had never seen him show that level of arrogance before. He looked over at Sadie who shared the same concerned look. They ignored the rudeness of the ask and grabbed Natasha and Aiden from the stalls they were visiting.

The Willow Pub was mostly empty, except for a couple loyal customers. Lyas and Callum had grabbed a large table but hadn't ordered any drinks for the group. As the four of them sat down, Joel could feel a sinking gut feeling that pulled from Sadie and then into him. He couldn't decide if the shared anxiety made the situation worse or somehow comforting.

"I found Morwin," Lyas said. Joel's stomach dropped from sinking to a sudden deep end. Lyas didn't wait for anyone's reaction. "He's in Fasdoba, of Lavendy. We all leave tomorrow."

The group was silent. Callum watched over everyone, waiting for a response and obviously having talked to Lyas about this mission already. Aiden and Natasha just looked at each other, knowing that they would go wherever the other would go. Sadie looked down at the table; she felt uncertain through the bond. Joel already knew his place. He wasn't a part of this family and would not be going. He knew his answer was clear when he looked up and found Lyas staring right at him.

Callum coughed to break the silence and spoke. "Veronica confirmed it too, and Rowan is making preparations back at home. This guy has no chance with all of us together. This is good news."

"Maybe together," Lyas cut in. "Joel? Will you be with us?"

Joel clenched his fists under the table. The audacity of this man. "You don't need to read my mind to know my answer."

Lyas scoffed. "After all the safety and comfort we've given you? And you still say no? You have the opportunity to silence the man you're so afraid of and you still want to run. A whole group of incredible people are ready to support you in this capture; that means nothing to you?"

"Fuck you, Lyas," Joel spit. "I knew you would eventually come calling for payment. No matter what I said, what I asked from you, it would still mean nothing, because your priorities would always come first. This safe haven you promised was a fucking lie."

"Joel, please," Aiden softly pleaded. "We could use your help."

"No," Lyas said harshly. "He's been given every opportunity to change his mind, but all he's proven is that he's still driven by selfishness. I invited you here, Joel, to be safe and to learn. I showed you your potential. I begged you to help with Morwin. I thought that deep down you would see a greater purpose for yourself, for this family, but nothing about you has changed. I'm done asking with kindness. You either come with us and protect the family that has been protecting you, or you leave the farm."

Joel's jaw began to hurt from clenching. He wanted to jump across the table and knock Lyas's teeth out. The promises made that morning at the cafe meant absolutely nothing. He was tricked and was now being guilted into a life he clearly stated he never wanted. Thoughts flew through his mind at light speed, not being able to stay still and make sense of the best path. Anger pulsed within him as Lyas's words echoed. If he didn't go to find Morwin, he would abandon the people that kept him safe. He would abandon Sadie.

Blood boiled violently within until he could feel the silver rings on his palms vibrate. His vision tunnelled onto Lyas. The reality of being betrayed bolded itself and demanded vengeance.

Everything led to Lyas, until a soft calmness laid beside him. He looked over at Sadie who pleaded with her eyes for him to stop. He could feel her grief; she knew everything he felt.

Joel stood up from the table and rushed out of the pub. He didn't stop walking until he hit the ocean tide. He was alone. No one was around him. His breath was rapid and strained. Joel wanted to scream forever, unleashing pure chaos into the world in front of him. His hands begged for a reaction as the rings vibrantly sang. Who did he owe? What was the answer here?

He didn't need to understand it. Joel knew that. His grief could wait. Those were Sadie's words, he remembered. His breath slowed as Joel closed his eyes and listened to the ocean waves. She wouldn't expect him to bend to the demands that scared him. Whatever decision he would make, she knew it was best for him.

Joel felt his anger dissipating. Thoughts that scrambled his mind seconds ago laid still. He stood on the wet sand, trying to understand the feeling of relief that had just blanketed him. Joel knew he wanted to avoid Morwin with every inch of his life, but what would that mean to the burden of the people he failed?

Joel let his body slowly fall to the ground until he was sitting on the damp beach. He let his mind wander with the wind. Nothing would make sense of his guilt until he finally had all the pieces. All he knew was that whatever he needed to do, he needed to speak with Sadie.

CHAPTER 23

When Joel found the courage to return to the farm, the sun had set well past the horizon. The cottages were shadowed by the dull light of dusk that creeped over the surrounding hills. The paths and main road were illuminated by warm light pouring out of each house's windows. The darkness made Joel feel sleepy. He thought he would soon need the rest he had been waiting so long for.

Joel headed straight to Sadie's house but noticed the inside was only lit by a small candle. He felt the pull lead him away from her cottage; she wasn't home. When he turned towards the pull, it led right to his abode.

Joel opened the door to his cabin and found Sadie sitting in his living room. She had turned on a few lamps and helped herself to a cup of tea. It looked like she had been waiting there for some time.

"Sorry, I helped myself in," Sadie said. She stood up from her chair and slowly walked towards him. "I wanted to give you some space, but I want to talk to you."

Joel nodded. "It's okay, I was looking for you too."

"I need you to know I had nothing to do with this. I always stood by what I promised you when you came here," Sadie said.

"I know."

"That was cruel of Lyas... what he said." Sadie paused as she gathered her composure. "But he isn't entirely wrong."

Joel stared at her, baffled at her belief. He scoffed and walked away from her towards his bed. He sat down on the end of his mattress and took his boots off. Exhaustion weighed heavily on his neck.

Sadie followed him into the bedroom, holding her hands anxiously. "He was wrong when he expected your help as some form of payment. Your time here should have always been treated on your terms. But don't you have any concern for us? Morwin is dangerous."

Joel let go of his unlaced boot and rubbed his face in the heels of his palms. "Of course I do, Sadie."

Sadie walked up to him and knelt down until she was face to face. She put her hands on his knees; he felt an unexpected shock of static run through his legs. He looked up and met her eyes, which pleaded with him. "Joel, I need your help protecting this family."

Joel shook his head. He could feel the wells of his eyes strain. "They're not my family."

"What am I to you?" Sadie whispered.

Joel stared into her brown eyes. He didn't know the answer. He cared about her, but didn't want to hurt her. With each passing day, it became harder to believe he could leave her side for a life of exile. At first he thought it was just the bond holding them together, but now he knew it meant more. She stared back into him, silence held as they felt the strain of grief and sadness between them.

"If I allow you into my life, then I have something to live for." Joel croaked.

Sadie tilted her head in confusion. "Is having something to live for a bad thing?"

"For me, yea," Joel said. "Life has given me nothing but pain. I was born to suffer. I've tried in the past to work towards being better, but I always find myself back in the same hole. I wish I could change, be happier, and accept goodness. No matter how hard I try, the universe denies me. And I've tried so hard. What kind of living is that? I don't want anything to live for, because I want this life to end."

Sadie's eyes watered. The sadness between them amplified tenfold. "Tell me more," she carefully asked him.

Joel's eyes drifted down to his palms in his lap. He realized he had never said any of this out loud or to anyone. The silver rings reflected the lamplight of his house, shining, flaming chrome. Sadie let go of his knees and softly embraced his hands with hers.

"The cycle never ends. The moment I became old enough to understand my moms abuse I knew I was doomed. I was around thirteen, fourteen years old. Nothing would change her, and I was forced to carry on. Every solution led to me just not existing anymore," Joel spoke as he tried to force his throat to loosen.

"When I left home, I thought the sadness would go away. I could live my life the way I wanted and leave her behind. For a time I had… hope. I got a job, a place for myself, a purpose. I met a woman, her name was Beth, she made me feel important. She put in so much effort into our relationship and I felt appreciated for who I thought I became. Life pointed towards the goodness I so desperately wanted." Joel cleared his throat and wiped the corners of his eyes.

"And then, for no reason, I just felt the sadness again. I couldn't kick it. I became angry and blamed it on the fuckups of the world. It bled into my home, into Beth, and life became meaningless again. I had no reason to spiral. I have no idea why I did," Joel looked back up at Sadie. She hadn't moved her attention from him. "And then today, I felt clarity. The thought of you eased my mind. I've only known you for so long, but in the short time you've been in my life you have shown me what real purpose looks like. Every wrongdoing and mistake I've committed doesn't have to control me, and I learnt that from you. Do you understand how important you've become to me?"

Small tears ran down her pale cheeks. "I think I do," Sadie said. She squeezed his palms and held them tight. "Thank you for telling me all of this."

"If I stay here, then one day that purpose is going to leave like it has before. I know it will kill me if your love is taken away. I'm so scared of building this life only to repeat the past. My life has been doomed from the start."

"I won't ever leave your side, Joel. I know you're scared and I am too," Sadie whispered. "Let me protect you."

Joel choked back his tears. "There's nothing to protect."

"That's not true," Sadie said. "I see you, for who you are. I have felt beautiful emotion and honour within you. I do not believe for one second that you can't make a purposeful life for yourself."

Sadie gripped his hands tighter and leaned in closer. Joel could smell the scent of rain and juniper on her hair. "None of your past is your fault, but it has defined the man I see."

Joel fought back tears. He didn't want to cry in front of her. "What do I do? How can I be happy?"

"I don't know," Sadie said gently. "In time, we will find it. I'm going to help you get there. I promise to keep you safe and protect you. I know I can trust you. Please trust me."

Joel nodded through the grief and closed his eyes. The pull between them surged with an intense mix of hope and love that he had never felt before. He knew she was true to her words. He could trust her.

"I'm so tired. I think I need to sleep," he said.

"I could too," Sadie said. "Let me stay with you?"

"Of course."

* * *

Dawn crept through the thin blinds of Joel's bedroom window. He had maybe slept six hours; the exhaustion was gone from his body. For the first time in a long time, his mind rested at ease.

Sadie was still asleep. The two of them were wrapped up in each other's arms and her head rested on his chest. She felt warm and comforting. The bond had never felt this strong before. They had fallen asleep shortly after his confession and stayed with each other the entire night. No woman had ever made him feel safe. Beth made him feel important, but vulnerable to losing what made that importance strong. He would never hold any contempt towards Beth. Everything that led to the demise of their relationship was because of him. Those same feelings should have scared him from loving Sadie, but she promised to protect him from the chaos of what made him into the man he hated. He believed her, without an inch of doubt.

But it wasn't just himself Joel needed protection from. He was forced into choosing a path towards facing Morwin or leaving Sadie and the farm behind. The thought of Morwin's torment haunted him; he could never unsee the gore and violence of his attack. The man wanted Joel dead or dominated, and if he faced him, then he would only be giving him the chance to multiply the chaos Joel was forced to commit.

If Joel refused to face him, then Sadie would no longer be in his life. As much as Joel believed in Sadie's promise, she would be faced with a difficult decision of abandoning her family for him. He didn't want that for her. Sadie always talked about the importance of her family, and Joel refused to steal that from her. If Joel refused to face Morwin, he would have to hurt Sadie and break their trust.

Either decision would not be easy to make. He wanted to believe there were other choices, but Lyas's words rang inside his head and forced him to believe the two choices were absolutes. The amount of what-ifs ran through his head in multitudes. What if he didn't go and Morwin got a hold of Sadie? What if he went and Morwin got a hold of him? Any decision led to the impending risk of someone or himself getting hurt.

Joel thought about the people he killed in downtown Mercer. If he wasn't there, would someone else just take his place? Would Morwin have eventually turned to violence on that scale? Joel reminded himself he stopped Morwin and killed innocents because he lost control. Now he had control. He could take down villains, like Morwin, and avoid killing others in the fallout. He could save people.

Not just people close to him, like Sadie, or the family. People with no connection to him, caught in the crossfire of villains who prey on them. Joel knew he could stop the cycle of violence, and he could end it without exiling himself to a place of loneliness. Joel now had a duty to use his control to protect the ones vulnerable, just like Sadie would do for him.

He looked down and watched Sadie sleep. Her hands were tucked under his body and her nose moved lightly as she breathed. Blonde curls fell over his chest; she had let it out of its usual ponytail. She would protect him, and he wanted to return the favour. Joel could only make sure Sadie was safe if he stayed with her.

Everything he believed before the farm was manifested out of hate. He hated where the world was driven, how his home fell to the corrupt, and the suffering that was carelessly accepted by people who don't care. He thought about the hate he carried, and how he did nothing to change it. The world was evolving in front of him. He was faced with the decision to finally face that hate. Face Morwin.

Joel was tired of being selfish; he wanted to pursue the potential revealed to him by people he trusted. The world would stay the same if he exiled himself. But maybe he could make it a better place if he let himself try.

Joel took a deep breath in and held that decision in his head. Was he ready to bring change? He wanted it; he wanted the world to be a better place. Life could have meaning if the world was saved. If the world had meaning, then Joel would have meaning.

Joel let out a long exhale and decided. He needed to speak with Lyas. Joel took another look at Sadie, appreciating her beauty as she slept deeply. Her mind felt peaceful in its rest. It was time for Joel to take the responsibility given to him.

Chapter 24

The streets of Fasdoba overflowed with people and bikes, like a burst dam flooding a river. Sweat dripped down Morwin's face as he watched the crowd. These people carried their lives as if their day was the most important cause in Aross. If only they knew how insignificant they were to the real world.

Morwin wiped the sweat away on his forehead with the back of his hand. He noticed a tan forming on the pale skin of his once dismembered arm. Even with the tan, the skin would never look the same. Losing the pureness of his body should have bothered him more, but Morwin knew where his priorities lay.

Lavendy was a beautiful country. If you stayed in the central area of the country, you would have warm weather year round. Morwin thought it would make a nice place to settle one day. Even the cafe he found was surprisingly quaint. It was a shame it would eventually die to evolution. An espresso this good held no comparison to the importance of his vision.

Morwin finished the rest of his drink and leaned back into his chair. Dozens of humans refilled the street as the river of people moved through. Fasdoba was the largest city in the province Manzera. It brought in tens of thousands of tourists every year, and this was their peak busy season. Because of Manzera's popular climate, it had grown into one of Lavendy's biggest money-makers. However, that also meant Morwin was limited in his work. Unwanted attention from these cockroaches could derail his mission.

Morwin finished with the people-watching and left the outdoor patio. He walked down an older cobble-stone back alley until he found a hidden corner. Quickly collapsing into the mycelium-realm, he carried himself back to his lair under the city. The closed tunnels made for perfect privacy. No one would enter unless they were intentionally wanting to explore its maze, and even then Morwin's lair was blocked off by a collapsed wall.

Morwin reformed on the slimy walkway. Bodies of his experiments plastered the walls, half eaten by mold and slime. Most of them were just homeless, used to feed his rumbling hunger. Then there was the odd tourist who had 'gone missing' and publicly blamed on the misdeeds of Lavendy's infamous trafficking ring. Those bodies were used to strengthen Morwin's desires.

Sitting on a cot and staring into the rotten eyes of a specimen glued to the tunnel wall was Morwin's ally. The man, named Garem, was found in Seraleveli. Morwin didn't give him the chance to decide for himself. He needed allies and muscle. Garem needed to sacrifice his will to aid Morwin with his vision. It was out of pure necessity.

Morwin walked up to face him and studied the new growths on Garem's head. His eyes had turned pale, filled with wriggling parasites. He blinked when he saw Morwin, meaning his vision was still intact. A large conk had spread across his temple and ear. Since Morwin's last visit, the fungus had grown out of control and needed pruning. Morwin grabbed the bulk of the growth and snapped it off. Garem didn't react. He just looked up to meet Morwin's eyes. Morwin could feel a deep, pleading cry out in Garem's mind.

"Are we close yet?" Garem mumbled.

"Yes," Morwin brushed residue off of Garem's cheek. "A beacon only they could find has been lit."

"And then I can die?" His eyes peered past Morwin and into the sockets of the rotten face across from him.

Morwin looked over at the body. Its jaw had been ripped down from the vining mold. He could still feel flashes of life in the body's brain. "No, Garem. I will need you for what's to come. But I promise you, you won't suffer the same fate as these experiments."

Garem nodded. He didn't break eye contact with the displayed cadaver. With each visit, Garem talked less and less. Morwin didn't enjoy seeing the fading soul of an evolved, like him. Garem deserved to see where the new society would be taken. But with each delay, his body lost more and more of itself.

Eventually Garem would become a bumbling simpleton, which Morwin didn't exactly see a downside to. Garem was muscle. All he needed to be was muscle. Garem's sacrifice wouldn't go unrewarded. When Morwin would ascend the new race to its rightful stand, he would give Garem the glory he deserved.

"We are close, Garem, you're going to do what is right. We cannot afford those who stand in our path, and I need strength on my side."

Garem continued to nod in silence. Morwin didn't appreciate that. He could tell the fringes of Garem's past life were surfacing again.

"Talk to me."

"I can feel you burrowed into my spine now," Garem said plainly.

"No, speak of something else!"

A tear fell down Garem's eye, but his expression stayed cold. "I miss home. I wonder what my family is up to... Do you miss home?"

Morwin sat himself on the other end of the cot. "Not really. Mercer was filled with disgusting people. Before I got my powers, I realized the truth behind the human race. Have I ever told you this before?"

Morwin faced Garem. The idiot was still staring across the tunnel. Morwin could feel his auditory cortex still intact. He could still listen.

"It felt like I was cursed for knowing the truth," Morwin said. "I had all the answers; I could change the world if I was ever given the chance. But no one cared. People online listened., They agreed with me, but no one would take the jump to create change."

Morwin sighed as he looked down at the pale skin on his hand. "I craved the power to be the one who could bring change. I know that makes me... imperious. But when no one else steps up, people like me need to take the stand by force."

"Did they call you a monster?" Garem asked quietly. He tensed as if he expected pain to follow.

One did.

The one we hate.

Morwin nodded. Those who called him that were as just as ignorant as the people killing the planet around them. "They called me a monster because I acted on what every single person wanted. Real change. Those against us saw what I can do, and they screamed to the masses that I was doing it wrong. The people after me will tell the world they have the answers, but will just keep doing the same thing leaders and politicians have been doing for years and years and years. Leaving the world to die."

Morwin breathed in. These thoughts agitated him dearly. "Once you and I remove their tongues, dominate their minds, then we can finally bring the change the world so desperately needs."

"What if they don't want it?" Garem asked. His eyes glazed over as the parasites wormed their way deeper into the sockets.

They will.

Even if you have to make them.

Morwin sighed longingly. "Despite their weaknesses, the humans of Aross are ready to leave the path to us. They will want my change, simply because they're too tired to try. No part of me will miss them, but they will leave a legacy behind that I can't afford to ignore."

Garem shifted on the cot and sighed. "I don't think we should dominate the new race. I think we should kill them."

Morwin tilted his head, confused by Garem's desire. "But we need the ascended to save this planet."

Garem nodded. Black goo fell out of his nostril. "But if they're dominated, all they will want is to die."

Morwin scoffed and stood up. The will of the ascended did not matter to him. It was simple. Join Morwin, or sacrifice your mind to save the planet. The new race was brought to Aross for a specific reason and it couldn't afford the debate of morality.

Morwin, frustrated by Garem's opinion, walked away from the lair. He thought the growths might have been eating Garem's brain too fast. Morwin made a mental note to alter the bacteria to slow down. He needed him in a functional state when the time was ready. There would be enough of this moping and gloom.

He walked over to his bag and pulled out his notebook. There he had kept notes and pictures of everyone he knew of with abilities. Outside Garem and himself, the rest fell under Lyas's family. Morwin had spent some time earlier searching for others, but failed miserably. A part of him believed his list had everyone ever to exist with abilities. That kind of doubt was dangerous, and he needed to believe there would be more. Without a world of ascended, there would be no saving.

Underneath Lyas's name, read the names of his family members. He gathered eight to ten members, guessing from the conversations he overheard back in Mercer. Morwin knew he could handle that many, but only in small groups. The full force of the group, together, could potentially stop him. All that stood in the way was one name, one member of the family. Joel.

Those who could oppose Morwin's will were an immediate risk to the vision. Joel and his damn helmet, he spit.

Rip it off his head.
Let us eat his flesh.
He will ruin EVERYTHING.

FORREST C. RICHARD

Morwin already knew that. He waved off the voices and returned to the notes of his ledger. He lightly stroked Lyas's name. In time, that man would serve a purpose greater than himself.

A furious coughing fit from Garem distracted him from his notes. When Morwin approached him, he found puddles of black stained blood at Garem's feet. A slow drip oozed from his mouth as he leaned over the cot, staring ahead at the specimens.

Morwin sighed disappointingly. "I think you may want to change into your stronger form... Give yourself some time to heal."

Garem stayed still, remaining in his human form. Morwin could feel a pull of slight resistance within Garem, defying him with what little will he had left. Morwin felt he was getting sloppy.

"Change!" He screamed.

In fearful compliance, Garem turned into the beast he was created to be. He stood from the cot and grew until the ceiling above broke from his towering height. Plates of dark armour enveloped his entire body as it expanded into a meat grinding mass. He was perfect, and frightening. The scaled plates looked as if they could resist even the greatest bomb man had made. Only Garem's head showed an anomaly. Morwin noticed the conk on his head had also been enveloped by armour and taken into his monster form. Regardless, Garem had become a machine made of barbaric death. He would be unstoppable, and Morwin had him on a tight leash.

Deep and grainy breaths released from the vents covering Garem's mouth. The cold, humid air of the tunnels fogged his breathing, as if he was releasing thick steam from a forge within.

His eyes were covered by thick plates, but Morwin knew his vision was amplified by an intense sensitivity. He hoped the parasites in Garem's eyes wouldn't affect his reactivity.

"Stay in this form for the time being," Morwin demanded. "We will be called to the surface soon, and your suit will heal your wounds in the time between."

Garem nodded without a word. He was under complete control; Morwin couldn't even fathom the level of destruction he could make Garem commit.

"Now stay here," Morwin said before he collapsed into the layers and roots that intertwined in the dirt below the city. The humidity of the country gave him endless potential for fungus and mycelium scattered around. He brought himself back to the dark alleyway of the cafe he enjoyed. He walked to the same patio seat and returned to people watching. Now that he finished checking on Garem, he could truly enjoy the warmth of the sunny weather. Seeing the crowds in front of him, and the idea they would soon cease to exist, excited him.

It was too bad that the city and cafe he lounged at would end up as ruins. He had come to enjoy the menu the owners had spent so much time perfecting. In the end, these enjoyments were merely a blip in the sacrifices that needed to come for his future.

To celebrate, Morwin decided to order a glass of wine.

CHAPTER 25

Sadie slowly awoke to the movement of Joel leaving the bed. She thought he was getting up to get water or use the washroom, but heard his front door creak open and shut. With any other, she would have been worried. But Joel felt determined through the bond.

Sadie let Joel speak for himself. She guessed whatever he had to say, it was to Lyas, and it was about to seal his future. Sadie thought she knew what Joel would do, but she wanted to let herself open to the possibility he would leave. She needed to be prepared to get hurt.

She watched the dust of the room settle as the light peered through the thin curtains and softly illuminated the room. Her body felt rested. Spending the night with Joel was comforting. She needed that, especially with the mission they were about to embark on. She wondered what she would do when they found

Morwin. She wanted to trust Lyas, that he would capture Morwin without anyone getting hurt. But if Morwin was left to live, then that gave him a chance to hurt someone again.

What would Joel do? She thought to herself as she laid in his bed. Would he kill Morwin? Nothing was stopping him from grasping revenge, other than the question of morality. She believed Joel was an honourable person. Beneath the rage and pain was a man who just wanted to live a normal life. He was robbed when he was a child and ever since he has desperately searched for what was taken. Sadie felt his pain. She remembered feeling the same way when she killed her parents. All she wanted was to go back in time and take her normal life back. Now she understood there would be no returning to the past. There would be no finding what was taken from her youth. She needed to make a new life for herself, and she wanted to help Joel get there, too.

Sadie slowly fell back into a hazy sleep. Fuzzy dreams of her home fell in and out of cognizance. She remembered the coasts of Titalfjord and the old streets of Kyve where her parents would bring her to watch theatre shows when she was young. The land of Arsacadia had a supernatural beauty to them. Wherever you went, you would find ancient mountains with great, pointy crowns and rolling hills shaped by volcanoes. A part of her wanted to go back. She wanted to show Joel. The beauty, the people, the land should be shared. Shared with the people close to her and those she loved. They made her appreciate the world, past its flaws. Going back with Joel felt inspiring. Maybe after the mission, she would leave on a little trip with him. She would show him where she grew up and the trails she ran through when she was a child. They could return to a small life of normalcy for just a bit.

The door loudly creaked open and Sadie woke from her extra moment of sleep. She could tell it was Joel; the bond held closely. She did not know if an hour had passed or minutes, but he felt purposeful.

The bedroom door opened to Joel, carrying two ceramic cups of coffee. Sadie sat up on the bed and smiled.

"Can't remember a time when a boy brought me coffee in the morning," she smiled. She tied her hair back with her ponytail as it was falling over her face and irritating her. She noticed Joel was smiling. He carried less tension.

"I should be making you breakfast... but I don't think either of us is hungry," Joel said.

"Coffee is perfect," Sadie said. She took the hot mug from him and sipped lightly. He made it strong and with the perfect amount of cream.

Joel looked into his mug and opened his mouth. He tried to find the words he wanted, but nothing came out. He looked her in the eyes; the dark brown could have been as dark as a smouldering log on a dwindling fire. Sadie leaned in closer.

"Thank you for letting me stay," she assured him.

Joel nodded his head and looked back at his mug. "It was nice. I haven't slept that soundly in a long time. I don't know what this is, but... I care about you, Sadie."

She placed a hand over his arm. "I care about you, too."

Joel smiled at her. The squint of his eyes furled with his cheeks. A jolt of relief shocked through them. She was happy. All they needed in that moment were those words of assurance. She knew he had more to say, but could tell he didn't want to ruin the memory. The two of them sat on the bed, holding their coffees and leaning into each other until they rested on the other's forehead.

Sadie could feel his warm breath and smell hues of cedar and pine on his shirt. The pull between them felt stronger than ever, holding an iron grip of affection.

She had never felt this way before with anyone. The bond she had with Joel made a definitive difference, but she had never found any semblance with another. Every attempt she had when she was younger ended with her either hurt or disappointed. All she wanted was someone, who was not her parent, that carried a fountain of respect and patience for her. Someone who made her feel safe. After she got her abilities, she thought her chance was gone. No one would want to spend the rest of their life with a woman so unnatural to the real world. She watched others on the farm grow closer to each other and ached for something similar. Being able to trust a man with a universe of love would have made the loneliness she felt disappear. And now she has found someone who trusts her as much as she trusts him back. The proof was within the bond.

Joel leant back and took one of her hands. She could feel the frigid steel ring against her skin. "I came back from talking with Lyas," he said.

"Wherever you go, I will follow," she assured him.

"I know. I can't separate you from your family, but I also can't leave you. I'm not about to decide what's best for you, but I thought hard about what would be best for us," Joel whispered. "Wherever you go, I go. I want to protect you like you protect me. This bond we share is a mystery, but it's proven my feelings for you go beyond it."

Sadie gently smiled and squeezed his hand. "Are you sure you want this?"

I am," Joel said. "I'm absolutely scared. I don't want to face Morwin ever again, but he stands between me, you, and a bizarre life that awaits. I never wanted to have these powers as my burden, but you make me feel I can use them for good. You have shown me I don't have to fear them."

"We are going to do this together. Morwin will be taken down and put behind us. Whether that's capturing or killing him, we won't let him continue haunting you," Sadie said.

Joel sighed deeply. Hope sparked between them. There was no debating the challenge of facing Morwin. They both understood what he was capable of and could escape again. The two of them leaned into each other again, resting their heads together. They held still until their coffees fell cold. Lyas would soon call for them all, so they got out of bed and poured themselves a hot refill. They waited and sat in the living room in silence.

Joel and Sadie needed no more assurance between themselves. They only needed to say it once to completely understand one another. Whatever happened from now on, the two of them would do everything in their power to protect the other. In time, Sadie would teach Joel how to protect others, vulnerable to the evil deeds of the world. Right now, she was just happy that he had hope again. No one would hurt him; she would be sure of that.

* * *

The family gathered in Lyas's living room and waited in silence for everyone to show. Aiden and Natasha were the last to arrive, shortly after Sadie and Joel. Natasha's eyes looked puffy and irritated, and Aiden carried a sadness rarely found in his charm. No one spoke of small talk; the room felt too tense. Sadie and Joel sat on a worn down couch together that faced Lyas. Rowan was occupied tying a string for her bow, but would occasionally shoot a concerned glance at Sadie.

Lyas held himself high with confidence, no doubt feeling like the winner in forcing Joel's hand. If only he knew how close he was to losing Joel. When Aiden and Natasha sat down in the living room, Lyas immediately began to explain the details of his plan.

"Now that everyone is rested... In an hour, we are all going to drop on Fasdoba," Lyas boldly said. "There is enough evidence to conclude Morwin is in that city, looking for another gifted person."

"What evidence?" Natasha demanded. She had her arms crossed as she usually had, but held an icy stare towards Lyas.

"Through the minds of several intelligence agents around the world, I placed deep conscious thoughts on Morwin's description," Lyas explained. "Even though he can hide from me, he failed to avoid surveillance technology. An agent from Lavendy spotted him in Fasdoba yesterday and I was notified."

"How sure are we that it's him?" Sadie asked. She never remembered Lyas seeing Morwin for himself.

"I immediately had Veronica search the city for his presence. She couldn't find him, but she found a very faint signature of a different gifted. From what I've gathered about Morwin is that he's after gifted people for his 'new race'. This gives me enough to believe he is after this new gifted while actively hiding from us," Lyas said as he looked over the faces of each family member.

Callum nodded. "The guy is getting to them before we are. We need to get the jump on him before he leaves the city with the gifted."

"But how much do we know about this new signature, Veronica?" Aiden asked her.

Before Veronica could speak, Lyas interrupted her. "It's enough. Whoever is in Fasdoba is slowly becoming stronger and will soon awaken. If we get to them before Morwin, they have a chance to survive."

The group fell silent. Lyas quietly waited for more questions to bluntly quash. Sadie felt a rising angst within Joel.

"This feels like a trap," Aiden said.

"I agree," Veronica said. "The new presence is too faint."

"This is the closest we have been to Morwin since Mercer," Lyas boomed. "He has no idea we are coming, which gives us the best possible chance to get the jump on him."

"But you said it yourself," Sadie interjected. This plan had more holes than she was comfortable with. "He will be hiding from us. How do you expect to surprise him if we can't find him in the first place?"

"Because we know where the new gifted is. Once we have them, then Morwin will come," Lyas said.

Natasha scoffed. "So, we are bait then?"

"For fuck sakes!" Lyas yelled. "What's wrong with you all? With all of us together, Morwin doesn't stand a chance. He's outnumbered and will be focused on reaching the new gifted before us, which has him distracted."

"It's not about our advantage, Lyas. It's about making sure each of us comes home at the end of the day!" Natasha argued.

Aiden nodded. "She's right. From what Joel has told us, Morwin is dangerous and intends to kill."

Sadie looked over at Joel. He was staring at the floor and rubbing his palms. Fear boiled inside him.

"We have all the tools we need to make sure he is incapacitated before that ever happens," Lyas shouted.

"Those who rush through the door are eaten by the door," whispered Veronica.

"Everyone, enough!" Callum shouted over the group. He took a long breath in and composed himself. "I think it's only fair if we all vote on this. The majority decides, and we have to abide by whatever is chosen."

Silence followed the proposal, and was soon agreed upon by the nervous nods of each family member.

Lyas nodded and sighed deeply. "Anyone who wants to go ahead with the mission, raise your hand."

Lyas, Rowan, and Callum raised their hands. Callum looked at Veronica with a disappointed stare, as she kept hers by her side and sunk in her chair. Aiden and Natasha held their arms down defiantly.

Sadie looked at Joel and he looked at her back. They held their stare longingly, feeling what the other was feeling in that moment. Wherever he'd go, she would go.

Joel nodded at her and raised his hand. "I'm going."

Sadie raised hers in succession, apologetically frowning at her friends who voted not to.

Lyas clasped his hands and sighed in relief. "Morwin's terror ends today. Go collect your gear and gather at the main road in half an hour. We need to beat Morwin to the new gifted before he reaches them."

The group got out of their seats and headed towards the door. Sadie stroked Joel's arm and excused herself to her cabin. She hurried down the main road, entered her cottage, and turned off any lights she left on. She wasn't sure how long the mission would take. In her room, Sadie grabbed her thin windbreaker and changed out of her slippers into compact boots. She gave her face a quick wash to fight through the anxiety of the mission to come.

When she finished changing and left her cabin, she found Joel standing outside. He was looking up at the sky, studying the moon that showed itself clearly in the bright morning sky. He wore his usual jacket that he was given from the thrift store on his first day at Conqet, and the boots that Aiden made for him. She looked down the main road and noticed almost everyone was gathered together.

"Are you ready?" Sadie asked.

"I think I am," Joel said as he stared at the moon above.

"Remember to stay by me, okay?" Sadie said.

Joel looked at her and nodded. "I will."

CHAPTER 26

Veronica's portal opened like a doorway bordered with red mist. As Joel stared through, he watched as each team member entered and stepped into the city of Fasdoba. The portal was a seamless tear in the fabric of reality. He noticed Veronica needed narrowed focus on the task; the amount of effort looked like it had a significant cost to her vigour.

Joel stepped through the doorway and only felt a sharp change of humidity from Lavendy's famous warm climate. Veronica was last and closed the doorway as soon as she stepped through. She had brought them to a secluded row of a grapevine crop. Around them stretched acres of a peaceful vineyard. The crop was built on the side of a hill that overlooked the city of Fasdoba.

A great, winding river carved through the city and glittered crystal blue under the hot sun. Kilometres of buildings and roads surrounded the river on both sides. Fasdoba was a gemstone to the country of Lavendy. It brought in hundreds of thousands of tourists every year and prided itself on being a staple vacation destination. Most people thought that the city only produced lavish wine as an export, however, the city also manufactured complex equipment for major pipelines that single-handedly flourished its economy. Joel's youngest brother explained the oil production hierarchy to him one Christmas. Most of it flew past his head, but he remembered that Fasdoba stood out.

"Veronica, do you feel him?" Lyas asked. "I can see them faintly, somewhere in the central district."

Veronica closed her eyes in silence. "I can see them too, barely."

"Good enough for me. Alright, listen up everyone." Lyas turned to face the group. The sun was already beginning to bead sweat on his forehead. "Myself, Rowan, Callum and Aiden will approach them on an introduction. The rest of you will station in the area, keeping an eye out for Morwin."

One by one, Sadie teleported each member to the centre of the city in only a few seconds. When the light returned to Joel's eyes, he was standing in an old hallway leading from an outdoor patio to a quiet road. Once everyone was gathered, they stepped out onto the street and followed Lyas.

Around Joel were dozens of bicycles and small cars parked up and down the street. Every building had an awning at street level, sheltering entrances to cafes, clothing stores, and restaurants. There weren't many people out, but enough to make Joel nervous. Everyone looked happy. He imagined Morwin hiding behind every face, waiting to strike at any moment. Beneath the hot sun and flowers covering the building walls, were people only there for the beauty of the country. None of them expected a sinister mind hiding amongst them. When he found Morwin, he would have to act fast, for the sake of these people's innocence.

The group stopped when Lyas halted in front of an older cafe. A barista clearing tables noticed Lyas was staring at him. He awkwardly smiled and approached Lyas. "Ciao, vuoi un... umm table?"

Lyas closed his eyes, and the man swayed as if a bout of vertigo had just hit him. Once he opened his eyes, Lyas faced his family and gathered them in a group. "Morwin was here many times. Everyone keep vigilant. We will split into our groups from here."

Without another word, Lyas marched up the street with his assemblage. Joel, Sadie, Natasha and Veronica stood watching the other four walk away into the growing crowds. Shared looks were enough to acknowledge that no one felt good about this plan. Joel wouldn't have split the family if it was up to him, but he realized he was more paranoid than the rest. They all continued to walk up the street, keeping a distance from Lyas's group. Once he was ready for an approach, they would set their perimeter.

"Lyas is withholding something from us," Natasha growled.

"No, I don't think that's the case," Sadie said. "He's just trying to justify a plan with little to no evidence."

"I tried telling him. I told him multiple times the signal here was too faint to be certain," Veronica said.

Joel shook his head to himself. Even with a plan as weak as the one Lyas had made, one thing was for certain. Joel was the bait. He looked over at Sadie and noticed she was intently watching the crowds as they walked. She wasn't about to let Morwin surprise them. That made Joel feel a little more safe; she was true to her word when she said she would look out for him.

The four of them continued down the street until Veronica came to a sudden halt. A second later, all of them heard Lyas's voice echo within their minds.

"The gifted is moving, southbound. We are about to close in," Lyas whispered.

"I see them too," Veronica said out loud. "Sadie, take us to the rooftops."

In quick, consecutive flashes, the four of them appeared across flat rooftops that overlooked a cathedral square. It was packed with tourists and local vendors pushing small carts of food or handmade garments. Joel's eyes strained themselves as they adjusted to the light change; he tried squinting to see where Lyas's group was. Sadie kneeled beside him and pointed towards a far corner with a marble statue.

"There's Lyas," she said.

Joel focused his vision and saw Lyas standing next to the statue. Rowan stood beside him, but Joel couldn't see Aiden or Callum.

"There's too many people here," Joel grunted.

"We should clear the square, force the gifted out," Natasha said.

"No, keep as covert as possible," Lyas's voice echoed.

"They're moving," Veronica called out. "Towards the church!"

Joel watched as Lyas and Rowan left the base of the statue and made their way to the cathedral entrance in a hurry. He noticed Callum and Aiden approaching from the other end of the square, politely pushing their way through the crowd, trying to catch up with Lyas.

"That church is going to be packed to the brim," Joel said.

"I'm taking us in," Sadie said.

Joel found himself in a dark empty hallway, only lit by stained glass and the blue flashes that followed Sadie's jump. The room smelt heavily of old carpet and incense.

"Mi scusi! No visitors for this room," a guide called out as he walked past an open door.

"I'm sorry, we just got lost," Joel said. The four of them exited the hallway and walked into a room funnelling dozens of tourists into the nave. They ignored the scoffs and comments from the odd tourists offended by them cutting the line.

The entire floor of the chapel was filled with people taking pictures of the marble columns and stained glass. Dull, warm lighting cast a gothic mood, making it difficult to see the finer details on faces around him. In another time, Joel would have wanted to visit a building like this. The hairs on the back of his neck screamed danger. He could feel his helmet itching to snap on. There was too much risk being in a dense crowd that possibly harboured a psychopath.

Across the room, Joel saw Lyas. He was hastily looking around him, trying to pinpoint the direction of the gifted.

"I think they are leaving the chapel," Lyas said in Joel's mind.

"Wait, I don't see them anymore," Veronica said out loud.

Lyas was already walking away, with Rowan trailing behind. Joel quickly lost eyes on them as the crowd flowed between. He glanced over at Sadie; she looked furious. Lyas was rushing beyond a safe pace.

Joel leaned towards Sadie and whispered. "What do we do? This doesn't feel right."

Sadie frustratingly sighed. "I know. Let's just keep Lyas within our view."

Sadie and Joel parted through the crowd towards the exit Lyas's group had just left. Veronica and Natasha were close behind, blocked by a river of tourists.

Joel stepped into the centre of the nave when the back of his mind flared with peril. Before he could even consider donning his helmet, a brutal crash contacted his back and plummeted him into the ground. Screams and gasps of the crowds around him deafened the sounds of grinding tile beneath his head. He tried to open his eyes, but the excruciating pain filmed his vision with tears.

Joel reached to the back of his head and found a large iron hand grasping it tight. His helmet tried to fold over his skull, but was blocked by the bulky steel. Blood dripped down his eyebrows from the crushing squeeze.

Joel screamed out in anger and tried to aim his hand towards whatever monstrosity was standing on him. His arm was instantly pinned to the ground and the weight on his spine grew heavier.

"Keep still," a voice behind him boomed. Joel tried to fight harder against the weight, but felt completely restrained. There were too many people around him to lash out blindly.

Across the marble tile flashed reflections of blue and white. It took him a second to realize that Sadie was unleashing a storm of lightning onto the mountain holding him down. Joel could feel his neck being crushed as he tried to force out a scream.

"Run!" Joel yelled.

The cries of the crowds echoed louder when a large black tentacle burst from the ground and slapped Sadie across the room. People became a blur as they ran in each direction. The breath in Joel's lungs strained as it struggled to replenish. He needed to get out. He needed to get to Sadie.

A man, shadowed by the dark lighting, formed in front of Joel. Alarms set off in every corner of Joel's mind. Morwin knelt down till his eyes met Joels. An unsettling smile stretched underneath the familiar rotting deer head.

"I told you I'd get that helmet off," Morwin whispered.

A creeping knife stroked the back of his mind. Joel's thoughts and memories cracked under the impending incision. Morwin had him.

Rage instantly killed the fear. Everything Joel thought he had under control was released from its prison and burst from its surface. Nothing around him mattered, except seeing the blood of Morwin on his hands.

Morwin's face turned concerned when Joel lifted himself off the ground. Blood dripped down his cheeks as he pushed against the brutal monster on top of him. He could feel his body and mind quivering under the immense pressure.

Joel popped up on a knee and grabbed the steel hand holding his head. He pried the thumb away and spun to face the attacker. Joel's helmet instantly formed once freed, and Morwin's grasp lost all restraint on his mind. He faced the abomination in front of him. Flaming anger bled into Joel's strength. The monster tried to grab Joel's other arm, but was too late.

Chaotic rage blinded Joel as it released from his will. Everything around him became enveloped in a bright flash, disorienting him from every sense. Screams of people became silenced in an instant, replaced by the booming thunder that emitted from Joel's hands. Nothing would stop him; he didn't want to be stopped. The rage would be unleashed until Morwin was killed for good. Only pure chaos would grant him that.

His control was handed to the deeply rooted wrath that he had been holding onto for so long. He would not be enslaved to the sinister beings that wanted his power. All he wanted was peace, and those who stood in his way would fall to the destruction of his anger.

Peace was with Sadie. A thought graced his mind, asking where Sadie was. Did Morwin get to her? Or did he? A rope to pull back control revealed itself and Joel grabbed it. His rage and anger settled as his eyes adjusted to the bright sky above. Joel heavily breathed through the adrenaline that pumped through his body. He felt disoriented. He knew he was outside, but remembered being inside a church.

Dust surrounded him. Joel knelt down on the ground, glassed over, as it smouldered wisps of smoke. As the dark clouds raised with the wind, Joel saw nothing but burnt land around him. Nothing remained for as far as he could see. No building was left standing, no person raised from the rubble.

"I killed him," Joel grunted as he gasped for air. "I finally killed him."

Morwin and his creature were gone. Wiped from the sheer violence that Joel conjured. He looked around him, searching. No one could have survived the blast. No one but Sadie.

"Sadie? Where are you?" Joel called out. Only the wind could be heard.

Joel reached out into the bond to find her. The bond was empty. He felt nothing.

"Sadie?" He whispered. Why did the bond feel empty? It felt ripped from its existence. A gaping hole wept within him. Sadie was gone... killed in the blast that he created.

Joel frantically searched in every direction around. No one remained. The city held millions. It had the family that sheltered him. All of them were gone. He forced himself to stand, pushing through the feeble shaking that made him want to collapse. He couldn't believe she was gone. She would have escaped the destruction.

"Sadie?!" Joel yelled. Silence held under the phantom wind that gusted across the barren wasteland.

Each step forward felt as if it carried bricks of lead. His arms crossed over his stomach to hold in the impending realization with each second passed. Joel wasn't sure how long he had lost himself, but whether it was mere seconds or hours, nothing remained. No one was coming to help him.

Joel wanted to cry. He wanted to wake up from whatever nightmare he threw himself into. He made so many promises to never hurt an innocent again, and the cruelty of his reality allowed him to take an entire city full of them. Even the one person who understood his pain fell to his recklessness. Sadie was nowhere to be seen, absent from the bond, and wiped from his embrace. All of this death, her death, was his fault.

Joel's life, the attack in Mercer, the destruction of Fasdoba, all pointed to the failure of his existence. No matter how hard he tried to change his luck, it would eventually return itself to its rotten core. It was evident that life would not allow him to change for the better. Sadie entered his life as a gesture of good faith from the universe, only for it to immediately take her away when he finally tried for a better life. For as long as he would live, Joel knew he would be stuck in the endless cycle of failure and sorrow. Nothing would steer his path to peace.

Nothing but his own death.

Joel looked at the silvered rings on his palms through the steeled sockets of his helmet. They reflected the light of the sun that escaped through the layers of dust and smoke. These rings, these powers, would only be controlled when no one would be there to use them.

A silent and peaceful end was always what he yearned for. Joel never wanted to feel pain when the time came. Tragic methods required some form of hurt that made him hesitant in the past. But now he deserved it. Now was the time to follow through.

Joel looked up at the dark dust filled clouds, peering into the faint sun that barely breached onto the nuked ground. He could not die like a regular human. His body had grown too tough and resilient. His options had become limited. Joel would have to suffocate himself in an endless void. The empty darkness above called for him, beckoning him into a cold, airless grave.

In the space filled with nothing was the only place that would grant him death. No one could touch him. His body would float on forever, and far away from the home he hated. The rings pulsated with anticipation. Joel held them at his side and looked up into the sky, ready for the embrace he wanted so badly.

In a split second, Joel propelled himself up and away from the wasteland below. At the speed he entered, he jetted out of the atmosphere faster than he realized. Sound fell far behind its ability to reach him. He could feel the freezing touch of the vacuum wash over, but he didn't stop flying. Joel forced himself to go faster, beyond the grip of the planet left behind.

Joel faced the billions of stars ahead of him. They shone through the dark blanket that was the empty universe. This was his destiny, to die alone in nothing.

Joel's eyes began to fade. He watched the stars slowly crawl to the centre of his vision until they became one pearl sized cluster. It cried for his name, begging him to follow into the light. Joel closed his eyes and let the dying light take him.

CHAPTER 27

Tiny, white fluffs of white floated across a cloudless, blue sky; a warm and gentle wind kept them afloat. At first Sadie thought it was snow, but realized it was cotton-like fluff once her vision stopped blurring.

As she tried to sit up, a sharp pain shot through her shoulder and down her arm till it made her fingers numb. Her back thumped back on the ground when the pain became too great to move. Sadie noticed she was grinding her teeth and her breath was frantic. Something was wrong with her body. Something was wrong with Joel.

"Sadie! Sadie!" A woman was yelling but Sadie couldn't make out who. Her ears were ringing a terrible pitch.

"Over here!" She managed to call out. Her working hand reached to her side, feeling long tufts of grass. Sadie had no idea where she was. Her head was spinning too fast to even start fighting through whatever injury she took on.

Natasha appeared over her. Fiery ginger strands dangled from her face, failing to hide the many open and bleeding scars that ran down her cheeks and neck. Her eyes were focused on Sadie, widened with shock and fear. "Hold still Sadie, I'm going to sit you up."

Natasha took hold of Sadie's free arm and braced her back. Searing pain spread through her entire body, forcing her to shake out of the dizziness and stop herself from vomiting. Natasha continued to hold her up; her body desperately wanted to lay back down. Sadie lifted her head and couldn't understand what she was seeing. She was nowhere near Fasdoba, or Aross.

Hexagonal pillars the size of mountains breached from long, brown grassy fields and soared impossibly high in the air. There were hundreds that scattered themselves in an organized pattern, stretching far past the horizon. Each pillar leaned at an angle that should have toppled its mass; they looked to be made of a yellowish translucent material that gradually became faint emerald near the bases. Four winged creatures flashed white as they flew between the pillars and perched on ledges. At their distance, they were too far to make out fine details, but Sadie knew she had never seen anything like them. Her breath became faster as she realized everything around them was alien.

"Stay still," Natasha said. "You're losing too much blood."

Sadie looked down at her shoulder. A long, rusted rod of rebar had pierced her chest at an angle and exited out of her left shoulder. Blood oozed out of each wound at an uncomfortable pace. She noticed the skin on her hands had multiple small scars; she knew by the heat on her face that it had not gone untouched.

She looked to her side and found Veronica standing away from them. Her hands were wrapped around her chest and she was facing a horizon of the pillars. White fluffs flew past her; ones that got too close clung to wet blood that ran down her back and arm.

"Veronica, come here now," Sadie gasped.

Veronica slowly turned to face her. Tears streamed down her face as she winced in pain. "I'm sorry. I'm so sorry."

Sadie needed to keep her focused. Shock had already taken her sister. "Come to me. Please Veronica, come here."

Veronica stumbled towards them and knelt down in the grass beside her. Long scars ran from her neck, stomach, and legs. Many of them cut deep.

"Veronica, look at me," Sadie wheezed. "All of us are hurt. My heart is pierced; I'm dying fast. I need you to heal us. Now."

Veronica rubbed tears from her face and looked at each one of them. Her eyes darted back and forth to each injury. Her eyes filmed with more tears about to flood.

"Breathe," Natasha whispered. "Breathe and focus."

Sadie nodded and grabbed Veronica's hand. Veronica rubbed her eyes with her sleeve and took a deep breath. A quiet incantation, that Sadie couldn't understand, escaped Veronica's lips. She took hold of the rebar jutting out of Sadie's chest, and in a few seconds the rod became as limp as a wet noodle. Veronica braced her hand over the wound and base of the rod and slowly slithered it out. Sadie bit down on the inside of her cheeks as the pain burned within. Once Veronica had fully removed it, the pain lightly subsided and blood poured out of the open wound. Veronica tossed the limp rod to the side, watching it curl like a snake as it hit the grass.

Veronica then placed her hand over the bleeding hole and mumbled the beginnings of a spell. Sadie could feel the hole in her heart mend back together. An invisible stitch spread across her body, sewing every other wound until she looked completely untouched. Her head stopped spinning and felt as if she just awoke from a deep rest. The fading tiredness from the blood loss had disappeared.

After Sadie was healed, Veronica reached over to Natasha and then herself. Once the last wound closed, Veronica rocked forward as a wave of exhaustion hit her. Sadie and Natasha caught her before she fell and braced her body so she could sit and rest.

"Stay awake, Veronica," Sadie said, rubbing Veronica's back. She looked back up towards the pillars to make sure she wasn't hallucinating earlier. In every direction, all she could see were the gigantic pillars. The grass rippled with the flow of the wind, giving life to the endless field of brown hairs speckled with tuffs of cotton. Chirping calls echoed down from the winged creatures as they soared above. High past the pillars, past the atmosphere, she could faintly make out the outline of two planets, or moons. Sadie closed her eyes and reached out for a source of energy. Other than the elements of nature, there was nothing to grasp.

"Where did you take us?" Sadie asked as she brushed off white fluffs that landed on Veronica's cheek.

"I don't know," Veronica mumbled. Her eyes were close to closing. "I panicked and picked a place at random."

"Was that Joel?" Natasha asked. "Did he make that blast?"

Sadie nodded and felt her stomach lurch. She couldn't feel the bond between them; she felt robbed and empty. "Yeah, I think so. Veronica, you saved us. Thank you."

"I didn't save the rest of us," Veronica quietly cried. "That horrible blast... so many people are dead. The rest of our family is dead."

"Don't say that," Sadie ordered. "We don't know if they escaped."

She remembered right before she fell through Veronica's doorway there was a thunderous explosion that Joel created. The whole attack was a blur. She tried to get the plated monster off of Joel, but something strong attacked her. Before she could try anything else, the explosion came and Natasha tackled her into the gateway Veronica had made. She would have been dead if it wasn't for her sisters. She was lucky to escape with just a rod in her chest. Sadie dreaded the moment they would return. If they barely survived, then everyone else in that church, or the city, could not have lived through the pure chaos that Joel conjured. She had no idea how to face the aftermath of what had occurred.

"Veronica," Sadie faced her and locked eyes. "I need you to bring us back."

"I need a moment. I'm... so tired," Veronica said. Sadie believed it. The effort to cast all of those healing spells had drained her.

"Where are we? Is this our universe?" Natasha asked.

All Sadie could guess was an alien planet somewhere across the stars. She had read books in school about the probability of alien life existing. But before she could speak, Veronica fell into a trance.

"No. We are still on Aross," Veronica breathed hauntingly.

Sadie looked all around her and chalked it to an omen. At least that's what the damage-control impulse told her.

The three of them sat in silence, backs to each other, listening to the tempered breeze and strange birds singing in chirps. As time passed, Sadie could only describe this world as frighteningly beautiful. If Veronica had been too injured to heal them, they would have been trapped on this alien planet forever. Nothing that could help them would be within reach to survive. They had come too close to an ending on a bizarre, pillar filled planet. She thought about Veronica's omen, and what it meant to where exactly they had been placed. Despite its unimaginable bearing, it was better than sitting with the impending confrontation of what they needed to return to. She needed to return to Joel, and hope there was something left to save.

"Okay. I think I'm ready," Veronica said, breaking the silence.

Sadie wiped a white fluff from her nose and stood up. She helped Veronica stand and noticed she still swayed. Sadie knew her sister was suppressing her exhaustion just to get home.

Veronica lifted her hands and drew patterns in the air. She had her eyes closed, but frowned with frustration. Minutes passed as Veronica tried over and over to conjure a gateway. Sadie was about to recommend more time to rest until a red misted gateway unfolded the fabric of reality and opened a door to a devastated land.

The three of them stepped through, and the doorway collapsed behind them. Veronica leaned into Sadie as exhaustion took hold of her. They were surrounded by flattened ground. The only indicator that Fasdoba existed here was the river that the city was built around. Debris jammed the waters from shore to shore. The ground around them had been glassed over in an emerald hue. Dust and smoke filled the sky as the wind carried it up into the atmosphere. Sadie knew they were back on Aross. She could feel the life of electricity miles from the blast zone, but she couldn't feel Joel.

Tears formed in her eyes as she realized the gaping hole in her soul would not be mended. She thought once they returned, she would feel his presence again. She had grown used to the bond's comfort; it reminded her he existed. The time spent turning the pull from distrust to a warm affection had been ripped from its roots. Now it was gone for good, burnt in the chaos of himself.

"Joel's gone," Sadie choked. She brought her hand to her face to wipe her eyes. Natasha stroked her back, trying to comfort her. She wanted to deny it, but the emptiness made it impossible. She cherished her love that she had grown, but the cruelty of life needed to remind her she would never keep love ever again. Anger filled the empty wound within as she looked over the vast wasteland, wondering what extent it would take to hold on to something good.

A gust of dust and wind appeared below Aiden's feet as he blurred in front of them. He immediately rushed towards Natasha and pulled her into a tight hug. He had arrived so fast that Sadie couldn't comprehend he had actually survived.

"You're alive. I can't believe this. You're alive," Aiden gasped. He hesitantly pulled out of Natasha's embrace and hugged Veronica and Sadie. "I thought you guys were dead."

"Veronica saved us," Natasha said. "Are you... the only one left?"

"No," Aiden quickly answered. "I was able to run the rest of the family, and maybe fifty civilians out, before the blast became too great and fast. I tried to keep up, but eventually I became gassed. I tried to find you three, but..."

"It's okay," Sadie assured him. "You did good, Aiden."

"I don't think Joel made it. I'm sorry Sadie," Aiden said.

"I know. I can't feel him," Sadie whispered.

One by one, Aiden ran the three of them to a mountain far from the remains of the city. Once Sadie regained her balance, she looked up and found the rest of her family sitting down. They all had minor wounds, except for a large splinter poking out of Rowan's leg. Veronica rushed over in her tired state and cast healing spells over them. Sadie peered down the mountain and knew they were nowhere close to Fasdoba, but the towns below them had been crumbled to sticks. The touch of the blast exceeded her guess.

"They're all dead," Lyas mumbled. "Thousands, if not millions, are dead."

Sadie stepped down from the overlook and kneeled beside him. "We need to look for the wounded and take them to get help."

Lyas locked eyes with her, glaring with hatred. "Do you know how many are screaming out right now? The blast didn't just level the city. It reached miles past the city. And that was only the core. The aftershock rolled over every surrounding town until it reached cities far from Fasdoba. Millions are gone, wiped from existence."

Guilt washed over Sadie. She never wanted this destruction.

She needed to get Lyas in focus. "Then let's start somewhere," she said.

Lyas's head fell into his hands. "I should have never taken Joel in. This is all my fault. I should have seen the risk he posed."

Sadie felt a tinge of rage. Joel didn't kill the city on purpose. Morwin had forced him into it. She wanted to defend Joel, but the weight of the lives lost weighed her to defeat. Lyas was not about to listen to her. There was no way he would understand what she had just lost.

Sadie stood up, facing Lyas. Her hands gripped into fists. All of this was his fault. He rushed in, and Joel was gone because Lyas couldn't bother to see the true risk.

"I'm not about to listen to you tarnish his name. I'm going to look for wounded, and I expect you all to do the same," Sadie fiercely said.

She immediately dropped into a flash of electrons in the realm of energy. The world around her buzzed with panic. She could see a flow of electricity border an enormous circle of blackout that was the fallout zone. The search would be difficult, but would distract her from what was about to cripple her will. The emptiness of the bond weighed on her with misery. People desperately needed saving before she could let herself mourn. She would go as long as she could to pull people from the rubble, solely created by the person she had grown to love. Only after the fall from exhaustion would she let herself curl into painful grief she never thought she would experience again.

CHAPTER 28

Garem's armoured body flailed across the factory floor like a fish out of water. His injured cries annoyed Morwin, and the factory walls buckled with each rabid spasm.

"Stay still, you oaf!" Morwin shouted. It had no effect on Garem's panicked state. The ground shook as Garem's remaining hand slapped the floor, shattering the concrete beneath.

Morwin had enough. He raised thick vines from the ground and pinned Garem's body down. Garem struggled through the restraint, snapping through tendrils that didn't wrap around fast enough. Garem screamed out like a wounded dog; the shout echoed off every wall of the abandoned factory.

The tendrils finally grabbed each limb and held him still. They strained under the immense strength of the metal monster; Morwin knew they were about to split apart. He quickly jumped over to Garem's head and placed his hand over his plated eyes. Blood was pouring out of each crevice in the armour. Morwin weaselled his way into Garem's mind and commanded him to sleep. The beast slowly stopped moving and fell to a dead rest. His breaths were raspy and wet.

Morwin stepped back to get a better assessment of Garem's injuries. Underneath the tightened black vines was a mangled body. Garem's right arm had been stripped off right at the collar, and one of his legs appeared to be twisted around three times. Blood seeped under every steel plate. Morwin wondered what the internal damage looked like.

When he reached out with his mind and combed the entirety of the body, he found every organ bruised and bleeding. However, Garem's healing ability was already taking effect. Morwin became confident Garem would survive.

"You did well, friend," Morwin whispered. "Now sleep and heal."

Morwin stepped back and collapsed onto an old bucket. He let himself take deep breaths, reminding himself that he survived. Barely. He was only seconds away from becoming disintegrated by Joel's power. Unfortunately, Garem took on the full force of the blast. He was found miles away from the city, thrown by the shockwave into a farmer's field. Without the armour, Garem would have been instantly wiped.

Morwin grinned and laughed. Joel had gotten so close to killing him, but in the end, Morwin was the winner. He had hoped to dominate Joel's will; he had his mind within his grasp, but Morwin could accept the death of Joel as an appropriate success. Either outcome was desired. And all he had to do was piss Joel off enough to blow himself up.

He leaned back on a steel post and watched Garem struggle to breathe. The meathead had made so much noise, Morwin was thinking someone would show up to investigate. He had found the factory long before the operation in Fasdoba. It was far enough away that it could be used as a safe-house. Luckily, it was just near the edge of the shockwave, managing to hold strong through the shaking of its foundation. Some town called Cerosmos owned it, but they deemed it derelict years ago. Even if a curious resident heard Garem's racket, it would not matter. No one could stop Morwin. The only person on Aross that could fortify their mind was turned to dust.

What of the others?

They have strength in many ways.

"Not like Joel's," Morwin said out loud.

You are forgetting the mind reader.

Lyas? No, that man was weak. But useful in time. Morwin hated to admit he could use the man's help. Joel wiped clean from the board did reveal all sorts of possibilities with the remaining family members.

We should strike now.

The blast must have killed them.

Morwin didn't think so. If he survived, then there was a possibility the others escaped as well. The ones that didn't never meant to carry forward with the future. In time, he would search for them, watching from the dark corners where they couldn't see. The idea of continuing the plan was enticing, but he needed Garem for his strength. The beast needed time to heal, so Morwin would then wait. As he laid back, revelling in the success of his plan, Morwin took off his deer mask and pulled out his notebook. He crossed off Joel's name with a sharp line. He hoped his death

252

didn't happen quickly; the man deserved to feel every second of his body being violently eaten away. Along with every single weak, inferior human that existed within the blast.

It was time to choose the next city. The remaining family members could wait for now; they would be easy to find. He knew where their little village was. They would be on edge, so he would have to act carefully. While he waited for the long process of Garem's rehabilitation, Morwin pulled out his world map and searched for his next snare.

* * *

A long black tendril slithered across the dusty concrete floor, pulling a limp body that had wandered too close to the factory. It dragged the slab of meat up the wall and plastered it next to the other bodies collected over the past few weeks. Mold already crawled towards the fresh meal, covering the body with yellow and blue slime. Morwin could feel the fungi jitter with excitement.

Morwin drew a circle around a city in Yanda. Nasmachi, fairly large and densely populated. The world-wide guide for tourists book he found was outdated by a few years, but estimated the population to be well over two million. He listed it as a secondary; he needed something larger.

He heard a grunt behind him and turned to face Garem. The beast was still in his armoured form. Morwin refused to allow him to change back. He was hunched over his knees; drool was dripping from the plated head. Morwin noticed Garem's injured arm had now regenerated past the elbow. His brain had kicked its coma a couple days ago and his blood had stopped leaking between crevices. In its place, a yellowish-brown crust was scabbing all over his armour.

His flesh is delicious.

"He's not food!" Morwin shouted. "Find something else to eat!"

The growls in his stomach rumbled in disappointment. The monster was of no use to him if he turned to slop.

Garem grumbled again and shifted back. The metal armour screeched as the plates ground against each other. "Please... just let me die."

Morwin sighed and set down his pen. He wished the oaf didn't require so much maintenance. He approached Garem and took hold of the hulking head. He could feel that Garem's brain had been completely washed over with infection. If let to continue, his mind would be devoured till his skull sat empty. Morwin squeezed most of the mold out, leaving just enough to keep his leash. For a brute that was practically impenetrable, he sure had soft insides.

"No, I need you still," Morwin said.

"For how much longer?" Garem mumbled.

Morwin winced with frustration. He has had this conversation too many times, and he was repeating himself. "Until someone else comes along that's as strong as you, then you'll be set free."

Morwin stepped away and walked back to his map. He looked at a city named Yavbai, in Tunland. The book read one and a half million citizens. He felt that was weird, as every single inch of Tunland was packed to the brim and the number should have been higher.

He flipped a few pages and came across a picture of a city named Tem-Mire. Capital of the province New Vessel, in Morwin's home country of the Northern Union. He had read lots about Tem-Mire back in school. It was a port city on one of the great lakes. It had a population of about three million; that was propitious.

It was a major producer of hydro-electricity and freshwater transport. What made the city interesting was its collection of skyscrapers. It was exactly what he needed. It wasn't peak summer season, but the winters there were fairly warm and wet. The city would be packed with bodies, regardless.

"I think I found it, Garem. I think I found our sacred ground," Morwin said. He ran his hand over the map, tracing the larger municipalities that surrounded Tem-Mire.

"Do they all really need to die?" Garem cried silently.

"Yes," Morwin said. "You'll never understand what humanity has taken from this planet. Your simple life in Lavendy kept you happy and fat. How much did you care for the suffering outside your country?"

"I cared..."

He twists the truth.

Your control is slipping.

"I can feel your mind lying," Morwin uttered. "You couldn't leave your precious city because it kept you distracted from what you feared. It's better to feel blind ignorance than face the issues ruining the world, eh?"

"I was just one guy," Garem said.

"And now? You are a steel brute capable of raising a riot wherever you please. You could have used that to make actual change, and you ignored your destiny!"

"I never asked to be this... monster," Garem cried.

"None of us asked for this. It was bestowed. And I chose to actually follow through," Morwin said, gritting his teeth. "The plague that is humanity needs to go. The world needs to heal from its wounds, and we will take their place as its caretakers. You could have been a god, but you chose to hide. I refuse to let you flee."

"I understand," Garem wept under the scaled helmet. Morwin thought he was pathetic. He could feel Garem's mind trying to mourn for the millions lost from his country. Morwin waved those urges aside.

Morwin grabbed his notebook and tossed it to Garem's feet. "Memorize these faces and names. They were there in Fasdoba, and they will try to stop me when the time comes."

"Do you want me to kill them?" Garem asked.

"Only if they overwhelm you, which I doubt they will. The one who controls metal will be a problem for you, which I believe you will figure out in time. I would prefer them all alive, but even if they have to die, they will soon be replaced by another," Morwin said.

"And this one, Lyas?"

"He's the one the others will try to stop me from taking."

"I understand."

"Good," Morwin said. "Because you're crucial in this. Without your riot, I will be vulnerable. If I'm stopped, the world dies."

Garem nodded slowly, still hunched over his knees as he looked down at Morwin's drawings. He could feel the brute stir with heavy hopelessness.

Morwin sighed deeply. "If you succeed in stopping the family from reaching me, I will grant you death."

He could feel a spark of desire within the mold ridden mind that festered under the armour. Garem truly wanted an end to his purpose, but yet he proved so useful. Morwin would reconsider once he was faced with the reborn world at his feet.

"Imagine, Aross protected by the evolved," Morwin said. "With every mind and ability combined, we could create so many unimaginable solutions. No weak human would be there to stop us. Our future is a paradise, and we are so close to reaching it."

Chapter 29

The upside down roof creaked under Sadie's hands as she lifted it. It belonged to a completely different home, and the house it landed on was crushed under its impact. Sadie easily lifted the metal and wood rooftop up on its side and tossed it next to the demolished walls. At the height she was at, she could see every tree in the area toppled over like toothpicks, pointing in the same direction. Any tree that managed to stand, had all its branches ripped off.

She could still feel the cell phone receiving a signal. Whoever owned it, she hoped they were alive. It had only been three days since Fasdoba was destroyed; anyone stuck in the rubble still had a chance.

Sadie had come across this acreage when scouring the zone for any possible hidden wounded. Lavendy's army and support from other nations arrived shortly after the destruction, but were still mobilizing and focusing on densely populated towns and cities that neighboured Fasdoba. Nothing was left to save out of

Fasdoba; every building and road had been thrown and levelled. It was clear to first responders that nothing survived, so they began in areas that weren't directly in the vicinity of the heat dome. Those searches still posed a challenge, as the deadly aftershock flew miles past the city centre. But it gave Sadie and her family time to help any town the army and aid had yet to reach.

A large wooden beam was pulled out from under her feet, revealing the body of a middle-aged man. Once Sadie removed more debris, she discovered that the man was dead, but was covering another body. When she flipped the deceased man, she found a woman underneath. Her breathing was short and grating. Sadie pulled more debris off of her and dragged her out carefully. The woman couldn't even open her eyes; she was too weak to move.

Sadie grabbed her water bottle and poured a little into the woman's parted mouth. She coughed as she drank, but was able to consume just enough to help her. Sadie noticed a gold band on her ring finger and a matching band on the man's body. That was her husband, she assumed. They probably didn't even have time to react before the blast hit them.

Aiden appeared out of a blur at the base of the crumbled house. He was carrying Rowan. "Alive?" He asked in a huff.

"Just one so far. I haven't had time to search the rest of the rubble," Sadie replied.

Aiden climbed the debris and took the injured woman in his arms. In a blur, they were gone. Delivered to a nearby medical station where people would find the woman and tend to her.

Rowan pounced up towards Sadie and knelt beside her. Rowan closed her eyes and breathed deeply. Sadie tried her best to stay as still as possible.

"No heartbeats," Rowan solemnly said. "If there were more people inside this house, then they can't be saved."

"At least we found the woman," Sadie sighed. Now that she was sitting down, she could feel the exhaustion settle. She had been searching the affected zone every minute since the blast. There was still enough gas in her to keep going for longer. Dirt and grease covered her face and hands, but that was of little importance. Rowan looked just as dishevelled as her.

"Onto the next?" Rowan asked. She nodded her head towards a neighbouring farmhouse.

"In a second," Sadie said. She picked up the husband's body in her arms and slowly brought him down towards the yard. She laid him down softly. She wished she had time to search the rest of the house, but that was an ongoing wish with every other pile of rubble they found. Sadie turned to Rowan and wiped the man's blood onto her shirt. "Where are the others?"

"Callum and Lyas are in Wakeajero. The army is crawling all through there. And Veronica and Natasha are in a town some ten kilometres that way. Its name is Villaneuvaz. Nat is taming the fire, but the town is already half consumed," Rowan explained. She pointed in the direction of her friends and Sadie spotted the large plume of smoke rising in the air. It was easy to find, as it was the smallest of every other plume across the horizon.

Sadie dropped her head into her hand. "Hells, we aren't doing enough here."

"We have to be careful, Sadie. One small misstep and all eyes will be on us," Rowan said.

"I know. I'm just speaking out loud," Sadie sighed. "C'mon, let's go to the next house."

Sadie took hold of Rowan and disappeared in a flash. At the house not too far over, the two of them reappeared out of blue light and searched for any life under the debris.

* * *

Two weeks had passed in the rescue of anything in the affected zone, and every day was proving more and more difficult to avoid the army. They built an emergency assembly and had successfully rooted themselves within each city and town around Fasdoba. But their reach could only extend so far, and they still missed hidden corners where trapped, wounded or dead sat waiting.

Aid and support from other nations poured in. Lavendy held a special place in people's hearts, and seeing footage of the destruction had shocked the entire world. No matter how much was given by donations, it still would not replace what was lost. The tally of dead had past five million, with millions more severely wounded. The gift of being a beautiful country cursed it with a dense population.

Sadie sat atop a sandbank, feeling the ache of denied rest, weight on her back and shoulders. She knew she needed to rest, and maybe something to eat, but she wasn't ready to stop. Only until Natasha yelled at her to sit for ten minutes did she listen. If she wasn't moving, then she was remembering. But Natasha was about to murder her, and Sadie decided to entertain the order. Once those ten minutes were up, she would return to whatever town needed help.

She overlooked a long and wide beach that was popular amongst tourists. Sadie watched as Callum braced himself on the sand, lifting a giant cargo ship from the ocean. The shockwave had flipped the ship, most likely drowning everyone on board. Regretfully, every rescue group was occupied elsewhere, and no one was checking for survivors.

The metal hull creaked shrilly as it was lifted out of the blue waters. Storage containers fell and splashed into the ocean once the weight shifted. Callum's invisible hand carried it up through the surface and over to the sandy beach where he gently laid it down. Once it was rested, Callum and Natasha cut holes through the hull, letting the water drain that flooded the entire interior.

Sadie heard footprints behind her and turned to see Lyas walking up the bank. He looked tired, and his hair was greasy from not washing it. From the direction he was heading, he was approaching her, and she really wasn't in the mood to speak to him or anyone.

"Hey," Lyas said. "Are you doing alright?"

Sadie shrugged her shoulders. For the amount of bodies and gore they had come across over the past two weeks, no one could say any of them were alright. Lyas sat down beside her and picked up the white sand in his palm, letting it pour down between his fingers.

"Is anyone alive?" Sadie nodded towards the ship.

Lyas shook his head side-to-side, sighing deeply through his nose. "All the crew drowned. I've already let Callum and Natasha know; they're just making it easier for the rescue groups to reach the bodies."

Sadie closed her eyes and rubbed her nose, trying to fight off the creeping tiredness. "We were too late."

"Because we were elsewhere, helping others," Lyas assured. "Think of how many lives you've saved these past couple weeks."

"I wish it was more," Sadie sighed.

As they sat in silence, Sadie felt an inching feeling that Lyas had more to say. He was just trying to find the courage to say it. She had hoped he would regroup with the others once he checked in with her, but the longer he sat, the more she built her walls to prepare.

"We need to talk," Lyas said. Sadie remained silent. He didn't need her permission to continue. "I need to know we are okay. This team… this family, is crucial to our survival. Morwin got the jump on us, and now we all suffer because of it. If we don't have our heads together, that will only make us weaker."

Sadie turned to face him. His eyes pleaded for forgiveness. "Morwin trapped us because of your plan. We rushed in too fast and we failed because of it."

"You agreed to the plan. Putting the fault on me is not fair," Lyas carefully said.

"Because you didn't give us any other options!" Sadie shouted. "We were given an absolute. There was no preparation or consideration. Do you not feel sorry at all?"

"I only feel sorry for the pain we've experienced," Lyas said. "But I did what I thought was right, and I acted on discretion. Any of the family could have stayed at the farm; I don't command any of you."

"You're supposed to be a leader. We listen to you because we trust you, and you fumbled that trust," Sadie snapped. She wanted him gone from her sight. For as long as they lived, he would give her no apology.

"No. I won't accept this. But I understand why you're mad at me. Joel's death was by Morwin's hand. I know you cared about Joel, but you also care about everyone else in this family and we can't fail them now," Lyas spoke softly.

She didn't want to talk about Joel. She didn't even want to think about him. The man she loved, that left a gaping wound in her soul, was gone and she failed to protect him. What followed was the death and slaughter of millions. She couldn't protect anyone.

"Leave me alone," she ordered. If Lyas sat beside her for a minute longer, she knew she would say things she could never take back.

Lyas hesitantly stood up and wiped the sand off his pants. Before he stepped away, he turned to Sadie. "We are returning to the farm soon. The army has almost covered the entire affected zone. If we linger any longer, someone will discover us."

As he walked down the sandbank towards the ship, all Sadie could feel was hate and betrayal. Part of her told her it was unfair to feel so; Lyas has guided her through dark parts of her life and was a good friend. But with the empty wound that pierced her affection, it reminded her of what was taken.

What would life look like when they returned home? She thought. Would they just go back to normal? Would they viciously hunt for Morwin? After everything that had happened in Lavendy, the entire fabric of their family has been permanently altered. The millions of lives lost, the life of Joel's, could not be easily forgotten. For the rest of her life, their deaths would haunt her until she died. There would be no forgetting the failure that she experienced. She was no hero. Heroes don't pick up the pieces and body parts of a society they tried to save.

Sadie picked herself up and walked away from the beach towards a parking lot of flipped and crumbled cars. Rows of helicopters flew in the distance, transporting food or injured people. No one could be seen around her. This area had been evacuated a long time ago. Wherever she looked, she was reminded of the destruction that had occurred. She was relieved they were almost done, but no part of her wanted to return to the farm. Wherever she would go, ghosts were bound to follow.

CHAPTER 30

Dark blue storm clouds sat above the low mountain range, rumbling with thunder. Lighting jetted downwards, behind the round peaks. She could feel each bolt before it struck. Sadie gave it thirty minutes until it reached the town. The storm was carrying a torrential downpour that would flood the desert fields until the dry dirt and sand pulled it into the ground below.

Sadie lifted the purple and white flower between her fingers. It had a fuzzy centre, with white petals that turned to a dark purple as they extended. The desert wind shook it in her hand. The storm would arrive fast and leave as quickly as it came.

The old wooden porch she was sitting on creaked as she shifted. Despite the clouds, the owner did have a nice view of the range. The woman let her take a rest when she noticed Sadie was struggling in the heat. Arsacadia was too far north to experience dry heat like Jaussa. They were lucky to get even a little in the summers. She decided to take the offer as she had just finished her scouting and needed to wait for the others.

A stronger gust of wind kicked up loose dust and freckled her face. The sleeves of her t-shirt flapped freely; the sweat on her back made her shiver. The sudden drop of dry, searing heat to a mild chill was unfair for what Jaussa usually offered. A jacket was not brought on this mission for that very reason.

"Quieres un té?" The Jaussian woman poked her head out of her front door again. This was the third time she offered Sadie tea.

"No, no thank you," Sadie smiled and shook her head politely. Without Veronica around, she was very limited to what the woman could understand. But the woman seemed to get it as she returned a smile and closed the door behind her.

Sadie looked down the town street and saw Veronica and Callum walking back towards her. They kicked up dust with each step. She imagined Veronica was happy to be among her people again. Before Veronica came to the farm, the people of her village practically treated her like a saint. Any illness or issue was cured by her spells. They believed she was a witch, but only gave her the utmost respect. The people of Jaussa would accept any help they could get. Their government sure wasn't providing any. So when Veronica discovered her magic, the people of her village took it as a gift from the gods. Whatever they needed, Veronica asked for nothing in return. Once they were done in this town, Wesso, they would pay Veronica's hometown a quick visit.

"Ugly storm over there," Veronica said. "Anything on the plains is about to drown in a flash flood."

Sadie nodded. She hoped they would leave Wesso before the storm reached them. "Did you find him?"

"In the orphanage, yea," Callum said. "We made sure to comb the entire town, too. I think we're safe here."

"Okay, let's go then," Sadie said. She dropped the flower onto the wooden porch and dusted off her pants as she stood. "Nothing is here on this side of town."

"Double checked?" Callum asked.

Sadie frowned at him; his tone was critical.

"I'm sorry, I didn't mean…" Callum stuttered.

Sadie interrupted him. "Whatever. Let's go."

Veronica and Callum followed Sadie as she stood up from the porch and walked down the gravel road. The town of Wesso was small and had not changed since Jaussa's coal boom in the forties. Everyone was too poor to maintain their infrastructure, and any home not made of brick or concrete toppled years ago.

Unless you were within the ranks of its military or government, every citizen of Jaussa lived in extreme poverty. Many towns across the nation started to depend on the support of whatever cartel owned them in their territory. But gang war and extortion were quick to crush whatever promises were made. Wesso was considered forever cursed by the debts of a once great cartel that had almost swept the entire country. Whenever life began to look up, ghosts of its past came through for payment.

Ahead of her was the orphanage they were there to visit. Half of its windows had been boarded up with old wood, and the roof was missing a chunk of tile shingles. She watched as a group of kids ran around from the back, chasing a scared feral cat. They cackled amongst themselves as the cat burrowed itself in a hole under the building's wall. With little to do in the town, they had to entertain themselves somehow. Every kid seemed to take part in the game, except one that sat on the front steps.

"That's him," Sadie said. She nodded to the lone kid. He was sitting alone, separated from the other orphans in their game of chase. Sadie could feel an aura of power emit from his body. Whatever he was capable of, he carried a well of light.

"Yes," Veronica said. "His soul is as radiant as the sun. It's almost blinding."

Sadie let herself take a deep breath. The boy was young. Every gifted they had ever met was at least an adult. A part of her felt the cruelty of his life. He must have been eight or ten. He didn't even get to live through the innocent youth he was owed.

"Let me talk to him. You two stand watch," Sadie said. She didn't wait for the others to object. The boy looked scared and alone. She didn't need a posse behind her.

As Sadie got closer to the boy, she noticed he had a ripped piece of fabric tied around his eyes. Pink scars peaked from under the cloth. A small TV, playing a fuzzy news channel, sat close to him, with an extension cord running from inside the house. She thought the boy was using it for the comfort of noise; his sight served him no help. Surprisingly, the boy looked up to meet her eyes when she approached.

"Why do you glow so bright?" The boy said. Sadie could see thinner burn marks running down his arms. He was frail, and his clothes were many sizes too big.

"Your English is good," Sadie smiled. "Can I sit with you?"

The boy stole a quick grin and nodded yes. She placed herself next to him, studying the extent of his injuries. The blindfold covered most of the scars over his eyes, but from what she could see, she knew it was permanent. Sadie looked over at the vintage

TV; the video signal was poorly tuned. But from what she could see, the channel played a recap of the rescue efforts in the Fasdoba area.

Sadie turned her attention back to the boy before she was pulled in. "You can see me glow?" She asked.

"Everyone has a glow. But you are really, really bright. Same with the other two down the road," the boy said as he pointed towards Callum and Veronica.

"Those are my friends," Sadie smiled. The radiant aura was consistent within the boy, but she could tell by his frown that he was slightly anxious. "You don't have to be worried. I will not hurt you."

The boy nervously nodded. Sadie struggled to think about what to say. She expected to find an adult in Wesso, not a child. The crackled static of the TV filled the silence between them. She watched as the group of boys ran around the side of the orphanage, chasing the spooked cat and laughing together in their mischievous game. They paid little notice to Sadie and their blind bunkmate.

"I'm Sadie. What's your name?" She asked the child.

"Nathan Dagal. But I like Nait," the boy said.

"Nice to meet you, Nait," Sadie said. "Your scars look painful. Are your eyes okay?"

Nait solemnly shook his head. "Not much anymore. I miss being able to see normal."

"What do you mean, normal?" Sadie asked.

"Everything is surrounded by light."

Sadie sighed. This kid's world violently changed without a chance to fight it. Everyone in town must have treated him like an outcast; she didn't even want to think about where his parents were. What fairness could she give Nait that the world hadn't already taken?

"I glow bright because I have these special abilities," Sadie explained carefully. "My friends also have them. And I think you do too."

"My nanny says I'm cursed," Nait mumbled.

Sadie looked down at her palms, torn between revealing the reality Nait faced or completely walk away to leave only fate behind to guide him. "There will be people in your life who just can't understand what has happened to you. Whether you see it as a burden, a purpose, or curse, life is going to make you fight for your own understanding of it. These abilities you hold can hurt people; sometimes they're so overwhelming you lose all control."

"That's how I hurt myself," Nait stated.

"Yes," Sadie said. "These powers are dangerous, and I'm sorry they hurt you. A part of why I'm here is to teach you to never let that happen again. You glow bright too, you know? I believe you wield great things. You can use them to save the people that evil chases."

"I can't help people if I can't see," Nait said sorrowfully.

"But you can see the light around them?"

"Yea, like sunlight, but it hurts my head to look at. Nanny told me not to talk about it or I'll get in trouble," Nait said quietly.

"It sounds like to me that maybe there is a way for you to see. This light around people is a sight unique only to you. I can teach you how to make it hurt less, and you'll be running around with your friends in no time." Sadie smiled. She didn't know this boy, but already knew he deserved his childhood to return. Sadness weighed her head. She choked as she mustered a reply. "I knew someone who thought he was cursed, too."

"What happened to him?" Nait asked.

"He died. I didn't fight hard enough to protect him."

"What's going to happen to me? Am I going to get better?" Nait said.

Sadie had no clue how to answer that. She thought she was finally figuring out how to navigate her new life and then a part of her was ripped out, leaving her to wonder why it existed in the first place. She wanted to be a guide to those who were lost, like her. If others were shown a way of hope, then that gave her purpose. She wanted to give Joel hope, and be his guide, but he was dead and she was left to question if her purpose had meaning. Now this boy sat beside her, looking for hope and his destiny in her hands.

"I don't know, Nait," Sadie said. "Life isn't going to get easier from here. I could take you with me, show you what this new life means. But I'm thinking I don't even have that answer. Hells, you're only a kid. You never asked for this."

Nait slowly rocked forward, holding his knees between his arms. Blazing heat washed down as the wind opened a gap in the clouds, letting the sun boil the desert beneath. The chills down Sadie's back disappeared and left behind a cold sweat. The TV played footage of a crane removing pieces of a collapsed hotel outside of Fasdoba. After it showed an air view shot of the levelled city. The news anchors were speaking in Jaussian; she couldn't understand what they spoke of. But it was enough to remind her what was lost on that day, two months ago. Alongside millions of wounded and dead, the tragedy in Fasdoba would forever remain on her conscience.

"I don't want to leave. All my friends are here," Nait said. He wiped away a tear that escaped his blindfold.

A stabbing wrench tore through her gut. This kid didn't deserve misery past what he had already endured. "Are you treated well here?"

Nait hesitantly nodded. "Nanny is sometimes grumpy, but my friends are nice. Wesso is my home."

Sadie looked over as he sat beside her. Life held nothing back on his suffering, yet he managed to hold on to small joys that gave him hope. If she took Nait with her, she would only rob him of what separated him from his abilities. Would life be better for him at the farm, or would it forever change the hope he had for his destiny?

"Can you tell me about your home?" Sadie asked.

Nait smiled and quickly began to tell her of his town and the friends within. During their talk, when he got really excited, Nait would fall into Jaussian speech, but quickly corrected himself when he realized Sadie couldn't understand. Nait shared stories that made him laugh, and stories that made Sadie hurt. She told him memories of her home and her family. She made him buckle over, laughing with a story about her ruining her mother's dishwasher. He was amazed when she told him about snow; and he asked dozens of questions that Sadie couldn't keep up with.

As time went on, Sadie put the pieces of his story together. Through the poverty and suffering, Nait and his family appreciated the life that they were given. As long as he was with his people, he could fight through whatever misery befell them. Nait watched his parents and brothers succumb to the wormwood plague; luckily the town and orphanage were immediately there to take him in. He had only discovered his powers a year after his family passed. The town had concluded that Nait had touched an exposed live wire, but only Nait knew his injuries were by his own hand. Since then, his vision was taken, and the world was moulded into a different perspective. Despite all he lived through, he had succeeded in keeping his innocence.

After a couple hours passed, Sadie noticed Callum pacing and looking down the road towards them. It was almost time to go. Sadie knew what they were sent there to do was not the right choice for this boy.

She leaned into Nait and took his hand. He squeezed them back, letting her feel the burn scars on his fingers. "Nait, I can take you with me or let you stay. I made a promise to someone I loved to protect them, and I failed. You don't deserve my failure, but I want to be there to protect you. The life ahead of you is dangerous, nothing says you have to do it alone. Whatever you want to do, I'll follow."

"If I stay, will you visit me? Maybe you can teach me how to see?" Nait asked.

"Of course. Any chance I get, I'll be there."

When she stood to leave, Nait jumped up and hugged her waist. Sadie hugged him back, said their goodbyes, and she walked back to Callum and Veronica alone. Callum looked confused and angry. He leaned in to quietly shout at Sadie when she reached them.

"What was that? We can't leave him behind," Callum said.

Sadie squared herself in front of Callum, refusing to be intimidated by her friend. "He's just a kid, Callum. He deserves to grow up with his friends and the people raising him."

Callum scoffed. "This entire town is starving. There's no quality of life here. Besides, he needs to be taught control. Look at Morwin, Garem or Joel. That's what happens when we fail to restrain these powers. What happens if he destroys this town or country?"

"I am done trying to control whatever these powers are," Sadie said sharply. "Our strategy has failed. We can't change the fate of others through this promise of safety. I can't, in good conscience, take this kid away from the only thing he has hope for, and try to force him into something we don't even understand. I will look out for the kid, but he remains in a place that keeps him with a good heart."

"Joel's death isn't on you," Callum said with sorrow. "You don't need to let it bleed into your life. We will do better with the kid."

"No. We have no control over this. He doesn't deserve more suffering than he's already experienced. And you will quit bringing up Joel?" Sadie gnashed her teeth.

Callum leaned in closer. "Morwin will get to him. You can't watch the kid forever, Suds."

"Wait, we can," Veronica interrupted. "In a way. I can cast a hex over him. It won't last forever, but it will hide him for now until I find a better solution."

Callum looked towards her, annoyed and with piercing eyes. After a long sigh, he nodded in agreement. Veronica quickly cast a red hex over her hand and let it dissipate. No one would touch him without them knowing. Nait was hidden, for now.

Sadie felt a touch of accomplishment; she was a step closer to protecting the boy. She rubbed Veronica's arm in thanks and kindly smiled. "I need you both to understand my decision. We can't force this life on a kid. Leave Lyas to me, I will explain what happened."

As the blazing sun disappeared behind the incoming storm, the three of them walked towards a hidden corner to teleport from. Sadie took one last look at Nait. He stared towards her, peering right through his blindfold. He gave her a small wave goodbye, and Sadie waved back before she jumped her friends back home.

CHAPTER 31

"They don't have much, but the longer the search goes on, the more footage they'll find." Aiden explained. He swiped his tablet to the next video showing collaborations of security cameras, cell phones, and dash cams capturing the destruction of Fasdoba. Most of the footage seemed completely unusable. The moment the bright green flash arrives, the source of the footage is rocked by a blast seconds after. Each video twisted Sadie's gut a bit more. She imagined Natasha and Aiden felt as uncomfortable as she did.

"This is what some radical outlets are focusing on. Conspiracies are already pouring in on social media," Aiden said as he pulled up footage from a camera facing a downtown street of a town nearby Fasdoba. Sadie watched a lightning bolt arc across the sky. Her lightning bolt. To her, she was just jumping from one pile of rubble to the next. But to a regular human, watching, this lightning was of questionable behaviour. Alongside reports of strange folk using 'magic', they were dangerously close to the public realizing the family's existence.

"Shit. At least my face doesn't appear." Sadie sighed.

"Yet," Aiden said. "There are still years of search and rescue planned. At any time, someone might come across more convincing evidence. Any of us in the affected zone could have been recorded."

Natasha rubbed Aiden's back. She looked concerned. And rightfully so. There were family back in Revenland that needed to believe she was still dead. "Can one of us somehow wipe any of this off the internet?" Natasha said.

"Maybe. Lyas could, maybe. But we would risk opening the floodgates to more questions," Aiden said.

"I don't think we need to panic just yet. Most of the public still believes in stories that point away from us. We helped a ton of wounded in those first days and got out silently. We would know by now if people knew. It's been months," Sadie said.

"A part of me still believes we should announce what happened," Aiden said. "If we get the truth out there, then we can give the people Morwin's information. Every eye on Aross can help us look for him."

"I don't think it's a good idea," Sadie interjected. "That would risk us and any other gifted to be hunted down. People are way to upset to be presented with the actual truth right now. If we give it more time, the conspiracies will fade beneath whatever new story the world offers."

Natasha bit down on her lip and frowned. "We need to get Morwin's face out there. Even if we reveal his picture without all the details, it gets us closer to finding him."

"I'm worried Morwin would retaliate. Like release our information or kill another city. Some of us still have family out there. The people wouldn't stop at us. They would go after everyone with any connection," Sadie said.

Aiden nodded. He still visited his parents, back in Port Grald of the Rown Isles, at least once a month. He was able to hide his secret lifestyle from them, but if the family was exposed to the world, he risked his parents' safety.

Sadie sighed and rubbed the bridge of her nose. Each day that passed since Fasdoba had new and terrible reports surface. The weight of their involvement was overwhelming. She could feel the tension and anger all around the farm. The family getting revealed to the world would be the cherry on top of the clusterfuck they were already dealing with.

"Let's remember to keep our focus on finding Morwin," Sadie explained. "We are still a secret to the world, and we aren't going to worry about it until it's actually happening. Like any self-destructive person would."

Aiden anxiously chuckled and changed the screen on his tablet. Any effort to sweep their existence off the internet would take all of their minds combined, and the family was in no mental space to do that. All they could do in the moment was keep their heads afloat while they tried to sort out their situation. Which, unfortunately, was the impossible task of finding a psychotic mass-murderer.

"Are you leaving today?" Natasha asked. "Aiden and I were going to cook some prawns."

"Yea, I promised Nait we'd help his town dig a new well. Veronica's coming," Sadie said.

"How's the kid doing?" Aiden asked.

"He's feeling better. He got along well with Rowan… but Lyas still refuses to meet him. A part of me thinks it's for the better."

"When will you be back?" Natasha asked.

"I don't know," Sadie sighed. "After my visit with Nait, I'm going to comb through Cas Cabian. It's about five hundred clicks from Fasdoba. Close enough for that scum to hide in. I appreciate the heads up on the footage. I'm going to have to be more careful."

"Sadie…" Aiden sighed sorrowfully. "Rest a little. You're telling us to focus, but you haven't let yourself recoup here at home?"

"My focus is on Morwin," Sadie said. "I'm useless here. If I'm not searching for Morwin, then that only gives him more time to find Nait or concoct another attack. I can't just sit by here only to remember what once was…"

Natasha tenderly smiled and took Sadie in a gentle hug. She held Sadie for a long time. Natasha's touch helped push back the guilt that was bubbling through. As tough as her friend was, Natasha picked the right times to show her compassion.

Sadie let go of her friend and wiped away a small tear. "I'll try to be back as soon as I can. We can all go for pints on the boardwalk."

She then walked out of Aiden's cabin and looked down the gravel path. The bushes and vines outside her cottage had gone unattended too for too long. When she got back, she would tend to them. But she would not touch the empty cabin that was once Joel's.

Sadie walked towards Veronica's cabin to bring her to Wesso, where Nait's village would feel a little more reprieve.

* * *

The physical world reappeared out of the familiar blue flash when Sadie landed back at the farm. She had just finished a visit with Nait; she brought him to a nearby town where a traditional parade was happening. The visit left her feeling happy, but a hot shower was greatly needed and definitely made her self-conscious of her hygiene. Nothing about the Jaussa heat would be getting used to.

Spring flowers bloomed in the garden beds of her cottage. Although the winters in Lohwem were nice, the springtime doubled it in beauty. Soon, the rolling pastures would somehow become greener than they already appeared. But as wonderful as the weather and scenery were, it wasn't enough to keep her there for long.

Sadie entered her cottage and gave her shirt a quick sniff test. Before she could strip down for her shower, a knock on her door was heard. When Sadie opened it, she found Lyas standing there.

"I saw you were back. I was hoping to catch you before you left again," Lyas said.

Sadie left the door open as an unspoken invitation and went to her kitchen to get a glass of water. She watched as Lyas leaned on her wall, holding the same frown he carried whenever he wanted to be serious.

"Any luck on your searches?" He asked.

"Nope," she paused to drink from her cup. "You?"

"No, nothing. I haven't even felt a gifted awaken since… Nait."

"Well, I guess that gives you more time to find Morwin, eh?" Sadie said.

Lyas stared sourly at her. She had poked the bear, but she didn't care. For all the things he said to her between Fasdoba and Nait, he deserved a little tough love.

"How long are you going to babysit, Sadie?" Lyas snapped. He was quick to reveal the true motive behind his visit.

"Until Nait asks me not to," Sadie barked back. "I don't care how long that takes. And you have no right to judge me. I've searched for Morwin in more places than you could guess."

"You are wasting your time. You are searching for a needle in a million haystacks and on top of that, Nait could be here, being trained by all of us," Lyas said.

"We've already talked about this," Sadie said sternly. "He is just a kid. He deserves a childhood, and not some false promise you believe in!"

"That was once a promise you believed in!" Lyas shouted. "You believed in our cause, and then hated it once Joel died. You can't blame yourself for his death and take it out on us."

"The only person I blame is you!" Sadie cried.

Lyas's face winced in betrayal once the words left her mouth. Although she hated Morwin for taking Joel from her, she never stopped holding Lyas against what happened. Some days, she felt unreasonable for believing so. But if it wasn't for Lyas, Joel would still be with her.

Lyas looked down mournfully at his feet. The tension between them made her want to scream. He had no right to make her feel bad for her anger. She deserved to be angry; she deserved to make him feel her hate.

"All I want for this world is to make it a better place," Lyas quietly spoke. "I thought I could gather incredible people, and make them into a family, so that we could steer Aross on a better path. Now I realize, with every passing day, how impossible that seems."

The two of them stared at each other across the room, waiting in silence for the other to share their misery. A thousand thoughts turned in Sadie's mind, wanting to scream out. The hole within her love was gaping because the man standing in front of her decided the interests for the entire family. Now all of them carried pain and grief from the suffering that happened in Fasdoba.

"I think…" Lyas paused. "I think that you've lost too much. You lost your family, you lost Joel, you lost in Fasdoba. The grief you carry cannot be denied, but I think it is clouding your judgement when it comes to the safeguarding of our family."

"Fuck you," Sadie snapped.

"I'm sorry, Sadie. I still love you, you're still my friend. I will continue to let you visit Nait, but when the time comes, when Nait loses control, I will bring him here. This family, and myself, will teach him what he should have been learning a long time ago. You can be a part of that, I hope."

Lyas turned around to face the door. She wanted to scream every obscenity at him, but the tears in her eyes and swelling of her throat forced her not to. Before he left the cabin, he turned around to speak one last time.

"Joel's death is on no one but himself. We brought him in, we gave him the tools for control, but in the end he could not endure the challenge of his own strength. What separates every person on this farm from him is that they were all able to fight through their own challenges. Even you. I know you loved him, and I can't understand what his loss means to you, but his demise was his own doing. Please, for the sake of his memory, realize where the blame falls."

Once the door shut behind him, Sadie collapsed to her kitchen floor. Tears flooded from her eyes as she crushed the water glass in her grip. The glass shards couldn't cut her skin, but she wished they had. She cried out through the pain, fighting through the endless flood of misery that had forced itself out. Nothing about her grief made sense; Lyas had made sure to tangle her own beliefs.

The memory of Joel was not meant to be tarnished. He gave everything in his will to change his life. The pure effort he showed was what made Sadie grow to love him. He didn't deserve to be remembered as a failure. The memory of him was a part of her now. It was a constant reminder in the form of a missing part of her soul. Deep down, she knew nothing would mend the wound she carried. Like their powers, the bond between them was an equal mystery. The only people that could understand what the bond meant were Joel and herself, and he was gone.

Sadie couldn't find the courage to stand. She sat crying in a pool of shattered glass and water. She needed to leave, but her body wouldn't allow it. Letting herself succumb to the grief was only good for Lyas. She wanted to be stronger. She needed to know she could fight through any pain. But she realized that the more she lost, the harder it became to believe in a future that she could save.

CHAPTER 32

Darkness surrounded him. Nothing but a pitch black canvas was there as Joel slowly opened his eyes. The silence was so loud he couldn't even hear himself breathe. Was he dead? He thought. He wasn't sure. If he was dead, his body wouldn't be feeling a frigid numbness.

As his eyes adjusted, the dark void manifested faint dots of light. With every blink, each pin of white became brighter. Stars. As dense as he ever witnessed them.

Joel couldn't comprehend if he was alive. Nothing could survive the fatal grip of outer space. At least, that's what he was taught in school. Nothing was meant to live in a vacuum, but yet he was different.

He tried to stay as still as possible, waiting to be yanked into some corporeal afterlife or endless sleep. He was too scared to move. It reminded him of when he had dreams of monsters standing over his bed, and any sudden, slight movement made them strike. There was a mounting tension that could not be denied.

In his peripheral, through the visor, entered a bright curve from the top of his eyes. With each second, the curve grew wider. The curve lowered itself down his sight until it became a hemisphere, painted crystal blue with wisps of white. The hemisphere descended further until it became a full circle. Puzzled with masses of green and brown, Joel slowly realized he was facing a planet.

Was it Aross? He knew he threw himself into orbit, but the pictures he had seen of his home, captured by astronauts, looked entirely different. This planet was dominated by land; he could only spot a few large bodies of water. Maybe he was fed a lie? How were they supposed to challenge the view of Aross from space?

The blue and green circle eventually sunk past his vision. At that point, Joel knew he was floating. He twitched his muscles slightly to test himself. Nothing happened. He then looked around and relocated the planet. When he took in more of his surroundings, he found two, then four moons, circling the grand marble. He couldn't see any blinking lights, like the ones he would watch back at home. Satellites soared the sky of Aross in droves, so he should have been able to spot at least one here. But as time went by, he couldn't find anything.

Joel was still convinced he was dead. He was floating in purgatory. But the sphere in front of him teased him with curiosity. Joel lightly let streams pulse from his hands. He could feel his body move in motion, but it was difficult to tell if he was gaining any distance. As he increased the intensity, the planet slowly grew larger in his vision.

FORREST L. RICHARD

Clouds, coasts, and continents became easier to make out in detail as the marble grew. Eventually, it was expanding too quickly, and he adjusted himself to slow down. He took a minute to realize how natural it felt to move himself through a vacuum.

The circle soon enveloped his entire perspective. He pointed himself feet first towards what he believed was downwards. He could see streams form beneath his feet, quickly heating to jets of fire. This was the atmosphere. The fire wasn't painful, but he slowed himself further so his clothes and shoes wouldn't melt off.

A roaring sound returned to his ears as clouds flew past his head, starting from thin sheets to billowing giant pillows. The ground beneath his feet enlarged with each second. Soon, the darkness of space only could be seen above his head, and the horizon of the planet consumed his surroundings. He felt he was falling too fast again; he released more pulse to match the fall.

Past the clouds revealed mountain ranges with snowy peaks, vibrant blue rivers that crawled through the ground like a nervous system, and rusty brown land with green patches that stretched in every direction. There were no roads, no buildings, and no people. This was not Aross.

The ground beneath Joel's feet flurried with wind and mist as he lowered himself to the ground. He was landing on a rocky outcrop, sitting on top of a hill that overlooked fields of rivers and rust. When he guessed he was only a few inches from the ground, he cut off the power to the pulse that lifted him. The dirt below him was soft, cushioning the short fall. Upon a closer look, he realized the ground was a reddish and brown moss. It stretched in every direction. Green bundles that resembled more moss popped out at random, giving the land a dotted vibrancy. Joel could feel the moisture seep out under his feet.

Joel looked up and across the landscape. He didn't feel dead. The land all around him felt incredibly real. If this was hell or purgatory, it was empty and alien. The mountains looked similar from the ranges back home, if not a little rounder. The moss fields were unlike anything he had ever seen. When he looked up towards the sky, he noticed the atmosphere had tinges of pink and orange. The clear blue skies of his home were absent. The silhouettes of moons filled the hemisphere; some were close enough to make out individual craters. Looking down at the wet moss carpet, he spotted tiny insects that did not exist in his memory.

Then it clicked for Joel. This was alien. There was no banishment to hell or death; he had only brought himself to another planet somewhere in the universe. He felt too alive for anything else to make sense. He threw himself into the vacuum and was carried to an alien world. His plan to kill himself in the cold void had failed.

He had tried to kill himself. He left Aross because the pain had become unbearable. Pain from killing an entire city, and the pain from killing Sadie. Flashes of the explosion rocked through his mind. He remembered being restrained, forced to submit his mind. He fought back but had succumbed to the flurry of rage so he could protect himself. In the fallout, the family, the city of Fasdoba, and the woman he had grown to love, became consumed by the rage.

The embrace of Sadie's bond was gone. It was an empty wound that sat like a rock in his soul. The bond was there to remind him she was alive, but he was the culprit who ripped it out. The chance to start over, to make up for the shit he had done, was extended and stolen in quick succession. This is what he deserved. He would never experience the comfort of love and his only cure was death.

But he couldn't even grant himself death. Joel had hurled the surrender of his life into an empty void, hoping it would lay him in an infinite and endless grave. Not even space would kill him. It allowed him to live, bringing him to an otherworldly place. Death was not deserved, a lifetime of suffering was.

Joel forced his helmet open and sucked back the first breath of air. It tasted sour and humid. Moisture rested over the pores of his face, letting him feel the warm touch of the climate. With each breath, he expected his lungs to be poisoned. But even with the strong taste of sour gas and wet dirt, it was revealed he could even survive the air of an alien world.

Joel collapsed to his knees, letting the squeeze of numbness take hold. Death was an impossible dream. No matter how hard he tried, he could not take his own life. His body shook, his eyes welled with tears. Joel's whole life he had suffered, and he knew he tried so many times to change it. Suffering was his destiny. Every attempt to gain control was either denied or stolen. Tears streamed down his face, dripping into the brown moss below. His eyes locked ahead, blankly staring through nothingness. His throat swelled, making it difficult to breathe. He wanted to cry out, but he felt too weak to do so.

He sat there, ignorant to the new planet around him, yielding to anguished rigidity. There was nothing else for him to do but rot. Joel did not rest. He felt the onslaught of memories beat him down into a pathetic shell of a body. He was alone. The only company he had was the chatter of alien bugs call into the pink skies above.

* * *

Hours, or a whole day, passed by. Joel wasn't sure. Time passed differently here. He could feel it in his bones. Joel felt the urge to move. He had spent enough time marinating in his own misery. Whatever he was going to do, he had no destination in sight. He could try to find some semblance of reason on this planet, or he could throw himself into space again and hope for the best.

Nevertheless, he was tired of sitting. Joel stood from the ground, feeling the dampness on his clothes cling to his skin. In front of him was an endless field of moss. Behind him, a wall of mountains. He pointed towards the snowy peaks and walked without haste. The only semblance of life he came across were more tiny bugs and red fish that skimmed the surface of the creeks they swam in. With each step he took, his boots became more and more soaked. It didn't help that he had giant holes carved into the bottom of them, but it was better than going barefoot.

It wasn't until the third hill he scaled he heard a low, booming drone. He instinctively dropped his body close to the ground. The sound had come from the direction of the mountains. Joel held still, keeping himself lowered and ready. A few minutes passed until the sound echoed out across the land again. Joel crawled closer to the top of the hill, looking toward the mountains.

At the base of a sharp faced mountain cliff, Joel could see stones and boulders rolling down. Was it an earthquake? Another loud drone called out, and the mountain moved. Tremors grew under his feet as the mountain rose.

The mass that was rising took form. Rocks, gravel, and dust rolled off its body and pelted the ground below. The beast stretched itself out, nose to trail, encompassing the enormous distance of three mountains, side-by-side. Its skin was dark and dusty. Joel couldn't see any eyes; if there were any, they were incredibly

Forrest C. Richard

small. Six enormous paddle fins flapped out from under its body, stretching further than Joel could have guessed. The creature rose higher, grunting more droning noises. The ground stirred with each flap it took to soar higher.

Joel tried to comprehend what was in front of him. The creature was something straight out of an imaginative mind. It seemed too impossibly big to exist. With each flap, it dominated more and more of the sky. Every call it boomed echoed across the mossy land. It was beautiful. It was a leviathan. It was a whale.

The whale split the clouds apart as it accelerated. Wherever it was going, it would reach the destination fast. Joel wanted to get closer and spotted a large hill close to him. He could get a better view there. To close the distance, Joel launched himself into the air with a short but strong pulse. Before he reached the hilltop, he eased his landing with another pulse. He needed to catch up before the whale was completely gone from his sight.

Joel ran the remaining distance to the hilltop and immediately, in his sight, at the base of the hill, was a large and shiny metal object that absolutely looked abnormal to the rest of the planet. Its body was entirely chrome and looked like an outstretched starfish.

Beside the object, tiny in comparison, was a person. At least they looked like a person to Joel. They had the shape of one. The person-thing had a dark skin, or shell. It had the head of a bug, antenna and all. It wore a long coat with similar make to the chrome of the metal object. The beetle-like creature was standing by a thin, shiny tripod with a long scope.

Before Joel could finish slowing himself to a stop, the chrome object trilled two short hums. The beetle man turned its head towards Joel's direction, and in an almost instant succession, it spun its body and drew something from its belt.

The ground exploded beneath Joel's feet, shattering rocks and moss into a messy cloud. Joel's body was blown backwards with the blast. He was thrown down the wet hillside, rolling vigorously, with debris falling from the sky. Joel tried to stop himself, but the blast had stunned every useful sense. As Joel's body came to a halt, the sudden realization that he was just attacked rushed his adrenaline. He ordered his helmet to form, but noticed it was already on. It must have snapped over right after the explosion. He knew he needed to act fast, but was torn between either running or fighting back. There was no expecting what an alien could do to him.

Over the crest of the hill rose the chrome star. It released a series of hums as it raised higher in the air. Pink sunlight reflected off the chrome body; each point of its star shape glinted with deadly sharpness. It was a ship, Joel believed. Either that or some other creature all together. There were no jets or signs of propulsion lifting it, but the ground beneath it sprayed mist and wind. The ship floated with a haunting grace and silence, setting cold, unseen eyes upon him. Regardless, he needed to act fast as the ship pointed towards Joel and let out a low hum.

Joel pounced to his feet and raised an arm with an open palm, pointed directly at the chrome star. If they wanted to attack him, they were going to feel the full force of a plasmic knife. The ring in his hand vibrated, about to unleash, until Joel spotted movement in the corner of his eye. Near the top of the hill was a blur of the beetle man. Before Joel could turn and shoot, the ground exploded at his feet again. Joel was sent flying like a ragdoll. Through the crippling shock, he was feeling annoyed at this alien's audacity.

Joel's back hit the soft red moss. He wouldn't give the beetle another chance. Launching onto one knee, Joel braced his arm and pointed towards the alien beetle man. He heard a sharp hum come from the chrome ship in the sky, and in a second it released a pulse from its nose. Joel's sense and sight immediately went black the moment it hit him.

CHAPTER 33

Joel awoke with a pounding headache and an immediate impulse to protect himself. He kicked himself backwards, hoping to gain space between whatever had just attacked him, only to feel hard steel rattle against his back. His helmet bounced off the metal, echoing a high pitch ring in his ears. When he oriented himself, he looked up and found the alien crouching in front of him.

All four of the creature's black, marbled eyes stared directly at Joel. Its arms rested on its pointy knees, baring its long, dark, shelled fingers. It held no weapon. Joel wasn't about to take any chances. As he raised his hand to defend himself, the alien held up its palms towards Joel. The alien was still and did not try to run or attack first. Its black eyes showed no expression, but Joel felt an odd gaze of curiosity overwhelm the space between them. Amongst humans, a surrender would have been the understanding. But this was an alien. Joel wasn't sure how to react. He waited, but remained ready. The creature's antennas bobbed as it tilted its head, watching Joel. Hidden mandibles along its jaw opened and rubbed together.

They were in a well lit room, surrounded by slanted chrome walls and terminals with illuminated screens. On one side of him were four hallways and a seat that faced a blank, solid wall. On the other was a ramp that led down to a lawn of red and brown moss. The chrome star was a ship; finer details of the interior were difficult to make out as his focus held firm on the alien. The ramp to the outside called for him to make a run for an escape.

A light chorus of clicking noises sang from what must have been the insect man's mouth. It slowly rolled a pea sized cylinder up between two gangly fingers, and very slowly the alien extended its hand out towards Joel, offering him to take the object. Joel didn't want it, but the alien's intention had surprisingly turned from attacking him to showing him this trinket. He wondered if it was poison or a weapon that could hurt him. He continued to anxiously wait, but the alien would not relinquish the trinket. What was the worst that could happen to him? He thought.

Joel quickly reached forward and snatched the item from the alien's hand. Nothing happened when it fell into his grip. It only began to softly vibrate when the alien made more clicking noises. The insect man tilted its head down and pointed to one of its antennae; although it was difficult to see, Joel spotted a similar cylinder at the base of where it pointed. It trilled a short series of clicks and continued to motion towards its antennae.

"I don't know what to do!" Joel accidentally blurted. The completely empty gap in communication made his anxiety worse. The thing obviously wanted to talk, but Joel didn't speak in bug. Joel decided he had enough and shot himself up from the steel floor. He continued to face the alien, walking backwards down the ramp. He held his hand up, ready to blow the alien into pieces. The creature didn't pursue him; it only turned to face Joel and continued to point to the small item on its head.

Halfway down the ramp his curiosity got the better of him. He still held the item in his hand, and the alien hadn't attacked him yet. The trinket must have a function for communicating. To Joel, that was impossible, but a small part of him nudged him to try.

Spurred by the moment, Joel foolishly collapsed his helmet and held the cylinder to his forehead. The alien tilted its head again, probably surprised by the reveal of his true face. As it clicked again, Joel felt the item vibrate in stronger waves. Still, he felt nothing. The alien continued to point towards its antenna.

Frustrated, Joel moved the item to the back of his earlobe. The item stuck to his skin like a suction cup. This was his last attempt; after that, he was leaving. The alien clicked in a patterned sequence. Joel knew the attempt had failed until a familiar sound brushed his hearing.

"...Ja..." His hearing resonated. Joel stepped back in disbelief. Was the item working on him?

"...Ja..nak..." Joel heard. The item vibrated with each click, but the sound came from the alien's buggish mouth. The alien noticed Joel's surprise and turned its finger to its chest.

"Janak," it said.

The word was unknown, but it was easy to assume by its body language that the alien was saying its name. How it could be translated was completely baffling. This moment gave Joel the opportunity to entertain this wild dream. He knew he could run; he could put this encounter far behind him. But a deep part of him wanted to try something else.

"Joel," He said, as Joel pointed towards his chest.

The alien pointed a finger towards Joel and uttered quick ticks. "...Joel."

Joel nodded. He collapsed his readied hand and pointed back towards the alien. "Janak."

The alien mirrored Joel's nod. "Janak."

Joel lowered his arm and exhaled a strained breath. This alien's intentions were past hurting him. It wanted to talk. The edge to defend himself offered a moment to relax. If this Janak wanted to talk, Joel would talk. But at any moment it showed a sliver of hostility, Joel would make sure to send it to its grave.

"...No... *click click click*... no ha... *click*... no harm," The common language sounded as clear as day. Whatever technology the item functioned on, it was far beyond anything on Aross. There was no part of him that could understand how it worked, but Joel understood what Janak meant in the moment. He never thought there would be a day he could speak with an otherworldly alien.

Joel raised his palms in surrender. "No harm."

* * *

The bug man, Janak, furiously scribbled away at the glass tablet on his lap. They sat across from one another on two damp rocks. The creature had taken off its chrome jacket and wore a gray long sleeve, tucked into brown cargo pants that were rolled up at the ankles, revealing his shelled bare feet. Joel waited patiently, giving Janak time to catch up on notes he wanted to take. The sun had barely moved in the many hours of their conversation; its warmth felt nice on Joel's drenched boots.

The process that Janak used was long and tedious. Once they had identified their names and lowered the gates of aggression, they began to slowly use the translator to make his and Janak's language one. From the simplified explanation Janak gave, the translator subconsciously compared each word, conception, and structure with what available linguistic counterpart existed. Anything that the brain couldn't comprehend was translated to what Janak described as a 'universal list'. Many hiccups made the conversations slow, but with each exchange, the translator collected more and more data to make the dialogue easier. The impressive piece of technology turned what should have been a decade long challenge to a chat over coffee.

"So," Janak paused. "It's armour of an unknown entity? And not your exo-shell?"

"Right. I have no clue where it came from. The people of my planet don't share the same ability," Joel explained.

"Interesting," Janak's clicking murmured under the translator. "These abilities transported you to this planet. But you're not an explorer?"

"It's a long story," Joel said.

"I understand your reservation," Janak said. "I hope in time you will share more."

"I need you to understand this is a weird encounter for me," Joel tried to explain informatively.

"It is weird for the both of us," Janak clicked. "I have never met a species of sentience."

Joel laughed. "But you attacked me?"

Janak titled his head in confusion. "You found that funny? I apologize. My... *click click* Voidante... read a spike in energy and identified you as hostile."

"Yea, I'm sorry too. It was my abilities that I told you about," Joel said.

Janak mirrored an expressive nod that he had quickly learnt from Joel and looked down at his tablet to scribble more notes. Joel was impressed by the alien. Janak carefully took his time to understand Joel's language and meaning. Joel had learned that Janak was an explorer, and it was his duty to record every planet assigned to him. It was still a mystery to Joel where Janak came from, but the alien was quick to assure him that there was still much to reveal. A part of Joel wanted to know more of Janak's origin sooner than later, but he knew he needed to give the translator time to complete its work.

Joel looked over to the chromed ship as he waited for Janak to finish his entry. The star-shaped ship glinted sunlight so blinding that it made the hull look radiant white. He couldn't spot any windows or propulsion system, leaving him to assume the technology surpassed his imagination. It was as beautiful as the planet around it. The moons of RES 9, which is what Janak had called it, dominated the sky in their full glory. Joel was still confused as to why the sky was amber pink; the science behind it must have been something Joel missed in middle school.

"That's your ship, your Void...ante?" Joel asked.

"Yes. And also me. There is a connection. I am Voidante. The vessel is Voidante," Janak said. "I still don't understand how you traversed here without a vessel."

Joel exhaled a deep breath. It was embarrassing how little he could give this alien. "I don't know either. These abilities are a mystery to me. Even my friends didn't understand them."

"Mystery? Friends? There were others like you?" Janak said curiously.

"There were…" Joel said mournfully.

"There were, as in past tense?" The alien carefully asked.

"I killed them all, by accident," His chest weighed heavily as the words left his mouth. What left did he have to lose in a confession to a bug-man?

The Beetle stared blankly into Joel's eyes. Without eyebrows, or any familiar facial cues, it was difficult to gauge what the alien was thinking. With each second of silence, Joel waited for the anvil of the Beetle's judgement.

"By your words, you sound remorseful," Janak said.

"I don't think I've fully comprehended yet what I've done, what I lost. There was this girl, her name was Sadie. She was… important to me," Joel spoke quietly.

In a hushed and embracing voice, the Beetle reassured him. "In your grief, I share with you."

Joel nodded, trying to shake away tears building beneath his eyes. Becoming vulnerable in front of an alien made him want to fold over in embarrassment. Yet, the comfort of the Beetle's words felt good. In a universe that seemed so empty, he had somehow found someone kind enough to guide him through the atrocities committed by his hand. The empathy was undeserving.

"You shouldn't," Joel croaked. "I'm a monster."

Janak shook his head side-to-side in his exaggerated fashion. "In front of me, I see awareness of guilt. No monster wields such strength."

Janak slipped his tablet into his pant pocket and rose from the damp rock. "Now, I suggest we leave for the Seekers. I think your discovery will be of high interest to them. Their wisdom is invaluable. Maybe they could help with these abilities?"

Joel stood and shook his head. "No. I should go my separate way. I am not safe to be around."

Janak stepped towards Joel to get closer. "I disagree. You could have killed me when you awoke, yet you granted me opportunity. Does that not contradict what you believe of yourself?"

"It's not that simple," Joel frustratingly rubbed his temple. "Besides, I have no idea what you'd be bringing me into. I could be walking into a trap for all I know."

Janak tilted his head, confused. "Manipulation was left far behind in the early evolution of the Seekers. I only suggest a meeting!"

Joel groaned and waved the Beetle away. There would always be an ulterior motive with higher power. He began to walk away from the alien before Janak called out behind him.

"Do you have no interest to discover more of your universe?" The Beetle yelled.

Joel turned to face him. "I have bigger problems than searching for answers."

"Answers?" Janak pressed. "Whether it's the void or the heart of creation, you will find no answers. The universe gives no answers. It is our duty to discover what we yearn for. In the short time we have spoken, I have seen that you run from duty. You speak of loss and grief, but how long will you go until you finally turn to understand its meaning? The pain you have inherited is too great for me to fix, but I can at least try to help. As hesitant as you are, you may just discover a sliver of duty from the Seekers. Come with me. Meet them."

Joel looked up at the sky, afflicted with the decisions and doubt that exhausted him. The clouds reflected a spectrum of oranges and pinks. In the distance, one of the flying whales breached and soared at heights he couldn't possibly fathom. The universe never stopped surprising him. Why would it stop here?

"And you're just ready to leave?" Joel asked the Beetle.

Janak looked up at the flying whale. Even without facial expression, Joel knew he was filled with awe. "Although I will miss this planet, I know that what's next will be discovery beyond value. It always is, each time."

CHAPTER 34

The journey back was earlier than scheduled, but for Janak that was okay. Finding a 'Human' named Joel was an incredibly rare happenstance. It gave him more than enough reason to abandon his expedition for a briefing with The Seekers. Luckily, his time on RES 9 was already at an end, and it would be up to the drones to complete the rest of the catalogue. The planet would live on to be a jewelled discovery for The Seekers, and cherished memory of Janak's. What was left of this galaxy's unexplored corners would have to wait.

Meeting his first sentient being, on a planet that wasn't its home, was a theoretical possibility, but not on his guess of events in his lifetime. He had been preparing for this moment for his entire career; he just didn't think it would happen like this. Still, the man named Joel was an interesting and complex alien. His access to powerful abilities added to the enigma of his existence. Nothing could traverse the empty reaches of space without advanced technology, and yet Joel was proof it could be done.

Soon after Joel agreed to join Janak on the journey home, Janak began the preparations for a return trip. With their languages still intertwining in translation, it was difficult for Janak to explain the finer details of the mechanics. Without a Rail Station, closing the distance between this galaxy and The Seekers would take thirty days of the Celestvendora calendar. Joel seemed surprised when he was told that, but Janak assured him they could use that time to iron out the translator.

As they left RES 9, Janak spoke his traditional goodbyes to the planet. Its beauty, its species, gifted him valuable research for the Seeker's expansion. It was always hard to comprehend that a planet so rich like RES 9 was only a tiny drop in an ocean that was its galaxy. Space was unimaginably big, and he just happened to run into a sentient alien at impossible odds. After his mission to bring Joel to The Seekers, he could return to this galaxy to find what else it offered. But he found it difficult to look forward to that when a discovery of his lifetime sat beside him. The atmosphere roared behind them as the Voidante breached the clouds, leaving the moss, Yen and everything between behind in their wake. Goodbye was always hard, but the future compelled him forward.

As they reached the vacuum of space, Janak activated the distance engines for a jump. He tried his best to explain to Joel every step and process. The ability to fold space and time was gifted by The Seekers upon his people's discovery. The Voidante would skim the layers of reality, finding a shortcut to their destination, making a journey decrease from hundreds of light years to only a handful of days. Having a Rail Station would lessen that time by a significant amount more, but Janak was returning from the frontier of the unknown. When Janak initiated the fold, Joel made a comment that confused him. There were no visuals to see;

the fold would always be incomprehensible to the naked eye. But Joel had asked if the sensation was normal for everyone. Over the next thirty days, they work out the wrinkles between languages and stare at a starless black void.

Joel was quiet and reserved over the first few days of travel. Janak attempted many times to spark conversation, but the man always seemed to return to a withdrawn state. From what Joel told him during their first contact, Janak knew he suffered internally. For that, Janak knew to respectfully tone down his excitement to learn more. It was on the fourth day that Joel entertained Janak's curiosity.

"Division of group, culture and race is to be expected," Janak assured Joel. "It took years for my people to unite under one banner, and that was years after The Seekers revealed their existence."

"It just seems impossible to unite everyone," Joel quickly replied. "The people who live on Aross are selfish. Everyone is content when they only satisfy themselves. You could never convince them to set aside their hunger for a promise of unity."

"You're right and wrong. Out of five sentient species discovered, three have made it work with The Seekers. Only two have failed. How can you decide the failure of your species when they have yet to be given a chance?" Janak said.

"Wait, that's it?" Joel asked, disappointingly. "You guys explore a universe of billions of galaxies and have only found five races?"

Janak sighed. "Well, no. That would be a very simplified interpretation. There have been a handful of species discovered, and only five capable of understanding the Celeste Expanse, The Seekers Mission. Remember, space is ancient and ever-expanding. Even if more sentient races existed out there, what if they only existed outside our timeline? Species come and go with the ageing of the universe."

Joel held silent. With the placement of a second pilot chair, it was created behind Janak's main seat. He wished he faced him during these conversations to understand his human facial expressions.

"So what did the two races that failed, do?" Joel asked.

"They couldn't unite. Evolution led them astray down a path of violence and competition. They were far too dangerous to accept into the mission. The interesting part of both their histories is that they both live in the same solar system! Isn't that rare?"

"Sure," Joel said quietly. "So what's the catch? Were they killed?"

"What? No," Janak said. "The Seekers would never intervene like that. They simply don't have access to technology and advancement they would receive if they could unite under the Celeste Expanse. It is unfortunate, but species too violent to evolve end up wiping themselves from existence anyway."

"If The Seekers are as benevolent as you say, wouldn't it be their duty to change violent species for their survival?" Joel asked.

"The existence, and survival, of life in the universe is valuable. And The Seekers understand that. But they cannot risk the safety of every other living species with the moral obligation to allow violence to breed. So instead of helping, or intervening, they simply just leave them alone. How they survive and evolve is then up to their own actions."

"You said your home had billions of your people before The Seekers discovered them. How the hell did your people convince every single Idelvin to unite?" Joel said.

Janak pondered the question. The Idelvin fought many wars and disagreements over many generations before The Seekers. He was born after the fact, so it was difficult to imagine his people at odds. By hearing Joel's disbelief in his own species, Janak compared it to how his ancestors spoke to each other long ago.

"You have no faith in your species. I think you fail to see that life can unite under the right circumstances. The Seekers provide change so powerful it may just surprise you how your people would react. There is hope to be made, Joel," Janak said.

He could hear Joel sigh heavily. "You don't know my people. They're cruel to each other. They would do everything in their power to strip your masters of whatever value they hold."

Janak turned in his chair to face Joel. "You hold such hate for them. Even though I haven't met them, I have met you, and I believe they could change. And the Seekers are not my masters. They are guides."

An awkward silence held between them. Janak felt he had stepped out of line, but speaking a complex dialogue with a sentient alien was incredibly surreal. He had not prepared for this moment, and he could only let the conversation flow in the direction it wanted.

"I'm sorry," Joel said. "I didn't mean to offend you. I just have seen so much hate in humans. It's hard for me to believe in redemption."

Janak peacefully nodded. "That's okay, I'm sorry too. Have you thought about what you represent when you finally speak with The Seekers? Will you hold yourself as an emissary or are you here for yourself?"

"I… don't know," Joel said. "With all the pain and death I've caused on Aross, I don't think I would be a viable candidate to speak for them. Back home, I'd be considered a villain."

"So you don't want them to survive?" Janak questioned.

"No. I don't want them to die. But I don't know if I can save them. Every time I try, I just end up hurting more of them. I tried to be that guy who helps, but I just ended up killing someone who didn't deserve it — many who didn't."

"Ahead of you lies a rare choice then," Janak said. "Will you continue as a lonesome explorer of the cosmos, or bring the change you wanted in the past?"

He could hear Joel shuffle out of his pilot chair behind him and walk away from the cockpit. Janak wondered if he offended the interloper. Joel's struggles were so inherently strong that even an alien, like Janak, could see them on the surface. Janak wanted to help. Purpose and duty was a responsibility that seemed impossible to deny. He needed to understand that Joel was different.

A couple hours later, after Janak felt he had given Joel a respectable solitude, he found the alien sitting on a bench in his laboratory. His fermenter hummed across the room; its subtle vibration sang a quiet song as it stirred a batch of Bonmoc. Janak noticed Joel was holding a tablet, swiping through pictures of species catalogued throughout Janak's career as a Voidante.

"There's so much out there," Joel said. "Creatures beyond my imagination."

"But none that can comprehend their own worth. Would you like a drink?" Janak asked.

Joel looked up from the tablet to meet his eyes. "Can I even… digest it?"

"Hmm, take this pill first. It will line your stomach with assimilating enzymes and proteins," Janak explained. He grabbed two cups and filled them with the yellow spirit from his cherished fermenter. He anxiously waited for Joel's approval of the Bonmoc as he swallowed back the pill, and shortly after, took a swig from his cup.

"Gods, that's bitter. But good. Is this alcohol?" Joel asked. Janak tried to decipher his satisfaction through his complex facial expressions. Joel's whole face seemed to twist and squint.

"Yes, a drink reserved for gatherings, celebration and contentment. I made this batch myself, but it will never match the purity you could find on Ceyillin, my home planet," Janak said. He dragged a chair over to sit and face Joel to enjoy the spirit together.

Joel looked into his glass, swirling it in circles. "Thank you for sharing with me. I'm sorry, for earlier, I let my emotions take the better of me. I speak so unkindly of my species; it's probably not what you had expected on your first contact with an alien."

"You don't need to be sorry," Janak said. "Forgive me for overstepping, but the blame you hold on yourself, and humans, carries a deeper weight. You have mentioned loss a couple times since we've met. The one you lost; her name was Sadie?"

Joel sighed deeply. "I didn't know her for very long. But in the short time she entered my life, she taught me a love I thought I'd never experience. Through her eyes, I saw a world where I could fit into. I could share her hope. I could finally find a purpose. All of that was ripped from me, and it was my own fault."

"And what was this hope you speak of?" Janak said.

"Even with the mistakes we both made in the past, she could still find hope in herself and the people who need it. She knew we could do better with the goodness in us," Joel said.

"How does this idea not correlate to what you experience now? Do you not hold on to those beliefs in her memory?" Janak asked carefully.

Joel locked eyes with Janak. "She believed that good could persevere, and was killed for trusting so. People like her work so hard to prove the world can change, only to be disappointed by realities cycle of misery. If Sadie survived, she would still see hope within. I am not Sadie."

"No, you are not. You are Joel," Janak said. "And at one point, Sadie showed you the cycle can break."

Joel took a hesitant swig from his glass and mournfully looked down at his feet. Speaking of loss was difficult, and vulnerable. If humans shared any range of emotion like the Idelvin, then Janak knew the torment that pulled at Joel's heart. His words were enough to show him of the pain Joel suffered.

"We carry one's memory by the hope they shared," Janak said. "Tell me, what did Sadie see in humans that you cannot?"

Joel quietly nodded as he thought. His eyes darted as Janak watched him find an answer. "She could see the innocence in people. But the older one gets, the more innocence they lose."

Janak breathed out slowly. "Yet, I see yours."

CHAPTER 35

"We will exit the fold in five minutes," Janak hollered from the cockpit. "You should buckle in."

Joel quickly tied off the last stitch on the shoulder of his jacket he was repairing and tossed it into a garment locker. He jogged over to the copilot seat behind Janak and pulled the crossed straps over his chest. Before he reached for the gimballed arm to view the exterior cameras, Janak speedily pressed a few buttons on his command console and a large screen took form on the hull in front of them. Multiple angles from the ship's exterior began to broadcast, only showing the pitch-black fold around them and the speck of light that was their destination.

Joel had lost track of the amount of days that had passed on their journey. Janak assured him it was thirty-two, but from his calendar. Without a watch or proper sleep schedule, Joel had no clue how to figure out how many of his days he lost. To kill time on the return, Joel learned a couple of board games from Janak's people, ironed out the translation between their languages, and talked about the many planets the Beetle had visited. Joel felt comfortable around his alien pilot. Janak had made the bizarre shock of his predicament feel natural enough for him to feel engaged. The many opportunities to learn more of the alien's life was a good distraction from the grief that haunted him. He could easily fall into it's grip, but the Beetle and his ship offered an open book of knowledge Joel could escape into. Now he was only minutes away from meeting the beings that Janak basically worshipped.

"The Seekers, they will be able to understand me, right?" Joel asked.

"Oh yes," Janak said. "Once we exit the fold, your language will be uploaded to the network, and your translator will download every other language in the Celeste Lexicon. You'll be able to talk with every species that is part of the expanse. But speaking with the Seekers will be much easier as they communicate telepathically."

Joel wasn't aware of that detail. Thoughts of a trap and betrayal began to graze the back of his mind. He had no intention to let anyone violate his memories ever again. These Seekers could have an ulterior plan with him; force him into submission or pick away at his brain. He could wear his helmet, and have Janak translate for him. That would be the safest option. The darkest parts of his mind screamed danger; he wished he was told this before he set foot on the ship.

"Is there a way I can speak with them that's not telepathy?" Joel asked carefully.

Janak turned in his chair to look at him. "We could get a translator, I guess. But why would you? It's a great honour to speak with the Seekers on a pure tether."

Janak turned back to face the broadcast after Joel shrugged. He felt he could trust the Beetle, but it would be stupid of Joel not to remain vigilant. The meeting with the Seekers quickly approached them; Joel only had moments to decide what he was going to do.

"Exiting the fold, now," Janak said. As he pressed away at his console, a loud descending noise echoed through the ship. The prick of light at the centre of the broadcast exploded into a bushel of stretched light. Every star they faced extended into thousands of bright strands, racing to return to their place in the void. The tail-end of each line followed shortly behind, leaving the lone prick of light behind in their wake and glittering the pure black canvas into a celestial painting of starlight. As each strand compressed to a stationary speck that was their star, the universe materialized in the blink of an eye.

Giant structures immediately filled the horizon as they exited the fold. The ship lurched forward, but Joel barely noticed it. What he faced, as he watched on the broadcast, left him in awe. The ship was flying towards a large planet, completely enveloped by a greyish blue casting and surrounded by dozens of moons of a similar hue. In every direction ran what looked like bridges, or wires, but in impossible sizes and lengths. In a satisfying pattern, they hovered above the planet's surface and stretched into the far depths of space. Each bridge pulsed with blue flashes and a deep red fog, casting an ominous perception of a godlike web.

The space around them held no likeness to the dark void. Millions of stars, each casting colours across the spectrum, filled the surface of an infinite background. Some clusters were so close together Joel felt overwhelmed just trying to make sense of how many he was actually looking at. Beautiful nebulae filled and intertwined the gaps between the stars. Their dark purple and blue glow were incredibly vibrant among the blinding starlight. The dense collection of radiance almost removed any existence of space's black emptiness; everything here was illuminated by what Joel thought was impossible. The beauty was terrifying.

"This is the Seekers' home?" Joel said. His eyes stayed locked on the broadcast.

"This IS the Seekers," Janak said, gesturing his dark, shelled hand towards the entirety of the horizon. The alien swiped a galaxy spanning map onto the wide screen they faced. A blinking dot showed Joel where they were for context. They were at the centre of a massive celestial wheel. "The Seekers are one being, with a collective mind. Their reach encompasses this entire galaxy."

"Nothing that big can exist. That's impossible," Joel said sternly.

"But it exists in front of you," Janak said. "Their body, their mind, their soul, all exist within every system part of this galaxy. No star or matter goes without function. Everywhere you look is part of the celestial body the Seekers evolved into."

Joel could feel the gears grinding in his mind. To fathom the extent of their existence overwhelmed him. To achieve such a task must have taken millions of years, maybe billions. "So what is this planet here?"

"This planet that you see is a waystation for Voidante. One of fifty. They are used to upload the mass of data we collect after every expedition. Here you will meet the Seekers at a contact node," Janak explained.

The chromed ship soared towards the station, passing between the enormous bridges in their methodical glory. As they approached the planet's surface, Joel could see that the entire terrain had been transformed into a mechanized environment. There were no natural formations, oceans, or rivers. Only intersections and lines of trenches, each with a purpose unknown to him. The atmosphere held no clouds or disturbances, except for the glitter of the chromed hulls of other Voidante entering and leaving the station. Their star-shaped ships flew with an extraordinary grace Joel had yet to witness; each one carrying an explorer like Janak, to discover the infinite unknown. The beauty of his surroundings was difficult to fully appreciate as they neared their destination. Once they landed, Joel would be forced on his decision to speak with the creators of this terrifying system or flee.

Janak pointed the nose of the ship towards a towering cliff face that seemed to stretch on forever. Above it sat a completely flat and silver plateau with antenna scattered across its field in the dozens. Joel could see wide vents etched into the steep cliff face. He guessed it was their landing bay, as many Voidante ships flew in and out at safe speeds. But Janak didn't fly them into the bay like the others. Instead he flew the ship above the cliff face and banked towards a large silver disk. The hull vibrated and quietly groaned as Janak brought them to a slow brake. He landed his ship in the middle of the silver disk with ease and unbuckled from his seat the moment the landing gear touched the surface.

Joel turned in his seat to watch the ramp open near the back of the ship. As the door lowered, he could see the flat, metal surface stretched long past the horizon, only broken by the ominous, pointed antenna in their separated spaces. He watched as Janak walked towards the ramp, looking back to see if Joel would follow. The impending hand was closing on him. Would he trust his gut? Joel thought. Or would he fall into the workings of sinister motives, again?

Joel unbuckled from his pilot chair and slowly walked towards the ramp. His helmet snapped over his head the moment he willed it. His eyes stayed locked on the surface, waiting for something to meet him. He carefully stepped down the ramp and found Janak pulling a thick hose out from the ship's belly. The Beetle yanked the hose downwards and plugged it into an outlet carved into the ground that misted thick cold fog.

"I'm just uploading my archive," Janak said. He pointed towards the edge of the landing pad that overlooked the cliff face. Voidante ships flashed like fireflies as they flew across, catching the sun's reflection. A blue night sky chased the warm starlight above his head. The planet's red sun was beginning to descend into the horizon, but failed to dull the dominating veil of stars and purple nebula clouds that filled the background of space.

"Why do you wear your helmet?" Janak's question shook Joel out of the fleeting gaze into the sunset. "Do you not wish to speak with The Seekers?"

"I... I don't trust this," Joel stuttered.

Janak stood from the hose and placed his buggish hand on Joel's shoulder. "I will not pressure you, friend. If it is your decision, I will translate the gap, but please consider the experience you face."

Janak's antenna bobbed as he motioned towards the cliff face. Joel followed him as they walked from under the chrome body and approached a waist high block that raised from the edge of the disk. Joel let himself peek down the face of the cliff, immediately knowing this was the highest height he has ever stood upon.

He became dizzy, as the drop was so steep and wide his balance mistook it for the surface he should have been standing on. The faint gravity of the planet didn't help.

Joel stepped back from the edge and joined Janak at the block. Janak nodded at him, then placed his hand on the block. The alien took a few steps back, promoting Joel to do the same. They watched as a red, fleshy spike raised from the block's surface and continued to rise higher up, slowly expanding in width. As it reached twenty feet, the spike blossomed and grew multiple branches across its entire trunk. Each branch stretched outwards, growing smaller branches in every direction until the space it occupied was full. Every branch then exploded with thousands of velvet needles, sharply pointed with ruby tips. The object towered above them, standing defiantly in front of the glittered sunset. Its shape held rigidity and a semblance of intent. But it was familiar, in the shape of a tamarack tree from back home. A tree that Joel loved and missed. When the flesh tree ceased its growth, every needle across its body slowly pointed towards Joel and Janak. The trunk of the tree hummed with a low whistle and pulsed as if it was breathing air for the first time. The tree held life. Life so evolved its reach encompassed an entire galaxy. And standing before all its might and knowledge was a scared man with no direction in the chaotic path of destruction he had sent himself on. It was so absurd Joel could laugh. But he was tired, and distrustful. No decision felt right to make.

Joel felt a hand lightly pat between the back of his shoulders. Janak stood beside him, encouraging him to press onwards in the supernatural convocation he had found himself in. His bug-eyed stare felt comforting, despite its murky gloss. "I will translate for you. What would you like to say?" Janak asked.

Joel looked back at the red tree, canvassing its shape from the trunk and upwards. Using Janak as a translator was the safe option. He promised himself no creature or being would pierce his mind ever again, but he had found an unexpected trust with Janak. He gave the Beetle the opportunity to break the barrier of speech. Now he was at the feet of whom Janak held immense respect for. Joel's paranoia only served himself. If the universe wanted him dead or dominated, it had gone to extreme lengths to get him here. The conflict in his mind rammed into itself; if he wanted death, why did he fight so hard against it? Maybe he was too tired to care, maybe he was done fighting the universe's plan.

The helmet collapsed in its hidden fold as Joel willed it. He could feel Janak's surprise just as a warm air enveloped the skin of his face. His mind felt caressed with open arms; every inch of Joel's restraint fought to hold fast, keeping his helmet at bay. If The Seekers sought death, it came in the design of a sedative embrace. Joel waited for whatever was to come.

CHAPTER 36

"Welcome, Joel Robson," a brilliant voice sang throughout Joel's mind. He could feel his soul tremble with a devastating intensity and quickly submit into an embrace that was promised without words. He had wished there was warning for this alarming experience, however it was manageable as he gained composure.

"It is a pleasure being in the presence of a unique explorer," the voice resonated. "I am The Celestvendora. You may call me The Seekers, if it aids you."

Joel vigorously shook his head as he found balance beneath the soles of his feet. The scarlet tree filled his vision in its towering might. Joel knew he could shift his focus, turn away from the connection, but the celestial presence held an intoxicating gravity.

"I'm sorry," Joel stuttered. "I didn't expect this... feeling."

The Seeker's voice fluttered across his mind. "I understand. Every species reacts differently to this technology. If you need more time, we can delay..."

"No," Joel interrupted. "I'm okay. I just needed to regain myself." He looked up at the tree, unsure where to lay his eyes. He wasn't even sure if he was speaking out loud or only through his mind.

The tree hummed as its trunk gently twisted. "Your first contact with Voidante Janak is a rare event. He has spoken very highly of you. Discovering a sentient species is a phenomenal achievement of the highest honour among his guild. I hope you can appreciate the effort he has pursued to bring you here."

"I do," Joel said. He looked over at the Beetle, and hastily returned his gaze to the tree's gravitation. Suspicion creeped up his spine as he questioned its dominant aura. "He's kind. And a friend."

"He has done well in preparing you with our universal dialect. Your language is most interesting, and highly complex. Please forgive me for any errors during our exchange."

Joel strained the back of his eyes as he fought against the psychic tide. Summoning his helmet would be easier. "You seem to be speaking it just fine."

Silence held between them as Joel's suspicion grew. He wanted to trust the assuring embrace. Its presence was too kind. His mind raced between trust and doubt, placing him in the middle of a conscious game of tug-o-war. He knew the Seekers were aware. He could feel their godly stare. Were any of his thoughts his? Or were they placed there by the intruder?

"Joel…" A soft voice rang. "I know you do not trust me. The intensity of the connection goes away with submission."

Joel snapped a deadly stare up at the red tree. Intentions would always surface with time. "You want me to submit? You want to use me like everyone else?"

"No," the voice cut defiantly. "I only wish to understand you."

Joel's breath raced with the tipping scale of his impending choices. This situation was too surreal, like a sick nightmare he couldn't wake from. Where he placed trust, or hate, he would always fall down the destructive path. Whether it was his mother, Lyas, Morwin or Sadie, he brought it all down with fire and torment. There was no escaping what the universe planned for him. He could fly millions of light years away and still find himself at the feet of a deceiver. The only one whose intentions were pure was Sadie. The brief time they had together had left its deep scar. She would wish him to trust again. The love they shared would follow him to the centre of another galaxy, and each thought of her brought a gentler breath.

Joel studied the red tree and each branch that faced him. He took a long and deep breath, held it in his full lungs, and exhaled slowly. The tempest in his mind flattened to calm waters. His mind submitted, and the tree's gravity returned his vision to its natural will.

"I can try," Joel said.

The tree hummed like a graceful wind. Empathy washed over his entire body. The Seekers had kept their word. "Creatures of sentience would not hold their rarity if it weren't for their complexity. A mind that yearns for purpose will always fight against itself. I understand the labour of your battle."

"My distrust isn't personal," Joel said. "I am not here as an explorer. I never meant to place myself in this predicament in the first place."

"Expectations for this meeting were never written," The Seekers said. "If you wish to continue speaking, we can start with the simple stuff."

Joel chuckled at its wit. He slowly paced across the tree's base, studying its composition and motions. A slight tinge of embarrassment pricked him for his outburst. Asking any question could break the awkwardness he created. He motioned with his hand at the tree's structure. "So is this your body? Or part of it?"

"No, I have no body. My consciousness is spread within a physical-based network across this entire galaxy. But many species within our collective refer to the galaxy as my body. What you see in front of you is only a communicating node; a design to create a telepathic link to ease the overwhelming input," The Seekers explained.

Joel found it funny that this was what they considered easier. "But why does it take the shape of a tree?"

The Seekers hummed in question. "I can see the resemblance, but it's unintentional. Does it resemble a tree from your home?"

"Yea, something like that."

"Alright. Question for a question," The Seekers said. "I have studied the data Janak had gathered on you. Everything I know about your species has been through your personal knowledge. Do you possess an archive with you of your people's history? To help me better understand human's nature?"

"I got nothing," Joel replied.

The tree's hum dropped disappointingly. "I see. Forgive me if this comes as any offence, but your perspective comes as rather cynical. Do all humans possess your beliefs?"

Joel scoffed to himself. The alien wasn't wrong. Joel had no patience for his kind; he hated them. "I've known a few people who believe in good, in worth, but that belief tends to bring disappointment when everything comes crashing down."

"Is failure and disappointment controlled within your society?" The Seekers asked.

Joel's mind grinded. "Well... no, maybe sometimes," He said.

"So where does the motivation to enact good come from?"

Joel let out a long breath as he thought about the question. "Some people just have morals, I guess. If they can avoid evil deeds, then they can believe they still hold honour."

The crimson branches shifted slightly. "Is there benefit, or reward, for honour?"

"No. Just the people closest to you see the effort. They see you're a good person," Joel replied. "Now it's my turn. Why are you searching the universe? What's the goal for adopting species into this 'Celeste Expanse'?"

"My purpose is to find civilizations in the ever-expanding void of space and ensure their survival," The Seekers hummed. "The universe is chaotic, and growing, and it has no consideration for what it has created. I want to preserve all life, simple or unique, and ensure they have the tools to advance into their full potential."

Joel nodded his head, dissecting each part of the answer. "Okay, but there are races out there that you have knowingly chosen to avoid?"

"Yes," The tree sang. "The Yvern and Falleg. Both live in violent desires, and have refused any cooperation for the betterment of their evolution. If they were given my technology they would pose tremendous risk to other civilizations. Because of that, I only observe from afar, and leave them to their own engagements."

"So you get to decide what is and what's not too violent? Right?" Joel pressed.

"I sense accusation of hypocrisy," The Seekers gently said. "I can understand that perspective. Joel, I am four and a half billion years old. I've been through five drastic evolutionary changes, extinction events, wars, and everything the universe has created to wipe my existence. But with each endeavour, I survived and adapted. I realized there is potential in advancement, and an endless frontier to explore. If you could, why wouldn't you want to see the infinite creation untouched? To see and find the persistent life that exists? My purpose is to ensure other civilizations have the same opportunity. Their survival depends on it. But if violent nature cannot be overcome, then I am forced, by my principle, to withhold until that nature evolves into one of purpose."

"And my species?" Joel challenged. "Would they be given the same opportunity?"

"Do you have faith they could?" The Seekers said.

Joel thought he knew his answer, however, as he opened his mouth he thought about the truth in his perspective. Good people existed, like Sadie. They would advocate for humanity, because they truly believed in them. Joel wasn't a good person. His whole life he tried to change that. But with each doubt in himself, all he could feel was Sadie's belief in him.

"I... I don't know," Joel stuttered.

A consoling cry washed over Joel's erratic thoughts. It felt apologetic; all the grief he carried must have been felt by The Seekers. Opening these emotions and questions of humanity exhausted him. The tree's voice arose as it composed its next question. "For my curiosity, how did you possess an ability to traverse the distance of space? Without technology?"

It wasn't the question, but why the alien was asking, that puzzled Joel. The Seekers already had the ability Joel possessed and used to get here. They created the ability long before him. "Well... A part of me was hoping you could tell me that."

"How so?" The Seeker asked.

"You're a galaxy-wide hive mind," Joel felt confused about the point he was trying to make. "How have you created this much, and ask me that question?"

The tree hummed defiantly. "The question comes from innocence of the unknown. I only asked how you achieved a great feat, without a vessel. Your methods could be completely different from our own."

Joel could feel his skin become hot. His anger was unjustified, but felt deserved nonetheless. "You're telling me, after this entire living galaxy that you created and the billions of years you lived, that you can't tell me why I have these abilities? If anyone knows why I'm like this, it's you!"

"I can sense I upset you," The Seekers said calmly. "Perhaps we can re-centre on a different question."

"No... No!" Joel yelled. "I deserve an answer! I never asked for these abilities. They came unto me without warning or an explanation. All they have ever done for me is fury my anger and destroy everything around me. I tried so hard to learn control, but it's hopeless. Do you understand how many people I've hurt? Who I've killed? I killed the only woman who believed I could have a purpose. She taught me I still existed beneath what I could wield; that I could use this power to save others and be a man of a good heart. But like the rest of my fucked up life, these powers reminded me who I am. Nothing. I am meant to suffer. The only solution is my death. I know you can feel this. I know you can feel my pain. How do you not know why I am like this?!"

"You expect me to have an answer to your mystery?" The Seekers asked.

"Yes! Look at what you've achieved, what you have created! You have surpassed an advancement that I thought, what humanity has thought, to have been impossible. You are billions of years old, with knowledge born far before life existed on my planet. You should have the answers to the universe. You should know why I have these powers! I need to know. I deserve to understand why I am like this," Joel yelled. His mind scattered with the boiling rage he let loose. His eyes and body strained with the anger that demanded answers. This ancient alien needed to have this knowledge. How much farther would he have to cross in the universe to find the answer?

The tree sang in remorse. "I had no idea you felt so passionate about this interest. I believed you carried answers to the nature of your powers; they are unlike anything I've seen in a species, despite what has been achieved across time. I never meant to offend you."

"That's not good enough!" Joel screamed. "You're a god! Look at what you've made! How can you not explain why I have these powers? Answer me!"

A deep breath soared across the branches that faced him. "The evolution of life is chaotic, but it has a destination. One that's infinite and defiant, beyond our ability to control. Despite my advancement, I have no choice where the universe leads me. It's on a path that will never be altered, and we just have to survive through it. Have you ever considered that maybe you have these abilities... for no reason? That you are the way you are without a guiding path that brought you here?"

Joel's mind sunk to its depths. His remaining crumbs of hope died as he realized there would be no answers to his misery. Tears pooled beneath his eyes and mourned for the purpose he desperately wanted his entire life. "I can't accept that," Joel cried. "I cannot accept that."

"I am sorry, Joel," The Seeker said. "I can feel your grief. I know you didn't want this life. I understand why you would be angry when you felt so close to the explanation you deserve. But some questions for the universe will scatter to its emptiness. I wish I could explain why you have your abilities; even my existence and reach has limits."

The rage settled as Joel nodded in response. Violence or anger wouldn't bring him what he needed. He was tired. Joel had come so far, fleeing from his mistakes on Aross. But no matter how far he flew, he would still be the same person he hated. There was no grand design. Sadie died for nothing. He would live the rest of his miserable life without knowing its purpose.

"Can we continue this later? I need to think," Joel said.

A wave of assurance acknowledged his request, and Joel watched as the crimson tree retracted all of its needles and branches towards its trunk and sank into the silver block. He could feel the telepathic connection sever, leaving a longing for The Seekers presence. Joel turned around to find Janak standing behind him. The Beetle was silent; Joel wondered if the alien knew what tears meant for him. Joel walked past Janak, towards the ship. He would find a secluded corner and allow himself to mourn what he had just lost.

Nothing would offer what he searched for. Despite wanting to refuse The Seeker's belief, deep-down Joel knew he could spend the rest of his life searching for answers that didn't exist. Every moment of pain and loss had no defining place in the universe. All of it was random. Each memory that pleaded for an end to his suffering was just a mask for a desperate attempt at purpose. Death or survival. Joel knew his story would fade into the nothingness of the universe.

CHAPTER 37

The mountain creek outside of Wesso was slow, cold, and unclouded. The only shade that could be found next to the water were the shadows of eroded banks with vibrant, layered sediment. Little plant life could be found here, other than cacti and spindly pinyon trees. The two kilometre hike up the desert mountain had broken an incredible sweat under the sun's scalding heat, but Sadie had promised Nait she would take him. It was one of his favourite places to spend his time. Since his injury, his visits to the creek had halted.

Sadie sat on a flat rock shaded by a curved bank. She had taken her shoes off to let the sand and gravel cool off her feet. In her hands she held her book, but her attention paid no heed to the story. The still, humid air pulled her into her thoughts, challenging every worry she relentlessly tried to avoid. She had started this day anxious and fidgety. This day was for Nait, and her attention demanded her elsewhere. In the back of her mind, she hoped he wouldn't notice.

Nait waddled upstream at a careful pace. The water splashed just below his knees as he slowly stepped forward; his head hung low and towards the riverbed, looking for interesting rocks despite his blindness. His vision was a mystery to Sadie. One would think the kid was completely blind, but he carried a certain balance to the way he moved and navigated the world. Each day Sadie spent with him, she watched him slowly become more familiar with his new vision. His progress was impressive, and she was proud of him.

Her attention drew back towards her book; she couldn't even recognize what page she was on. Sadie set the book down beside her and sighed. Her restlessness had become annoying.

"Are you staying in town tonight?" Nait asked across the creek. His blindfolded eyes looked towards her. "We can come back here tomorrow and catch pececillos."

Sadie smiled. A month ago, she would decline, leaving that time to follow any lead she could find. But with each day, her drive slowly died. Some of her family had come to terms that Morwin was dead. Sadie refused to believe that. Now she wasn't so sure. Her time with Nait made her feel safe and purposeful. These moments became more valuable with each failed attempt to find Morwin. For her own sake, her efforts had more worth when spent with Nait. Yet fleeting moments, like now, reminded her what was possibly out there.

"If you'll have me," Sadie replied. "But tomorrow we are tele-porting here. The heat almost killed me!"

Nait laughed. The climate was second nature to him. Sadie was used to the cold, alpine weather of Arsacadia.

"Deal!" Nait chuckled.

Sadie grinned and looked back down at her book. Her smile disappeared when her gaze drifted to her bag. In it was her phone, which she was intentionally avoiding. Every time she picked it up, she was bombarded with texts from her family or the latest news article to come out of Fasdoba. It had become a taxing reminder. Stashing it away didn't kill the looming feelings of its summon. Its battery pulsed with each text that called for her.

"Did I make you angry?" Nait glumly asked. "You feel sad."

"Nait, no," Sadie quickly assured. "I'm just feeling a little low today. None of it is your fault."

"Your soul is dim. It makes me feel bad," Nait said. His supernatural sight made Sadie wince in discomfort. Sadie could see the flow of electricity in any form, but Nait could see the light that life carried. Part of it felt like reading her mind, but she knew he came from a place of innocence.

"I'm sorry, Nait. I just miss someone. But I truly am having fun with you here. Don't worry about me, okay?" Sadie smiled. She watched a smile gently lift on Nait's face. He turned his focus back on the riverbed and began to sift through more rocks. Soon she would have to teach the boy to be mindful of others' privacy.

Nait pulled his hand out of the water, holding a sharp, red rock. He juggled it between his fingers before throwing it back in. "Is it Joel? The person you miss?" Nait asked.

Sadie had told Nait about Joel before, but each time was never easy. Every reminder reopened the wound that was the empty pull. For months, she could feel a crucial part of her soul missing. She had come to terms it would never heal. "Yes. I don't think I'll ever stop. Some people just happen to leave a lasting mark. Like your parents."

Nait nodded mournfully. "I do miss them. They would really like you."

Sadie smiled softly. "Joel would have liked you, too."

A cheeky smirk flashed across the boy's face. He continued moving upstream, splashing through the cold water and soaking his shorts. Sadie watched him stop at a shallow rock the size of a tire and flip it easily. He could only use his true strength around her; he risked too much if people saw more than Sadie was comfortable with. The rock slapped the surface as it tipped over and Nait rummaged through the soft gravel beneath it. His enthusiasm was quite entertaining.

"What are you looking for?" Sadie laughed. "Is there some treasure under there I don't know about?"

"No!" Nait shouted defensively. "I'm digging for the gold strings!"

Curious and amused, Sadie knelt forward between her knees and continued the banter. "That sounds like treasure! What are gold strings?"

Nait chuckled louder. "You know! The strings that trees and plants grow. Below them! I can't remember the word in English. Raíces."

Sadie felt more confused. "You can see roots?"

"Yea! They glow bright," Nait said. "My tío told me plants are alive. Just like us, and some are even connected. Like these trees, all of their... roots are touching."

"And you can see the life in them?" Sadie asked with growing curiosity.

"Can't you? I learnt that there's electricity in us. And plants too!"

Forrest C. Richard

"Well, yes, sort of. It's a bit more complicated than that, but…" Sadie paused in thought. Her abilities could only see the power in hardware; anything manufactured. But yet, there was a deeper level that could be felt beneath the flow. Like a wind so gentle you couldn't pinpoint its direction. If Nait could see the light in life, maybe she could find a current similar to her sight.

Sadie closed her eyes and listened. The sounds of the river, wind, and wildlife dissipated away. The world became dark. Sound took form in the rapids of electrons. The battery in her phone glowed brightly. Streams of radio waves shot up from the cell and across the sky, connecting to thousands of lines between each satellite that glittered the atmosphere above. Lights and machines could be felt from the town of Wesso and other nearby towns, kilometres away. Despite being in the middle of nowhere, it was all too loud to feel anything beneath the sound. If anything was under the chaos, it was never meant to be found.

She took a deep and long breath, letting her mind become still. The sounds around her were pushed away, leaving a bubble that commanded silence. Without a source of energy, the world felt quiet and alone. Removing the presence of electricity made Sadie feel uncomfortable. It was like cutting out parts of her soul that remained from what was already butchered. She braced herself to let the energy flow back in, but stopped when she felt a new trickle of sound.

Below the ground, blue light faintly pulsed. Sadie forced her focus onto the new light, and the veins amplified all around her. Roots of every tree and plant that surrounded her formed a maze of capillaries that streamed needle-thin rivers of electrons. All of them reached as far as they could, creating a network to feed and survive. Many intertwined together, using the connections to communicate with other trees and plants of their shared community. Hidden from the roar of electricity made by man, was a secret layer of life. The discovery was beautiful. And then a sudden realization hit her.

Sadie snapped out of her sight and gasped. "Nait, I need to go home."

* * *

A flash of blue left Sadie's eyes as she appeared in front of her cottage on the farm. The cool air of the Isles immediately soothed her skin. She would take the salt in the wind over dusty, arid desert air any day. An apology to Nait stirred in the back of her mind; she dropped him off at his home abruptly and without explanation. She would make it up to him later.

Sadie turned to find if there was any company around. Every cottage was silent. No one seemed to be working the barns or moseying about. The only thing that greeted her return was a highland cow, staring at her across the road and grazing on long grass. Her family must have been busy. But if her theory was correct, she hoped they would return soon.

The wooden door of her cottage swung open and thudded against the wall as Sadie rushed in. She looked around the room, deciding where would be the best place to sit. The blinds in her living room were too thin to block out sunlight, but her bedroom drapes were thick enough to make the room as dark as night. That's what she needed.

She closed the bedroom door behind her and pulled the drapes closed. The cloth kicked up clouds of dust as they billowed shut. It had been a while since Sadie had stayed here. Once she was satisfied with the lack of daylight, she jumped on her bed and sat with her legs crossed. Sadie began to take deep breaths, slowing down her anxious heartbeat. She needed to be calmer.

Breath escaped her lips as she exhaled. Her eyes closed, greeting her with shadow and the call of energy in every anode, wire, machine and conduit that made the farm alive. Blue light pulsed as the flow took shape. She could feel each stream and deficiency. They all outlined the home her family created and beckoned her to reach further. When she did, she felt the pull of telephone wires that ran along roads, cars coasting to their destination, rivulets of signals shooting through the air and satellites soaring across the planet. All of it painted a world only for her. Every electron singing to be shaped to her will. This was her domain.

Getting lost in the beauty of her sight felt like a warm caress she desperately needed, but now was not the time. Sadie cut off every current around her. The farm temporarily would lose its power, but she was sure no one was home. A dome shaped itself across the farm, outlining every electron trying to follow its designated route. For now, none of it would reach its destination, and only Sadie could open the gate. She needed silence.

Sadie took another deep breath and extended her mind. When she was at the creek with Nait, she was slow to see the hidden layer. Now she knew what she was looking for. She grasped onto the pulse that crawled through the dirt below, allowing the light to amplify and trace every root and plant that existed where her sight fell. First she focused on her house plants that sat on her windowsill, and then onto the vines that were suffocating the outside of her walls. She reached further and felt the motion of every blade of grass that littered the pastures. Millions of them, absorbing the sun's energy and converting it into the trickle of energy that nourished them. They carried their current below the ground and into the vast delta of roots that seemed impossible to organize. The mess of the vascular organs felt overwhelming. With this much life, it was difficult to tell what belonged to which plant. But as she carried the flow of electrons, she discovered how truly all of it was connected.

Hidden below the surface was the native system. One that was similar to what humans made, but created in the wild programming of nature. A network that existed long before humans, constantly evolving to survive and grow. Sadie could feel each pathway, finding sources of stronger reserves and pockets that absorbed more sun. The plants spoke to one another in a language alien to her, across a vast labyrinth that dug incredibly deep. She could fly the route of each root and get lost forever. A feeling of wonder that she hadn't felt since she first accepted her powers filled her. A whole new world was there to explore.

Sadie took another deep breath, preparing herself for the next difficult step and possible disappointment to follow. Sifting between the roots, she sought out individual species through the different wavelengths each plant sang. She traced the roots of old trees, the flowers and grass around them, and the negative spaces between that was lifeless dirt and rot. Hidden in the corners of the labyrinth were the clues that she was seeking. Matter and life that held a silent and unusual tune. The moment she grasped onto a strand, the entire ground amplified in the organism's shrouded reach. Mycelium.

The fungus stretched as far as every living species in the ground it shared. It connected itself to the network that fed it nutrients, absorbing the sun and dirt to bloom its offspring. Most of it was dormant, waiting to activate with the right conditions. Sadie collapsed her reach into its grid and blossomed as far as her strength would let her. Her mind strained as it expanded further and further; Sadie guessed she encompassed half of Aross in seconds. Power surged through her body as it fed her increasing demand

Her vision enveloped the planet. She could feel all of it. Every living being that carried energy through its form. The cacophony of Aross overwhelmed her mind, begging her to let go. She only needed a few seconds. Just moments to find what she needed.

Sadie could feel her vision collapse on itself, forcing her to submit. The pain was unbearable. Just as she was about to release her grip, she felt a cluster singing a song of agony. Sadie focused her reach onto the cluster, feeling the power that crawled through an unnatural rot. It was buried under the city of Tem-Mire. Beneath a city of millions. Every vein and root of fungus pointed towards the cluster, grown in a dense web and into the bodies of decomposing souls. The remaining life in them screamed for death as the rot fed on their flesh. This was a lair. This was what she was looking for.

The world of static vision disappeared from her eyes as she opened them, facing the door of her dark, empty bedroom. "I found you."

CHAPTER 38

The sun was setting over the pasture that Lyas's cottage overlooked. Sadie had been waiting for him to return home for a couple hours now; the lack of wind made for a quiet evening. Only the calls of the cows and creaking of the rocking chair she sat in were there to keep her company. She had sent him a couple texts, but never got a response.

An anxious tick urged her to find him. The lead she discovered was too important for her to wait on, but she needed to compose herself before she faced her friend. Sadie wasn't sure how Lyas would react to the news; she wasn't sure of many things about her friend these days. The doubt she had in him forced her to stop and think about what she wanted to say. The time spent on his porch turned out ideal for exactly that. He had a peaceful view of the farm.

She tapped the arm of the rocking chair impatiently. Should she just call him? Sadie thought. They had gone for too long without a lead on Morwin. They needed to make a plan quickly. One that was fleshed out, and wouldn't steer anymore of their family to an unpreventable death.

Just as she was about to grab her phone, Lyas appeared out of a misty, red gateway conjured in the middle of the main road. He stepped out with Veronica and Callum; all of them carried a shadow of defeat. None of them shared a goodbye as Veronica and Callum veered off to their cabin. Lyas paid them no attention; his gaze fell on Sadie. The red portal collapsed in on itself behind him as he trekked the short walk up to his cottage.

"Sadie," Lyas nodded, eyes locked on the wooden floorboard of the porch. He tried to make for his door before Sadie stopped him.

"We need to talk. It's important," Sadie blurted. She stood up from the chair to face him.

Lyas halted with his door half open. He sighed heavily. "Can it wait?"

"No," she stated. "I found Morwin."

Lyas's head lifted as he looked toward her. Concern filled his eyes. He let the door close behind him and walked over to the same rocking chair she was sitting on earlier. His body thudded as he dropped himself into the seat.

"I just came back from Yanda, following a lead that Veronica thought was him too. Guess what we came back with? Absolutely nothing. I'm tired, Sadie. Maybe Natasha is right; I'm starting to believe too, that Morwin is long dead. Disintegrated in Joel's blast. All of us have been searching for months now. We should put this to rest," Lyas said bitterly.

"It's him, Lyas. I know for certain," Sadie protested. "I found his lair. He's holed up beneath Tem-Mire, of the Union. Read my mind. See for yourself if you don't believe me."

Lyas waved her off lazily. "I don't need to do that."

Sadie stepped closer to him. "I need you to believe me. It's him, he's right there."

Lyas glanced at her from the corners of his eyes. "How do you know?"

"I was told - I found out I can see the electricity that flows through plant life," Sadie desperately explained. "I saw a whole new world that exists, all of it intertwined and communicating. Once I searched deeper, I found routes of mold, and it led me straight to Tem-Mire. Morwin is planning something there. He's already captured dozens of people."

"And this lair," Lyas spoke with caution. "It's been used recently?"

"Yes," Sadie gasped. She felt the doubt chipping away. "The people there are suffering; they're being fed to something growing under the city. It's like what we found in Mercer, but so much worse."

Lyas stood from the chair and grabbed onto the porch rail. He looked towards the row of cabins, silent in his thoughts. Sadie faced him, impatiently waiting for what he had to say.

"If we do this," Lyas said. "We do this with everyone."

"He won't know we are coming this time," Sadie asserted.

Lyas let out a long breath as he stared across the farm. "If we do this, I have one condition."

Sadie tilted her head in confusion. Deep within, she knew what he would ask of her. Her anger didn't even have the chance to spark before he spoke again.

"Nait needs to be brought here. For his own protection and safety," Lyas said. He couldn't even find the courage to face her on his ask.

Sadie's fury made her blood hot and skin red. The feeling of betrayal assaulted her unexpectedly in a horrible heartache. "Are you fucking serious?"

Lyas fiercely spun to face her. "You absolutely know I am. I have said my piece on Nait and I will say it to you again. The boy needs training. This family needs to guide him together before he chooses a path that cannot be reversed. You can accuse me of selfishness all you want, but I have heard your reasons and the only one being selfish is you. Nait needs a family. Not a grieving woman, pretending to play mom."

Sadie's tears pleaded for release. The friend she had grown to trust and love was not standing in front of her. Pain and misery fought against the tides of anger as they both got pulled into the blackhole that was her gaping bond. "Is this where you've set the bar, Lyas? Or can it go lower? How much lower do you need to go to belittle me?"

Lyas's frown furled inward. "You've forced me to come to this. I have tried the compassionate route. I opened my arms to help you and you pushed me away. At some point, I need to stop being a friend and reveal the hard truth."

"You didn't try jack-shit," Sadie spat. "This 'leader' responsibility overwhelmed you, and blinded your ability to see the obvious. Fasdoba was your fault, and the only way you can save your pride is if you have control. It doesn't take a mind reader to see that this family has lost faith in you."

"This family depends on everyone, together!" Lyas yelled. "They see you leaving for days on end, prioritizing a kid over them. I've been here! I have been the one protecting them! How can you accuse me of wanting control when you have abandoned every single one you love?"

Sadie furiously scoffed. "Protecting? You threw us like bait in Fasdoba. You promised Joel protection and fucking lied. Why would I trust you with Nait after that? You can't protect anyone!"

"Neither can you!" Lyas screamed.

Sadie's bond ached with loss. The last few words Sadie shared with Joel echoed in her mind. She felt like a hypocrite. Was she deflecting by keeping Nait to herself? Her world was spinning before her and fell apart with each word Lyas threw at her. She thought she knew her friend. The trust and faith she had in him died, maybe long ago. She could keep screaming at him, letting him spit hurtful words right back at her. Sadie came to him with a desperate ask. Now, she knew nothing would change his mind unless he got what he wanted. She would never give up what was necessary. Nait needed a childhood in the world of his choosing, and Morwin stood in the way of that. Maybe what she thought she believed wasn't needed at all.

Sadie stepped closer to Lyas, seeing the unravel of the weakness behind his dark eyes. "I haven't abandoned this family. I will never give you Nait. I will kill Morwin with or without you. The rest of the family doesn't need your blessing to choose for themselves either."

With nothing left to say, Sadie spun around and stormed off of Lyas's porch. He didn't shout after her, nor did he try to stop her. Her image of the friend she had was left behind outside that house. There would be time later to add it to the pile of grief she already battled. Tem-Mire called for her, and she would answer.

"This goddamn city," Aiden swore. "There are too many choke points. Crowds will jam at every major roadway, regardless if they're in their cars or not." He pointed to multiple intersections on the map of Tem-Mire displayed on his tablet.

Sadie tapped her fingers next to the map, contemplating any idea hidden in her thoughts. "How many gateways can Veronica open?"

"I've only seen her open ten at the same time and that was pushing it," Natasha replied. "The people would also need to be convinced to go through. No one is going to trust a magic door."

Sadie sighed. "We have to persuade them somehow."

"Maybe with Lyas, this evacuation could be done orderly?" Aiden cautiously asked.

"Give it your shot if you want to talk to him. I was already given my answer," Sadie said.

The three of them stood in silence over the map. Sadie had yet to speak to her other friends, but the moment she brought the proposal to Aiden and Natasha, they immediately agreed. Their strength combined made her feel more confident in her plan, but she still needed more. There was only one shot at a mass evacuation. Any delay could inspire Morwin to attack at will.

Sadie looked up from the tablet to the sound of her door opening and was greeted by Rowan's gentle smile. Aiden and Natasha shared a silent nod of agreement and passed by Rowan as they left the living room. Sadie appreciated the privacy; she hoped Rowan came as a friend and not a messenger.

Rowan joined her next to the tablet, looking over the dense city blocks and streets laid out before them. She reached out and brushed the screen to see a wider view. Sadie knew she was seeing a crucial point they missed; Rowan couldn't help but strategize any challenge set before her.

"Are you doing okay?" Rowan asked.

Sadie shrugged. "He said things he can never take back. All I can do is do this without him."

"I'm sorry," Rowan whispered. "He only told me fragments, he was pretty upset. Sadie... you need to think about what you're about to do."

"I've put more thought into this plan than Lyas did with Fasdoba. This time, we won't be walking into a trap. I gave him the opportunity to help and he spit in my face."

Rowan sighed. "We should go after Morwin with everyone."

"I agree," Sadie said defiantly. "So are you coming?"

Rowan locked her in a steel glare. The slant in her eyes made them difficult to read, but Rowan could look intimidating when she demanded it. "I want to. You know I want to."

Sadie leaned in closer to her. "Lyas doesn't know what's best for us anymore. You don't have to follow him blindly."

"It's different when you're in love," Rowan said quietly.

Silent defeat filled Sadie's lungs. She leaned onto the table and rested her head in her hands. She felt Rowan lay a hand on her back. "Can't you just talk to him again?" Rowan asked.

Sadie raised from the table and faced her friend. Pride was an awful feeling. When millions of lives were at its mercy, it was wrong to cling to. How much of it could she sacrifice to save the world she promised to protect?

"I thought I could be a hero," Sadie said. "I wanted to do good by my parents, and by Joel. I believed Lyas would lead me there, but now I stand here questioning the very fabric I thought I was made of. Lyas gets no apology from me. But I won't stop him from coming with me to Tem-Mire. I will do whatever I have to do, to finally end the terror that Morwin has put this family and world into. With or without Lyas. If I give up Nait, to appeal to Lyas's demands, then I've only proven that I can't protect anyone."

"And what of the rest of your family?" Rowan said sternly. "If they die facing Morwin, what does that mean for you?"

Sadie readied her breath. "It means exactly what Lyas fails to see. Everyone on this farm wants to protect the ones they love."

"Lyas loves this family, including you," Rowan said.

"But only this family," Sadie shot back. "The rest of us can see a whole world needing to be saved. If they want to risk their lives for the same purpose I follow, then I can't stop them. All I can do is fight along their side and kill whatever threat we both seek. Should I die, I could die content, knowing that's the best protection I could offer someone so willing to throw themselves to a cause we share."

"Aiden and Natasha? This is what they want?" Rowan asked.

"They see the upper hand. They want this and I know Callum and Veronica will want the same."

Rowan exhaled heavily and averted her eyes back to the tablet. Sadie wasn't sure what else she could say to convince her, but before she could speak again, Rowan drew on the map. "In this lair, could you see Garem?"

Sadie felt a glimmer of hope gifted from her sister. She was a step closer to putting an end to Morwin's chapter. "Yes. He was there. I don't know how he survived, but he's riddled with mycelium. I think that's how Morwin controls him."

"Then we need to separate them. To here," Rowan pointed down on the map. "Garem's form is metal, so Callum and Aiden should force him to this rail yard while the rest of us get the jump on Morwin downtown. We will evacuate the city centre first, and the rail yard is large enough to be empty of civilians. This is the best path for no casualties."

Sadie gently grabbed her friend's hand and squeezed it. "Thank you, Rowan."

"This is how we owe the people we've failed. We put Morwin in the ground for good," Rowan said. Sadie released her grip and watched her friend leave the cottage. Sadie assumed she was leaving to speak to Lyas; it wouldn't be an easy conversation. Callum and Veronica were hers to convince. She couldn't imagine they would refuse an opportunity where they had the surprise on Morwin. If they all failed, they wouldn't be given another chance.

Once every family member decided for themselves, Sadie would gather them to iron out every wrinkle they could think of. She wanted each and everyone of them to come home. They wouldn't repeat the same mistakes that took Joel away from her.

In the meantime, while she waited, goodbyes were in order. Nait would want to know what happened if she failed to return. He was too young to understand the risk that hunted him if left unattended, but they have grown a bond together that she couldn't ignore. The upcoming path was the answer to protect Nait. If she succeeded, the life Nait could make for himself could grow into something beautiful. The cost of losing that was too great.

One day, he would understand the sacrifices and challenges that followed the desire for purpose. The world was ready to turn its back at any failure, but the spark to continue on should remain ablaze. Whatever prepared him for the day he realized that was a step closer than nothing ever given. If she could teach him that life, then maybe Nait could be the hero she wanted to be.

CHAPTER 39

A thin swarm of Voidante ships sailed through the deep, lineal canyon in an organized pattern. Their chrome hulls glittered the pink sunlight that seeped past the shadows of the bridges that floated above the planet's surface. Swarms like this one would enter the trenched ravine every ten minutes or so; Joel wasn't sure what they were accomplishing, but it gave the giant, empty canyon life to entertain the view.

Joel's legs dangled over the side of the canyon, with his back to the face of the cliff they landed on. After sitting in Janak's ship to calm himself, he flew himself away from the landing pad and found a quiet spot to observe the mechanisms around him and keep himself from remembering what he just experienced. The embarrassment of his behaviour would have to be acknowledged at some point. For now, he just wanted to watch spaceships fly.

The sound was the first thing he noticed when he was finally alone. Beside the roar of the ships that echoed across the ravine, the only noise was the groans of the bridges above. From where he sat, the groans were as quiet as a distant animal calling. If next to, he guessed, they would be like standing next to speeding trains. The mass of data that was pulled across this galaxy required a tremendous amount of energy. To Joel, it was inconceivable. To The Seekers, it was just like an organ working without thought. The significance of its existence made Joel feel like he was a bug under a boot. How this entity possessed no answers for him became more outrageous with each grasp of its size.

Behind Joel, footsteps could be heard. When Joel turned, he found Janak approaching. The Beetle carried a careful posture; Joel assumed he would try to find him at some point. He just wasn't sure how. "Did you walk here?" Joel asked.

"Below the surface is a widely accessible transit system," Janak explained as he sat next to Joel. The tough shell on his legs tapped against the hard surface. "You can get anywhere you need to."

Joel nodded in acceptance. Every inch of this planet had purpose, no amount existed that had gone untouched.

"I am sorry if we have offended you in any form," Janak chittered. "How are you feeling?"

Joel heavily sighed. "It's not your fault, it's mine. I am a full-grown adult, and I just had a tantrum in front of a galaxy-spanning alien. I am the one that should be apologizing. I'm sorry, Janak."

"I did not know the stakes of what you sought. If I knew, I could have better prepared you for your meeting," Janak said.

"How could you?" Joel smiled. "I was too busy learning about the planets and creatures you discovered."

Janak chuckled through the translator. Through the aiding voice was a series of excited clicks. "I guess there are some things we cannot prepare for."

Joel shared a laugh as he rubbed the bridge of his nose. "I should probably go apologize to The Seekers."

Janak shifted his hips to face Joel. "I wanted to give you privacy, but I came here to ask you something. How many times do you need to apologize until you change what you are apologizing for?"

Joel, confused and taken aback, turned to face the Beetle. "What?"

"Countless times you have apologized for your anger," Janak explained. "Over many memories you've shared, you have described your grief for your actions, but continue to experience said grief. I see a repetition that continues despite your feelings towards it. Why do you do this? Is this a behavioural trait of humans?"

Joel stuttered as he contemplated the question. "I… I don't know."

"But there must be a reason," Janak insisted.

Joel sighed cumbersomely. If there was any truth to the answer, it laid in the buried past that was Joel's miserable life. What did he have to lose at this point? "I… I deserve it. Pain will follow me wherever I go, because that is my inheritance."

"Someone gave you this pain?" Janak asked.

"In ways," Joel said woefully. "My Mother made sure to remind me, all my life, of my worth. She died not too long ago. I thought, with her, my past would die. I'd be given a clean slate and I could start over without her existence haunting me. Turns out I couldn't escape it, even with her gone. A black cloud follows me, making sure my life suffers. No matter how many times I've tried to change it, I am brought back to the grave made for me."

"And this pain, you take no responsibility?" Janak said.

"Haven't I? Have I not proved my innocence through so many attempts to live differently?"

Janak clicked quietly. "In some ways, yes. But at your roots, you are the only one who can herald the change you seek. Not destiny itself. I could tell you stories of my past, or someone else's, to inspire change, but none of it will matter. Until you are ready to stop blaming the path of life you believe exists, the life you yearn for will fall to evil design."

In an earlier life, Joel would have been angry with the alien. But this time, he wanted to hear more. "Life is supposed to have purpose, a destiny. This belief that life is on a chaotic path is absolutely wrong."

"Is it life, or the individual, who seek purpose? There cannot be both, so in this reality, it is the individual," Janak replied.

"After everything you've seen and discovered, you truly believe it is the individual? Buddy, how many planets with life have you studied? We are insignificant to the purpose of the universe, and the life that is created out there is proof that the individual holds no grip on our so-called path."

"No it isn't," Janak replied with confidence. "The universe laid out the building blocks. Just that. The individual took those components and built something greater. That is evolution. Anything that exists out in the beyond exists because it put itself there willingly. It has survived because it understands the absurdity of all of this and has chosen to forge a path it deems purposeful. That is why The Seekers see any form of life significant. You have significance, Joel."

Joel shifted uncomfortably. "Even if you were right, Janak, what am I supposed to do? Do a few kind words just forgive every horrible thing I've done? Sometimes, people can't make a path for themselves because it's too late. People like me, who have gone too far. I've killed so many people. I killed the woman I love… I watched my own mother die, and I hated her more for it. I'm an unredeemable monster."

"So you just let yourself fall back into the cycle? Commit evil actions, feel sorry for yourself, and continue living without changing anything? What will it take to end the cycle?" Janak persisted.

"My death," Joel snapped. "I've tried desperately for it. You know how many times I've tried to kill myself? First time, I was just a kid. The second time, I failed to hang myself in the forest I worked in. Third was when I threw myself into fucking space. I can't die. Three times I've tried to end this miserable joke that is my life. You know what the worst part is? I only want death if it's by my hand! There's been so many chances Morwin could have ended me. But I got scared, and for some stupid fucking reason, I defended myself. Why couldn't I just let him take my life? Why is it so difficult for me to die?"

Janak stared into Joel's eyes. The four black marbles across the alien's face absorbed him like black holes. "You beg for death because you think it's deserved? The past that was inherited is not your fault, Joel. The past you control is the purpose yet to define you. Why let death be your legacy when, deep down, you believe another exists? End the cycle on those terms. For not just the people who care for you, but for the sole worth hidden within yourself. You have worth, Joel."

Joel held the cold stare right until the wells of his eyes began to drown. Joel forced his face into the palms of his hands and wept. In another life, his skin would have crawled off of his body in embarrassment. In this life, there was nothing left to lose. His body shook as the tears rained and flowed off the back of his hands. How much further in the universe would he have to go to finally accept his fate? What The Seekers offered, what Janak offered, made too much sense for him to accept with grace. His destiny was to suffer and feel the pain he has endured on others. He wasn't supposed to feel the acceptance of suffering the aliens offered.

As Joel wept, he felt the steeled arms of the Beetle reach around his body and squeeze. Joel was at first taken back but then fell into the embrace his friend offered. His tears were unyielding, submitting to the years of his past that bruised his body relentlessly. Joel wanted to stop, but the part of him in control knew this was needed.

The two of them sat together, accepting the hold of a companion offering his aid. As time passed, the embrace was released, and they returned to watch the ships fly in and out of the canyon. Nothing more was said for a few hours. All that was needed was silence and the respect made for one another. They both looked on, letting the dense starlight wash over them. As more time passed, they began to share stories and jokes. Joel wasn't sure who spoke first, not that it mattered. In that moment, the only thing that mattered was realizing someone cared for him. The first since Sadie was taken. And as they cared for Joel, he would return the care that was given.

In a moment to catch their breath through laughter, Joel asked his friend a question. "What do I do, Janak? Where do I go from here?"

"Where does your mind lead you?" Janak replied.

Joel shrugged, watching a diamond form of Voidante soar in front of him. "I don't even know what my options are at this point."

Janak readily sighed. "Well, there are a few options. You can stay here and teach The Seekers more of your species. You have also been permitted to travel alongside me, should that be your wish. Or, you return to your home planet, Aross."

Joel shook his head in confusion. "I can't return home. I don't know the way."

Janak raised his hands in excitement and leaned in closer to him. "The Seekers believe they know the way. Their theory is that the data is in your helmet. They have the technology that could decipher what it hides, but they will only do it with your permission."

His confusion only grew as the offer settled. "Why would they want to know where my home is?"

Janak placed an assuring hand on Joel's shoulder. "Because any life that exists deserves a fighting chance. Think about what opportunities you can offer to fix everything you've identified! You are the herald, the messenger, for your planet. Like my home, yours can grow into the utopia your people deserve. Joel, everything you've told me about 'humans' can be changed with the technology The Seekers have created. All the hate and distaste you carry for them can be the past. It is my belief that the hero you want to be, the purpose you seek, is in this opportunity to unite our species. I wouldn't be asking you of this if you didn't trust me."

"But... they can't be changed. Violence is in their nature," Joel whispered.

"Species tend to surprise you with the gift of unity," Janak said. "Look at you. You've made friends with an alien. Trust in the good that humans can carry. I've seen it in you."

Joel looked towards the canyon floor. The decision for humanity's survival was on him. As much as he didn't like it, this was the purpose he could forge for a better path. "What if they fail? Will The Seekers banish us? Will I be able to defend them?"

"Against all odds, I met an alien across the stars and space between. You showed me your nature, your spirit. If they're anything like you, I believe they have a chance."

As he contemplated the offer, many outcomes ending in consequences rattled his mind. What if The Seekers were using him? What if humanity retaliated? What if he failed? So much was written to end in disaster, but if intentions were true, then maybe the change his species needed could be obtained.

Joel looked over at his bug-eyed friend and breathed deeply. If he were to be the herald for humanity, he would bring them the guidance that he was given. He whispered. "I need to speak with The Seekers."

CHAPTER 40

The ruby tipped needles of the alien, coniferous monolith stretched out in every direction, greeting Joel in its host form. He absorbed the deafening hum with a willing brace. Now that he understood the rules of its nature, it was much easier to handle.

Janak stood beside him, entering the telepathic handshake with Joel's permission. He could feel every fold of the Beetle's mind. Memories and thoughts danced across the surface; many could be felt locked away, requiring an invite. Joel assumed his mind mirrored the same sensory visual. But with all three minds connected, his focus narrowed to the gathering Joel requested.

They had returned to the same landing pad where Joel made his first contact, but this time the cliff hosted multiple other Voidante ships. The landing pads were distanced apart, but close enough for Joel to see each pilot on either side of them. They both were speaking with a Seeker node similar to the one Joel faced. He pondered the energy needed for The Seekers to stretch and extend their consciousness across an entire galaxy for any Voidante needing an audience. How much of that consciousness was fixed onto him?

"Celestvendora," Janak echoed across the three connected minds. "Thank you for agreeing with this meeting."

The crimson tree hummed vibrantly. "There is no need for formality, Janak. There is no sacrifice, nor labour, of my time requested by you."

Joel could feel a surge of appreciation glow bright in the Beetle's mind. Beneath was a great layer of respect that Janak built and cared for across the decades of immortality gifted to Voidante. Feeling the trust firsthand would have been helpful to have during Joel's first, distrustful impression.

"Joel and I have spoken at great length," Janak explained. "And he has decided to return to Aross."

A curious murmur stretched past Joel's ears like a gentle wind. "Is this your decision, Joel? I must admit, I believed you would choose isolation, or at least a partnered voyage, over returning to your home. You spoke of such a heavy animosity for 'humans'; I didn't think you'd entertain the position of a herald."

Joel's breath held tense before he spoke. "I haven't. There are conditions that must be met before I agree to my return."

"That is understandable," The Seekers echoed. "Any contingency or question will be met, of your asking."

"If I return home," Joel declared. "Then I need to bring back something that guarantees its survival. Something that can save humans from the destruction they lead themselves onto. I need this because... I need to amend the atrocities I've committed. If I return with nothing, then I bring no promise of the change I want to believe in."

"You want proof of what we've accomplished?" The Seekers asked suspiciously.

Joel solidified his belief through his mind. There would be no turning back now. "Yes. They will refuse to believe me with no evidence. They need proof that unites them."

The Seekers hum withdrew with a cautious silence. "Civilizations demanding proof is a familiar encounter, but you must know this violates the rules set forth by my own will. Doing what you demand results in the meddling of my influence before I could even lay the foundation of my existence. Think of the consequences, Joel. Should it take me centuries to reach your galaxy, what will happen with the development of said technology you bring? What if your species abuses it, or cross-engineers it to something violent? How can I aid through my own accountability if I'm not even there?"

"Because I'm ready to be the person it is burdened to." Joel accepted. "It will be my responsibility to protect them until you arrive. This is how I repay the ones I hurt. These powers I wield may be unknown, but this is my path for redemption and I need to follow it."

The minds of The Seekers and Janak skimmed the edges of the telepathic circle as they anticipated with thought. Joel knew he was asking for a substantial gift, but he needed the trust of this galactic leviathan if he was going to advance humanity far past any capability of survival. Should they refuse, Joel would learn to adapt from that. But without a unifying entity to heal them, Aross would never live past the ending they have already written. If he was going to be a hero, a hero that Sadie wanted him to be, then he needed to at least try and convince The Seekers to put trust in him.

"Joel…" The Seekers spoke. "Do you make this ask for humanity, or for yourself?"

The question pushed Joel off from his stand, built from confidence. He knew his interests were for humanity, but maybe there was some truth to The Seekers' wariness. Where was the proof of the care for humanity he should have been carrying all along? He arrived at the feet of a hospitable alien as a desperate failure, wielding power beyond belief. He had shown no evidence that humanity or his world were in The Seekers best interest. Joel could even feel similar hesitation within Janak's mind at that moment. The truth would only be revealed with what Joel was hiding from himself.

"For myself," Joel said without restraint. "I have made this ask for myself. Selfishness is no stranger to me. Only these past handful of months have shown me I can love, or care for something that's not me. Each of those moments were blinded by my own rage. The constant cycle of hope and misery has beat me time and time again. I don't know who I'm supposed to be."

"And you wish to introduce life-changing technology to a species unknown to me, to test your character?" The Seekers questioned.

Joel nodded. "If I am meant to create a purpose beyond one of death, then I think this is how I do it. I want to be a good person. I want to save those who share the same chaos, or face nightmares beyond my own experiences. I'm tired of believing that I am meant to die alone. For years, I've struggled to understand why I was placed in this universe, and I am not the only human who questions that. The only difference between me and them is that I was given powers. I thought they were meant to destroy and discovered they were meant to bring me here. This is how I save humanity. This is how I become the hero others believed I could be."

The Seekers breathed deeply within the conscious space shared between them. Their hum sang of profound respect that hadn't been felt since Joel was last on Aross. "There is no greater purpose than one of acceptance. If this ask is what you truly want, Joel, then I will honour it. It is my belief, you will bring the change you want to believe in. Wishing for a purpose given is dangerous and will lead to disappointment. But you have shown the purpose is found within. Become the hero you have promised me to be."

"Thank you," Joel exhaled blissfully. A blanket of assurance fell onto him. It was familiar; in the past, disappointment followed. But this time, if failure followed, he believed he could truly stand against it. Fault, in the past, would only extend to what he inherited from his mother. Everything past was a making of his own. Whatever was in his control would no longer drag him under. Purpose was found in the individual choices that the universe could not give.

Between Joel, Janak and the flesh larch that was The Seekers, was a silver pedestal that raised from the seamless ground. It stopped as it reached his waist and was approximately the size of a dinner table. Joel assumed the pedestal had something to do with the gift, but seemed absent from anything recognizable to his knowledge.

"Joel, please place your helmet onto the table," The Seeker requested.

Joel let himself take a deep breath, then summoned the dark green helmet over his head. In two consecutive sharp crashes, the helmet enveloped his entire face. The alien world in front of him narrowed to the thin slots meant for his eyes. He could feel the connection to the aliens slice away, leaving him feeling alone in empty silence. Joel raised his hands to the jaw of the helmet and willed it to disconnect. The face plate extended out, allowing him to pull the cold metal from his head and let the connection of The Seekers flow back into his mind.

Flipping the helmet around in his hands, Joel faced the glare of the helmet that was as alien as the universe he found himself in. The hard stare of the visor peered deep within. It commanded fear and power, even within his own grasp. He had practised this before, back on the farm. But the stare of the lone helmet was unsettling. It cried of a thirst for knowledge, so he hadn't tried it again. Until now.

Joel approached the pedestal and placed his helmet down. The metal against metal rang with a cutting chime. As he stepped away, the empty but cold stare demanded a return of his touch.

"What I'm about to use is technology derived from the Tolrek. They were the third sentient species to accept The Celeste Expanse. As part of the exchange of our technology, they gave us this organic software that can diagnose any machine. There have been some added functions of my contribution, but I believe it will be a useful tool in understanding your strange armour," The Seeker explained.

From the silver box, five orange rods rose until they stood level with the crown of his helmet. With an unsettling squelch, the rods spat out orange and yellow webbing until the dark green metal was barely noticeable. The wet veins began to beat rhythmically. An itching urge to wipe the helmet with sanitizer sat heavy in the back of his mind.

Seconds after the webbing was ejected, a soft hologram of a blank, black canvas appeared above the rods. Strange symbols flooded the screen in formulated lines. Joel thought his eyes were deceiving him, but soon the symbols blurred into numbers and letters he could understand. An assuring thought from Janak reminded him the translator was at work.

Even though the data was translated, he still couldn't understand it. Every second filled the screen with formulas and equations he hadn't seen since grade-twelve physics. He wasn't sure if he was the only one not following, and felt the awkward need to ask for The Seekers to slow down.

"I'm sorry. What am I looking at here?" Joel asked politely.

The tree hummed behind the busy hologram. "There is a substantial amount of data collected in this helmet. Nothing that explains the origin, but I can see detailed, live recordings like heart rate, adrenaline spikes, energy discharge... It is difficult for me to compare this helmet to a form of technology, but rather as an appendage of yourself. It is in a constant state of vigilance and attention."

Joel stared deep into the helmet's eyes as he tapped his foot in thought. Unsurprisingly, he only had more questions and no answers. "Is there anything else?"

"Maybe start at the recent records?" Janak asked. "Start backwards. See what we can recognize since RES 9?"

The screen blinked and quickly filled with different sets of streaming columns. Joel might as well have been reading instructions for a rocket.

"Incredible," The Seekers whispered. "This data shows recent distances covered, speed, trajectory, but... it doesn't seem possible."

The screen switched to a finely detailed diagram showing a planet and a directional line. Joel appreciated the visual, but felt slightly embarrassed he couldn't keep up with the aliens analyzing the data. The Seekers hum excitedly reverberated. "This shows your relative position as you approached RES 9. Your helmet records every single coordinate value. Follow the line away from the planet, Joel."

Joel traced the thin line from the moss covered planet until it reached empty space. At the end of the line was nothing; a sharp cut that pointed towards the dark void. He still wasn't sure what he was looking at. "Is there data missing? I see nothing."

Below the cut line dropped a box. Numbers in powers of ten read with a range of values. The Seekers began to hum again for his attention. "Right at this point is an incredible discharge of energy. You exited the fold. Your abilities allow you to cross space and time… It's incredible. Groundbreaking. Travelling the distance of space was thought impossible without technology, yet you have proved that law wrong."

Joel felt a wave of disappointment follow. "So that's it then? This is all we can trace back to?"

"No," The Seeker said. The holographic map shot outwards, revealing hundreds of stars. The map fell back further until he could see the entire galaxy, then its neighbouring bodies, and then dozens and dozens of glowing galaxies. The map didn't stop flying until the screen seemed to show the entire universe, or more specifically a very small part considering its size. The map then began to zoom inwards, focused on a small prick of light. The light slowly grew into a galaxy. Further, it revealed the vast field of stars that the body hosted. The flight of the map fell into a single, orange star, and then into a blue marbled planet.

Aross. There was no denying it was his home. He could recognize the continental shapes from the distance of its moon. They found his home, across an entire, unknown frontier of galaxies yet to be discovered. His helmet held the map, all this time. As the planet grew nearer, a similar finer line reached out from Lavendy and into the empty void of space. It shared the same cut end, with a sheet of data reading a massive spike of energy. An enthusiastic hum escaped the tree's mind. "This is you entering the fold. Amazing."

As relieved as Joel was, The Seeker's excitement confused him. "I'm grateful you found my home, but why is this impressive? You possess the same technology."

The map instantly zoomed outwards until it revealed the great field of galaxies that glittered the screen in the thousands. Joel watched as a thin line traced from his home galaxy to the one they were currently in. The path flew past at least a hundred celestial bodies; even Joel could understand the distance was great.

"Because, Joel..." The Seekers said. "The time and distance you have accomplished is legions past what my technology is capable of. It is my dream to reach past the limits of the universe's wilderness, and you have the ability to do so with the power of your own command. Now I see... The universe is your frontier. You can go wherever your heart desires without restriction. I hope you can understand the awe of your existence I hold dear. Without change, our species would never have survived. What took me billions of years to grasp has been given to you to forge the change that will define you. This life continues to amaze me..."

The webbing from the rods snapped away from Joel's helmet as the rods returned to the seamless surface of the pedestal. His helmet lay bare, menacingly staring into Joel's soul. He watched as a branch from The Seeker's node extended out towards the dark green metal and touched it with a single sharp needle.

Down the plate of the left eye, a long rectangular strip of thin, chrome metal fabricated itself vertically into the helmet's surface until it reached the jaw. It reflected the deep blues and purples of the sky above, leaving a bright mirror within the emerald darkness. Joel reached out his hand to touch it, feeling the warm boundary of the chrome strip that merged with the familiar, cold steel.

"Joel," The Seekers droned longingly. "I give you an archive port that will allow your species to access a vast library of information about my existence. It contains my history, mission, blueprints, and findings of our shared universe. With you, I trust that you will lead your people into unity and preparation for acceptance into The Celeste Expanse. Show them this data. Convince them what exists out there beyond the empty void."

Joel looked up at the tree in anxious wonder. "Will you be able to cross the distance in time? What if I can't save them before you arrive?"

The Seekers sighed an air of content. "Because with time, comes change. My story is yet to reach an ending. I believe that as the expansion grows, we will discover ways to reach everything beyond your galaxy. I trust you will help them, Joel. Aid them, and when I reach you I will ensure their survival across the time this universe has left."

The branch that graced his helmet pulled back into its original form. The shape of the tree relaxed and washed a deafening,

FORREST C. RICHARD

blissful hum over the two of them. Joel slowly picked up his helmet and studied the gift that ran down the cheek. He watched his own reflection of his eye glimmer with light.

"Joel, my history is a long one," The Seekers warmly shared. "Back in our carbon form, before a universal language was created, we titled our greatest adventurers a rank that held an incredible honour. This title passed on as we evolved; its meaning held close to our character and history. The Celeste name Voidante was derived from this title. Each explorer we employ carries a great burden of the design we envision for this universe. For that, we hold the highest of honours for them. Joel, I haven't known you for long. I see you as a complex, powerful individual with heavy, internal battles. The burden you carry across space and time cannot go unnoticed. And with this new mission to aid your species into evolutionary change, I truly believe you have shown your motivation goes above your self-interests. Risks must be taken to prove the individual purpose we carry. For that, I gift you the title shared among ancient adventurers and explorers soaring between every star and planet around us. You are Ver'Nova."

CHAPTER 41

The sound of Tem-Mire was the first thing Sadie noticed the moment they materialized into the physical world. Jammed traffic, ongoing construction, the scrambled voices of hundreds of people walking by. All of it mixed together to create a flood of music singing the tune of a densely populated city.

Rowan, Natasha, and Sadie stepped out of the hidden back alley and onto the sidewalk that hugged one of Tem-Mire's downtown roads. Crowds of office workers swerved through the clumps of tourists taking pictures of the famous highrises that towered above them. Cabs and cars packed the road, bumper to bumper, while bicycles zipped between them. This particular street seemed to be tailored towards tourists, as every second storefront was either selling the same nationalistic merchandise or expensive and mediocre 'exotic' food. Despite their apparent price-gouging, they were still full of bodies. The city was alive, and that made the imminent situation all the more critical.

This was Sadie's first time visiting this city, and she had to admit it held a certain beauty to its claustrophobic design. Downtown was filled with glass skyscrapers of unique, architectural design. A short walk from the core would take you to the boardwalk, which overlooked one of Aross's largest lakes. Cargo ships and yachts filled the harbour while ferries from neighbouring cities floated along the coast. Historically, warm air from the great lake made for miserable but short winters. This late in the season made it feel like Sadie was standing in the humid heat of an early summer. Springtime in the Northern Union felt unnatural.

Why Morwin chose this as his next hiding spot held no mystery. Tem-Mire was incredibly large and was one of the Union's jewels. It generated more wealth than the entirety of Arsacadia, and for that had become a regular callout in every article reporting the top ten most expensive places to live. Not long ago, five neighbourhoods that surrounded Tem-Mire's outer territory decided to separate into their own municipality, in hopes to ease the pressure of the growing population. It only took a couple years for those towns to match the same quality of living. Settling in the Tem-Mire area was undeniably popular. People flocked to where the money was. Sadie remembered a night where Joel told her about the city. Everything she knew about it was from him. That knowledge was now helping her understand why Morwin had chosen it for his lair.

With a city packed almost shoulder to shoulder, came the opportunity for people to vanish. Whether they were homeless or people found in the wrong place and time, the trail of their disappearance would quickly fade. Police were simply too busy with chasing spontaneous crime or trying to pick away at the pile of paperwork that filled their offices. Morwin was smart. Attention wouldn't be drawn to a few missing persons that carried no interest to unwanted eyes. He played the system for every flaw he could exploit; he had learned that since Mercer.

"There's so many people…" Natasha whispered. She seemed frozen in place, trying to comprehend the task they were about to take on.

Sadie agreed with her sister, but she needed to believe the challenge ahead of them could be done. A few blocks ahead of her, Callum, Veronica, Aiden, and Lyas would step out of a gateway, placing themselves in position. There would be no turning back now, especially since Lyas had agreed to join them.

Before the family left the farm, Sadie called for a meeting to go over the plan one last time. To her surprise, Lyas walked into the room. Rowan must have convinced him, as he didn't seem too enthusiastic about his involvement. A part of Sadie should have guessed he would show up last minute; Lyas wasn't stupid enough to leave his family at death's door without him being there. Still, he had no words for Sadie during the meeting. In this moment, all he was to her was another tool to protect the people of Tem-Mire and her family from what was to come.

Grazing the back of her mind, Sadie felt a chain of consciousness touch her mind. Soon she could feel the same anxious anticipation from the rest of her family. The connection completed with Lyas knotting the ends, allowing all seven of them to speak through the telepathic conference call he created. Behind it, she could feel a bubble wrap itself around the loop. Lyas wanted complete concealment from any wandering minds; only one man in this city was capable of that, and he wanted them all dead.

"Is he still there, Sadie?" Rowan said through the connection.

Sadie inhaled a deep breath and closed her eyes. In an instant, she bloomed her sight until every electron illuminated around her. The world was painted into a different picture. Every living being and organism carrying energy shined a beautiful blue. Sadie silenced them, and focused on the target buried beneath the concrete forest. It pulsed like a dying heart. Now that she was finally close, the energy felt tainted and cursed. Each innocent soul, forced to live through the feast, cried for death. In the middle of all of them was the rotten life that was Morwin, completely unaware of their arrival.

"He's there," Sadie shared. "Right under us."

Lyas's voice jumped into the connection. "Let's do this, now."

Waiting on Veronica's move, Sadie grabbed onto Rowan's and Natasha's arms. She watched as Rowan pulled out her collapsed compound bow, snapped it open, and notched the special arrow she engineered. Sadie could feel electrons around them begin to boil excitedly in anticipation; they needed to be fast.

Before passers-bys could gawk at Rowan's weapon, each head on every body that filled the traffic-jammed vehicles or crowded the sidewalk swivelled towards the nearest end of the block. Wide gateways, fringed with crimson mist, tore open mid-air and expanded until each intersection near them was now a door to a large, empty park field a few clicks outside of the city. Every block within Veronica's sphere would see the same destination within the magical portals.

At the same time, Sadie quickly awakened every alarm within the city's emergency system. Lyas could only extend his reach so far. The same with Veronica. Their hope in the rest of the city now relied on the public's better judgement.

Scores of hypnotized people parted the street like organized drones. Every building around them poured out bodies with one aim injected into their minds. The evacuation was in place. Now they only had a few seconds until they would lose the advantage they needed.

Sadie dived herself and her sisters into the realm of energy. Her body and mind flooded with the familiar embrace of electricity. The entire world around her pulsed into the veins of every conduit and atom that painted her domain. Beneath her, she could see the stagnant tunnels of the city's old sewer system, and the dark lair where Morwin was standing. In less than millisecond Sadie jumped the three of them to the door of the monster's cave and sprung them back into the material world.

Rowan only needed a moment to orient herself and mark her target. Morwin, who was standing near the middle of the sewer chamber, couldn't even turn to face the unknown visitors before Rowan's arrow impaled the back of his shoulder. Sadie watched the man they hunted shout out in pain as the arrow's impact sent him stumbling forward. Four wires sprang from the arrow-tip embedded in his body and punctured the ground around him. Morwin lost his balance with the mechanism's trap, and was forced to his knees as the wires tightened into a snare.

At the opposite end of the room, a red portal tore open. Lyas, Veronica, Aiden and Callum jumped through. Grinding metal groaned from the shadows of the chamber and an armoured monster slumbered into their light. Sadie's heart fluttered as she remembered the last time her eyes fell on the beast. She felt tempted to strike out, but before she could, Callum sprang forward and the metal monstrosity fell back into the cobbled ground. Callum kept his arms raised while forcing Garem to hold still. The beast's strength must have been incredible, as Sadie noticed Callum's arms were beginning to quiver.

Lyas nodded towards Veronica. "Train yard. Now."

Veronica's hands danced in front of her and blood red light from the new gateway reflected across Garem's steel body. Simultaneously, Callum pushed Garem across the rank floor and into the conjured door. The metal of his armour ground and shrieked against the invisible grip. As Garem was moved into the train yard, Callum and Aiden followed and disappeared with the closing of the misty gateway behind them. The light of the red magic faded, leaving the rest of them standing over Morwin and the pool of blood that he kneeled in.

"It would be fatal to flee," Lyas hawked. "That arrow tip is laced with a very potent mix of fungicide and poison. If you move a finger, I'll release the entire dose. It may not kill you, but it will for sure hurt."

Morwin grunted a painful laugh as he pulled against a tight wire beneath his collarbone. "I can imagine."

The five of them circled their capture. Sadie could feel each and every one of them anxiously vigilant through the psychic connection. No one was ready to allow an opportunity of escape. Morwin turned his quivering head to examine each of them, meeting his dark, empty eyes upon theirs.

"Where did you take my goon?" Morwin asked. Sweat beaded across his pale skin, clinging strands of his black, greasy hair along his cheeks.

Lyas scoffed and took a closer step to him. "Somewhere where we can hold him until we deal with you. I'm confident we can figure out how to burn out the corruption you bled into his mind. I can't say you'll get the same treatment."

Black blood shot out of Morwin's mouth with a cough. "Good luck. You'll find he may be too far gone."

Sadie felt a panicked strain flare within Aiden and Callum's mind. Something was wrong. When she looked at her sisters, they shared the same worried stare.

"So…" Morwin whispered through heavy breaths. "Now that you have finally found me, what is your plan? Are you to be my judge and jury?"

Lyas stared upon Morwin with hateful eyes. They were taking too long. They shouldn't have been stalling. She only stood a couple feet from him. At this distance, she could put a lightning bolt right through his head with a quick snap. The idea played in the back of her mind as she watched the man who killed Joel stall for a few more seconds of life. Sadie prodded Lyas's mind to hurry but was waved away.

"There are many ways I can think of to repay the souls you've carelessly taken. You deserve pain and punishment beyond what is honourable. Look around you. Look at the death and torture you've caused," Lyas said.

Sadie stole a quick glance at the plastered cadavers that were displayed around them. Blankets of tendrils and slime covered the walls of the sewer chamber. Beneath them were the decaying heads and limbs of Morwin's latest victims. All of them were denied a quick death, forced to feed the monster's twisted dream.

That remaining life they held was what brought Sadie to his hidden door. Once this was all over, she would end the suffering they were forced to live through.

"And what do you know about what is right and wrong?" Morwin asked Lyas. "Despite being superior to them, you still hold on to their old world law. What will it take for you to realize we have evolved beyond humanity? You possess power greater than they could conjure, and you refuse to believe you could do something better in our image. All of us in this room are beyond and above what has no right to exist anymore. Yet you still play human."

Lyas shook his head and laughed in disbelief. "Listen to yourself. Morwin, you are absolutely delusional. What you speak of is insanity."

Morwin smiled and revealed his bloody, stained teeth. "I'm not insane. I'm calculated."

"I've heard enough from you. It's clear to me you will refuse to change. I'll give you a choice, Morwin," Lyas said as he took a step back from him. "Do you want death, or have your brain reduced until you're a drooling idiot? This is purely for the sake of my own conscience."

"Neither," Morwin grinned.

"Death it is, then," Lyas sighed.

Across the mental circle, Sadie felt a surge of power fill the connection. Lyas closed his eyes as he directed his focus onto his execution. In seconds, Morwin's mind would be melted into nothing.

Silence lingered as they waited. Sadie heard a grunt escape from Lyas's lips and noticed he was starting to sweat and shake. A scowl stretched across his face as if pain was coursing through him.

"Lyas. What's wrong?" Rowan asked with hastened concern.

Lyas said nothing. He continued to cough in discomfort while keeping his eyes locked shut. Sadie looked down at Morwin. His neck was exposed. She could kill him right here in an instant.

"Lyas!" Rowan shouted. Right as Sadie raised her hand for the kill, a shrieking pitch echoed across the connection.

All of them reached for their ears to block out the sound. The pain made Sadie's knees buckle. She looked up and saw foam pouring from Lyas's mouth. His eyes had rolled upward, and his body was beginning to violently seize.

Disabled by the psychic sound, Sadie could only watch as Morwin slowly ripped out the arrowhead from his shoulder and pulled the anchored wires from the cobblestone floor. He tossed the restraints aside and carefully rubbed his wound. Studying each of his intruders, he looked at Sadie last, and wormed his dark gaze into hers.

"Might want to find your other friends. A riot is in the train yard," Morwin whispered to her.

Around them, the walls exploded in a horrible earthquake. The ground erupted beneath, covering them in falling stone and concrete. She tried to reach for her sisters, but the psychic scream pulled every muscle apart. Light from above broke through the crumbling sewer, spotlighting Morwin as he gracefully rose from the rubble with Lyas crippled at his side.

The last thing she felt was the surface of a city crumble down to bury her.

CHAPTER 42

The projector hardware had a satisfying click as Janak gently placed it beneath the right eye socket of Joel's helmet. As it did with The Seekers gift of an archive port, the helmet accepted the new implant without rejection. Whatever origin the helmet possessed it had a clear nature of adapting to whatever Joel needed. It truly was programmed to respond to his will.

Janak grabbed his fusion tool from the table and noticed Joel was staring at a screen displaying the port side of the ship. The screen showed the entirety of a rail station they were parked just outside of. This was one of three main stations used to shorten the gap between every celestial body The Seekers have visited. A square grid of parked ships ranging from Idelvin carriers, public cruisers, and Voidante waited in queue for their turn to join the steady stream of vessels entering the station's highway. Janak had yet to join the queue; he needed a little more time to finish the pre-trip duties. He didn't think Joel minded the wait. These would be the last few hours they had before they would meet again at his home so far away.

A bright flash illuminated the screen as the station ejected the next group. Joel watched without turning an eye. Janak wondered what kinds of thoughts were playing in Joel's mind. The moment he felt Joel's conscience helped him understand the complexity of the human's pain. There was mounting pressure when Joel decided to return home, and with each passing moment, Janak believed the pressure would become greater.

"Where are they going?" Joel asked across the hub. "All of these ships here. Where are they going?"

"Hmm, depends," Janak murmured. "The Voidante, they could be going anywhere. Each one has a specific mission at any unexplored or explored system. The other ships are of Idelvin or Tolrek make. They're probably moving resources or civilians. I see some Querell drones too."

On the screen crossed a giant hauler that was entering the queue. Joel pointed towards it and asked. "What's that one? It's huge."

"That's an Idelvin carrier. Probably moving ore or water," Janak explained. "Even though the reach of The Seekers is small in comparison to the universe, they still have settled on many habitual worlds. Whatever community made landfall on those planets still needs many resources and aid that would take decades to make if they were left alone. Part of the Celeste Expanse is to make sure those settlements thrive."

Joel's mouth parted in thought as he stared at the giant hauler. "There's thousands of ships here... there must be billions of citizens part of the expanse."

Janak nodded in agreement. "Trillions. My people are the majority; the other races have more intricate breeding practices. But regardless of where they were born, they are all working towards the vision of The Seekers. That's why it's so important that we ensure everyone's survival. This life is plentiful, but fragile."

"Were you born in a settlement?" Joel asked.

"No, I was born on Ceyillin, of the Grendah Lav Galaxy. It is the Idelvin home world. I wish we had time to visit it," Janak said. "My home is beautiful. The Idelvin have created incredible wonders there. I think you'd have found it fascinating to see."

Joel let out a heavy sign and turned away from the screen. He leaned onto the table and looked closely at the implants Janak had just added. "We can still go. We don't have to leave for Aross just yet."

"You would delay? Are you having second guesses?" Janak asked.

"I always second guess myself," Joel smirked.

Janak flipped the fusion tool between his fingers. The idea to see Ceyillin again was tempting. "There will be other chances to see what this universe offers. Returning to your home is no end to your story."

"I know," Joel sighed. "If the circumstances were different, then maybe it'd work. I know I need to return to Aross."

Janak leaned in closer to the open face plate and held the fusion tip to the edge of the hardware. He carefully activated the tip and watched the tool weld the projector into the helmet. "For explorers like us, home becomes harder to remember as the distance and time between stretches. But it always remains a place we miss deeply. No matter how many details we forget, we will always remember what meaning it holds. Returning home is an honour, Joel. Us Voidante treasure the moments we have when the time allows. You are hesitant now, but there may be a time when you appreciate a reunion personal to only you."

Joel nodded gently and watched the careful hand of Janak's weld. "Maybe. It's hard to think about seeing Aross through a new perspective. The hatred I had grown for so many years was deafening. No matter how many cities and provinces I tried to restart in, I could never escape what made me hate the world. The easy path would be to just leave Aross behind in the past, but…"

"But it would eventually follow," Janak quietly added.

Joel nodded in agreement. "As much as I'd like to see the universe, I will never stop thinking about the ruin I left back home."

Janak cut the power of his tool and set it down on his table. He took a long inspection of the projectors' fixture and felt satisfied. "I understand. One's duty is a powerful bond."

"I need to do right by my promises. But it terrifies me that I'll fail again," Joel said.

Janak pinched the other projector and brought it up to one of his eyes to check for any deformities. "Failure is part of the burden Ver'Nova carry. There is no reason to fear it. The honour falls when failure's change isn't understood."

"Does it ever overwhelm you? The thought that honour within Ver'Nova can fall at any time?"

Janak breathed deeply through his nose ducts as he thought about the question. "There was a time when it did. A time when I put my purpose to question. Our personal turmoil will never stop, Joel. We have a duty to break its control. You'll learn this realization again and again, as time keeps throwing whatever absurd realities it has left in stock. I believe that you have come to understand that."

"If it wasn't for you, or The Seekers, I don't know where I'd be now. Maybe I'd be wandering aimlessly, or dead, but you showed me it doesn't have to end that way. I hope you know I'm thankful for that," Joel spoke.

He looked up to meet Joel's eyes, finding what Janak thought was an expression of sadness or content on the human's weird skin. If it wasn't for the translator, Janak would have missed the tones of honest gratitude.

"I'm thankful for you too, Joel. You showed me friendship where I believed only loneliness existed. I am looking forward to what stories we will create in the future," Janak said.

The two shared a respectful nod over the silent hum of the ship's engines. Joel looked back at the helmet and pointed towards it with one of his pale fingers. "How's the implants coming?"

Janak dropped the second projector into place and quickly fused it into place. "I'm done now, but I need to run tests to confirm it works. Can you put it on?"

Joel reached over the table and picked up the dark green steel helm. He put it over his swept back hair and the plate closed with a hard chime. Joel began to slowly look around in every direction, watching the holograms activate.

"I think it's working," Joel said excitedly. The silver strip of data glinted light from the ship's ceiling as Joel moved his head. Janak could barely see the screens within the sockets; it was as if they weren't even there.

The thrill of invention made Janak's mandibles chitter proudly. "Fascinating! You should be able to shift through any form of data the helmet collects. Try thinking of the path back to Aross. The same one The Seekers found."

"Found it," Joel said. The data was showing instantly. "It's like a direct line."

"Good," Janak nodded. "You are set to head home now."

Joel looked back at Janak and collapsed the helmet into whatever hidden pocket it folded into. The human looked concerned. "Are you not coming with me? I thought we would be flying together?"

A sigh escaped Janak's mouth as he prepared to disappoint his friend. "I will be coming to Aross, but you need to understand the difference between your capabilities and my ship's flight tech. Even with the full output of a rail station, it will take me some time to reach your planet. You however, according to your helmet, can make the journey in a significant fragment of time."

Joel shrugged his shoulders. "Okay, so I push through the long flight with you. Doesn't matter to me how quick I can get there, I want to do this with you."

Janak shook his head respectfully. "No, Joel. You are needed on your planet at a time where they need you the most. There is no need to worry for me. I have the coordinates. I just have to make sure I don't get lost."

"No," Joel protested. "We should be doing this together. Especially if there's a chance you can get lost! I want to do this with you, Janak."

"Joel, your duty as Ver'Nova, as an explorer, is to face the unknown with courage. I face the same challenge; the dark depths of the universe is no stranger to me. These gifts we gave

Forrest C. Richard

you, the trust we have instilled, would not have been given if we didn't believe you could achieve this. I know you can save your world without me. And in time, I will meet you there."

"How much time?" Joel mournfully said.

"With the data we have, it will take me maybe ninety six Celeste-calendar days by rail station. But the distance in between is greater than any Voidante have attempted. We don't know what obstacles lie between here and the destination. I need to prepare for any interruption possible."

"So you're unsure," Joel pressed.

"It's much easier to theorize on paper, but yes. This journey has uncertain risks," Janak said.

Joel scoffed under his breath. "All the more reason I should be with you."

"My friend. I need you to trust me with this burden, as I have trusted you with yours," Janak whispered.

Janak could see Joel's eyes begin to water. Goodbyes always held a certain grief to their nature. Joel stuttered as he spoke. "If you don't make it... then I'm responsible. I can't keep being responsible for the deaths of my friends."

Janak reached out his hand and rested it on Joel's shoulder. "You were never responsible for your friend's deaths. They knew the risks that followed your burdens. They would have never agreed to them if they didn't believe in you."

With his sleeve, Joel wiped away the tears beneath the whites of his eyes. "A bit difficult if you don't know the risks, no?"

Janak slapped a firm pat on Joel's shoulder and leaned back into his chair. "The day I let risk change me is the day I retire my ship."

The two sat in silence, and that was all that was needed for the recognition that their reunion would come one day. As they turned their focus to watch the bright flashes of the station fill the screen, Janak quickly left the table and returned with two glasses of Bonmoc for a final salute. The ring of their metal cups rang as they gave a toast, and Janak let the warmth of the liquor wash his throat as he shot it back.

He would truly miss Joel. There would be a day when they would reunite, but as an explorer he needed to state the truth that there may not be a day that would come. The universe was too big and chaotic to allow such ease. Janak knew he should have told Joel sooner, but like his friend, he too hated goodbyes. All they needed in that moment was to believe they would both reach Aross. Maybe not together, but reunite there nonetheless.

When Joel was ready to leave, Janak quickly ran a few more diagnostic tests on the helmet's implants for the sake of his own assurance. He watched as Joel grabbed his jacket from a locker and zipped it up close to his collar as if he was entering a snowstorm. Janak tried to insist upon a vacuum suit, but Joel declined. He didn't need it. Another anomaly that came with the human's powers.

Joel stepped into the airlock and turned back towards Janak. Between them was the track of the door to seal them. The two phased clank of Joel's helmet echoed in the airlock. The lights glimmered the pure chrome strip that carried The Seekers' legacy. Janak thought back to the day he and Joel crossed paths. Joel wore the same outfit and helmet when they first saw each other. Janak thought he was facing down an imminent threat, signalled by his Voidante. The two shared a deadly and short exchange of power available to them, and luckily ended the confrontation with the help of curiosity. Now they faced each other again, but shared a goodbye. It was always Janak's dream to find a sentient species. The day he became a Voidante, he knew he would find a planet that hosted life beyond comprehension. He just never would have guessed one would become his friend.

Joel held out an open hand, held sideways and flat. Janak was shown this by Joel once before and quickly he returned the exchange of respect Joel was offering. Right after, Janak turned Joel's hand and clasped the top with his other palm. An Idelvin handshake. Much similar to humans, just only a couple steps apart.

"I'll see you on Aross, okay?" Joel said.

"On the day, Ver'Nova."

Joel stepped further back into the airlock and Janak closed the door. Once the air cycled, the exterior door opened and the darkness of space expanded. Joel stepped out into the vacuum and floated past the ship's hull. He turned to face Janak, waved goodbye, and then jettisoned himself away from the ship and far into the vacuum.

Janak kept the door open to watch Joel leave. For a second, his friend held stationary. Then in a quick, green flash, the man was gone. In only a second, Joel was hurtling across space and time to the home where he was needed. Janak would follow, and one day he would get there. The emptiness of space still held horrors beyond the unknown, and it was his duty to cross it.

The airlock door closed shut and Janak began the final pre-trip adjustments. Once ready, he joined the queue and waited patiently for his turn in the station. The Seekers gave him a priority request, but Janak decided to wait in the line. In moments like these were when he felt the true worth of his purpose. Waiting for the journey to carry him to the next discovery. These moments could never be replaced; their value was beyond any memory he held deep within. This was his purpose. Being a Voidante meant crossing the unimaginable. On the other side were wonders yet to be discovered, and he would risk everything to see them.

CHAPTER 43

Asphalt, concrete and dust billowed around Morwin as he rose from the sewers. He pulled Lyas close behind, using the man's own power against him. Everything around Morwin pulsed with excitement. The released floodgate of Lyas's power filled Morwin with a cold, intense rush. He could feel Lyas recoil in pain. Neither of them had felt this much power before.

The two of them rose higher, above the ground between the towers that stood over downtown. Morwin unfolded the possibilities of Lyas's potential the higher they rose. The levitation would prove useful, but the man had failed to see what he was hiding beneath his own moral restraint. He could feel Lyas try to fight back, but the torrent of power rushing through him now belonged to Morwin.

"There's no use fighting," Morwin exhaled blissfully. The rush was euphoric. He imagined what it would be like with hundreds under his thumb; anything above this seemed almost impossible.

"Stop!" Lyas screamed out. "What are you doing to me?"

SILENCE HIM.

More! MORE!

Morwin laughed. In time, he would understand.

With his connected mind, Morwin reached out further and deeper into the material layers that surrounded them. He could feel and see every individual molecule, submissive to his will. It was a whole new world. A hint of jealousy hit Morwin the longer he combed through it. Lyas had this entire realm available to wield, and yet had refused its offer. The waste of it was tragic.

They stopped just below the peaks of the skyscrapers. The cold rush of power was deafening. Morwin could barely grasp the world around him and could only see the excited pulse that brightened his vision. He altered the torrent a touch and let his vision return. Pain from the Yandian woman's arrow finally rushed in. His black blood, tainted with their poison, poured from the open wound. The throbbing pain was noticeable, but it wouldn't be lethal. It wouldn't be long until it healed over. Lyas's family had come sooner than he expected, but his trap worked nonetheless. At some point, they would have found him here. Tem-Mire was large, but part of a pattern they seemed to have discovered.

The city of Tem-Mire was beautiful at this view. Green mountains surrounded the giant city on one side, and a crystal blue harbour on the other. Hundreds of thousands chose to live here for its disgustingly extravagant lifestyle.

Hundreds of thousands of people should have been here. Morwin snapped out of his euphoric trance and expanded his mind in a panicked search. The entirety of downtown was almost empty of any humans. Reaching further, he found that a significant portion of the city's habitants were emptying out.

"You evacuated the city?" Morwin asked angrily. He turned to Lyas and found him curled in a fetal position. A faint pink hue glimmered around him. The psychic power they emitted begged to be expelled.

He ruined our plan!

NO! We can still FEED!

Morwin reached out to find any cluster of people that remained. There were a few, but not as many as Morwin wanted in Tem-Mire's destruction. He chose this city for a reason. But now he had what he truly came for. Those who escaped the city would eventually find the death that was coming for them.

In his rage the towers around him vibrated in the psychic sphere.

"My body..." Lyas quivered. "It hurts."

"It's not pain you feel," Morwin said. "Start learning to enjoy it."

He reached his mind towards the rail yard and found Garem. The beast was in a frenzy.

In the prison at his feet, Morwin felt Lyas push against the torrent. All of his energy and will, fought against the hand that forced him down. Enough power to level a city tore through his mind, and he would only find to be denied of its grace. He was a conduit. He would spend the rest of his days as a battery. All of that untouchable potential would ruin a man's spirit. Yet even against the raging torrent the man managed to raise his head and meet Morwin's eyes. It was like watching a child rise from a fall.

"Your mind is tainted black. I can see it. You haven't erased all of my will," Lyas grunted.

"Not yet, but I will learn," Morwin spat. "What you can see, I can see tenfold. No amount of effort will break through the chains I have on you. It's pathetic to see what you failed to use. All of this power, and you thought the higher road was to be... responsible?"

Lyas painfully groaned as his legs became limp. "Do you actually believe any sane person would see your perspective? The power we have, untapped, is only good for people like you. Monsters. Villains. Pure evil. I held restraint because I understand responsibility."

"Responsibility is what holds us back from evolving," Morwin said. "You and your whole family, completely wasted. You could have rolled over every nation in a day. This world could have been yours to mould."

"It's not mine to rule. It's no-ones," Lyas said.

"No," Morwin spat. "You have no clue how wrong you are. Gifted like you, your family, me, are the next step in Aross's evolution. Humanity had its chance and failed this planet in every aspect imaginable. Aross created people like us to save it. I know this because it *speaks* to me."

"So the cure is... just genocide, then?"

"Absolutely," Morwin stated. "I will no longer waste anymore time on patience. I will erase every weak, pathetic, human meat bag that walks this planet."

Lyas exhaled in a sharp grunt. "What the fuck did they ever do to you?"

They hurt us.

THEY HATE US.

"They failed to evolve before me. Simple as that."

"So why keep me prisoner? Just kill me. Spare me this prophetical bullshit."

Morwin shook his head. "I need you, Lyas. I need you for your mind. You feel all that cold energy? That's all you. That's how much power even just one of us can wield. You needed guidance. You needed that 'awakening'. But for the sake of this planet, it is best if I'm in control."

Morwin lowered himself till he was face to face with Lyas. He reached out and grabbed Lyas's jaw with a firm hand and squeezed. The fear in his eyes was maddening.

"Can you feel what I feel? The jealousy?" Morwin whispered. "Joel, Garem, you. Those who I've connected with... all hold so much more power than me. It sits there waiting to be used, but all of you believe... believed you were part of some higher purpose. There is no honour waiting for you. Your vision of helping humanity is a non-existent virtue. Really, think about how they would react to our reveal. They would hunt us, shame us, hate us. They would do everything in their power to eradicate us because humans need to be the predators. If they aren't at the top of the chain, their minds explode out of panic. They would never accept that we exist."

"You're wrong," Lyas gasped.

"I see, deep down, you agree with me. They won't share this world. They will never give us a chance to protect it. Humans want to be the knight facing down whatever planet killing threat faces them. They're so far up their own asses they actually believe they can win. They can't. I've dreamt it. Before I found my powers, I saw the horrors that will engulf Aross in an instant. The universe is unforgiving; it is hungry. And only we can save it from this planet's doom."

"If you wipe out humanity," Lyas groaned through Morwin's hand. "You kill the chance of more gifted rising. Without humanity, there are no gifted."

"Wrong again," Morwin squeezed harder. "When I'm done, it will just be me and your family left. They will all submit to my mind. We will create our new race, of only those who wield power like us. That is our evolution. And they will understand this planet's importance because I will teach them."

Lyas tried to lift a limp hand. It fell against Morwin's chest, just below the wound Lyas helped cause. "You can't beat them. My family will come for you. They won't stop until you're a cold body."

"You will find the hope you dearly cling to is useless," Morwin said. "Right now they struggle to face Garem. They are hurt, they are scared. They will not see me until it's too late. Your family didn't realize; I expected you this entire time. You believed you had the upper hand, but you walked right into my open arms. I needed you, Lyas. I lured you here. I never intended on being captured, but to use you specifically. They will see your face besides mine and their last conscious thought will be 'why are you betraying me?'"

"Let's go then," Lyas laughed. "Go find them. I wanna watch you fail."

Morwin slowly released his grip and stood above his prisoner. "Humanity goes first. I hope you feel every second of it, knowing you were the conduit to their demise. Thank you, Lyas. I couldn't have done this without your mind."

Enough! Consume him!
Abuse his power within!

The two were raised higher above the towers. Morwin spread his connected minds outwards. He surged the power from Lyas into his psychic reach. Energy rushed into him like a freezing blizzard. From him, he shot it across the city and past. He could feel thousands, then millions of minds connecting to his reach. The power didn't falter. He had unlimited potential. Morwin knew he could connect every human mind across the entire planet, and sever them in an instant. He needed a rooted grip first; it would be slow, but it was possible.

So many souls...

End their existence!

Morwin hadn't noticed that the power he wielded was manipulating physical material around him. Buildings in and around the entire city began to levitate and raise from the ground they were built on. Rubble, cars and broken roads smashed between the walls of the floating towers. The air filled with debris and anything that wasn't nailed down. Every molecule moved with Morwin's expanding reach.

The psychic dome forming around the city must have been a discharge of the power that now blanketed the planet. The destruction of Tem-Mire was beautiful, even more so than it was before. He chose a proper place to create his vision.

He looked down at Lyas and found him passed out. The man couldn't handle the ongoing assault of power that flowed through him. At least he was quiet now. Morwin turned his focus back onto his reach. The edges of his mind were a quarter way across the planet's surface, linking to every mind under his shadow. It would only be a few more minutes now. Time was difficult to tell, unfortunately. The euphoric rush of power filled him with ecstasy that crippled his senses. The prospect of letting it go angered him. However, the planet that awaited him held a higher award. It would be a world without flaws. A world he deserved. A world he controlled. And under him, an army of those who would love him.

CHAPTER 44

The rubble that fell around Sadie's body didn't hurt her, but the panic of seeing her family in danger set in quickly. She materialized to an open pocket within the collapsed sewer and found sunlight from above shined on. Dust smeared her clothes and skin. Part of her mind was stuck on Lyas being taken. However, she needed to pull out her friends first. She couldn't chase after Morwin alone.

Sadie reached out with her mind until she felt the beating hearts of her three trapped sisters. Morwin's words of trouble in the train yard rang in her ears. She felt pulled in every direction; she was spread too thin. Sadie flipped the butt end of a demolished cab forward and found Rowan underneath. She seemed uninjured, but a deep fear glared from within her eyes.

"He took Lyas," Rowan gasped.

"Help me dig out the others," Sadie said.

Rowan shuffled out of the rubble and the two of them quickly tossed shattered concrete off of Natasha and Veronica. When Natasha found her bearings, she grabbed Sadie by the arm and pulled her in close.

"Aiden is in trouble. I can feel it," she snapped.

Sadie held Natasha's arms and reaffirmed her. "I'm going with you. Veronica and Rowan, you chase after Lyas. We will join you once Garem is restrained."

In a second, Sadie took all four of them up to the surface. When the sunlight settled in their vision, they noticed large objects suspended in the air, stripped of their gravity. Buildings around them vibrated with a concerning intensity. She couldn't see any civilians, but Sadie wasn't confident they got to them all. The city was falling into chaos, and Morwin was nowhere to be seen.

Sadie grabbed Natasha's hand and shot towards the train yard in the city's industrial zone. She wasn't sure where to land, but found a small electrical junction where they could start looking.

The two of them materialized into the physical world. Around them were lines of rusted rail lines, black tankers, and vandalized box cars. The ground kicked up fine dust as they landed. The middle of the large train yard was mostly empty, except for Garem standing there in his armoured form. Without the low ceiling of the crammed sewer, Garem towered eight feet above the ground. Every limb was thicker than a tree trunk, covered with dark silver metal plated over each other like scales. A sharp, hole-less helmet wrapped around his head. Yellow discharge leaked from the thin slits that connected each plate.

In one giant hand, he held Aiden's limp body. In the other was Aiden's head. When Garem caught Sadie and Natasha in his sight, he threw Aiden towards them and they watched his lifeless body roll over the rails.

"He couldn't outrun me. None of you can," Garem boomed through his plated head.

Sadie could feel an intense heat form beside her. Before she could stop her, Natasha stepped forward and unleashed a jet of white hot fire that consumed the space ahead of them. Her mournful scream was muffled by the raging fire. Steel rails next to the flame instantly glowed bright red and curled upwards. She couldn't see Garem through the flames, but she felt a panicked intuition they wouldn't be enough to stop him.

Sadie grabbed Natasha by the arm. Right before Sadie blipped them away she saw Garem leap through flames; he was inches away from grabbing them before she was able to teleport to a safe distance. She landed a few hundred yards away from the beast. Natasha's flame fizzled out, but she forcefully shoved Sadie away once she gained her footing.

"Let me go, Sadie!" Natasha cried out. Flames burst around her legs and she shot up into the air above the trains. Fireballs the size of cars arched from her fury, hurled down towards Garem in a fiery rain. The armoured man absorbed and stepped away from them like they were only cusps of wind.

Aiden was gone. Sadie wanted to mourn, but death was only a moment away. If Natasha wasn't careful, Garem would easily catch her. Callum was nowhere to be seen. She needed to act fast.

Garem grabbed an oil tanker still connected to its adjacent tankers. In one effortless toss the tanker broke off from its connections and soared directly towards Natasha. Sadie unleashed a deadly bolt of lightning and watched the tanker burst into an oily fireball. Fire from the explosions, moulded by Natasha, arched in two different directions and back towards Garem. The sticky flames plastered his armour as it rained down. He carelessly wiped it off without a thought.

Sadie stepped forward and raised her arms towards the sky. Lightning crackled in the clouds above. She threw down her brewing storm and dozens of blue bolts shot down onto Garem's body. Lightning arched across his armour and stuck to the rails that lined the ground beneath. Sparks danced in every direction with each strike. She heard him grunt, but it wasn't enough to hold him back from leaping towards her. Sadie dropped away in a flash, just missing Garem's fatal blow.

In a second, she reappeared behind Garem. She needed to keep her distance; she could get drowned in Natasha's fire or caught by Garem's unexpected speed. She conjured a heated bolt of lightning, but before she unleashed her strike she noticed something in the corner of her eye.

Across the yard was a damaged box car thrown off of its rails. It was folded inwards, and a black boot was sticking out of the torn metal. Callum. Sadie instantly teleported beside the body and found Callum crushed in the mangled box car. Blood poured down his head. His short black hair was wet and plastered to his skin from an open wound. She could see him still breathing; she could feel his heartbeat.

"Callum!" Sadie called out. She looked behind her to check for Garem; he was occupied with Natasha's fire storm. Sadie knelt down and tried shaking Callum awake. He was knocked out cold. Sadie placed a hand over his chest and fired an uncomfortable amount of voltage into him. Callum's eyes shot open, and he sat upwards with a quaking gasp. Sadie grabbed his jacket and shook him forcefully. "I need you now!"

Callum's eyes met hers. She could see the delirium slowly leave. He must have taken a horrible hit to get him this shaken. "Huh, what?..."

Sadie turned around again to check for Garem. She couldn't see him, but she could hear commotion somewhere in the yard. "You need to help with Garem right now. He killed Aiden. We need to stop him."

"Aidens' dead?" Callum asked with concern.

"We will all be if we don't do something quickly."

Callum sighed in pain. His hand wiped away blood that smeared his cheek. "I can't, Sadie. He's too strong for me. He resists everything I throw at him."

Sadie turned and pulled him up to his feet. "If we don't try, he will kill us all."

Leaving Callum to finish waking up, Sadie blipped back into the train yard and found Natasha and the beast in a close spat. Natasha jetted a bright flame so hot that Sadie could feel its heat at the distance she stood. Garem was on one knee, using his arm to shield himself from the flame. Beneath the flames, Garem's armour was slowly heating to a glowing orange. But Natasha had stepped too close.

Garem grabbed her by the leg and the flames whisked around them as she was pulled off her feet. His other hand shot towards her head and enveloped it with his massive palm. Her fiery, red hair spilled out between his fingers. Natasha rolled out of Garem's grip the moment Sadie's lightning bolt connected with his face. Garem held his head as if he was in pain and stumbled back. The sharp crack of the bolt thundered across the yard as the heated air collapsed back into itself. Sadie saw her window and materialized in front of the beast. She threw her weight forward into her fist and sent the steel monster flying backwards. The connection of her fist to metal pitched a reverberating song of violence. They would only get a few more seconds until he was back on his feet.

Sadie picked Natasha up and her sister immediately found her footing as if she wasn't just a second away from dying. They watched as Garem picked himself up and kicked away a pile of steel rails that piled into him. His chest slowly regained its dark steel colour as it cooled and lost its hot, red glow. A black burn mark smeared his face where his right eye should have been. He could be injured. It would be slow, and dangerous, but they could do it.

Around his feet, the long bars of rails began to vibrate and snaked around Garem's legs. More were raised into the air by an invisible hand and were thrown around his arms. His body slowly was plastered with layers of metal, forcing Garem to kneel against the weight that was piled on. Sadie looked to her side and found an injured Callum walking forward. He furiously picked up any metal beside him and shot it towards the beast. Rails, metal sheets and undercarriages flew across the sky and dove into the massive pile. The scream and crashing of metal tearing apart filled the air.

Garem burst from the metal prison and grabbed a handful of rails in his reach. He jumped towards Callum at a terrifying speed and swatted him away with a swift backhand of the rails. Callum's body forcefully crashed into the ground, kicking up dust and gravel. He showed no sign of getting back up.

Natasha burst into the air and jetted a white hot inferno towards Garem. He dodged away from its impact and tossed the rails towards Natasha. Her peripheral must have been enveloped by the flame, as the rails collided into her without so much as a reaction. A tail of fire twisted into the sky as Natasha fell downwards. Sadie looked up to find her, hoping to catch her midair. But it was a terrible mistake, as in the corner of her eye she saw a glimmer of silver.

The impact was so sudden that Sadie didn't know which way was up. She could feel her body tear through layers and layers of metal, then into what she believed was the ground. Dirt and concrete exploded around her. Her mind rattled through the onslaught of the furious tumble she was struck into. She tried to find a connection of energy to stop herself, but her lack of balance denied her.

The pain of the impact set in when Sadie collided with a solid wall that ended her crashing roll. She could see open, blue sky, and her back was against a hard surface. Her mind felt like it was thrown into a blender, and pain seared up her chest and across her arm. Every emotion poured into her body. Her mind tried to find balance, but the impact had crippled her to a point she wasn't sure if her body would continue working. She wanted to scream and cry. She felt fear of dying, and fear for her family. She felt the love she cherished escape into her memories for one final view. She needed to fight back. She needed to get up.

Sadie slowly crawled up to her knees; the pain became too great, forcing her to rest. She looked around her and found herself against the concrete ramp of an intersection deeper within the city The trainyard was nowhere in sight. She thought her mind was still settling as the air around her seemed to be boiling and more objects like cars and buildings appeared to be rising above the ground.

Her hand squeezed the arm that felt frozen. She was bleeding, but nothing felt broken. She still had a role in this fight. While she forced herself up, a crash in front of her sent shattered concrete in every direction. The metal monstrosity landed with a brutish charade. He slowly stood up straight, towering over Sadie. Being this close, she could see the tainted yellow discharge leaking out from under every plate. She could smell a sour rot in his odour that left a foul taste on her tongue. Was he here because he had already finished her friends, and she was all that was left? Sadie knew she wouldn't be spared, and she wasn't about to go out begging.

Before Garem could step forward, Sadie connected with each outlet and conduit around them that still carried even the slightest trickle of energy. The air around them became excited and raised the hairs on the back of her neck. A thick taste of metal coated her mouth, and she knew Garem could taste it too.

The beast stepped out of his crater and was greeted by a web of crackling lightning. The air screamed continuously as lightning blasted out of every connection and met with Garem's solid mass. Sadie pulled energy across the entire city and unleashed it into a violent, turbulent bundle. Garem tried to escape, but was locked in. The smell of metal in the air was replaced with burnt flesh. Sadie let the excited electrons carry her up till she was floating; her reach extended to pull in more power for her flood. She pulled power from the sky, across the land, and from the ground. Anything with voltage was sent flying towards the web that assaulted Garem.

When the power dwindled, Sadie cut every stream with a sudden halt. Below her, Garem knelt in a tangle of crystallized bolts that grew from the glassed ground. His body was covered with burn marks and searing metal. The ground sizzled and smoke slowly replaced every point of contact that was cooling. The beast painfully looked up to find her. The crystals around him began to crack and shatter as he moved his body. Like her, Garem wasn't about to give up his life. She wasn't about to give him a chance to save it, either.

Sadie drew in a terrible storm of energy, ready to unravel its fury. Garem began to stand and shake off the sharp, crystallized branches. The monster wouldn't stay down. Her mind and body filled with anger, followed by an unexpected feeling she hadn't felt in a very long time.

CHAPTER 45

Time within the fold of space was difficult to tell. Joel wasn't sure how long or how far he had travelled at this point. He remembered saying goodbye to Janak, but that seemed like days ago... or seconds.

Either way, it didn't feel like this when he jumped across the emptiness of space in Janak's ship. Maybe being exposed to the vacuum of space affected him differently? Whereas being inside if a ship helped equalize time's perspective? Joel wasn't sure. Physics and theory were never his expertise. In what seemed like ages ago, Joel pursued forestry because it allowed him to be outside all day. His job was to mark desired lumber and keep exploring until he was told to stop. That was a much simpler life. Now he was on his way home to aid humanity into the next era. An era of hope.

The darkness of the fold left Joel alone with his thoughts for too long. But just before he accepted a state of boredom, the holographic lens displayed a heads up display. It showed his destination closing in with units rapidly decreasing in light seconds. Joel waited until the metre cusped the edge of dangerously close and then dropped out of the fold. Stars shot back into place from an exploding lattice of light.

The planet of Aross suddenly ballooned into his view. The familiar continents of his home and neighbouring nations sat in a wide, blue ocean dotted by white clouds of every size. Cities in the shadow of dusk glowed a warm, speckled light. He could see the cities of Blackpine, Yarford and Golden basking in sunlight. He could outline the long range of mountains that ran along the spine of Lavendy, and the wide, flat deserts of Jaussa.

Against what seemed like impossible odds, he was home.

Before he could fly closer, a sudden and overpowering emotion slammed into his mind. An empty hole within his spirit was instantly flooded with the water that was desperately missed. His mind and body quaked with the return of what was stolen. The intensity screamed with emotions of fear and horrible pain. Pain of doom, grief, and failure. Joel felt like he was in danger and seconds away from death. The sudden surge that overwhelmed him was so powerful that he almost didn't recognize the emotions didn't belong to him.

They belonged to Sadie. She was alive.

Joel fixed onto where the bond pulled him and fired forward. The powerful release of energy brought him to a terrifying speed. Light around him began to blur and darken. Only a pinpoint, directly in the middle of his vision, remained definitive.

The edge of the atmosphere shattered around his body. The dense sphere of air tried to slow him and failed. Sound and light could not match his speed. The planet pitched towards him like he was a bug to a windshield. At the velocity he was travelling, nothing would be able to save itself from the impending obstacles ahead, but Joel's reaction to time at this speed felt almost natural. It was in his control. The distances of space and reality could be closed faster than light. Whatever he commanded, it was his.

At the last second, between Joel and the ground, he locked into a familiar mass of metal that had attacked him once before. Garem, in his monstrous form, shone like a brightly lit target. He stood there menacingly, frozen in time and unsuspecting Joel's arrival. The beast was too close to Sadie's bond for Joel's own comfort; now Joel knew exactly where to land.

Light rushed back into place the moment Joel made contact. The air around them was forced out; the impact between Joel's fist and Garem's head released a white hot rupture, and the ground caved into a deep crater. The blast shot debris and rubble in every direction; metal and concrete close to the impact vaporized in the heat. It took a few seconds for sound to catch up, but when the trailing thunder of Joel's flight met the core explosion, the city cried in an alarming song of a direct barrage.

None of it phased Joel. His eyes remained fixed on Garem's crippled body. The beast was buried under rolling concrete and dirt. His armour scorched fiercely, showing a large dent that caved in a portion of his head. As Joel floated above him, he felt a surge of disbelief and surprise pulse beside him.

Turning towards the bond, Joel found Sadie standing on the ground and lowering an arm that shielded her head. Her eyes met his. A doubtful shock grew stronger, and then weakened, as they held their reuniting gaze. Both of them fought against the belief that the other should have been dead; the void that was empty filled itself so swiftly it was difficult to accept.

Joel tightened the pulses that raised him and floated down towards her. He gently dropped onto the ground and collapsed his helmet. Her usually tightly wrapped ponytail had broken open and blonde waves poured down over her shoulders. Her deep brown eyes studied his face; she recognized what she had lost, but what was lost should have been gone forever.

"It's me, Sadie. It's just me," Joel assured. His throat struggled to speak through the swelling.

Sadie jumped forward and wrapped Joel into a tight embrace. Her nose could be felt against his neck; her familiar scent of rain and juniper filled his senses like a drug. His arms moved around her back and pulled her in tighter. What he thought was lost, killed by his hand, lived and breathed against his body. The bewildered scepticism fizzled, and Joel felt a surge of relief and love return in its place. The intoxicating feeling buzzed between them as it balanced itself into pure equals. Out of an entire, endless universe, this was where he was needed.

"I felt you die," Sadie cried into his shoulder. "I could feel your absence. You died."

Joel squeezed her tighter and noticed an odd assortment of floating objects drift around them. Buildings hovered above their broken foundations, and were slowly rising higher. The air around them boiled so subtly that he almost missed it. Joel realized this didn't end with Garem.

Behind them, a rumbling toil echoed from the crater. Joel turned and found the steel monster crawling his way out of the pit Joel forced him into. His caved head bled a thick, dark blood mixed with an oily yellow discharge. The lack of eyes made it difficult to judge where the beast was looking, but Joel knew they were fixed on them.

Joel snapped back towards Sadie and held her shoulders intently. "Sadie, there is a lot I need to explain. But what do you need me to do here?"

Sadie's eyes darkened as she leaned in. Fury hijacked her perfection. Grief and anger rolled into the bond between them and demanded blood. "He killed Aiden. Go for his head."

The imminent danger that posed itself could be fully understood with Joel's past. Garem had the jump on Joel once; the beast was answerable to Joel's eruption in Fasdoba. Even feeling the loss of Aiden through Sadie's bond was enough to convince him what needed to be done.

Joel faced the crawling brute and stormed towards him, unleashing an angled pulse. Garem was thrown backwards with savage force. His body slammed into the far end of the crater; his arms shakily reached out to grab onto anything near him. Joel leaped over the mouth of the crater and stomped onto the bulk of Garem's chest. In three swift punches, Garem's head was swallowed by the ground. Joel spotted a seam in Garem's helmet and he quickly took hold of its exposed edge with a firm grip. As he pulled, the sound of grinding metal on metal screeched like nails on a chalkboard. The armour was strong, but Joel could feel it move.

In the corner of his vision, Joel saw a glimmer of fast moving silver. Before he could react, the world around him flashed blue and then instantly rematerialized into its physical form. Sadie held onto his arm, breathing heavily. She had brought them maybe ten feet away from the crater; Garem crouched over the bank where Joel stood just a second ago.

The beast flung around and snapped toward his escaped prey. The brutes' speed surpassed what Joel had expected.

Lunging across the crater, Garem was met with an unexpected, concentrated explosive to his temple. Rowan repelled down from a tower floating above their heads and shot a couple more rounds of her engineered arrows.

Joel jumped across to Garem's flank and readied a hellish concussion. The moment Garem lifted himself from the crater, the shock sent him spiralling down the destroyed street and across a handful of torn foundations.

Sadie zipped to Rowan, then grabbed Joel, and placed them a few feet away from the shaken and dazed monster. As the light flooded back into Joel's vision, he unleashed a straight beam of plasmic energy dead centre into the brute. The green blade burned with a ferocious intensity. Anything, and everything, that the plasma has touched in the past had become completely disintegrated. Yet, the blade had only left a long burn mark on Garem's armour.

Garem rolled to his knees and sprang back onto his feet, giving himself distance from his attackers. Above him, a hovering tower began to descend. Garem grabbed onto the steel beams that dangled in reach, and the brute threw all his weight forward with the tower.

Joel watched as the tower crumbled towards them. It was like watching a cut tree slowly topple onto the lower forest beneath it. Sadie didn't give them time to react, as suddenly they found themselves blipped back into the city on the other side of Garem's home cooked weapon.

Torn metal and glass shattering roared towards them, as dust and rubble burst beneath the falling skyrise. The dust didn't even have time to envelope Garem's body before a deadly lightning strike crashed into his back. His body was thrown into the collapsing rubble, disappearing away from the clap of thunder that followed.

"One of us needs to tear away just one part of armour," Joel said, huffing through short breaths. "He can't be all metal underneath. He has to have some weakness."

Rowan swiftly snapped an explosive arrow to her bowstring. "Whoever gets there first, grab a limb and pin him down. Last one there goes for the kill."

A floating tower, wrapped in glass panels, descended along the torn street between them and Garem. Its base collided with the ground, grinding metal and glass in a destructive scrape. Bursting from its surface, Garem jumped through the tower's body, leaving a trail of shattered glass and rubble behind him. When he landed, the ground quaked and cracked beneath his terrible mass. Other than the dent along his head, the aberration showed no sign of injury or slowing down.

Using a jettisoned stream of concussive blast to move him forward, Joel hurled himself close to Garem and sent a low, wide blast beneath the creature's knees. Garem tripped forward and tried to brace himself for the fall. His hand was met with an exploding arrow, forcing his arm to shoot out from underneath him.

Before he could push himself up, a flash of blue sparked the sky and dropped directly on Garem's back. A painful grunt slipped behind his helm, and his arm tried to find a balanced support to escape the ground. The tower behind him continued to descend onto the streets it originally rose from. The blending of glass and metal screamed continuously and drowned every thought. Garem was staggered down onto his chest, and he was vulnerable.

A powerful burst of concessive waves sent Joel flying forward and directly onto Garem's arm. Across from him, Sadie appeared from a crack of lightning and grabbed onto the beast's other arm. Joel tried to grab and plant himself with the arm closest to him, but Garem cracked a fist that missed his face by millimetres. Sliding on the asphalt beneath them, Rowan ducked under Garem's thick wrist and wrapped herself around the metal trunk. All that was left was the head.

Like a bull by the horns, Joel grasped the exposed lip of Garem's helm and braced himself onto the bulk of the brutes' back. Joel could see Sadie on one side, and Rowan on the other, both holding an arm as straight as possible with all the grit left in them.

Garem thrashed his body side to side, trying to throw all of his assailants away. Joel held his grip with every muscle in his being, pulling it towards him till the sound of bending metal screamed out. His arms and legs quaked with the force he exerted. The girls most definitely experienced the same, or worse; failing his strike would most definitely lead to death.

Beneath his hands that grasped onto the folded plate was a layer of pulsating flesh. Yellow-stained liquid pooled between every crevice of the meat that hid under the armour. Branching tendrils of mycelium sprouted across every muscle, revealing the extent of how deep Morwin's influence had driven. Innocent, or guilty, the being suffered.

Joel shot forward one hand and thrust his palm into the tainted tissue. The beast's body halted the moment the green flash erupted from Joel's hand. Every tissue within the armoured husk immediately was burned to ash. Whatever wasn't touched by the plasmic blade fell or clung to the shell that was supposed to protect it. As Garem's fight was torn away, his lifeless body became limp and fell onto the shattered pavement with a loud thump. Joel let go of the helmet and rolled forward; he spun towards Garem, preparing himself for an unexpected attack. Nothing came. The brute was a dead, empty shell.

Rowan and Sadie rolled out from under the steeled arm they fought to cling to. Sadie gazed upon Garem's dead body, anticipating a startling revival of the beast. When it became clear to all of them he was dead, Sadie jumped to her feet and took hold of Joel's hand. The warmth of her touch was dearly missed; her grip was an embrace of assurance. Their fatigued breaths matched in unison, but held a looming suspense. The city itself told Joel it wasn't over.

Buildings, cars and rubble hovered around them, each in their own path and colliding in a disastrous crash. The air that surrounded them simmered with an unseen fever. Whatever city Joel had landed in, it was in chaos. The battle wasn't over yet.

Rowan snapped another arrow to her bow and tested its tension. She nodded to the sky above them. "Morwin is up there. He has Lyas."

FORREST A. RICHARD

CHAPTER 46

"This is from Morwin?" Joel asked as he motioned towards the flying interstate of mayhem around them. "How is he able to do this?"

"I don't know," Rowan huffed. "I think he hijacked Lyas's mind or something. I feel like he's watching…"

Joel looked up and tried peering through the jungle of rubble. Morwin was up there somewhere. Whatever intention he had with Lyas would not end peacefully. Joel needed to get up there and end this quickly. Above him, he watched a bulky, older building made of bricks dissolve into pieces as it flew directly into the hull of a cargo ship. The infrastructure of this city, Tem-Mire, Joel guessed, was gone. All he could hope was that everyone made it out alive before the havoc started.

Joel faced Sadie and squeezed her hand tightly. "I need to go alone. The minute Morwin sees either of you he will instantly have control."

"Not happening," Sadie said firmly. "I can jump away the moment he tries. I told you... I told you before you were taken, we'd do this together."

Joel held silent. He couldn't argue with her; they had promised to be at each other's side and he had always intended to follow through. Returning from the grave of deep space didn't change that. He gently lowered his head till it met hers. "Together."

He turned towards Rowan, foreseeing her disagreement. She had just as much to lose in this battle.

"My Lyas is up there. I'm going with you regardless of what consequence will follow," Rowan murmured. The woman's face was steeled, but her voice carried a hushed stress.

Joel nodded. He could not deny the fervour of a shared cause. "What of the others?"

"Veronica is with Callum and Natasha... Us three is all we will have," Rowan said.

Letting go of Sadie's hand with a reaffirming release, Joel stepped back until enough space was made for a safe liftoff. "Meet you up there then."

A sonic clap roared behind Joel's feet as he shot up. Rubble and buildings filled the sky with no room for passage, but Joel would just make his own path. He burst through the litter of glass, steel, and concrete at breakneck speed. In only a few seconds, he burst into open skies and pulled to a sudden halt. The sound of thunder followed his trail.

Hurriedly scanning the cityscape below, Joel looked for any anomaly or thorn that would give away Morwin. It wasn't long before a pattern could be traced into the hurricane of debris. What seemed like mindless chaos below now revealed organized entropy above. The towers and their remains floated in a wide circle that encompassed the entire city boundary. Layers levitated above or below the hurricane's horizon. All the debris drew a path towards an empty middle eye; what Joel searched for laid out in the open like a greeting.

Morwin floated there. Beneath him was a curled body, surrounded by a faint pink sphere. Joel never witnessed Morwin wield levitation. However he was able to conjure this destruction, was most definitely through Lyas. Joel only knew Lyas's abilities to an extent. The man had incredible psychic power, so it wouldn't be impossible for the man to manipulate matter with his own mind.

If a strong connection dominated Lyas's mind, would killing Morwin be Lyas's demise? If time could be exploited, maybe he could figure out how to sever the connection safely. But Morwin wielded a psychic nuke, and if Lyas was anything like Joel, then the bomb was about to trigger.

Holding hope for Lyas's survival, Joel drove near into the escape of light and planted his shoulder directly into Morwin's face. The sociopath was rag dolled across the empty eye, as expected. What was not, was Lyas's body staying near and fixed on Morwin's position, and the entire city, too.

From behind, a curtain of debris swallowed Joel like a raging sea. Morwin and Lyas vanished from his vision, and Joel's body tumbled into a sand pit of mangled rubble and crashing thunder. With a quick reaction, Joel unleashed a powerful concussion and burst through the waves. He found himself above the hurricane again. The eye was close, and in the middle he could see Morwin, searching angrily around him.

Morwin locked onto Joel. He began to move forward, pulling the anchored chaos with him. Joel let Morwin come to him; the pale man seemed to move with disbelief. Morwin stopped when he was eye level with Joel and they were a few feet apart. Joel knew he should attack right then and there, but he would send the city wherever he sent Morwin. He needed to get close.

"I must be dreaming," Morwin whispered. "Is this a vision of you, Lyas? Is this your attempt to buy humanity time?"

Joel could see the delirium in the man's eyes clearly. Fury and excitement filled them. His jaw clenched and grinded; the air around him boiled fiercely. A deep bruise formed where Joel connected, but Morwin seemed unfazed by its pain. Below Morwin's feet, Joel could see short breaths fill Lyas's chest. He was still alive, but locked into whatever prison Morwin held him in.

"Let him go, Morwin," Joel demanded.

The man seemed surprised by the vision speaking. His eyes gazed over every inch of Joel's body. An ethereal and creeping touch prodded the edges of Joel's helmet, trying to find a gap it could slither into. The realization on Morwin's face slowly shaped into anger. "You're... alive? How are you alive?"

"Release Lyas, now!" Joel shouted.

Morwin stared at Joel with gritting teeth. No amount of convincing would turn over Lyas; the power he wielded had already rooted itself as his own addiction. Morwin raised his hands and Joel felt an invisible strap wrap around his arms and pin them. But before it could tighten, a bolt of lightning flashed across the eye and a clap of thunder filled the air. Morwin reached for his scorched neck and tumbled forward.

Joel burst from the psychic cuffs and shot forward. He grabbed Morwin by the throat with one hand and used the other to twist Morwin's wrist into a straight and locked bar. Morwin's eyes burst with a fiery rage, locking directly into Joel's.

Morwin's mouth frothed as he screamed. "I won't let you stop me! DIE!"

Across the entire border of the eye, black and wet tendrils burst from clumps of ripped up dirt and rubble. Joel felt a snap whip across his back, which threw him off his flight. More tendrils wrapped around his limbs and began to pull him apart. Joel twisted one of his palms before it was completely stretched, and beamed hot, green plasma into the black mass. The monstrous mold whipped in a flurry as it was amputated, throwing dark goo in every direction; only for it to float against the psychic storm.

Joel swiftly cut free from the remaining tendrils and flew back towards Morwin. To his surprise, Morwin was prepared to counter his return. Joel's head and body were slammed downwards by what felt like an invisible hammer.

The hammer relentlessly continued to slam his back. Joel unleashed enough concussive force to keep himself airborne, but could feel his strength weakening.

In a quick escape, Joel sent himself flying backwards and out from under the psychic punch. He pivoted back towards the sky and sped past Morwin's tendril reach. In both hands, mounting energy grew in the vibrating rings. Joel thrusted his aim towards Morwin and a screaming, fatal ray of green illuminated the sky.

Morwin dived out of its path and the entire hurricane jolted with him. Joel tried to connect the blade with Morwin's position, but the intensifying energy burst through. His arms and hands started to shake and burn, overcoming his aim and forcing him to cut the power.

An unseen hand gripped Joel's throat and chest, immediately squeezing all the air from his lungs. He violently gasped for air and tried to reach for the phantom grip. His vision began to fade, until a blinding flash of blue filled the eye. Joel looked and saw Morwin turning and trying to find who had just attacked him. An arrow, smouldering with a brown sap at the tip pierced below Morwin's rib cage. Morwin flailed his hand against the injury with a manic hysteria. Joel trusted Sadie to move Rowan and herself away from Morwin's immediate reach, as Joel accepted what needed to be done.

The moment he felt Sadie's bond disappear into her realm, Joel sprang from where he stood and descended onto Morwin with all of his weight. Thunder cried from the forceful impact. Morwin dropped like a peppered bird, spiralling out of control. The city, and Lyas, fell along with him. The hurricane's body flattened itself into the ground with Morwin's telekinetic anchor, tossing clumps of concrete and destroyed buildings in every direction. The sound of a city crashing down echoed across the bay and mountains that it once stood between. Rubble poured like an avalanche into the harbour, turning the lake's surface a tempestuous white. Sections of skyscrapers, that had somehow survived the psychic hurricane, collapsed into dust. Gravity against Morwin, took everything down with him. The only thing that remained in the sky was Joel, flying above a disastrous graveyard.

With a quick descent, Joel landed and shattered the ground beneath him. Laying at his feet, he watched Morwin struggle to crawl up on his arms. Lyas's body was next to him. The pink hue had disappeared; short breaths could still be seen.

Morwin's chest was beginning to dissolve from the arrow's wound. It was slow, and Morwin's body actively was fighting to heal itself. The smell of liquefying flesh filled Joel's senses.

Morwin was using all the strength left in him to crawl away. His panicked breaths sounded like bones scraping each other as they rattled through his lungs.

On the other side of Morwin, Sadie and Rowan materialized with a quick flash. At first, Joel was filled with panic. Morwin could still dominate their minds. But Sadie held a reaffirming look, promising to break away if she felt anything unkind.

Morwin stopped crawling and flipped onto his back. He looked around, reflecting on the presence of Lyas and those who toppled him.

"Have you tried fleeing yet?" Rowan asked Morwin as she stepped around to face him. She knelt beside Lyas and placed her hand on his neck to check for life. "That poison sure takes the fun away, wouldn't you agree?"

"Fuck you, bitch," Morwin spat. Blood as black as oil spilled from his lips. He turned back towards Joel and scowled with a face of pure anger and pain. Joel felt a touch of pity for the man; his pathetic obsession with Joel was an illness he desperately tried to shake. "You should have stayed dead. Humanities' final breath was in my hands, and you just... took it away."

Joel stared down at him. He had nothing to say to this monster. Morwin had terrorized him from the start of this chapter of his life. This man thought he was entitled to some penance? Joel didn't believe any significance existed between them at all.

"What?" Morwin squabbled. "Nothing to say to me? No heroic speech of triumph for you? If you truly believe humanity will forgive you for this... you're terribly mistaken. These abilities we wield are too powerful for them to just let us keep them. They will come after you, and your take family. You should have just let me end them. I could have made this world a home for those like us."

Joel continued to stare at him. Words couldn't be found. Maybe Morwin had some truth to his hate. Humanity was once something Joel despised for being a part of. Growing to find a future for them was something that seemed past his acceptance. How much struggle would he and his family have to endure to finally build a better world? Even with the gift he returned to Aross with, would humanity give it a chance? Coming home was a gamble, but Joel was ready to try. The hate died with Morwin.

The crippled monster at Joel's feet began to froth at the mouth. His teeth gnashed as he screamed and cried. "Say something! I showed you who you are! I am part of you! I want you to remember what you told me when you finally realize humanity doesn't want anything to do with you! I want-"

The space between Morwin's jaw and chest instantly vaporized. The green flash of plasma was swift; its light dissipated with a sudden finish. He stepped closer to the body and released another short beam consuming the rest of his head. The ground beneath smouldered as the energy was cut. It was better to be sure, for if Morwin somehow returned, he would forever regret his mistake.

Joel knew he had killed before, but never had he killed with intent. Morwin's death was justified; life was precious, but Morwin was miles beyond saving. This day held no heroics, just a deeply hidden relief that the nightmare was gone.

Joel slowly stepped towards Sadie and embraced her longingly. He felt her arms wrap around his back with a hand gently cusped around the nape of his neck. A warm feeling of safety settled between them. His helmet collapsed away and the skin of his cheek touched hers. He was safe. He was with her.

"I'm so sorry," Joel said softly.

Sadie buried her face into the collar of his jacket and rested her head. "It's okay."

Rowan turned Lyas onto his side and placed his head into her lap. She looked up at Joel and Sadie with tears welling beneath her eyes. "Get the others. We should go home."

CHAPTER 47

Rowan carefully lowered Lyas's unconscious body onto their bed. She dipped his head until it was comfortably placed and removed his torn clothes. Joel could see Lyas's eyes unpleasantly darting beneath his closed eyelids. His breaths were ragged and short. Whatever battle raged in that man's head was not an easy one.

Joel and Sadie kept a respectful distance, standing in the entrance of their bedroom, watching Rowan wash away the dirt on Lyas's face with a damp cloth. Veronica knelt beside Lyas on top of the mattress and placed his head between her hands. A hazy crimson glow enveloped Lyas's face and cast a dull, red light within the room. Soon, the glow dissipated from Veronica's hands. She looked up at Rowan while mournfully shaking her head.

"Try again in an hour," Rowan demanded. She bent down to wash the dirty cloth in the bucket at her feet. "We have to keep trying."

Veronica shifted herself off the bed and left the room without a word. She looked exhausted. Joel had watched her spend the past hour conjuring whatever healing spells the family needed. The portal home seemed to have spent the remaining vigour left in her. Veronica needed rest as much as the others.

The family had left Tem-Mire pretty quickly. Once they had reunited, they spared no time in collecting Aiden's remains and leaving before the collateral truly began. Right before entering the portal home, Joel could see the military beginning to fill the air space. They would be combing the debris for any remains, and clues to the culprits responsible for the gruesome slaughter of their cherished city.

Setting foot back on the farm didn't change everyone's mood for the better. Natasha fell into a grief-stricken collapse. The safety of the farm must have triggered permission to mourn. She planted herself over Aiden's corpse and refused any help and comfort. Sadie stayed with her until she could finally convince Natasha to move.

Joel gave them space and offered Callum a shoulder to hold for balance as they walked up to Lyas's cottage. There in the living room, Veronica tended his wounds. The two of them could not stop glancing towards Joel. He felt like a ghost. Joel promised them he would explain everything; he just wanted them to settle in first.

When Sadie returned from bringing Natasha to her cabin, and swathed Aiden's body, she and Joel walked upstairs together and checked on Rowan and Lyas. All of them had lost in their own way. As badly as Joel wanted to talk with Sadie, he needed to give her time to tend to her family. He could feel her eagerness too; they both knew the time would come for just themselves.

"Why won't he wake," Rowan whispered. Joel wasn't sure if she was talking to herself. Loneliness was an unforgiving affliction.

"We will be just downstairs, okay, Rowan?" Sadie said quietly. Rowan nodded without looking at them and continued to wash away the grime on Lyas. Sadie looked up at Joel and tipped her head for them to leave. The two of them walked downstairs, back to the living room, and found Callum and Veronica watching the news on the TV.

The media was in mayhem. Dozens of clips and calamitous remarks played in a continuous stream. Whatever channel they turned to was centred on Tem-Mire. Some had already compared and theorized the connections with Fasdoba. Interviews of survivors and civilians played in short clips, focusing on available commentary that amplified the disaster's magnitude.

"We were evacuated without choice."

"My mind was taken over!"

"Everything, to my name, has been destroyed."

The anger and misery were justified. An entire city was levelled in less than an hour. There would be no celebration of life; no one would ever know the stakes that were at play. Humanity was seconds away from extinction, and they didn't even know. The lack of truth would drive them furious. Explanation for the losses of Mercer, Fasdoba, and Tem-Mire were desperately wanted. The planet was tired of disaster after disaster; Joel could only hope it ended today.

Conspiracies were rarely touched by mainstream media, however, whatever evidence was tossed up was picked apart as by ravenous vultures. Blame on foreign adversaries fell into a laborious cycle of revolving accusations. Clips of protests, spanning many countries broke out. Answers were demanded, but whatever was thrown to the hungry swarms was just not good enough.

"The Governor of New Vessel has placed immediate sanctions on Tunland-manufactured imports in an unexpected legislative motion. The Northern Union, Prime Minister, has condemned this decision, causing interpolitical tension."

"The Vallan government promised to escalate their response to eradicate the terrorist group, Saddars, in response to their alleged involvement in Tem-Mire's attack."

"Large protests have broken through police barricades in downtown St. Michael. Mayors of the surrounding cities are attempting to divert the thousands of refugees trying to find shelter."

The world is in chaos. People couldn't handle the lingering doom they believed would devour them next. Much of their pain was Joel's fault. He knew he had contributed to their anger. In some way, he had a part in Tem-Mires destruction. Maybe if he accepted his abilities sooner, he could have ended Morwin before the incidents. As much as he would like to return to a simpler time, he needed to face the consequences that lay in his future. It was now Joel's responsibility to make the world a better place than when he left it. However, as clips continued playing on TV, Joel realized that could be harder than he imagined.

Blurry videos and pictures of the family were wiggling into the media's spotlight. Stories and theories were attached to the mysterious people with mysterious powers. As the evidence continued to pour in, it became harder for the media to deny its presence. Accusations born from anger and grief were created; any explanation to make these anomalies make sense were born from the hundreds. Each member of the family was caught by some snapped picture and video. None of them were clear enough to identify a specific person, but that didn't stop people and media from making their own theories.

"These are government agents that were given weapons made with taxpayer dollars!"

"Dozens of reports are flooding in with confirmation of these 'unknown persons' were present at the sites of recent disasters."

"They're aliens! I saw them descend from the sky!"

"What right do they have to control my mind? It is a violation of privacy to use their powers on me!"

"I know the girl who controls lightning. She went to my high school."

The onslaught of insults and allegations were brutal to watch. But what right of it was Joel's to be upset? Unchecked power had killed so many loved ones, and the lack of explanation forced humanity to make their own truth. Now the entirety of Aross had grown a fearful hate of the family. How in the hell was Joel supposed to convince them of The Seekers' gift? The longer they remained unknown to the world, the harder his mission would become.

But no matter how hateful humanity would become, Joel would follow-up his promise. Too much blood was on his hands. Giving up because of humanity's villainous vision of them would not stop him from what he promised. Whatever future lay ahead, whatever obstacle blocked him, Joel would fight to make his planet a better place. Humanity would not be left behind.

"Let's turn this off," Veronica said. She grabbed the remote and powered off the TV.

The four of them sat in silence. There was no celebration earned; there was no victory in destruction. The longer they sat, the more Joel yearned to speak with Sadie. They looked at each other in agreement to leave, but stayed seated when they heard Rowan come downstairs. She joined them in the living room, sitting on a loveseat and tucking her knees close to her chest.

"We thought you were dead, Joel... If we knew you were alive, we would have tried..." Rowan stuttered.

"I don't think you could have, even if you knew," Joel responded. Trying to explain his journey through space was not something he had prepared. None of it would sound real, yet they were a group that wielded power beyond comprehension. Luckily, Joel had the proof with him. "Is this a good time to explain what happened? Everyone went through a lot today."

"I'd rather hear your side," Callum said. "If it's not your story, then I'll be sitting in silence or listening to more of the news."

Joel nodded and scanned the room. Everyone seemed in agreement. He could feel an uneasy anxiousness deep in Sadie's gut. All he wanted was time alone with her.

"After I lost control in Fasdoba, I awoke to everything gone. I thought I killed everyone, so I... threw myself into space, thinking it would kill me. But my powers, somehow, brought me across the universe. Many, many light years away."

Joel paused to gauge everyone's face. Everyone seemed patient enough. "I found this incredible planet. It was beautiful, and the creatures there... But I ran into an alien, like an actual alien, with a spaceship. His name is Janak. We had a messy introduction, but we became friends. He's a good friend."

"Janak searches galaxies for life. They go through meticulous documentation of every planet, every system, they come across.

He was studying the planet that I initially landed on. Janak convinced me to meet his 'employers' and we flew to the home of the Celestvendora. They are also called The Seekers. They were a different kind of alien, as their form is an entire galaxy."

"The Seekers… are incredible. They live to preserve whatever life exists out there. The technology and achievements they have made surpass anything we have here, and they have used those creations to aid other planets in evolving. There aren't many species that The Seekers look after, but that's because sentient life is incredibly rare within the universe. They showed me what is possible. They showed me a chance for humanity."

Joel paused. He knew some would be sceptical, and wanted to give room for questions. But everyone was intently listening. "I thought I left Aross behind, but what I saw across the universe was hope. The kind of change that is needed here. For the first time in my life, I truly believe we can make our world a better place. The Seekers found a way to get me home, and they gave me this gift."

Joel summoned his helmet and lifted it from his head. He turned it in his hands so the face was towards him. Its cold steel tingled beneath his hands. The long strip of chrome glimmered his reflection as he stared at it. Joel thought about how much hate he had for this hunk of metal in the past. Now it carried the purpose he defiantly carried. He picked at the chrome strip and plucked it from the helmet. It felt similar to removing a magnet from a fridge door. He held it up for everyone to see.

"What is that?" Sadie asked curiously.

"I'm not sure. Nor do I know how to exactly use this thing. Maybe if I just…" Joel carefully set it down on the coffee table in the middle of the room. He felt like it should have gone on a computer.

The moment his fingers released the strip, a seamless illusion of pictures, videos, and data illuminated the room. Everyone stood from their seats, witnessing the collage of creation present itself for their viewing. They stood in awe and silence, even Joel. He knew he didn't see everything The Seekers had to offer, but not to this extent.

Structures of extraordinary purpose displayed across a span of size and function. Stars surrounded by heat-absorbing transformers; ships the size of moons carrying colonists; bridges transferring data across systems; walking towers making an atmosphere breathable.

Machines tailored to essential disciplines showed how they make a community thrive. Medical advancements, created by the Querell, were shared across the galaxies; ships manufactured for dozens of different scientific fields conducted research on hundreds of planets; urban transportation spanning an entire world could give you access to limitless travel.

The citizens and their homes on core planets were utopias beyond suffering. Mega cities designed by Idelvins with complete efficiency. Opportunities could be accessed without barriers. Pollution and over-consumption were eradicated.

The Seekers had a promise; they created a mission and somewhere across the depths of time they had got themselves there. On their gift for Joel, they showed what possibilities lie ahead under a united duty. Life, in any form, was so precious that its preservation led to the realization of what potential exists.

The data strip revealed more and more, even when they thought nothing else could exist from The Seekers' mind. They believed Joel could save his planet, and they gave him the tools to do so. With this gift, Joel would aid humanity in giving itself a fighting chance. With this gift, The Seekers showed Joel his purpose.

The hologram collapsed when Joel picked the strip up from the coffee table. He held it close to the helmet faceplate, and the magnetic strip clung back to where it was originally placed. Joel took one last look before he put away the helmet, appreciating what the gift carried to aid them.

"Was all of that real?" Rowan asked carefully. "It was all… boundless."

"The grave of the cosmos holds the light to valour," Veronica mumbled. Callum put a hand on her back, awakening her from her usual trance. Her words hung on thin hooks near the back of Joel's mind.

"What do we do with all of this?" Callum asked. "Are these Seekers just going to give us these creations without repayment?"

Joel sighed to himself. There was no payment. There was just the potential to be denied. "We need to give it to the world. If we show this to every nation, maybe we can unite them. In this data strip, is every answer to what humanity has been fighting for. If we fail to convince them, if we fail to tame our violent impulse, then the worst outcome is exile from The Seekers mission. We would be alone in the universe, doomed to die by our own faults. Aross's survival begins with us; this data strip gives us the power to do so."

Rowan leaned forward in her chair, holding a piercing gaze with Joel. "This idea weighs heavily on the word of an alien only you have spoken with. So much of this feels too great to be true, and asking us to trust this path comes with immeasurable risk. We would need to announce our existence to the world; that alone is enough to risk our lives."

Joel agreed. It was an undeniable concern. "I hear you. That's why I invited Janak to meet us here."

"An alien is coming here?" Veronica asked with alarm. "What if they lied to you just to find out where we are?"

"No, I thought the same thing." Joel shook his head. "But I've seen what they're capable of. It's an entire community, united across lengths you can't even fathom. They have proven their mission works. We can be a part of that. We just need to try. I understand the risks that come if we reveal ourselves; I'm ready to face those consequences."

"And if humanity refuses?" Sadie asked quietly beside him. "What will you do then?"

Joel held her gaze and lightly squeezed her hand. Failure may come, but Joel knew he needed to try. That was the hero he promised to become. That was the man he promised Sadie to be. "I can't force humanity to do anything, but I'll do everything in my power to save them."

CHAPTER 48

The sun was beginning to set over the pastures when Sadie and Joel were finally able to break away from the rest of the family, and their many, many questions. Joel could feel a shower call for him; his skin was smeared with grease and dirt. But his attention was needed somewhere more important.

Sadie rubbed her tired eyes and leaned against the porch rail of Lyas's cabin. She felt tired, but anxious at the same time. Joel guessed she had a handful of questions she wanted to ask in private; he was in the same boat. He joined her at the railing and immersed himself in her features. Her hair was down and frizzled, and the small freckles on her face could be traced beneath the grease and dirt that covered her. Her subtle fragrance of rain and juniper his senses desperately missed, returned. It still felt surreal that she was alive; seeing her living and breathing next to him was an impossible dream not too long ago. He wanted to share with her how much it meant that she was alive, but with the bond, some things didn't need to be said. They could just be, and that's all they needed.

Sadie looked up at him. Her dark brown eyes held a thin film of tears. She couldn't believe his return was real, either. Her voice stuttered as she softly spoke, "I thought you were dead. If I knew you were alive... I would have crossed the cosmos to get you back."

Joel could feel her drown in regret. "It's not your fault, Sadie. It's mine. I thought I killed you."

She wiped her eyes with the back of her sleeve and rested her head on his shoulder. "It feels really good to have you back. The bond we have, it kills when it's empty."

"Feeling it completely gone was the worst part," Joel mumbled. "It was like a brutal reminder of your memory."

Sadie sighed heavily and buried her head deeper into his chest. Joel watched the orange and pink glow descend over the green fields and cast a gold radiance over her hair. He wasn't sure how he felt about the farm. It wasn't home, but it was a place of safety. It was the hearth of comfort for the person he loved. His relationship with these fields was welcoming, but a reminder of the responsibilities set on him.

He was prepared to embark on this mission alone. Returning to find the family still alive was an unexpected blessing. Although they were still wary of The Seeker's purpose, the family was given a chance to offer a gift of peace to humanity. Joel had brought them hope from the stars above; combining their abilities and the knowledge of the gift would bring the world to untold possibilities. No villains stood in their way. The family could become the heroes they wanted to be.

However they approached revealing the gift would come with great difficulty. Humanity would need time to fully commit. If The Seekers taught Joel anything, substantial change came with billions of years. Joel knew humanity didn't have that much time to spare, but he fully intended on succeeding. When the day The Seekers came to see humanity for themselves, the world would be ready.

Evil was loud. It blinded, deafened and buried any good around it. Trapped in the influence of anger and rage made the world a desolate place. Joel looked back on his worst days and remembered the hate he had carried. Evil had a way of making life absurd and beyond control. Purpose existed past the event horizon of rage, and it was found in believable hope.

Outside of evil's influence, was the good that so many yearned for. Once found, it told Joel how to face the absurdity and refuse its maliciousness. The planet would still float through the winds of space and continue living, but making a life worth remembering was possible for any who wished for it. Joel found that hope. He felt like he was out of the toxic pits. One day, he might fall back in. But today he could share that hope with the woman next to him and create a life together founded on goodness.

In the end, good would prevail. Humanity would join the forces among the vast cosmos and their legacy would be written in time. People would look upon what they created and remember their purpose was always to discover what potential existed here and beyond. One united humanity, sharing the good they carry to inspire what else existed out there. Joel and the family faced the beginning of that journey; it felt good to feel hope above that imminence.

An endless universe with endless potential. And that story began on the porch of a farmhouse. Joel smiled to himself. This planet was alright.

Sadie lifted her head, grabbed Joel by the wrists, and pulled him in close.

"What did you find up there?"

Joel felt like she wasn't asking for what was already shared.

"In a sense, nothing. Just a reminder that good still exists," Joel said.

Sadie's breath was warm and welcoming on his lips. "You always believed that, Joel."

"Maybe in another life," Joel whispered. "It took a galaxy wide alien to remind me who I could be; how I could fit into this universe. But that was all you, Sadie. I learnt that from you. You showed me what hope looks like. Without you, I would have never believed anything could be saved. That's why I came back to Aross. I was ready to follow your memory."

Kind eyes and a gentle smile filled Sadie's face. "I'm just happy you're back."

Sadie pulled him in and planted her lips against his. Her kiss was an old memory, reigniting every sense that desperately missed it. He wrapped his arms around her and leaned into her embrace. The bond between them ignited with a revived love lost with the chaos. All he ever needed in this endless universe was her, and feeling a shared desire was enough to make him whole.

When Sadie slowly pulled back, she continued to hold Joel's arms and kept him close. Her mind shifted to a flurry of anxious thoughts lost in a mess, attempting to unwind itself. She whispered with a tender ask. "I need to ask you of something. I need you to listen."

Joel held her loving gaze and nodded. "Of course."

Sadie breathed deeply before she spoke. "When you left, I felt the kind of grief I found when my parents died. The idea that the fault was on me crippled any notion of seeing it differently. The empty bond made our grief worse. An important part of me was ripped out, and I thought I would never recover from its wound. The time we had together before Fasdoba created something stronger than I think we both realize. When we were together, that's all that mattered in that moment."

"I was so close to giving up. I'm not sure how it would have happened. Some days I never wanted to leave my bed; other days I wanted to burn everything down. My memory of you reminded me every day what I lost. My grief had come so close to killing me, but I knew you wouldn't allow that to happen. I still don't know what kept me alive. No one just recovers from that kind of loss. One day you're completely in love, absorbing every single moment you share, and then the next day that person just ceases to exist. Their body is gone, the memory of them is fading and all you can do is become angry at that emptiness."

"Then one day I met this child. His name is Nait. He's gifted like us, but he discovered his abilities much younger than us. I saw pure innocence in him. Pulling him out of his world was something I couldn't live with. I fought with Lyas, demanding that Nait should be left alone. I spent whatever time I could find with that boy. I wanted to teach him how he could control his powers, but keep him in a place he was familiar with. I thought about you, and how I could have helped you like I was helping Nait. I dreamt about a life spent with you, learning how to navigate this chaos but under our own conditions. The memory of you, and what I could have done differently, flowed into the care I gave

Nait. Despite everything that life had robbed him of, that boy has held his grip on the life he wants. It's beautiful. I'm so proud of that boy, and I don't intend to ever remove him from my life."

"Nait is the galaxy spanning being I needed to pull out of my anger. I know you can appreciate that. The world is brighter with him in it, and now that I have you back, I feel like I'm flying above everything that can tear me down. This is the kind of hope I've always wanted; I wanted this for my parents, this family, and for you. If I can pass that onto Nait, then I know he will always be safe."

"I know you feel that hope, too. We face an uncertain future, but we carry hope so powerful that anything seems possible. You, Nait, this family, all of us, can make this planet a better place. I'll do anything to keep people safe, including the people I love. I want to keep you safe, Joel. You protect me, I'll protect you; we promised each other that. Our bond is strong, and together we will never stop feeling this hope that the both of us want. I need you by my side, Joel. I need you to promise me you'll never leave my side. Promise me, no matter what burdens we face, we will be together, always."

Sadie's eyes held in love and anticipation. No planet or galaxy held the same beauty as her. The whole universe could disappear, but nothing could kill her memory. Sadie was everything good about the world. She was his purpose. The path ahead would never change that. Joel pulled her in closer and spoke the shared truth the two of them felt deep within.

"I promise."

Thank you for completing *Ver' Nova*.

We would love if you could help by posting a review at your book retailer and on the PageMaster Publishing site. It only takes a minute and it would really help others by giving them an idea of your experience.

Thanks

PM Store Author's QR Code
https://pagemasterpublishing.ca/by/forrest-richard/

To order more copies of this book, find books by other Canadian authors, or make inquiries about publishing your own book, contact PageMaster at:

PageMaster Publication Services Inc.
11340-120 Street, Edmonton, AB T5G 0W5
books@pagemaster.ca
780-425-9303

catalogue and e-commerce store
PageMasterPublishing.ca/Shop

ABOUT THE AUTHOR

Forrest C. Richard was born and raised in Alberta. The range of Canada's wild diversity grew him a profound love for the outdoors and has inspired Forrest to pursue a career as an ecologist in conservation biology. Before Forrest pursued ecology, he worked as a Community Peace Officer for 7 years in the Edmonton area. In that time he met his now-fiance, Ashlyn, and found the drive to write his first novel: Ver'Nova. If you ever want to get his attention, talk about space or show him a cool looking bug.

www.ingramcontent.com/pod-product-compliance
Lightning Source LLC
Chambersburg PA
CBHW021121260626
47169CB00005B/1390